About the author

Jack Sutton was born in Wellington, Shropshire of Salopian parents but when very young moved with his parents to Lancashire. He is a retired engineer and lives in Merseyside which before boundary changes was South West Lancashire. Among his hobbies are photography and painting.

This is his first novel and set within a framework of industry whilst embracing the surroundings of his birthplace.

For Graham,
With best wishes and the hope that you enjoy the read
Jack Sutton

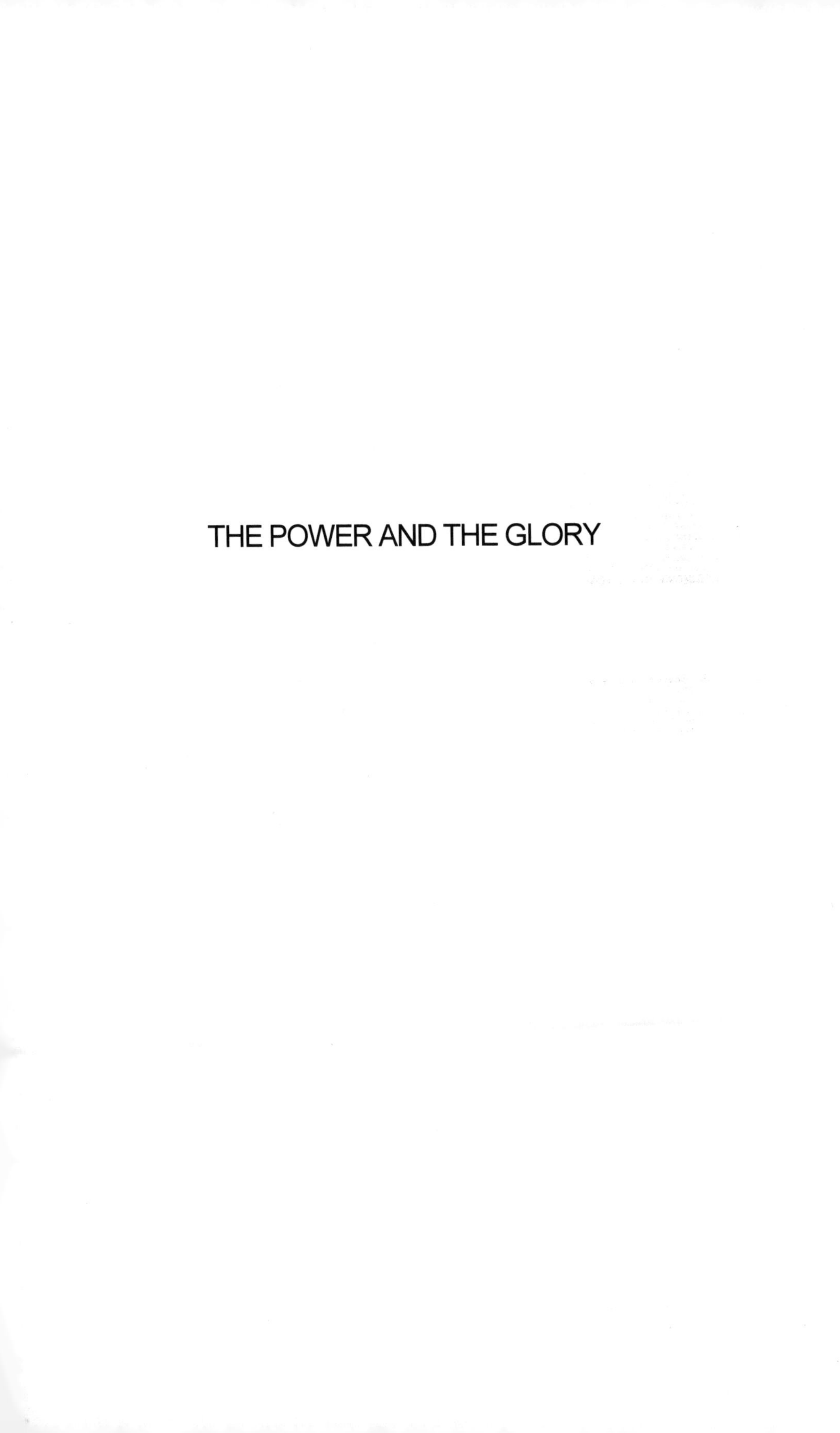

THE POWER AND THE GLORY

Jack Sutton

THE POWER AND THE GLORY

Vanguard Press

VANGUARD PAPERBACK

A CIP catalogue record for this title is
available from the British Library.

ISBN 978-1-80016-105-4

Vanguard Press is an imprint of
Pegasus Elliot MacKenzie Publishers Ltd.
www.pegasuspublishers.com

First Published in 2021

Vanguard Press
Sheraton House Castle Park
Cambridge England

Printed & Bound in Great Britain

1

The claxon sounded loud and clear signalling the end of the lunch break. The hubbub of conversation was essentially drowned out by the noise of chairs scraping over the floor as the men stood and began making their way towards the canteen door. They were the fitters, welders, plumbers and sheet metal workers employed on the major repair and tank furnace rebuild at the factory of Salopian Industries Limited in Telford, Shropshire. Salopian Industries manufactured thermal insulation products of glass fibres and phenolic foam boards. A medium-sized company but small in comparison with the main manufacturers in Britain, Europe and America. Nevertheless, the company held a significant part of the market.

Making their way to their respective work areas, several headed towards the tank furnace end of the production line, when one shouted a warning and ran forwards towards the body of a man lying prostrate on the floor beneath the tank furnace platform some twenty or so feet above. The body was under the large opening in the platform where the tank furnace would be situated, the base of which would be supported by steel beams stretching across the opening. The first man to reach the body could see at once the severe head injuries and he appeared to be dead. Recognizing the victim, he shouted back to the others as they approached, "It's Danny Drew. Danny the engineer." Looking up, seeing that they were under the edge of the tank furnace opening he said, "He must have fallen from the platform. Get some help quick." One of the men ran towards the production foreman's office at the far end of the production line and on his way saw the company CEO, Patrick Evans, standing and talking with the senior production foreman. Running up to them and without preamble, with panic in his voice he said, "Come quick, there's been a terrible accident and I think he's dead."

"Where? Who is it?" asked Patrick Evans as he and Don Phillips, the senior production foreman turned to run after him.

"It's Danny Drew, the young engineer in Mr Anderson's department."

Arriving at the scene, Evans could see the terrible head injuries and said to Don Phillips "Call 999 quickly for ambulance and police. Also, Health and Safety Exec. This is a disaster."

It was quite obvious to them all, that Danny was dead but what he had been doing on the platform or indeed any other part of the site without a safety helmet and at lunch time when everyone would be in the canteen was unexplainable. The fact was, he had no reason to be there since this work was being carried out by and under the control of Company Engineering Division. Input from Works Engineering Division was neither required nor desired.

The ambulance and paramedics arrived at the same time as a police sergeant and a police constable. They all agreed that the body should not be moved until the police surgeon had examined the victim. The police sergeant called through to the station to inform CID for it was his opinion, that this was not a straightforward accident and should be considered as a suspicious incident.

Some twenty minutes later, DCI Harry Davies arrived, accompanied by DI Bob Grant, DS Larry Robb and DC Jane Todd. The DCI, noting the position of the body which was lying face down and seeing the injury to the back of the skull spoke with the doctor, who had already examined the body and certified death. Addressing him he said "Paul, I don't think this was accidental. The injury to the back of the skull must have been sustained before the fall which must have been forwards since he is lying face down. I believe that this is a case of murder."

"I agree with you," he replied. "I suggest the weapon could have been a flat object, about six millimetres wide, and struck with considerable force, from behind."

Addressing all the other officers, the DCI ordered an immediate search for a possible weapon.

DI Grant and DS Robb climbed the stairway to the platform and began a painstaking search. The first thing they observed was a safety helmet lying on the platform as though discarded. There was no name on it or on the inside. It lay several feet from the opening through which the victim must have fallen but there was no sign of a weapon. The opening in the platform had a steel angle curb around the entire periphery, preventing foreign bodies being accidentally knocked over the edge and on closer examination, the DS called over to DI Grant,

"Sir, come and look at this," pointing to the angle curb.

"Looks like blood. Get forensics up here and get them to check this safety helmet for DNA because I think it belonged to the victim. It looks as though a struggle may have taken place during which he lost his helmet and then was pushed towards the opening but falling backwards before getting there and striking his head on the angle curb. This I have no doubt would have rendered him unconscious. The assailant must have then rolled him over and pushed him over the edge of the opening."

DCI Davies called for everyone to assemble in the canteen immediately so that he could address them all and take statements, meanwhile the forensics team would begin their examination of the site. Taking the CEO aside, DCI Davies asked if there was anywhere within the factory that could be allocated for the setting up of an Incident Room. Patrick Evans, without hesitation, offered the use of the main conference room stating that he would do anything to assist in their enquiries.

When all were gathered in the canteen, DCI Harry Davies introduced himself and the team and after a short pause, gathering his thoughts, he began to address the assembly. "I am quite certain that the incident here today was not an accident but one of murder and that the forensics team will confirm that. There is some evidence that suggests the possibility of a struggle having taken place, during which the victim lost his safety helmet. Also, that he was either pushed, or had fallen backwards, striking his head on the angle curb surrounding the opening, rendering him unconscious. It would appear, that his assailant then rolled him over and pushed him, head-first, over the edge of the opening in the platform." There followed a hubbub of conversation among the assembly, expressions of incredibility being the predominant sentiment. By now, everyone knew that the victim was Danny Drew, knowledge that stunned them all for although he was not a member of Company Engineering, he was well liked among the men. However, no one could think of a reason for Danny to be on the platform other than he had gone to meet someone during the lunch break when all would be in the canteen. But why meet on the platform?

DCI Davies told all assembled, that his officers would take statements from everyone in the room with, particular attention, to be paid to anything that anyone may have seen to be unusual before they had gone to the canteen for lunch. After giving their statements, they could leave but would not be allowed back on the site until forensics had finished their examinations which would not be until tomorrow at the earliest.

The news spread around the factory like wildfire, and it was difficult for anyone to come to terms with the fact that the victim was Danny Drew and that he had been murdered. He had been liked by all for his gregarious and happy-go-lucky way. Most people, women particularly, knew him to be a flirt but accepted that, that was Danny or 'Danny Boy' as he was often referred to, in friendly affection. He certainly had an eye for the ladies and the nerve to pursue his amorous inclinations wherever and with whoever may yield to his charms. That a lady might be married was no obstacle to his adventuresome spirit.

Sharon Sumner, the CEO's PA, on hearing the news, went to the Supplies Department to see Julie Phillips with whom she had become very friendly. Julie was the wife of Don Phillips, the senior production foreman and according to Julie, he had become difficult to live with. She thought that it was perhaps the difference in their ages that was the problem. He was twelve years older than herself, she, being thirty making him forty-two. She felt that she was stuck in a rut and had confessed to Sharon that the way Danny Drew flirted with her, every time he went into the Supplies Department, made her feel attracted to him. On one occasion he tempted her by asking her to go for a drink with him. She had, however, reminded him that she was a married woman and that Don wouldn't like it. 'He would not need to know' was his reply. 'We could go when he is on the afternoon shift and since that doesn't finish until ten o'clock, that would give us most of the evening.' She told him that he was incorrigible and that there was no way she could do that, behind her husband's back. He had laughed and said that anything is possible if you want it badly enough. She had confided in Sharon, telling her that she could not get Danny out of her mind, saying that he was exactly the opposite in ways and attitude to Don. When Don was on the night shift, she would lay awake for quite long periods thinking of Danny and imagining what it would be like with him lying beside her. Such thoughts usually got her aroused and with her mind on flights of fancy.

The next time Danny went into the Supplies Department he headed for Julie and having given her the requisition for the equipment he required, asked if she had given any further thought to his suggestion that they go for a drink. She shocked herself when without hesitation she agreed to go with him on the condition that she was home by nine thirty, well before Don would return. Without at that time realizing it, she had begun her affair with Danny.

Sharon knew only too well that Julie would be devastated by what had happened that day but unable to show too much emotion in public. As for herself, the situation she was now in was also one that had to remain out of public knowledge. If it became known that she was now in a torrid affair with her boss, Patrick Evans, the future for them both would be disastrous. The outcome would mean certain dismissal from their employment. Although she herself was single, Patrick Evans was a married man and would not only face dismissal but probably divorce also.

Sharon took Julie into the Ladies Rest Room where they could hopefully be alone for a while. Julie was devastated and in shock. She sobbed as she uttered the almost unanswerable question, "Who and why would anyone do such a terrible thing to such a lovely person?"

Sharon could only say "I don't know, love. But I am sure the police will find whoever is responsible."

The CEO gave the instruction for all employees to go home. All personnel working on the repair site, which was now a designated murder scene, to remain at home until the police gave permission for them to return. Those from other areas to return to work the following morning.

From the answers to questions put to the employees working on the repair site, the police now knew that prior to the lunch break, a number of men had been working on the platform and every one of them had confirmed that Danny Drew was not there up to the time that they left for the canteen, when the claxon had sounded.

On the morning of day two, the Incident Room was now set up and fully functional. DCI Harry Davies stood before the incident board looking at what little information was shown. Apart from the victim's name, his age, which was shown as twenty-five, details of the contents of his wallet and that his mobile phone was in his pocket, there was a blank board. Turning around to face the now assembled team, he stood for a few moments, hands in his pockets, looking at them. "So far we have bugger all to go on," he said. "However, I have received the post-mortem report from forensics. Death was due to a fall from a considerable height, compatible with a fall from the platform. There was, however, an injury to the back of the skull consistent with the victim's head striking the angle curb on the platform, which would have rendered him unconscious, but this was not the cause of death." Pausing for a moment whilst looking at the incident board, he then turned to them and continued. "We need to know why he was on that platform at the time when everybody, working on that site, were in the canteen having their lunch. That he was not there for normal work purposes is certain, but it would appear, that there was someone else up there at the same time."

"Perhaps he had gone to meet that someone," suggested DC Jane Todd. "Perhaps deliberately when nobody would be around."

"Surely, if that was the case, there must be better and safer places to meet."

"That would depend on who he was going to meet," she replied. "There may be something on his mobile phone to give us a clue."

"That is a possibility. Check that out."

The DCI continued, "The contents of his wallet were twenty-five pounds, a lottery ticket from last week, his driving license and a fuel bill from the local supermarket. There was also a photograph of a lady I think may well be his mother who we know lives in Liverpool. The Merseyside police have informed her of her son's death and that it is being treated as murder. They have also told her that an officer from here will go to see her and ask her to return here with him and identify the body. I want you, DI Grant to go there and take Jane with you. A feminine touch in this case I think would be desirable."

For a few moments there was general conversation amongst them as they discussed the various avenues of questioning and who might be the people most likely to give them the sort of information, they needed.

DCI Davies called their attention. "DI Grant and DC Todd, you had better make moves to get up to Liverpool as soon as possible." Then addressing DS Robb, said, "find out what the victim should have been doing at the time he met his fate. You will probably need to speak to Leslie Anderson, the works engineer. I am going to interview the ladies in the Supplies Department. It is highly likely that they knew the victim quite well because an engineer must have had regular contact with them requisitioning materials and engineering items."

The DCI introduced himself to the staff in the Supplies Department and explained that he would speak with them individually and in private. Also, that whatever information they could give him would be treated in confidence. Looking around the room, he noticed that one young lady seemed to be quite distressed and his keen eye told him that she had been crying. Although knowing that some women are more emotional than others, he suspected that this young lady may well have more to be upset about than the others in the room. He decided to begin his interviews with her. She told him her name was Julie Phillips and that she was married to Don Phillips, one of the senior production foremen.

"May I call you Julie?" he asked.

"Yes, of course. It seems less formal," she replied.

"I want to build a picture of Danny Drew as a person, his likes and dislikes and his relationship with others as well as his relationship with yourself. Anything you say will be treated in confidence and be assured that whatever you may know of his movements yesterday, no matter how insignificant it may seem to you, will be of great importance to the investigation."

Pausing for a moment, trying to interpret her facial expression, he then smiled and continued. "You must have known Danny quite well I imagine," he said more of a statement than a question.

"Why do you say that?" she asked guardedly and in defensive manner.

"Well, being an engineer, he must have had fairly regular contact with the department bringing in purchase requisitions and chasing up deliveries, perhaps."

"Oh, I see what you mean. Yes, he was in quite often."

"Was he a friendly person? Did he like to chat or was he more of a business only type of person?"

"He was always very chatty. A real live wire, so to speak and good fun."

Harry Davies thought he detected a faint blush to Julie's cheeks and wondered why that should be. He also wondered why Julie seemed to be on the defensive when he suggested that she must have known the victim quite well. He was forming an opinion that Julie Phillips was closer to Danny than she was prepared to admit. "I understand that he was a single man. Do you know if he had a girlfriend?"

"Maybe he had," she replied and then with some bluster, "I don't know."

"Did he come in here yesterday morning. Did he see you at any time?"

"I was very, busy yesterday morning. I don't remember."

DCI Harry Davies stood up. "Thank you, Julie, I appreciate your help and I do understand how difficult it must be for you to answer questions about someone, in such tragic circumstances, especially when it's someone for whom you have a liking and high regard. Should you remember anything you may think could be helpful to us, please contact me at any time or any other member of the team. I will give you my card which has the contact number, also my direct number." With that he shook hands with her and moved on to speak to the other staff members.

He received a similar opinion of the victim as that of Julie Phillips from all the others in the office, but he had formed the opinion that Julie new him better than the other members of staff.

DS Robb introduced himself to Leslie Anderson. "Mr Anderson, can you tell me what Danny Drew was working on yesterday morning and if he had any reason to be on the repair site during the time the workforce was in the canteen having lunch?"

"He should have been working on some minor modifications to be carried out in the phenolic foam department. What he was doing on the repair site, I do not know. I can only assume he was taking a short cut from the Drawing Office to the foam plant. However, I can give no explanation for him being on the tank platform. In fact, only Company Engineering personnel should be there. Works Division does not have input to capital projects any more. That has been the case for the last couple of years."

"For how long, was Danny employed here and was he always in your department?"

"He came as a graduate from Liverpool University about a couple of years back, around the time of the reorganization when Patrick Evans was appointed CEO. Danny had applied for a design engineer's post in the new Company Engineering Division but was unsuccessful, but I liked him and so offered him a position in Works Division which he accepted. He always got on well with the other members of the team and I had no complaints. There is no doubt that he will be a big loss to the department and will certainly be missed by his colleagues. His bright and happy spirit was quite infectious."

DS Larry Robb thanked him and left the department. He decided now to see the DCI.

DCI Harry Davies, along with DS Robb, went to speak with Patrick Evans. As they walked down the corridor, they saw him talking to his PA, Sharon Sumner, outside his office. Seeing them approaching Sharon went into her office, which was adjacent to that of the CEO, leaving Patrick Evans to greet them, shaking hands with them both. "Come in and please take a seat." He then offered them coffee, which they gratefully accepted having not had a drink since early morning. He then went to the connecting door to Sharon's office, opened it and asked her to bring coffee for all of them. Returning to his desk he sat facing them. "Gentlemen, how can I be of help?"

"I am given to understand that when the victim was discovered and the alarm raised, you were at the other end of the building talking to the senior production foreman. Is that correct?"

"Yes, that is perfectly correct."

"How long had you been there?"

"Oh, just a few moments. I had just entered the building and saw Don Phillips going into the foremen's office at the end of the production line. I needed to speak with him and as we began to talk, there was a shout from the tank end of the line and a man came running towards us shouting that there had been an accident. The rest you know."

At that point, Sharon came in with the coffee, placing the tray on the desk. The DCI thanked her, at the same time noting how attractive she was. She had on a beautifully tailored suit and light beige blouse with shoes that were obviously expensive. Her make-up had been immaculately applied and she had an air of sophistication that would impress anyone with whom she had to deal. There was no doubt that Patrick Evans had chosen well.

As she turned to leave, Harry Davies addressed her. "Miss Sumner, did you know Danny Drew?"

"Not really. I didn't come into contact with him very often. The girls in the Supplies Department knew him quite well I believe. I think Julie Phillips dealt with him on a daily basis."

"Have you any idea of anyone who may have had a grudge against him?"

"No, I haven't," she replied. "Everyone seemed to like him and his gregarious attitude."

"I think that at least one person disliked him for some reason. Thank you, Miss Sumner." When Sharon returned to her office, the DCI continued his conversation with Patrick Evans by asking, for how long the two Engineering Divisions had been operable. Evans told him that when he was appointed CEO, he was dissatisfied with the existing organization and so decided to establish a Company Engineering Division, to be responsible for all new capital work under the direction of a company chief engineer. This Division would also be responsible for all new design work together with a small development team to progress all product development and a Works engineering Division to deal with day-to-day matters including maintenance. Also, that department would be answerable to the company chief engineer.

Harry Davies, having finished his coffee, thanked Patrick Evans and he and DS Robb took their leave. Once outside, the DCI said to DS Robb, "I sense some animosity between him and Leslie Anderson's department. I think we should speak with Anderson and get his view of matters.

Having been shown into Leslie Anderson's office, Harry Davies introduced himself and said, "DS Robb you have already met."

"Yes, that is quite so," he replied and shook hands with them both and addressing DCI Davies, said, "Detective Sergeant Robb came to see me a short while ago. He wanted to know if there was a reason for Danny Drew to be on the tank platform. I told him that there was no reason whatsoever. Works Division does not have input in major capital works since the formation of Company Engineering Division a couple of years ago."

"So, I understand. Tell me about that."

"Just over two years ago, the then CEO had overseen the take-over of a small company in Cardiff, that was developing a new insulation board which did not give off toxic fumes at very high temperatures. However, the process needed to be developed into a financially viable operation. At that time, I was chief engineer and planning the development strategy. The CEO, who had held that position for ten years had reached retirement age and sadly left the company. The senior sales manager, Patrick Evans, was appointed to take over as Chief Executive Officer and I then knew that my planning of the development strategy would be overruled because we had been rarely in agreement on anything in the past. That was an underestimation of the situation. Patrick Evans dropped the bombshell that a new department would be formed to be responsible for all major capital engineering work including all process development and would be headed by a new company chief engineer. I was invited to apply for the position along with all external applicants. It is obvious that I was not appointed but offered the position that I now hold, works engineer, responsible for day-to-day work and plant maintenance. Patrick Evans, in his usual, smooth talking manner, said that he was sorry not to have appointed me, but the man chosen had higher qualifications and had held a senior managerial position with British Aerospace. In offering the post I now have, he tried placation by saying that it was not demotion but a sideways move with no loss of privileges or salary. However, I am answerable to the company chief engineer and in my view since I was answerable to the technical director originally, in effect I have been demoted."

"Have you not considered moving on?"

"Yes, but with a son aged seventeen and a daughter of fifteen, it would probably be too disruptive for their education if a move was to be of any distance, which it would most certainly be."

"Thank you, Mr Anderson for being so frank. It does give us a better perspective of the general situation although it doesn't help to explain the reason for Danny Drew to be where he was when he was killed."

The detectives left Anderson's office and made their way back to the Incident Room. Davies wanted to go through all his notes and try to get some order into the numerous pieces of information so far gathered. He had come to the stark opinion that, apart from knowing that the victim had struck the back of his head on the angle curb of the platform following a scuffle and without doubt had then been pushed off the platform deliberately, there was little else to give any further lead. The biggest problem was not knowing the reason for Danny Drew being on the platform. It seemed to Davies that he could only have been there for some covert reason. Probably to meet someone. But for what purpose he wondered.

Sleep that night, was for Davies, very disturbed. At the end of the second day of the investigation he knew only too well that apart from establishing the cause of death and that the victim had been deliberately pushed off the platform, they had little else to go on.

Morning dawned with some relief. He felt somewhat better having showered and had toast and coffee. Driving to work, his mind now clearer, he pondered the many pieces of information that was known at the present time. The gregarious spirit of Danny Drew and the impression work colleagues had of him. Also, there was the suspicion he had that Julie Phillips was somewhat closer to Danny than she cared to admit. After all, she was a married woman, the wife of the senior production foreman. On this third day of the investigation this was something to look into, in more depth. Parking his Jaguar, he felt a little more confident in that he had at least one line of enquiry to begin the day. Perhaps the other members of the team would have other useful information that would help to kick-start the day.

The murder investigation team gathered in the Incident Room for de-briefing. The DCI asked them for their reports on the interviews they had so far carried out, and if any significant facts had emerged or possible clues become apparent.

DCI Davies was, himself, the first to speak. "I talked to all the staff in the Supplies Department and the general opinion was that the victim was a happy-go-lucky type and humorous. Also, he liked flirting with the girls, a habit which they encouraged. There was one of them I thought had probably done a little more than flirt. Her attitude when I suggested that perhaps she knew him quite well, was without doubt, on the defensive. I did qualify my assumption by saying that being an engineer, he must have been a regular visitor to the department, at which she relaxed a little, although I believe her cheeks had coloured slightly. Her name is Julie Phillips and she is married to Don Phillips, one of the senior production foremen."

DI Grant reported that he and DC Jane Todd had visited the victim's mother in Liverpool and had brought her back to Telford with them for her to make a formal identification. This she had done and was now staying at the Queen's Arms Hotel until the body of her son be released for burial. She would then accompany the body back to Liverpool. She had been in regular touch with her son since he had moved to Telford two years ago after he had graduated. To her knowledge, he did not have a regular girlfriend as he had never mentioned anyone particularly, and he was quite happy at work. He had never spoken of anyone he did not like or with whom he had argued. There didn't appear to be any motive for anyone to kill him.

DCI Davies then told the assembly of the meetings with both Patrick Evans and Leslie Anderson. He told them that there had obviously been problems between them in the past although now, matters seemed to be normal. Neither men could give any reason or explanation for Danny Drew to have been where he was when he was killed. Also, it seemed that the murder had been made to look like an accident so could have been premeditated. The DCI summed up by saying that there appeared to be animosity and unrest and maybe sexual activities in existence under a thin veneer of normality. He paused, then made a statement with emphasis. "If we are to crack this case, I believe we must peel back the veneer and uncover the troubles that are fomenting beneath the surface.

2
TWO YEARS EARLIER

The sales/production meeting had just finished. There were, several heated moments when Patrick Evans, the chief sales manager, had almost thumped the table in his demands for a higher production output. His sales potential was being, as he put it, severely restricted. This was countered by the production manager saying that plant breakdowns have significant effect on production.

"What have you to say about that, Leslie?" Evans said, addressing Leslie Anderson, the chief engineer, in a smooth but condescending manner.

"The same comment I have been making for the last two months; your demands to keep the plant running for at least another two months is ridiculous. It should have gone down for a major repair and tank rebuild three months ago. Breakdowns are inevitable with anything that is virtually falling apart."

"Your usual excuse. Surely some of these problems could be sorted on the weekly maintenance drop shifts."

"You can't see inside a gearbox or the state of insulation on the windings of an electric motor on a drop shift."

The arguments continued throughout the meeting as was the usual case. There was animosity between Patrick Evans and Leslie Anderson. Almost everybody around the table was well aware of this and although they understood the chief engineer's difficulties and agreed that extending the working life of the plant could only lead to more breakdowns than would normally be expected, nobody seemed prepared to speak in his defence. They knew that Patrick Evans's smooth talking with the chairman of the board and the technical director put him in a dominating position. They were all afraid to upset Patrick Evans for although he was a smooth-talker and appeared to be the perfect gentleman, he could be vindictive, and woe betide anyone who crossed him. His ambition in life was to climb the professional and social ladder and he had no scruples about treading on anyone who might get in his way. It was also known that he was a, 'ladies' man and capable of captivating the attention of any woman he chose, almost without exception. Good looking, suave and smooth-talking — that was Patrick Evans.

The day came for the CEO to take his retirement. His secretary, who was now fifty-eight years old had also decided to retire and so there was now a place at the top not only for a new CEO but also for a new secretary. The position of CEO was taken by Patrick Evans and he wasted no time in appointing a young lady he referred to as his PA. He was now, in a position to dictate, without opposition, provided, that he continued to have the support of the chairman, Sir Ian Leighton-Boyce, and that he was determined to do. He had outlined his plans to establish a new engineering organization to be responsible for all major engineering and development projects, thus separating these from the day-to-day engineering tasks. These plans had Sir Ian's approval and so the changes were put into operation.

The majority of the morning, on the day he selected his PA was spent interviewing no less than six young ladies all of whom had good qualifications and CVs to match. His final choice was Sharon Sumner, a very, attractive young lady with a superb figure and a degree of sophistication above the other candidates. She was dressed in an impeccable navy-blue suit, white blouse and high-heeled shoes which were obviously expensive. Her make-up was expertly applied and her long blond hair, cascading to her shoulders, expressed her careful dedication to her appearance. In addition, her distinctive blue eyes gave the impression that she could see into one's soul with complete empathy. She lived alone locally, was not married, did not have a man in her life and at the age of thirty, she was perfect for the preferences of Patrick Evans.

At the end of the interview with Sharon, he asked her to have dinner with him on the following evening. He explained to her that this would be the final part of the interview in relaxed manner, although he had already made up his mind that she was the one for the position. A chance for him to talk with her, he explained, and for them both to discover if they were comfortable in the company of each other, because as his PA, there would be many occasions when such situations would arise. In his smooth and gentle voice, he told her that an evening such as this would enable her to make up her own mind, whether, or not to take the job should it be offered to her. He could tell that she was overwhelmed but with perfect grace she accepted the offer. He suggested they meet in the foyer of the Queen's Arms Hotel at seven thirty. He would order a table for eight o'clock. That would give them time for an aperitif as an overture to the evening.

The Queen's Arms Hotel was the most opulent in the area, an old building, richly carpeted and with soft lighting. The hotel boasted a superb menu with an excellent selection of wines and the service of traditionally costumed waitresses and a tariff to match. Cost was not an issue for Patrick as the company would be footing the bill. Patrick arrived early, to be sure of being there before Sharon arrived. He wanted to see how punctual she would be. He seated himself in a comfortable chair in a position that he could see the entrance and with a single malt to keep him company he waited patiently for Sharon's arrival. She came though the entrance at exactly seven thirty. Patrick wondered if she had waited outside so that she could enter at precisely the agreed time. He stood and she, seeing him, came directly over to him with the most charming of smiles. He shook hands with her and took her coat over to the cloakroom. Returning he then escorted her to the bar and having found a table, pulled out a chair for her and asked her what she would like to drink. She chose a white wine which he fetched for her and then they sat opposite to each other at the table. Once again, she was exquisitely dressed. This time she had on a very sophisticated dress, classical in style and with a single row pearl necklace. She was in Patrick's opinion a very classy and sophisticated young lady and he was now convinced that his choice was the right one. They went into dinner at eight o'clock and enjoyed a superb meal during which Patrick asked her many questions about herself, her preferences of food, entertainment, music and literature. She was perfectly relaxed throughout, her answers being confident and concise to all his questions. At the end of the evening, he told her that he had enjoyed her company and the meal, and offered her there and then the position as his PA and hoped she felt able to accept the offer at the salary that had been discussed at the primary interview. Sharon's face beamed as she thanked him for the job offer and accepted without hesitation, saying that she looked forward to working for him. He said that a formal offer would be in the post the following day with all the necessary conditions and salary offer included and he looked forward to receiving her official acceptance. With that he escorted her to the cloakroom to retrieve her coat and then at reception ordered a taxi for her and one for himself. He had now got a PA who he thought would suit him and help him in his quest to re-organize the workings of the company to his own liking. The next major job was to appoint a new chief engineer and he knew a man, who in his own opinion, would be an ideal candidate for the job. Having met him on numerous occasions over the past year or two, at business conferences and symposiums, he had found Frank Ebbs to be confident in conversation, almost to a point of haughtiness. Holding a senior position at British Aerospace and with high qualifications, Frank Ebbs would need a very, good offer to bring him to Salopian Industries, but Evans was sure that this was possible.

***

For the second time in a week, Patrick Evans entered the foyer of the Queen's Arms Hotel to meet someone and to have dinner. This time however, it was a man from Bristol, Frank Ebbs. The task of persuading him to come to Telford to discuss the possibility of him working for Salopian Industries had not been as difficult as Patrick Evans had thought it might be. Mr Ebbs had arrived late that afternoon and had booked a room for the night so that discussions need not be rushed and so could be relaxed. As Patrick entered the foyer both men, seeing each other, moved towards each other and shook hands. They then went to the bar, ordered a drink and sat down. Conversation at this point being casual and relaxed.

The meal was to the usual high standard and Patrick sensing that Ebbs was suitably impressed, launched his proposition that Ebbs come to Salopian Industries as the new company chief engineer. "Let me give you an overview of what I have in mind."

"Please do," Ebbs replied. "I find this very interesting indeed."

Patrick told him that the Drawing Office would be the nerve centre of the new Company engineering Division in which would be housed a new chief designer, two new project engineers and three new design engineers, one of the project engineers would take on the responsibility for developing the new phenolic board process into a viable production line. There are ten draughtsmen already employed but should the need arise, more could be recruited. “We still call it the Drawing Office although little actual drawing is now done. The computer and CAD have now taken over. The existing chief draughtsman, Arthur Brown will become one of the project engineers. I don’t suppose he will like it, but he will have no choice in the matter. His existing position will be changed and be replaced by the new chief design engineer.

“What plans do you have for your existing chief engineer?” asked Ebbs.

“He will be moved to head the newly formed Works engineering Division and will be responsible for all day-to-day engineering matters and for plant maintenance. He would of course be answerable to yourself should you accept the offer.”

“Does he yet know of your plans?”

“No, only the chairman is aware of my plans and he has fully approved them.”

“Suppose he doesn’t accept your proposal of being works engineer, what happens then?”

“I believe he will accept, although I think with reluctance. I know that he has two teenage children who are either taking or about to sit their GCSEs and he will not want to disturb their education prospects by moving away from the area, which he would almost certainly have to do to find another comparable job.”

“Do you have anyone in mind for the second project engineer and for the chief design engineer?”

“The second project engineer and all the other positions will be advertised. I would leave the selection of candidates in your hands.”

The rest of the evening was spent discussing all the possibilities that could possibly arise during the formation of such a radical change in organization. Patrick Evans was totally unaware of a man and woman sitting a couple of tables away, watching them with obvious interest. The table between them being unoccupied offered a good view, also, little snatches of conversation were audible. The couple were employees at

Salopian Industries and were man and wife. He was a senior production foreman, Don Phillips, and his wife Julie, who worked in the Supplies Department. It was not very often that Don Phillips took his wife out for a meal or indeed to go out for anything special, but this was an exception because Julie had nagged him for a week or more. She was bored of just watching TV in the evening. So far, they had gleaned that the new CEO was planning changes that would involve the chief engineer, Leslie Anderson, although they couldn't quite catch what the changes were to be and they had heard the words Drawing Office which, in their minds, implied that changes were to take place there too. Neither of them had any idea who the man with Patrick Evans was but it was obvious that he was being taken into Evans's confidence. Tomorrow, Julie would have plenty to gossip about with the other girls in the Supplies Department.

Despite Don Phillips telling Julie to keep her 'mouth shut', she couldn't resist the temptation of telling the rest of the staff what she had seen and overheard the previous evening. Such gossip always fuels speculation and usually leads to exaggeration. In a short time, a general rumour was circulating throughout the factory about forthcoming changes. It was some time before it reached the ears of Leslie Anderson. He was curious and suspicious about the referral to himself so decided to speak with Patrick Evans directly. Evans was taken aback and immediately denied the rumour, saying that he was indeed planning some changes to improve the running of the company but as yet, no specific decisions had been made but assured Leslie that he would be an important figure in whatever changes were decided upon.

Patrick Evans now awaited a decision from Frank Ebbs. Until he received that, he could go no further with his plans. He was furious that such a rumour had started about changes in the organization and specific mention of Leslie Anderson. Where and how this rumour could have started he had no idea. He asked himself the question; could Frank Ebbs have spoken to anyone from the company about the offer on the table and if so, who was that person?

Later that day, Frank Ebbs rang Patrick to accept the offer and to thank him for it, saying that he looked forward to taking up the position of Company Engineering Division chief engineer and to the future. It was agreed that he would start in one month from the following Monday.

Patrick asked him if he had, by any chance, spoken with anyone from Salopian Industries, other than himself, about the job offer to which his answer was no, he had not. It was now time, he realized, to make his plans known. Sharon Sumner was starting her new job as his PA next week, so then perhaps would be the best time to go public. She could arrange to have all advertisements placed in the press for a chief engineer and also project and Design engineers and having done that, he would tell Leslie Anderson that he was invited to make application along with all the other outside applicants and would be considered accordingly.

That evening, at home, Leslie Anderson felt very unsettled. His wife, Jenny, sensed his unease and pausing from bringing in the food she had prepared in the kitchen, put her hands on his shoulders as he sat at the table. "Darling, what is the matter, what is worrying you?"

For a moment he didn't reply, then placing his hand on hers he looked up at her. "You can read me like a book."

"You haven't answered my question. What is wrong?"

He then told her of the rumour going around the factory of changes in the organization which included himself and that he had questioned Patrick Evans, who had denied the rumour. He had however, admitted that some changes would be made to improve the running of the company. "He told me that I would be an important figure in any such changes and that is what worries me. That man is devious beyond words. He is so suave, speaks in such a friendly way and with a warm smile on his face but, figuratively speaking, would stick a knife into you at the same time if it would gain him an advantage. All he wants in life is the power and the glory and he doesn't mind who he treads on to get it."

"But darling, he can't sack you. He could be taken to court for wrongful dismissal."

"I wouldn't put that past him. He would be capable of concocting any kind of story to give reason for dismissal and with his smooth talking, would have a good chance of convincing any judge or jury."

"Let's not worry about it any more this evening, let us relax and have dinner in peace. Perhaps we could enjoy that bottle of Merlot and forget bloody Patrick Evans. He is no doubt nothing but a conniving bastard. Please forgive my language but to hear about his ways makes me furious"

Leslie was taken aback by her outburst. It was so rare to hear Jenny swear that it took him completely by surprise. He could not help but laugh and the tension was broken. They enjoyed their meal and afterwards sitting on the sofa, Leslie's arm around Jenny, they finished the bottle of Merlot. Tomorrow would be another day.

***

Patrick Evans and his wife Amanda were enjoying the evening at the Golf Club. It was the annual dinner and Patrick was making the most of the opportunity of talking with those members he thought of as influential, even though it meant leaving his wife to fend for herself for quite lengthy periods. Amanda was used to this and although she disliked being left alone, she had learned to cope and not to say anything to him for if she did, he would express his disapproval by telling her not to be so 'clingy', to be more extrovert and get out there and talk to people. One member he always ensured he had the opportunity to speak with was none other than the chairman of Salopian Industries, Sir Ian Leighton-Boyce. However, on such occasions he would make sure Amanda was with him. He liked to give Sir Ian the impression of them being the perfect couple for he knew that the chairman held family life with high regard. It was just so on this occasion. Having seen Sir Ian talking with the club captain, he interrupted Amanda's conversation with two of the members' wives and with the briefest of apologies escorted her away and headed towards the chairman. Approaching, he gave the broadest of smiles and said, with a hearty voice, "Good evening Sir Ian, I trust all is well with you," and with a gracious court bow included Lady Barbara Leighton-Boyce in his greeting.

"Very well thank you Patrick," he replied and then "Good evening Mrs Evans."

Sir Ian asked how he was settling into his new position and how everything was progressing with his re-organization programme. With the mention of a work topic, Lady Leighton-Boyce took Amanda's arm drawing her away. "Let them talk shop if they wish but we don't have to listen."

They went over to the bar, Lady Barbara ordering Martinis. She was a very gracious lady, easy to talk with and with an endearing personality that complimented that of her husband's. Their conversation continued until the gong was sounded, indicating that dinner was about to be served.

In contrast, the evening in the Phillips's household was not pleasant. Don had been on the day shift and by early afternoon he heard the rumour that had started in the Supplies Department. He knew only too well who had started it, despite him telling her to keep her mouth shut and say nothing. His shift finished at two o'clock and so he was at home well before Julie returned in which time his anger fomented. When she did at last arrive, he vented his wrath in a manner that unnerved Julie. She was, aware of his temper and that he had for some time been more verbally abusive of her for which, in her own opinion, was not deserved. But his anger on this occasion was greater than she had ever experienced.

She dissolved into tears and between her sobs, she said time and time again that she was sorry, but his ranting continued until, what seemed to Julie like hours, he gradually calmed down. One of his most hurtful statements had been that he didn't know why he had married her. This she would not forget.

With Sharon now in office, Patrick Evans had her arrange for the advertisement for the new company chief engineer and those for the project and Design engineers to be placed in the press. Before they would appear however, he called Leslie Anderson to his office to tell him of his plans, for the future.

"Please, take a seat Leslie," he said as Leslie entered the office. "I want to bring you up to speed with the changes that are going to be made." He then outlined the organization and explained how he expected the two divisions to work separately but with the new works engineer being responsible to the new company chief engineer who would have the overall authority in all engineering matters.

As Patrick talked on, Leslie began to relax mentally. He thought that he, as chief engineer at the present time, would automatically become the new supreme head. Then he heard Patrick say, "The advertisements for all these positions will be in the press within the next couple of days. You are of course invited to apply for the position of company chief engineer along with all the outside applicants."

Leslie Anderson was stunned by what he had heard. That he must apply for what he considered to be his own job. He sat for what seemed like an age, looking at Patrick Evans, with an expression of incredulity on his face. Then he said, "You expect me to apply for my own job?"

Before he had chance to say more, Patrick said in that smooth but condescending tone that he had, "Leslie, it is not your job. It is a new position in a new organization and as such you must make a formal application. I can assure you that you will be treated just like the other applicants, without prejudice of any kind." In that statement he was speaking the absolute truth. All other outside applicants would of course receive an interview, but those interviews would be for political purposes only. None of them would be selected because the new man was going to be Frank Ebbs.

Leslie made the decision to finish work early, something he rarely did but after that stunning news he felt so frustrated he could not concentrate on work matters. This, he thought, was going to be the end of his career because of the animosity that had existed for so long between himself and Patrick Evans. A situation not of his making but one that had grown from the ambitions of an unscrupulous man aiming to get to the top, whatever the cost to anyone who might get in his way.

He didn't go straight home but went to the Parish Church of St. Chad, where he was the organist. He was a very accomplished organist and would spend much of his spare time playing. Saturday afternoons, when there were weddings, he would of course play for the ceremonies but on the occasions when there were none taking place, he would give a short organ recital to which many parishioners and other townspeople would go to listen. Today, he was in sombre mood and the music he played reflected his emotions.

As Patrick Evans had promised, when all the applications had been received by the prescribed date, he announced the date for the interviews. He told Leslie that with respect to his present position in the company, his interview would be the first to be conducted. This would be with himself and the technical director and as they knew him, it would be a "fairly short" affair. Much shorter than for the outside candidates. The one thing he didn't say was that the technical director was unaware that the position had already been offered to and accepted by Frank Ebbs. He was quite confident that, whoever the technical director thought should be the one, and that might well be Leslie Anderson, he would be able to persuade him that Frank Ebbs was the best choice. In any case, as CEO, he could overrule the technical director.

Leslie's interview was a quite convivial affair. Patrick gave the impression of being a good friend of Leslie and expressed thanks, on behalf of the company for his dedication to his work, acknowledging the fact that without engineers, production could not take place. The technical director, Bill Hammond, concurred with Patrick, saying that he hoped Leslie would be able to give many more years of service to the company. When all was said that was necessary, Patrick concluded the interview by saying that he would be in a position within the next couple of days to give Leslie a complete list of all the appointments to the positions that had been advertised in the press.

That evening talking with Jenny, he said "I just can't figure out what is going on in Patrick Evan's mind. He gives the impression that we are all colleagues working for the good of the company in general, but I sense that beneath the friendly exterior there is poison there, ready to be used when the purpose suits him. Like a snake waiting to strike."

"You told me that Bill Hammond was at the interview and expressed his thanks to you, hoping for your service for many years to come. Surely, he of all people, wouldn't be so underhanded by saying such things and then dismiss you. Darling, I think you could be getting things out of proportion and worrying yourself too much."

"I hope you are right. Patrick told me that he would give me a list of all the appointments made to the positions advertised in the press but there is one position which he has spoken of but was not one of those advertised, the position of works division engineer. Why was that position, not advertised? It makes one wonder. Whatever the case, the truth of the matter will be revealed within the next few days."

The announcement of the new organizational structure was made along with the list of all the positions to be appointed. The list gave the name of Frank Ebbs as the new chief of Company Engineering Division and named Leslie Anderson as the new works engineer. This was in the form of a circular sent to all departments and displayed on all works notice boards. It stated that all other positions would be announced in the near future. When Leslie Anderson received his, he was stunned to see that he had been appointed to the position of works engineer. He regarded it as the greatest insult that Patrick Evans had ever given him. Without hesitation he went to see Patrick Evans intent on telling him just what he thought of him and that he could find someone else to fill that position. When he reached Evans's office, Sharon, who was just inside the doorway but on her way out, on seeing him said, "Mr Anderson, I was about to call you. Mr Evans wishes to see you and to introduce you to Mr Ebbs, the new company chief engineer" and she stood aside to allow him to enter the office. Leslie went in but before he could say anything, Patrick stood up and with such bonhomie, said, "good morning Leslie, let me introduce you to Frank Ebbs, our new company chief engineer. I'm sure you will get along splendidly."

Leslie, somewhat taken aback, shook hands with Frank Ebbs but then turned to Evans and said, "I didn't apply for the position of works engineer so why appoint me as such and without prior consultation?" He was furious and that was obvious to both Evans and Ebbs.

"Leslie, it was the obvious choice to make." Once again, he was using that smooth and friendly tone of which he was a master. "Unfortunately, you were unsuccessful in your application for the post of company chief engineer but your knowledge and experience within the company makes you the most suitable person to take on the position of works engineer. Besides, what else could you do in the company." This was said with a touch of nastiness which Leslie understood immediately but of which Frank Ebbs was unaware. Evans had now moved the one man with whom he had argued and disagreed in the past but who he had never been able to overrule.

"Patrick, let me think about it for a while and then I will let you know if I decide to accept." Leslie turned and without further remark, walked out of the office.

Evans had expected an adverse reaction from Leslie and had deliberately arranged for this expected confrontation to be in the presence of Frank Ebbs in order to defuse an angry scene.

"I am somewhat surprised that you hadn't discussed with him your proposals and your reasons for the decisions you have made," Frank Ebbs remarked.

"That wouldn't have helped matters in any way. Leslie Anderson would still have reacted in the manner you have just seen."

"Suppose that he rejects your offer, we then need to appoint someone as a matter of urgency but someone without the knowledge and experience of the plant that Anderson has."

"I don't believe he will refuse to accept the position because he knows that there would be nothing else on offer in which case his only option would be to resign from the company and seek employment elsewhere."

"He may well do that."

"As I have said previously, Anderson has two teenage children at school here, ready to take exams. If he resigned, he would certainly have to leave the area to find another job of equal status. That would mean the children moving school which I am sure he would not be prepared for them to do because it would be too disruptive at this period of their education. I am sure he will accept."

That evening Leslie again talking with Jenny, unburdened himself of the frustration he felt of the situation he was in and the anger he felt towards Patrick Evans. That man had, in his opinion, deliberately planned these changes in organization to move him away from engineering authority and put someone else in total charge that as CEO he could control and manipulate as required.

"Have you made a decision?" Jenny asked. "Will you accept the position?"

Leslie remained silent for a while, Jenny looking at him and trying to figure out what he was thinking.

Finally, he looked at her, his facial expression displaying his dejection and with despair in his voice he said, "I don't have much choice. If I refused to take the job, there would be no other offer and so I would have to leave to find other work. That would probably mean moving area with all the disruption that would cause for you and the children. Evans is aware of that and knows that to some extent he has me over a barrel. He says that it is not a demotion but a sideways move. That is obviously not true. It is a demotion, but the salary and general conditions remain the same. I will accept, I have no option to do otherwise but Patrick Evans will need to be very careful of what he does in future because I or someone else will ultimately expose him to everyone, for the devious, power-seeking and despicable person that he really is.

The following morning, Leslie rang Sharon and told her he wished to see the CEO. Guessing the reason for his request, she told him to come right over as Mr Evans had no one with him at that moment and she was sure that he would see him. Putting down the phone, she went into Patrick's office, using the communicating door and said, "Mr Anderson wishes to see you. I told him to come right over because I thought you would want to see him as soon as possible"

"Quite right, Sharon and I would like you to stay whilst he is here. Draw up a chair and have a pad and pen ready. You can take any notes that may be necessary."

Evans thought that with the presence of Sharon, Leslie would be inhibited in what he might say. Typical of Evans, such manoeuvring would, he knew, defuse a situation before it could be regarded with any significance.

Leslie arrived, knocked on the door and entered. Walking up to Patrick's desk, he said "I have come to officially accept your offer," this with a straight face and with no sign of pleasure or a smile.

Standing up, Patrick smiling and with his usual condescending tone of voice said, "Oh, Leslie, I am so glad that you have seen sense," he raised his arm offering to shake hands. Leslie just looked at him for a moment and without returning the gesture turned abruptly and walked out of the office. Patrick turned, both he and Sharon looked at each other, then shrugging his shoulders, he sat down.

It was a few days later that Leslie, now having moved into his new office, which was adjacent to the new works Drawing Office, received a phone call from Frank Ebbs asking him to go over to see him. When Leslie arrived, Frank greeted him with a warm and friendly handshake, thanking him for coming over and offered coffee. They sat in a relaxed manner, Frank toying with a pencil on his desk, then looking directly at Leslie said, "I realize this situation must be very difficult for you to come to terms with and I quite understand how frustrated and demoralized you must feel but please believe me when I say that you are a very important person in the company, and Bill Hammond has very high regard for you.

I do believe that he would, perhaps, have preferred to see you in this chair but we are where we are. I hope that we can be friends and deal with our respective responsibilities as colleagues. I should very much appreciate your input when the applicants for the positions of project engineer and design engineer are interviewed. In other words, I should like you to join me and Bill Hammond on the interview board. We must also select one of the design engineers to be appointed as the senior."

Leslie Anderson was surprised, to say the least, at this turn of events. Looking directly at Frank he said as much but, with a friendly assurance, said that he would be pleased to be of assistance. He was relieved to know that Patrick Evans would not be with them.

"How many applicants are there," Leslie asked.

"Five for project engineer for which we shall select one and Eight for design engineer for which we need three one of which will head the process development for the new Insulation Board under the direction of a project engineer who will be Arthur Brown."

"I need an assistant engineer in my department, that is, if you approve. Maybe one could be offered such an alternative if not selected for Company engineering?"

"I see no reason why not. You would have the authority to choose which candidate you prefer."

Later, contemplating the outcome of his meeting with Frank Ebbs, he formed the opinion that he was a much nicer person than Patrick Evans and that, maybe, he was a person he could work with without having to watch his back all the time. There was no doubt that events had taken a turn of which he had no control. When such a person as Patrick Evans was put into a position of authority, even people in the highest positions could be manipulated to suit his own purposes. However one looked at it, the situation that now existed was here to stay and one would have to accept that there was nothing to be done that could change matters.

The interviews were arranged to take place over two days. Ultimately the long and arduous job was done. Subject to receiving letters of acceptance, the project engineer and the three design engineers could now be named. Leslie Anderson had also made his choice of the person to join his Works Engineering Division. He was a young man of twenty-three years of age and recently graduated from Liverpool University with a degree in Mechanical Engineering. His name was Danny Drew.

3

The murder investigation team were gathered in the Incident Room. This was the beginning of the fourth day. DCI Davies addressed them with a trace of exasperation in his voice, understandable in the present circumstances. "Listen up all of you." The rumble of conversation ceased immediately. "This is, as you are all well, aware, the fourth day of enquiries and to date we have bugger all to show for it. Let us examine some of the facts known. The murder of Danny Drew was committed in a factory at a time when apparently all personnel working on that site, were in the canteen having lunch. The victim was apparently on a steel platform for a purpose unknown to us and there, met his assailant with whom, it would appear, he had a confrontation and almost certainly a struggle during which his safety helmet was knocked off. He fell backwards, or was pushed, striking the back of his head on the angle steel curb surrounding the opening in the platform over which the tank furnace will be built. This would have, almost certainly, rendered him unconscious. It would appear, that his assailant then rolled him over and heaved him over the curb, letting him fall to the concrete floor below." The DCI paused for breath and allowing the facts he had stated to sink in.

"This crime could only have been perpetrated by someone within the factory and we know that those working on the repair site were not there at the time the crime was committed. We can presume, therefore, that the murderer was from one of the other departments of the company or that someone who should have been in the canteen was not. In my opinion, the assailant was a man because the strength needed to roll the victim over, dead weight, and then heave him over the angle curb would have needed a great amount of strength. That, theoretically, reduces the number of possible suspects significantly." There followed several individual conversations among the assembly, discussing the facts and assumptions just outlined to them. Then the DCI once again called for their attention. "Questions that we must ask ourselves are, 'for what reason was the victim where he was and why at that time of day? Was the reason to meet someone and if so, how was the arrangement made? Most importantly what was the motive for killing him?'." It was clear to them all, that the answers to most of the questions just posed to them could only be obtained by questioning personnel. The DCI then told them to begin the routine questioning of people in all departments of the company including those who were supposedly in the canteen at the time of the incident. "One more thing, check with the gatehouse if there were any visitors in the factory around the time of the murder. If so, we need to know who they were, who they were to see and the times of arrival and departure. This will all be logged in the visitors' book." He then said that he wanted a thorough examination of the items recovered from the victim, particularly his mobile phone. "Check for emails also voicemail. Now get moving." He concluded by telling them to assemble again, here in the Incident Room at four thirty when they would report on progress and maybe put a few facts together that hopefully would begin to point them in the right direction.

***

It was around six months after starting work at Salopian Industries that Danny Drew began to chat up Julie Phillips whenever he went into the Supplies Department. To begin, it was just harmless banter and mild flirting. Danny had become known during the short time he had been with the Company, to be unable to resist flirting with all the women. However, he was particularly attracted to Julie Phillips and whenever he went into the Supplies Department, he chatted her-up in the hope that one day she would yield to his advances. This practise became a regular routine. It was only three months before Danny's murder that Julie had finally agreed to go for a drink with him. This, she told him could only be when her husband Don was on the afternoon shift, and she knew that she was living dangerously, for if Don found out there would be all hell to pay. But it was Don's coldness towards her that finally brought about her change of mind and agree to go for that drink.

Julie met him in the Crown Inn, a pub on the A5 just outside the market town of Wellington, which of course is within the new town of

Telford. The Crown Inn was not a pub normally frequented by people from work or indeed her neighbours, so was perhaps the safest place for them to meet. She had already made it quite clear to him that she must be home by nine thirty, well before the time that her husband would arrive home. This was the first time for weeks that Julie had been out for the evening and so it was particularly enjoyable to her to sit in a relaxed manner with someone so happy-go-lucky and humorous as Danny Drew. They had a few drinks throughout the evening and Julie, although not drunk, was feeling a little merry. Shortly before nine o'clock, Julie said that it was time to move if she was to be home at the time she had planned. She said she would order a taxi, but Danny said he would order one for them both to share. He had come by taxi because he wouldn't drink and drive. Danny ordered the taxi for nine fifteen, knowing that this would give them about a quarter of an hour to say goodnight. A great deal could be achieved in that time. He suggested they wait outside to which Julie agreed. They stood in the car park, in the shadows by the boundary wall. Danny put his arms around her, drawing her to him and kissed her. He sensed her freeze for a moment and then she relaxed putting her arms around his neck. He began running his hands around her body, down her back and her buttocks. The taxi arrived at that time cutting short his explorations leaving him exasperated by not knowing just how far he could have gone. However, he felt convinced that there would be other times to come.

She sat quietly in the living room with a glass of wine. To have a glass of wine at the time Don arrived home, would hopefully mask the fact of her being out drinking during the evening. When her husband finally arrived, he was not in the best of humour. "That bastard CEO has had me running around like a blue-arsed fly today. I have enough on my plate ensuring that the planned production schedule is carried out on time, and with minimum wastage at each product change without going to see Dick, Tom and Harry about this and God knows what." He poured himself a whisky and flopped into a chair.

Julie's 'bubble of pleasure' was burst in that instance. Here we go again she thought, grumble, grumble, bloody grumble. This attitude of Don's was becoming the norm. They didn't have fun any more, they didn't go out very often as a couple and the physical side to their marriage had become almost non-existent. She felt as though her life had become empty and useless with nothing to look forward to, other than going to work every day and bed every night. In fact, a life of 'bed and work'. She finished her wine and then said to Don, "I'm going to bed. Don't stay down here too long."

"All right," he grunted. "I'll be up shortly."

With that Julie went upstairs. Her mind drifted over the evening with Danny. What a contrast it had been to the life she was now experiencing with Don. She thought of the last few minutes she and Danny had together, waiting for the taxi. His amorous advances had not come as a surprise to her but her own reaction to them shocked her a little. When he was running his hands around her bottom and thighs, she had made no objection. She realized she had wanted him to do more. Had the taxi not arrived when it did, she now felt unsure how far things might have gone. The thought of how she would react when she saw him tomorrow troubled her. She wondered what he would be thinking at this very moment. Would he also be thinking, like she herself was thinking? The answer to all these thoughts she knew would come soon enough. If Danny should ask her again to go for a drink, she wondered whether she would say yes, or tell him that it could not go any further and put an end to their relationship. Endless mental questions and thoughts cascaded through her mind, on and on until finally she fell into a deep sleep, the alcohol and sexual excitement of the evening being the anaesthetic.

At work the following morning, Julie was at her desk sorting through all the recent requisitions when Danny entered. In his usual style and with bonhomie and a loud voice he said, "Good morning all, and what a wonderful morning it is."

They all, in almost unison, said "Good morning Danny."

He then went straight to Julie's desk and handed her a requisition paper which she looked at, ready to register it for action. What she saw was a message, hand-written, which said, "Thank you for a wonderful evening which ended far too soon. How soon can we do it again and please make it very soon."

Julie looked up at him, feeling her face going red, and said without hesitation, "Tonight if you wish. Don is still on the afternoon shift so provided that I am home by nine thirty, all will be well." Her voice, little above a whisper.

With a broad grin on his face said, "Can't wait. See you in the Crown at seven o'clock." His voice, echoing her own. With that he waved to the others and left.

The rest of the day Julie spent in excitement and with a little trepidation. At times, when thinking about Danny and the previous night, she became aware of her heart beating faster than normal. Her mind was contemplating the evening to come in a way that before now, she would never have believed herself capable. She felt almost like a teenager about to go out on a first date. Where this was going to lead, she was unsure. She was a married woman, thirty years of age and now about to go out with a man about five years her junior, single and with no responsibilities for anyone other than himself. Not only that but he was a man well known for his flirtatious adventures with a few women, although none of them being of any serious nature. She decided to close her mind to all that, have a lovely evening with him and let the future take care of itself.

***

Back in the Incident Room, the squad were waiting for the DCI to arrive. It was a little after four thirty when he hurried into the room, this time with a smile on his face. "I have been told by one of the women in the Supplies Department, that she was fairly certain that Julie Phillips was having a fling with Danny Drew. That is a suspicion that I have had since first I interviewed her."

"If that can be established as a fact, where is that going to lead the investigation?" put in DS Robb. "Could it be that he was murdered by a jealous husband?"

"That is certainly a possibility but with the knowledge we have, it would be very difficult to prove because he was actually talking at the far end of the plant with Patrick Evans, when the alarm was raised."

DI Grant then informed the gathering, that forensics, having examined the victim's mobile phone, had found two text messages in the memory. The first being a message from his mother and the second, a message from one of his pals back in Liverpool, suggesting that if he could get back home in a fortnight, they could go to Anfield to watch Liverpool play Arsenal. However, the most interesting thing was a very brief message in voicemail which said, 'make it twelve fifteen'. "I can only think that it must be referring to time. It could be just after midnight or just after mid-day but the latter would make the most sense in that the incident took place around that time which leads one to think it was a confirmation of the time Danny's assailant was making for a previous arrangement."

"Have you been able to trace the caller?" the DCI asked.

"Unfortunately, no I haven't. The call was made from a mobile belonging to John Preston, the engineer responsible for the development work, but he has a habit of leaving his mobile on his desk often unattended. I am sure that that habit continues outside of work and so anybody could have made that call. One thing is certain, it was not John Preston who made the call because the voice is a woman's".

"That means the caller could have been anyone and not necessarily a member of staff. However, if it were someone from outside the company and if that person did commit the crime his name would be recorded in the visitors' book at the Gatehouse. The person he was to see would also be recorded and, in this case, would almost certainly be Danny Drew. It was confirmed however, that Danny didn't have a visitor that morning and so the possibility of the perpetrator of the crime being from outside the company can be disregarded."

The DCI suggested that they should consider the most important thing in any crime — motive. "Here we have a victim who was, by all accounts, a very likeable young man with a gregarious nature and humorous attitude. However, he was a known flirt and one who had an eye for the girls and so this may well have upset someone, either man or woman, although we have previously thought that the crime was most likely committed by a man because of the strength thought necessary to heave the body off the platform. This brings me back to the belief that if Julie Phillips was having an affair with Danny Drew, her husband may have found out and committed the crime in a rage. There are a lot of 'ifs' that need to be made certainties, or not, if we are to solve this case any time soon."

With that, the meeting broke up, each one determined to make a breakthrough. They knew only too well that only good, old fashioned police work, would bring the result they all so desperately wanted for in this case. There was little forensic evidence to help them.

***

Julie and Danny met, as arranged at seven o'clock, in the lounge bar of the Crown Inn. She was wearing a trouser suit, a rather low-cut blouse which emphasized her natural attributes, much to Danny's approval, and a discrete amount of make-up. Seeing Danny already seated, as she entered the room, she quickly walked over to him and with a broad smile she said "Ohh, look at you, Danny Drew. You don't half scrub up well".

Danny stood up from his chair, over which his waterproof jacket was draped, his black hair of medium length and nicely groomed gave testimony of his Irish ancestry and crowned his fresh athletic features. His lemon- coloured polo shirt with a distinctive grey design down one side and light blue chino trousers suited him perfectly. With a smile to match Julie's, he replied "And you look gorgeous too." The time seemed to pass extremely quickly as is usual when having an exciting and pleasurable experience. They talked and laughed in a most comfortable and intimate manner, the drinks helping along the way.

At around a quarter to nine, Danny suggested they go outside and wait for the taxi that he had pre booked on his way to the pub. He had told the private hire driver, with whom he had become pally, not to arrive before nine fifteen so to have a little more time with Julie in the car park. They went outside as Danny suggested and stood by the boundary wall in the shadows at a spot where they couldn't readily be seen. Danny put his arms around her, pressing himself close to her and she responded, putting her arms around his neck, looking up into his eyes. He bent forward, kissing her gently, then more fiercely. Julie responded in a similar manner, pulling gently on the back of his neck. He ran his hand gently down her back, around her thighs then up the front of her body. His hand then found its way inside the front of her blouse and he felt her body tense for a moment and then relax and so encouraged he began further progress to feel her bra. Julie began to breathe in short gasps her mind in a whirl. Then it began to rain, suddenly, and with an intensity that might herald thunder. The spell was broken as though a bucket of cold water had been thrown over them. They ran quickly back to the pub doorway, sheltering from the rain and there to wait for the taxi. They were both breathless but not because of running to the doorway. They looked at each other but not speaking. Danny took her hand in his, she squeezed his hand in response.

Danny now knew that Julie was available and willing and now he must find a way of being with her in private, not just having a drink in the pub and a quick fumble afterwards. He wanted her in a big way.

Julie was feeling shocked with herself for not only giving into Danny's advances but for the feeling of delight she had experienced and the utter disappointment when it started raining and everything stopped so suddenly. She knew that she wanted him so badly and, in a way that she had never experienced with her husband. Her conscience told her that it must stop but she knew that really, she didn't want it to stop. Julie was already looking forward to their next meeting.

It was mid-morning of the following day when Danny Drew breezed into the Supplies Department in his usual buoyant mood and saying, "Good morning, fellow slaves." He went straight to Sue Thompson's desk and without preamble leaned closely to her and said quietly, in a conspiratorial way, "Sue my love, you look more gorgeous every time I see you. The name of this department is aptly named because you could supply all my needs."

Sue blushed and with a playful slap on his arm said, "Go away. You are nothing but a flirtatious torment," this in a voice loud enough for everyone to hear.

Julie felt a pang of jealousy when he went straight to Sue Thompson without even looking at her. Hearing Sue's retort to whatever he had said to her, told her without doubt that he was 'flirting' again and this hurt more than she thought possible.

"Take your requisition to someone else," Sue told him, laughing and pointing her finger in an action of dismissal.

Danny threw up his hands in mock despair, "All right, I know when my gracious and heartfelt comments are not wanted but you may live to regret it you know."

Still pointing her finger, laughing, she said, "Go."

With that, Danny turned and walked over to Julie and in a similar quiet and conspiratorial voice, bent close to her and said, "Just a little subterfuge so that people don't get the impression that I only come to you." He handed to her a requisition form but again handwritten. It said, "Last night was wonderful but spoiled by the rain. I could come to yours and bring a bottle of wine. That way we could be alone and not get rained on. Phone me and let me know what you think." With that he just said, "Thanks Julie," and left the room. This before the department manager, who had heard most of what Sue had said, could speak to him. Sangita Khan was furious and decided to speak to Danny about his attitude with her female staff the next time he came to the office.

Julie slipped the paper into a desk drawer and carried on working in usual manner, as though Danny's visit was just a normal act of business. Her mind raced through all the possibilities such an arrangement might present. If he were seen by neighbours, it would only be a matter of time before Don would know, so he could not come to the front door. The rear of the house backed onto a large playing field and there was a gate leading from the garden onto it, so that was a possibility. A short distance down the road was a car park for customers using the library and the few small convenience shops. He could park there and make his way to the house via the playing field. With no more ado, she sent him a text simply saying, "Yes. Come rear way only. Will arrange soonest."

When Danny received the text, he was overjoyed. He deleted it immediately for safety, that was a message he could not afford anyone else to see. He waited for her to call for nearly a week and began to think she had changed her mind but when the call came, he could hardly contain his excitement. Julie explained that he could only come to her home by the rear garden. That he could park his car in the car park and walk along the edge of the playing field to the rear garden gate, which she would leave unlocked and use the rear door of the house. "The following Monday, Don will start the afternoon shift so come about six o'clock," she told him, "but you must leave no later than nine thirty."

The following Monday, Danny did exactly as he had been told. Julie was watching the rear gate, through the kitchen window and when she saw Danny enter, she opened the kitchen door to let him in. The bottle of wine he was carrying he put on the kitchen unit, put his arms around her and kissed her, pulling her close to him. Julie responded immediately with no inhibitions. There, in the kitchen, he pulled her jumper up over her head, she helped by holding up her arms and he flung it to one side. Then they began where they left off in the car park. This time there were no inhibitions and no fear of being seen by anyone and to a finale like a volcano erupting. They stood for a while in close embrace and in silence, coming to terms with the last five minutes. Julie broke the silence by saying in a low voice "Danny, I love you".

"I love you too", was his reply and for the first time in his life, he meant it.

The next time was taken more leisurely. They had a couple of glasses of wine before Danny made any advances. He resolved to take things more slowly and gradually build up the excitement. Sitting on the sofa, he put his glass on the coffee table and then put his arm around her. She immediately pushed up close to him her arm around his waist. They kissed and his hand found its way to her thighs, gradually moving upwards.

Julie breathing in short gasps, pushed his hand down and said, "Let's go upstairs."

Danny didn't need to be asked twice. Without hesitation, he stood, took her hand and pulled her up off the sofa. Still holding hands, they climbed the stairs and Julie took him into the bedroom at the rear of the house. She drew the curtains, then started to undress. Danny did likewise and standing naked, looking at each other, Julie lifted the duvet and they both slid into bed. Finally, and once again, they experienced that explosive climax which left them feeling totally exhausted and it was only eight o'clock.

Sitting up in bed with his arm around her they chatted away for a little while, Danny wondering if they might do it again before it was time for him to leave. Suddenly, Julie sat up straight, her head slightly cocked to one side. "Listen." she whispered, """I thought I heard a noise. I'm sure it was the front door closing."

Before Danny could reply, a voice shouted, "Julie, where are you?" It was Don back home early.

"Shit," said Danny, leaping out of bed. He rapidly put on his clothes. "What the bloody hell is he doing back home at this time?"

"I'm upstairs, I'll come down," she shouted down to Don, as she hastily put on her dressing gown. She silently pointed to the window miming, "go quickly."

Danny opened the bedroom window, climbed through and jumped onto the flat roof of the living room extension and then to the garden below hurting his ankle in the process. Julie hastily closed the window, crossed over the landing and into their bedroom where she quickly turned back the duvet, making it appear that she had just got out of bed and made her way downstairs. As she entered the living room, her eyes saw the two glasses and the wine bottle, three quarters empty. Her heart was racing, and she was close to panicking.

"Who have you had for company?" he asked nodding towards the glasses then, "what were you doing in bed at this time of the evening?"

Julie amazed herself, as without thinking she said "Oh, Sharon called round earlier to show me her latest holiday brochure, so we had a couple of glasses of wine. After she left, I decided to have a read in bed. There was nothing of interest on TV."

"That stuck up cow," was his reply." I cannot see how you two have anything in common."

By the way he looked at her, Julie sensed that he didn't believe what she was saying but she could do nothing but brazen it out.

"Why are you home so early? Are you all right, is something wrong?"

"Nothing that I want to talk about. You go back to bed and your book," he replied. "I'm going to have a drink myself and relax for a while." Going to the drink's cabinet, he poured a liberal measure of single malt and seated himself in an armchair.

Julie didn't reply but turned and went back upstairs. She instinctively knew that he didn't believe her story and she wondered why he was home so early but wouldn't give her any reason. Her mind raced on until finally she fell asleep, her book slipping from her hands.

The next morning, Danny went into the Supplies Department limping badly.

Sue Thompson said, "What have you been doing?" She laughed, then said, "Something that you shouldn't have been doing I have no doubt."

Danny meekly replied, "I twisted my ankle."

Sangita Khan saw Danny come into the office and speak to Sue. She was about to go to him and give him a reprimand but changed her mind. Instead, when Danny left, she went straight to Leslie Anderson. Storming into his office and without preamble, she said, "Leslie, you must do something about your engineer Danny. I will not have him come into my department and speak to my staff in his sexist manner. I find it insulting and degrading".

"And good morning to you too, Sangita. Please have a seat and let us calm down".

"I will not calm down Leslie, because I am furious". This she said with determination, and without trace of her native language.

"Tell me what you find offensive".

"It's the way that he speaks to the women. This is the twenty first century and women are not to be a butt for his sexist comments and innuendo".

"But Sangita, surely it's just banter".

"I don't consider it as banter. He should have a verbal warning".

Leslie could tell that he wasn't going to placate her so he said, "All right Sangita, I will speak to him and tell him what you have said".

4

It was a little over two weeks prior to his murder that Danny Drew witnessed something that astonished him. Having been asked by Leslie Anderson, to take the maintenance figures for the last three months to the CEO, he went directly to Sharon Sumner's office. He could see through her office widow, the blinds of which were very rarely closed, that she was not in. He went in, without knocking and walked across the room to put the file on her desk. The communicating door to the CEO's office was open and as Danny walked across the room, he glanced through the open doorway. Patrick Evans and Sharon Sumner were in a very romantic embrace which they broke instantly they heard him in Sharon's office but not before he had seen them. Danny turned, with his back to the connecting door, and walked across the room to leave but before he could exit, Patrick Evans called him back. In that instance, Danny wondered what the CEO was going to say, for he was sure that Evans knew that he had seen them in what could be described as a very intimate position and construed as a romantic embrace.

Before entering the CEO's office, Danny stood aside to allow Sharon to go into her own domain, which she did without looking at him, then to Patrick, "You called for me, sir?"

"Yes, I did call you."

Danny didn't know what was now going to be said but expected the worst. To break the tension in himself, he said, "I have brought the maintenance figures for the last three months. Mr Anderson said that you wanted to see them urgently."

"Thank you. Take a seat." Patrick Evans was not sure that Danny had seen Sharon and himself embracing, in a manner that could only be regarded in one way, but he knew that he had to do something to silence Danny in case he had seen them. After a short pause, which to Danny felt like an eternity, Patrick Evans said "Danny, you have been with us now for about two years and so I wanted to speak with you regarding your progress. I assume that you are happy here and I know that your work is good. Some of the work here is commercially quite sensitive. The process development for the new insulation board for instance because we must obtain patent rights before any other company can learn what we are doing. I cannot stress too much, the importance of keeping your mouth shut about matters within the company." Patrick Evans stared at Danny, then said, "Do you understand the importance of what I am saying, and that you have signed an NDA?"

"Yes, Mr Evans, I understand, perfectly and you can rely on me because I'm not a gossip." Danny knew what Evans was talking about and realised that a person such as him, would have no mercy whatsoever for anyone who betrayed him.

"Your satisfactory progress in the company, is quite evident, and so I think it is the right time to put you up to the next salary band." He then smiled at Danny. "How does that sound to you?"

"That sounds wonderful, Mr Evans. Thank you very much."

"That is all I wanted to say," Patrick said by way of dismissal.

Thanking Evans again, Danny left the CEO's office and made his way back to his own. He realised what Evans's little talk was about. He knew that the emphasis was really centred on the possibility that he had seen him with his PA in what could only be described as a compromising situation. The raise to the next salary band was really a bribe.

The amorous affair between Patrick Evans, CEO, and Sharon Sumner, PA, had been going on for around a year and before today's incident, a very private and secret matter. Now that they had probably been seen by Danny Drew, the cat could be out of the bag with disastrous results. Evans was without doubt a womaniser and he had fancied Sharon from the first day that he had interviewed her for the position of PA. However, he had gone no further than resting his hand on her shoulder from time to time or putting his hand gently on her back when ushering her through a doorway.

One evening, past normal finishing time, Patrick was standing in front of his desk looking at some papers when Sharon came in from her own office next door, walked over to Patrick's desk and alongside him placed a file for him to see. He instantly turned around to the right as she simultaneously turned to her left which left them very, close and facing each other. They both gave a little laugh and he instinctively put out his hands, gently holding her upper arms. For a few moments they stood in that position. Sharon made no attempt to move but calmly looked up at him, the expression on her face unreadable. Knowing that the building was now deserted and that no one would interrupt, Patrick very gently pulled her closer, testing her reactions. There was no resistance whatsoever and so bending his head kissed her lightly on her forehead. She lifted her head, looking into his eyes without the slightest hesitation, moving very slightly towards him. He then kissed her with gradually increased passion. Sharon responded and put her arms around his neck gently moving her slender fingers, caressing him. This increased Patrick's ardour and his hands began exploring her body, the body he had longed to touch for such a long time. Sharon writhed with a growing passion. He began to explore her body in a more intimate manner, and she pulled herself closer to him not resisting his advances. Emboldened, he pulled down the front zip of her trousers. They looked intently at each other for a few seconds, then he quickly undid the top of her trousers, allowing them to fall to the floor. Sharon kicked off her shoes and trousers and gazed at him with the most alluring smile as his hands touched her bare flesh. Her mind now in a whirl, that intimate moment that she had never expected, and he had only fantasised about came like an explosion.

Driving home that evening, her mind raced over the event that she could hardly believe had happened. She was certain that although this was her first time of intimacy with Patrick, it would not be the last. She had started an affair with her boss.

5

Detective Inspector Bob Grant, sitting at his desk in the Incident Room, was in deep thought. This was the sixth day of the investigation. Weighing up what evidence they had, related to the murder, he felt that Julie Phillips was concealing her relationship with Danny Drew and that the only way to get to the truth would be to ask her directly.

"Toddy," he said to DC Jane Todd, "Go to the Supplies Department and bring Julie Phillips here. Tell her I need to speak with her, then I want you to sit in during the questioning and take notes. At this time, we will not record the proceedings and she will not be under caution. I don't want to alarm her but rather that she felt we are having a frank discussion."

Jane said, "Yes, Sir, right away."

When Julie arrived with DC Todd, Bob Grant said in his most friendly manner, "Hello Julie. Please take a seat." Then shuffling some papers on his desk, he said, "would you like a coffee?"

Julie replied in the affirmative and seemed to relax a little, feeling that this would be just a friendly interview. Exactly the atmosphere DC Grant wanted. Then his very direct questions would probably shock her into telling more than she had to date.

Addressing DC Todd, he said in a most friendly manner, "Toddy, bring three coffees please and then you can take notes of anything Julie may be able to tell us, however insignificant it may seem, that will help the investigation." He looked at Julie for a few moments before speaking. "Julie, I want you to be frank and truthful when answering a few questions that I would like to put to you. I would also remind you that to deliberately withhold vital information or give deliberately misleading answers to a police officer, is an offense."

"Yes, I understand," she said without hesitation.

Then DI Grant asked, "Were you having an affair with Danny Drew?" looking directly at her, waiting for her reply to his 'shock tactics'.

For a moment, Julie looked back at him, a look of shock on her face. Bob Grant could see tears welling up in Julie's eyes, then dropping her head, twisting her hands together, she said in a very, low voice, "Yes, I was."

"For how long, had the affair been going on?"

"For about three months. It started after I agreed to go for a drink with him when my husband was on the afternoon shift. He had been flirting with me and the other girls since he joined the company a couple of years ago. I always rebuffed him in a friendly way, and he would, in mock despair, say that one day I would probably regret spurning him. I used to say, don't forget that I am a married woman, then he would leave in his usual happy-go-lucky way."

"Having rejected his advances for so long, what reason had you to go for a drink with him?"

"My husband's attitude towards me. He has become a miserable person, grumbling about everything and everybody. He was cold towards me and we went out together only on rare occasions. The marriage had become a sham in almost every way. When Danny, once again, suggested I go for a drink with him, I thought to hell with it all, I will go out when my husband was at work and he need not know anything about it. After all I'm only going for a drink and with a jovial and happy man."

"When you left the pub, did you go straight home, or did you dally elsewhere?"

"We went straight home by taxi, which we shared. We waited in the car park for it to arrive. We were in the shadows, where we could not easily be seen, and we kissed. He tried a few advances but on that first occasion, the taxi arrived before things got serious."

"You went with him on more than one occasion?"

"Yes, twice. The second time, again in the car park, he became more amorous and although I was not surprised at that, I surprised myself by going along with it. Before anything could develop, it started raining very heavily and we had to run back to the entrance for shelter. The taxi came shortly afterwards. The following day he suggested seeing me at home. He said he would bring a bottle of wine. We would not be seen and being alone, we could relax."

"That I gather was the real start of the affair."

"Yes, I suppose it was. When he arrived, he was very amorous. We were in the kitchen and we started kissing. His hands were all over me and I didn't stop him. It was a continuation of where we left off in the car park when it started to rain. Then we had sex. That was the first time."

"Did he come to the house frequently?"

"Whenever my husband was on the afternoon shift it would be once or twice in that week.

"Did your husband have any suspicions of what you were up to?"

Julie explained how her husband had very nearly caught them in bed when he came home earlier than expected and Danny having to climb out of the bedroom window in a frantic rush.

Bob Grant was inwardly smiling at this but kept the serious expression on his face.

"Do you think that he knew about it all and came home early to catch you?"

"When I asked why he was home so early, he wouldn't say or even discuss it. It was the following day that he accused me of seeing Danny Drew because he had seen Danny's car in the car park when he came home. I tried to convince him that seeing his car, didn't mean he was with me. I lied and lied but I knew that he wasn't convinced that what I was saying was the truth."

"Did your husband make any threats. Did he threaten you?"

"The only thing he said was that if he caught him here, he would break his bloody neck. That threat scared me."

DI Grant thanked Julie for being so forthright in answering his questions and asked her if she knew of anyone who might have had a grudge against Danny, other than her husband. To Grant's surprise she said, "Perhaps Mr Evans. I can't think of anyone else."

"Why do you think that Mr Evans might bear a grudge?"

Julie paused for a few moments to collect her thoughts. Then she told DI grant that Sharon Sumner had been to see her. "She asked me if Danny had said anything to me about seeing Patrick Evans and herself in the office. I knew straight away what she was referring to. Danny had told me in confidence what he had seen but he didn't know if the CEO was sure that he had really seen them embracing. He quickly put the file he had brought on Sharon's desk and was on his way out, when, the CEO called him back." Julie then explained how he had spoken to Danny and his raise to the next salary band. She also told him how Sharon had told her about her affair with Patrick Evans and how it had started, begging her to say nothing to anyone.

DI Grant stood, up and thanking her once again for her frankness to his questions, asked that should she think of anything else that could be of use to them, no matter how insignificant it may seem, speak to him, or any other member of the team. Julie was at the door, on her way out, then stopped and turned back to the DI. "There is something that I have just remembered. When Danny last went to Liverpool to see his mother, his long- standing friend, the one he used to go with to watch Liverpool play at Anfield, had told him something that he said would be a bombshell if it was confirmed. He wouldn't say more at that time, but he did say that the information had come from his friend's girlfriend who worked at Eco-Tech Insulation."

When Julie had gone, the DI said to Jane Todd, "I bloody knew it. I knew from the start that she could say more about her association with Danny Drew and now the revelation that Patrick Evans is having it off with his PA is dynamite. If that became public knowledge, his career with the company would be over. He is a married man and I do know that the opinions held by Sir Ian Leighton-Boyce are totally towards family unity and that he would not tolerate one of his senior executives committing adultery, especially with a PA." Then with a shake of his head, looking at Jane, he exclaimed, "Bloody hell, are they all at it do you think. Is this, a den-of-iniquity? That last thing she spoke of is very, interesting. I would think that when he referred to a bombshell, it would be the effect on Salopian Industries which he would be thinking about. Maybe we should look a little deeper, turn over a few more stones and see what emerges.

I believe that Don Phillips is our number one prime suspect but considering our latest information, we could, perhaps, put down Patrick Evans as number two. At the time the alarm of the incident was raised, Don Phillips and Patrick Evans were seen at the far end of the building and in conversation. We only have Evans' word that he had only just entered the building wanting to speak with the senior production foreman. Also, we don't know with any certainty where Phillips had been earlier. I believe that we should bring Phillips in, under caution, and interrogate him. I think that the DCI will agree but I'll put it to him before we act.

Whatever information Danny's friend gave him was probably connected to the business of this company. Since the source of the information was from someone working for a competitor, I would speculate that either product sales or product development would be involved."

The following day, Don Phillips was on his forty-eight hours off between change of shifts. When DI Grant and DS Robb went to the house, there was no reply, so they went to the factory to ask Julie where her husband might be, as they needed to speak to him. Julie told them that he often went fishing on his days off and that sometimes he would stay away for the two days he had off work. He usually stayed at a B&B in Ironbridge which, being close to the River Severn, was very convenient. She gave them the address and said that the name of the lady who ran it was a Mrs Addison.

When they went to see Mrs Addison, she confirmed that Don Phillips often stayed with her, but she had not seen him for a couple of weeks. With that, they returned to the Incident Room. Later that day, DCI Davies called the team together urgently.

"The body of a man has just been recovered from the River Severn, upstream of Ironbridge. From the contents of his wallet and his driving license he has been identified as Don Phillips. He suffered blunt force trauma to the back of his skull and then drowned. He was obviously pushed into the river following the physical attack. He had been fishing, his fishing tackle was found about five hundred yards upstream. He appears to have been alone but, with evidence of a struggle, he must have suffered an attack before falling or being pushed into the river. Since his wallet was still in his pocket and his fishing tackle was all there, robbery does not appear to have been the motive. That a stranger would come along the towpath, hit him on the head, with some type of weapon, and then push him into the river, I don't believe can be considered. That leads me to think that the killer knew him and obviously had a very, serious grudge against him, which is probably the understatement of the year."

"Bloody hell, he was my prime suspect for the murder of Danny Drew," exclaimed Bob Grant. "This is absolutely incredulous." Rubbing his chin in contemplative thought, he finally addressed the DCI. "Sir, do you think that these two murders are connected and if so, are we looking for one perpetrator, or are we dealing with two separate incidents with totally different motives?"

"I think that in the first instance we must consider both possibilities. It is important, I believe, that we look more deeply into the backgrounds of both victims. There may be some common factor that connects them. For instance, Julie Phillips was married to one of the victims and having a torrid affair with the other. She is a common factor. Unless she has a good alibi, Julie Phillips could be in the frame for the murder of her husband but in my opinion, not for Danny Drew. In such a scenario, we would be looking for two separate assailants with different motives. For the two incidents to be linked, we must look for a common motive. As I have already said, we need to examine the backgrounds of both victims. "DS Robb, you and I will do the search on the background of Don Phillips. DI Grant, you go up to Liverpool and take DC Todd with you. Speak with the Merseyside force, give them the facts of the murder of Danny Drew and request their assistance. Your first line of enquiry must involve Danny's friend, and the girlfriend."

***

DI Bob Grant and DC Jane Todd travelled to Liverpool by train. This trip was going to take at least a whole day, so they had been booked into a hotel on the waterfront. This was very convenient not being far from police headquarters. They had travelled late afternoon so that they could begin their enquiries, first thing the following morning. Taking a taxi from Lime Street Station, they went straight to the hotel. They decided to have a meal and then a relaxed evening. Maybe a stroll along the waterfront because in the evening, with the lights on, the view was quite spectacular DI Grant had been told.

The following morning, they went to police headquarters to speak with DCS Stuart, a friendly man but with a direct attitude. He was fully briefed on the reason for their visit and so the start of the discussion was easy. He had allocated a car for their use along with a driver.

Danny's friend was a man by the name of Paddy McGuire who, DCS Stuart confirmed had no police record and so he could not give them any information about his background other than his job was with a local firm of builders. He suggested, they go to the company's address, in Huyton, a suburb of Liverpool and they would be directed to the site McGuire was working on.

Paddy McGuire was a pleasant young man who was very, upset about the death of his friend Danny, who he described as his 'best mate', since school days. He was stunned when he received the news of the murder and couldn't think why anyone would want to kill him.

"We understand that you told him something, when you last saw him, that was very significant to him, so much so, that he apparently made the comment to a person he was close to, that if whatever you told him was confirmed it would be a bombshell to his company."

"I know what you are referring to. It was something my girlfriend told me. She works for Eco-Tech, a company making insulation products. They have recently started to make a new type of insulation board, in small experimental batches, that has some unique qualities. I don't know the details or how well they are progressing with the work, but my girlfriend thinks that, from something she overheard, someone from Danny's firm has been feeding them information on the work being carried out at Telford because apparently the chemical formulation was top secret. At Danny's firm, only two or three people knew the details. He told me that only personnel from, I think he said, Company Engineering along with the chemists, were allowed access to the development area. Security was quite strict."

"If your girlfriend learns anything further, would you please let us know. If what you have told us is confirmed, it would suggest, that something underhand is going on and could possibly have a bearing on Danny's murder."

They thanked Paddy McGuire for his help and took their leave. In the car, on the way back to Headquarters, Bob Grant said to Jane, "This new information puts yet another aspect on the case." Gazing through the window he said, in thoughtful manner, "What if someone believed

Danny knew what was going on and that he also knew the identity of that someone. That could be a motive for murder. If what we were told about security being tight is true, the list of suspects in such a scenario is reduced dramatically. It would, surely, have to be someone working in development."

Back in the Incident Room, DI Grant had given his report on his visit to Liverpool and put forward the additional aspect of industrial espionage being a possible motive for murder. The fact that two employees of Salopian Industries had been killed, although in different circumstances, there could be a possible link. After all, both victims had suffered blunt force trauma to the back of the skull.

DCI Harry Davies then addressed the assembly. "DS Robb and I have discovered some interesting facts concerning the background of Don Phillips. He was twelve years older than his wife, Julie, as you are aware. There is nothing unusual in that, but we now know that Julie was his second wife. He married his first wife when he was, twenty-five and she was twenty-two. They lived here in Telford and he worked for this company. They had been married for seven years, apparently happily, when his wife died in tragic circumstances. She had been vacuuming the living room carpet when she accidently tripped on the power cable, falling with considerable force, striking her head on the hearthstone. Don Phillips was at home that morning and it was he who called 999. The paramedics arrived within five minutes, but there was nothing they could do for her, she was dead. There was of course an inquest at which, when questioned by the coroner, the next-door neighbours claimed that they had heard raised voices that morning and assumed there to have been a domestic argument. Don Phillips denied this, saying that his wife was happily listening to the radio whilst she was working and he was reading the newspaper, having a cup of tea at the kitchen table. He suggested that what the neighbours had heard was the radio because the volume was rather high, so that his wife could hear above the sound of the vacuum cleaner. Finally, the coroner gave his verdict as accidental death because there was no evidence to suggest otherwise. When the police examined the scene, they confirmed that the she had indeed fallen, striking her head on the hearthstone and that her right foot was caught up with the power cable. The brother-in-law of Don Phillips never liked him, apparently a mutual feeling, and they were always at variance with each other. After the death of his sister, despite the verdict given by the coroner, he had accused Don of fighting with her and pushing her, causing her to fall with fatal consequences. He said that he was sure that what the neighbours had heard was a full-blown row and not the radio as claimed."

There was considerable discussion amongst the team. The possibility that Don Phillips' death was a revenge killing, could not be ruled out, was the general opinion.

DCI Harry Davies called for attention. "We now have much more information about the victims and their respective backgrounds. There is the possibility that Danny Drew was killed by a jealous husband or due to some connection with industrial espionage. However, the jealous husband has, himself been killed. Why and who by? If Danny's murder was in connection with industrial espionage. what or who is that connection? At this moment, there seems to be more questions than ready answers."

6

Julie Phillips usually cycled to and from work and during the week following Danny's death, going to her grandmother's, with whom she was staying, she was cycling along a narrow lane which these days was rarely used by motorised traffic, the new main road being preferable. A few moments before turning into the lane off the A5, she was aware of a car behind her and going very slowly. The lane was wide enough for one vehicle and had frequent passing places cut into the banking. As Julie cycled along, she became aware of a car behind her, so, she pulled into one of the passing places to allow the car to pass. The car accelerated as if to pass but steered towards the passing place. Julie jumped backwards, letting her bike fall to the ground. Fortunately, the driver of the car had to steer back to the road to avoid hitting the banking and then accelerated away. Julie was trembling with shock as she picked herself up, having fallen backwards into the long grass of the banking. Picking up her bike, which was unharmed, she continued her journey to her grandmother's house.

Telling her grandmother what had happened, she burst into tears. She said that the incident was, without doubt, deliberate with the obvious intention to injure or kill her. Her grandmother called the police and told them what had happened and that her granddaughter worked at the factory where 'that young man had been recently murdered'. The desk sergeant told them to remain indoors and an officer would see them shortly.

It was DI Bob Grant that arrived, accompanied by DC Jane Todd. Julie related to them the sequence of events. The DI asked her if she had seen the registration number, but unfortunately, it had all happened so quickly and in jumping backwards and falling into the long grass of the banking she had no chance of seeing it but she could tell them that it was a saloon car of medium size and in a dark colour, possibly dark blue.

When they finally took their leave, DI Grant said to Jane, "If what Julie Phillips has told us is in fact true, it was, a direct attempt on her life.

It makes me think that whoever it was, must have known about Julie's relationship with Danny Drew and is afraid of what she may know."

"Sir, I don't think she would make up a story like that. She did seem to be in shock."

"I don't mean that the event didn't happen, but whether or not, Julie has mistaken a bit of bad driving for a direct attempt to do her harm. If it was a deliberate attack, then the perpetrator must believe that she maybe a danger to him or her, because of what Danny Drew may have told her. This could all be connected to corporate espionage."

"Danny told Julie about his 'bombshell', without giving her any details but whoever is behind all this, won't know that Julie has no knowledge whatsoever. I think it could be connected to that company in Liverpool, in which case, I feel sure that you are right, Sir."

"It also means that the perpetrator knows that Danny Drew knew about whatever is going on. Since the information that he had, came from the girlfriend of Danny's pal, how did the perpetrator know that Danny was 'in the know'?"

At the briefing the following morning, DCI Harry Davies was given the details of Julie Phillips's encounter which he said gave him considerable concern. Her life could well be in danger. After a short time looking at the events board, he turned to the assembly and spoke with emphasis. "The facts beginning to emerge are leading me to believe that in the case of Danny Drew's murder, the motive may well have been connected to whatever information he had been given by his pal's girlfriend, in which case, we could rule out the work of a jealous husband. Also, we need to consider the death of Don Phillips, that too, may be connected in some way for he was the jealous husband but, for what reason was he killed and, by whom? We need to question, in more depth, the personnel working on the development of the new product because if information is being passed to Eco-Tech, it is essential that we discover who is passing the information and how they are doing it. With regard, to the incident involving Julie Phillips, we need to have her under surveillance because she could be targeted again. I will leave you to arrange that, DI Grant and I think you, DC Todd, should visit Julie Phillips again. Have a good chat with her, woman to woman, you know what I mean. We may learn more that way and it will help her feel more secure."

DC Jane Todd visited Julie at her grandmother's home, where she was living, for the time being. They could talk freely and privately which would not be possible at her place of work. Julie made coffee which she brought into the lounge and sitting comfortably, Jane told her to call her Jane and forget the 'DC Todd' because it was more friendly. Jane chatted to her, asking questions but in a conversational way rather than in the manner of normal police questioning.

"I know that you were very close to Danny and his death, being that of murder, must be terrible for you but now with the murder of your husband how does that make you feel?"

"I loved Danny very much and I miss him beyond words. My husband Don, had become distant towards me, didn't want to go anywhere or do anything as a couple. In that sense, I don't miss him. Even on his days off between shift changes he would sometimes take himself off fishing for both days, staying overnight at a B&B on his own. I sometimes wondered if he was seeing another woman. But, after all is said and done, he was my husband and because there was a time when I did love him, I mourn him. If only he had continued to be as he was when we were first married, I am sure that I would never have given way to the advances of Danny, but as things were, I was seriously considering asking him for a divorce."

"Would you have considered marrying Danny?"

"Yes, I would. In fact, that is what I told Danny's mother when she came to see me."

"When did Danny's mother come to see you?"

"Three or four days after he was killed. I cannot remember exactly when. I have been so upset with all that's happened, my mind seems to have been in a whirl."

"She, obviously, must have known about your relationship with her son. Did she say how she had got that knowledge and how she knew where you lived?"

"She had been in to see Patrick Evans because he wished to speak with her and to give her Danny's personal effects that were in his office. Afterwards, she saw Sharon Sumner, who told her about me. I had confided in Sharon and didn't expect her to say anything to anybody, let alone Danny's mother. She must have told her where I lived."

"Did she say why she had come to see you?"

"She said that she thought Danny had a girlfriend and when Sharon told her about me and that I was married, she wanted to see me and talk with me."

"What was your opinion of her?"

"I think that she was of the opinion that I was just enjoying 'a bit on the side' and not being fair to her son but I am sure that she changed her mind when I had been 'frank' with her about my marital situation. She said that no wife should be treated in the way that I described. Then she asked if my husband had any idea of what Danny and I were doing behind his back. I told her that he was suspicious of Danny because he had seen his car in the car park, lower down the road but that was all. We were careful to avoid being seen in any compromising way. I liked her because she listened to what I was telling her without appearing to be judgemental. She is a very shrewd person and what surprised me was that she had been an athlete her speciality being the triathlon, running, cycling and swimming. Although she is now in her late forties, she still goes to the gym on a regular basis."

They chatted for a little while longer, then Jane said that she would now have to leave but if Julie would like to chat further, she would be pleased to come again.

"Yes, please come again whenever you are able," Julie said. "I have enjoyed our chatting and it has been some relief for me under the present circumstances."

The following day, in the Incident Room, Jane gave an account of her meeting with Julie. The team listened with great interest and when Jane had finished speaking DCI Davies brought their attention to the events board and began writing items and headings, in an attempt, to summarise the knowledge they had so far obtained.

"I am now of the opinion that the murder of Danny Drew is directly due to industrial espionage, that being connected to the new product being developed here at Salopian Industries. I also believe that the 'spying company' is Eco-Tech in Liverpool. What we need to establish is who the actual spy is, and how the information is being delivered. If it is by electronic means, we have a good chance of tracking the person involved. If, however, it is by manual means, the job is that of identifying the carrier. Whatever the case, it is highly likely that the person involved is the person who killed Danny Drew because they were aware that he knew what was going on and who the culprit was."

There was general agreement of this theory. It made perfect sense and perhaps explained why Danny was in the unlikely place as the tank platform and at a time when there was no one around.

"With regard to the murder of Don Phillips, we must consider two distinct possibilities. Was it also connected to industrial espionage or some other reason in which case we cannot rule out Julie as a 'suspect'. We need to know her whereabouts at the time of her husband's death. But there may well be someone else with a grudge of large proportions or even revenge for some problem, or action, for which Don Phillips was responsible or considered responsible. We know that he would often go fishing on his days off work, sometimes he would spend two full days away leaving Julie at home. The B&B at which he stayed we know is operated by Mrs Addison, whom we have already questioned as to when she last saw him. She told us that she had not seen him for a couple of weeks, but we only have her word for that. Mrs Addison is a married woman whose husband works at the local fire station on shift work, he is a firefighter. It is a possibility that she and Don Phillips were closer than we are given to believe. Remember that Julie made a chance remark, that she sometimes wondered if he was seeing another woman. Check out that possibility."

***

It was one of those evenings when Patrick Evans would stay beyond the normal finishing time. The Head Office building being deserted, he could be alone with Sharon without fear of being caught. He would always ask her, the previous day, 'if she could stay late' tomorrow. Sharon knew of course, what was in his mind and on the day, would wear a trouser suit because trousers were much easier to kick off than dealing with skirts and tights.

Patrick held her in his arms, gradually moving his hands down her back and onto the back of her thighs, pulling her to press up to him. They kissed and then deftly Patrick pulled down the front zip of her trousers, undid the top and let them fall to the floor. Then Sharon kicked of her shoes and trousers, an action that she was now well used to, and he lifted her to perch on the edge of his desk. He pushed up to her with an urgency she hadn't experienced before.

Finally, their passion exhausted, Sharon sat forward putting her arms around his neck and said, "My darling, don't you think it's time we did this in a little more comfort than on the edge of your desk?"

"The problem is that I can't take you home. My wife would object," he replied with a laugh. "To use a hotel locally would be courting disaster because we would eventually be seen by someone."

"I am, well aware, of that but there's no reason why you couldn't come to mine."

"That would be wonderful, but when?"

"Tomorrow if you wish and whenever you are able to come."

"Tomorrow it is then, straight after work."

They both knew that what they were doing was highly risky but neither of them wanted to stop. It was important to Patrick, to keep up appearances of normality. That of a happily married man and a senior manager of a successful company but he was enjoying the relationship he now had with Sharon so much that he was determined to keep both, whatever he may have to do in order to do so. He wanted to 'have the cake and to eat it.'

Sharon had now developed other aspirations. She knew that the lifestyle of Patrick was good and one to which she aspired. She was aware of her own sophisticated presence and always felt confident in whatever company she happened to be. The truth of the matter was that she could now see herself in the position of Mrs Evans. It was perhaps a long shot, but slowly she could probably win Patrick around to those thoughts. One thing she did know for certain, Patrick Evans was a very sexy man and she knew that she was more than capable of complying to all his desires and wishes. Tomorrow might well be a glorious opportunity to impart to Patrick a feeling of what a normal domestic life with her would be like.

7

DCI Harry Davies accompanied by DC Jane Todd went to the Development Department to interview the personnel, making it clear to all that they were interested in learning anything that anyone may have seen and perhaps thought to be unusual on the morning of Danny Drew's murder, either within or outside the department. They began their questioning with Gwyn Thomas, the chemist from Williams Bros. Ltd, the company taken over by Salopian Industries, the company that began the development of the new insulation board but hadn't the financial resources to carry the project through to become a financially viable product. The company, Williams Bros. Ltd., well known in Cardiff, was family owned by two brothers neither of which had a successor capable or even desirous of carrying on the company name on their retirement. They were both in their mid to late fifties and so decided to sell the company and retire.

The core business was that of fabricating and selling insulation products to the industrial and structural market and had for many years used base products supplied by Salopian Industries. The younger brother was a qualified industrial chemist and it was he who came up with the idea of the new board. Needing practical assistance, they employed Gwyn Thomas, a very promising graduate, to progress the development and so he became the driving force behind the project.

Addressing Gwyn, the DCI asked, "Were you part of the deal when your old company was taken over, to continue the work into commercial status?"

"No, not in that sense, although Salopian did suggest that I continue the work at Telford, in their employment. At the time, I was not very enthusiastic about moving to Telford. I would have much preferred to have stayed in Cardiff but that would have meant finding another job. To find a job of equal status, as a young graduate, is not easy these days. There were a couple of other companies interested in taking over at the time, either of which would have been preferable to me because one was in Manchester and the other in Liverpool, both being big and progressive cities. Please don't tell the bosses what I have just said. I don't think Mr Evans would be very, pleased. However, when the decision was made to sell to Salopian, I accepted the offer to come and work here in Telford."

"How near are you now, to producing on a commercial basis?"

"We are virtually ready to produce boards, but we are still working on the manufacture of pipe fittings."

"Did Danny Drew ever come into this department?"

"Yes, he would sometimes come in to look at the production equipment. He was very interested in our progress. I suppose he thought that it wouldn't be too long before the equipment would be handed over to production and then he would have the responsibility of day-to-day maintenance."

"I was given to believe that there was strict security in here and only development personnel were allowed access."

"In the early days, that was true. The chemical formulation was particularly well-guarded but now it is necessary for all production staff to have full details, otherwise we would not be able to produce commercially. The production equipment also needs to be fully familiar to all concerned for obvious reasons."

"Am I correct in assuming any of the employees can come and go as they please?"

"In fact, only those who have need to come here, do so."

"Thank you for giving me the background to the project. I now have a much better understanding of the situation." After a short pause and looking directly at Gwyn, the DCI asked, "Did you see anything unusual or anyone acting in a suspicious manner on the morning of the incident?"

"I can't remember anything unusual. It was just a normal morning"

"Where were you between eleven o'clock and twelve thirty pm?"

"I was here in this department. The other members of staff will confirm that."

DCI Davies thanked him for his assistance and said, "We may need to speak with you again."

John Preston, the design engineer responsible for the project development under the direction of Arthur Brown, the project engineer was the next to be interviewed

"For how long, have you worked here Mr Preston?" the DCI asked.

"Since Company Engineering Division was formed. When the new positions required were advertised, I applied and was fortunate enough to be appointed. I was delighted when I was offered the position of senior design engineer with the responsibility of developing this new product to commercial viability."

"Who did you work for before coming here?"

"Ellison and Page, engineers in Liverpool. They are general engineers but do a lot of structural work as well as machine design and machine building."

"I understand that you are a married man with a family, is that correct?"

"Yes, my wife's name is Andrea and we have two children."

"Do they like living in this part of the world, quite a change for them I should think?"

"They all love being here. Although we originate from Liverpool and city life, we as a family have always loved the countryside. Here in Shropshire, we have some of the best in England."

"I am told that this new board project is virtually ready to go into full-time production."

"Yes, it certainly is ready, and I am delighted to say that the production rates we can achieve are well above the minimum required for commercial viability."

"All-in-all, a resounding success, would you say?"

"Absolutely. I now look forward to bringing the next phase to completion."

"Regarding the tragic incident that took place in the factory just over a week ago, do you remember anything unusual happening or seeing anyone behaving strangely."

"No, I can't think of anything at all. I'm sorry I can't be of more help."

"Thank you, Mr Preston for your patience. However, I must ask, where were you between eleven o'clock and twelve thirty pm?"

"Here in the department, although I did go over to Supplies around eleven thirty and I was away for around twenty minutes."

"Just one more question. Has the company made an application for patent on the product?"

"I believe the necessary documentation is now in the hands of solicitors in readiness for submission."

"I would impress on your superiors, that the sooner the submission is made, the better."

The DCI and DC Jane Todd left the department and headed for the Incident Room. There Jane thumbed through the notes she had taken during the interviews with the two leading figures of the development project. There was nothing that stood out as being significant when considering the possibility of industrial espionage. Both men had given the impression of being satisfied with their respective jobs. Gwyn Thomas had indicated that a move from Cardiff to either Manchester or Liverpool would have been preferable to Telford, but there was no hint of dissatisfaction such that would induce him to engage himself in the shadowy world of espionage. John Preston, a family man, appeared to be happy in Telford and seemed to be displaying pride and satisfaction in bringing the project to completion.

Despite all of this, DCI Davies remained convinced that there was betrayal somewhere in the scheme of things. "Jane, I am going to speak with Patrick Evans. I believe that we should, if possible, put someone in the Development Department undercover. We may then discover if there is some underhand work going on and hopefully by whom."

Patrick Evans was astounded by the possibility of details of the new process being given to a competitor, especially should it prove to be Eco-Tech. He was aware that they were the company in Liverpool that made an offer for the takeover of Williams Bros. Ltd. but could not imagine who they could have managed to persuade to steal information about the new process. He readily agreed with the DCI's suggestion to put in an undercover police officer, for if there was a mole in the department, then the work now being carried out on pipe fittings was at risk. Also, the final work on boards being in the possession of an opponent, who could very well beat them to obtaining a patent on the products. The mole must be identified urgently.

When about to leave, DCI Davies said, “Mr Evans, I am sure that you will be pleased to know that in a couple of days, we shall move the Incident Room back to Headquarters. I do thank you for your generous accommodation and for your patience with our presence. However, you will still be seeing us quite frequently during the next week or so as we continue and hopefully wrap up the investigation.”

“Perhaps I shouldn’t be asking this question but, have you yet any idea who could have committed this awful crime?”

“A number of facts are beginning to fit into place as we explore several lines of enquiry. I am confident that we shall soon be able to identify the person or persons responsible.”

***

PC Gail Sykes, now in her fourth year in uniform, was the chosen undercover agent. Prior to joining the force, she had attended college on a Business Studies course, and so it was thought could easily fit in as a clerical assistant,.

Sharon Sumner, at Evans’ request took Gail into the department, introducing her to the staff, after having taken her to see John Preston. Patrick Evans had previously told John of her appointment Preston was delighted to have the assistance and had told Patrick Evans that it would make his task a little easier. He welcomed Gail with a genuine warmth and explained the kind of things she would be doing.

After her first day in her new situation, she reported to DI Grant, at Divisional police Headquarters. She must not be seen by anyone speaking with the investigation team or her cover could be compromised. Everything had gone well for her and she was comfortable with all the staff. However, one thing that caught her attention was the fact that the computer in John Preston’s office didn’t appear to have a password which surprised her because this was the machine that John used to store technical data and send technical reports to Patrick Evans and outside destinations as required. DI Grant told her to watch for anyone else, other than Preston, using that computer and that he would speak with Evans, recommending that a password should be introduced.

Patrick Evans told Sharon to speak to John Preston and tell him to introduce a password immediately to ensure security, and conform to legislation, which she did, explaining that security was of prime importance as it was thought that technical information was being given to an outside source.

"Whoever would do that?" he asked in astonishment.

"Whoever it is that is trying to obtain the product patent. There must be a mole in this company"

"A mole, here in this department!"

"It's almost certain, so we must be vigilant at all times. That's why Mr Evans has ordered that a password on your computer is essential. The only people who will know the password will be you, Mr Evans and myself. We have already talked of being vigilant, let us use the word VIGILANCE as the password. Quite appropriate don't you think?"

"Yes, you could say that."

8

The investigation team now back at Divisional police Headquarters, assembled for the morning briefing. DCI Davies addressed them, saying, "I am now of the opinion that there are two possibilities in this case that will give us the motive for the murder of Danny Drew. The first being that of a jealous husband, feeling betrayed by his wife. The second possibility is that of industrial espionage. Considering the first, the obvious suspect is Don Phillips. We know that he was in the building when the victim was discovered, although at the far end of the area and talking with Patrick Evans. He could very easily have quickly made his way back there, after killing Danny. However, we must not forget that Don Phillips was, himself, murdered. For what reason and by whom are two big questions that at this moment in time I have no idea. Then let us consider the second possibility, that of industrial espionage. In this case, it would be fair to assume that Danny knew the identity of the mole and that the mole was aware that he had been discovered. We have questioned the reason for the victim being on that platform many times but have been unable to come to any satisfactory answer. Perhaps he was lured there, but if so, what could have been the 'bait', do you think? My thoughts go back to the statement that Julie Phillips made about Danny telling her about something that he had learned from his pal up in Liverpool that would be a bombshell if it became public knowledge. He didn't tell Julie what that bombshell was but since it originally came from his pal's girlfriend who worked at Eco-Tech, I suspect that it was something that connected the two companies. Maybe espionage. DI Grant, I think that you should go back to Liverpool and interview Danny Drew's pal again. Find out what this bombshell was. Take Jane with you and if possible, try to speak with the girlfriend. If industrial espionage was the motive, we must consider if the killing of Don Phillips was connected or was it for some other reason, in which case we are looking for two separate killers."

***

Back in Liverpool, Grant and Todd, having travelled by train walked from Lime Street Station to Merseyside police Headquarters. It was good to have the exercise after the train journey. DCI Davies had already spoken with DCS Stuart and as on their previous visit, a car and driver had been arranged for the following morning. They were well received by DCS Stuart, who gave them his assurance of help and cooperation in their investigation.

They arranged to have dinner at seven o'clock, which they enjoyed in a relaxed manner accompanied by a bottle of Cabernet-Syrah. Conversation soon centred on the reason for their visit to Liverpool. What could possibly have been so sensational for Danny to say that it would be a 'bombshell' if it became known publicly? They talked round and round the subject but could not come to any plausible reason other than the possibility of it being in some way connected to the theory already put forward. That of industrial espionage.

Having finished dinner and being only eight-thirty on a late April evening they decided to take a walk from the hotel, along the waterfront, having enjoyed a lovely meal. Dusk, with the lights illuminating the iconic Cunard building and the other examples of a period of architecture long since gone, was uplifting. The lights being reflected in the waters of the River Mersey, echoing the picture before them and the Mersey ferry, almost at its destination of the Liverpool Pier Head completed the scene of tranquillity. They had walked some distance without speaking. The scene and atmosphere occupying their minds, such that the reason for their presence in this place, was for a short while, pushed to the back of their consciousness. The spell was finally broken by the sound of a motorbike accelerating along the road and passing them along the way.

"Perhaps we should make our way back. We can have a nightcap in the bar before we retire. What do you think?"

"Yes Sir, that would be fine with me."

"Whatever you do, don't call me Sir in the bar. I don't want to draw attention to ourselves. Just call me Bob and I will refer to you as Toddy, is that ok?"

"That will be fine, Sir. Sorry, Bob."

They both laughed and made their way back to the hotel.

The following morning, having breakfasted together, DI Bob Grant and DC Jane Todd left the hotel and walked to police Headquarters. It was a lovely bright morning with that atmospheric feeling that spring had arrived. The city was already very much alive, the amount of traffic and the bustle of the populace making their way to their places of work giving testimony to the fact. Finally arriving at police Headquarters, they made the acquaintance of their appointed driver and so to the allotted car arranged for their use. The driver was the same officer that had driven them on their last visit.

"Good morning, sir," he said, addressing the DI, then "Good morning Ma'am," to Jane. "I have been instructed to take you to the building company in Huyton, that you visited when last you were here."

"Yes, that is so," replied Grant.

They were soon being whisked through the city traffic with the skill and assurance that comes with the daily experience of such conditions.

"The person we wish to speak with will most probably be on a building site away from the yard," Grant said to the driver. "I just hope that it's not too far away."

"In all probability, it will be the same site as last time, Sir."

And, so it proved to be. Paddy McGuire was surprised to see them, but DI Grant quickly reassured him and put him at ease. He explained that, when they last talked, there had been mention of something that had been said which Danny Drew had thought to be highly significant.

"I understand that your girlfriend had either seen or heard something which Danny said would be like a bombshell if it became known. Can you remember what it was?"

"It was someone that Sophie, my girlfriend, had seen at work and knew that she worked at Danny's place. She mentioned her name, but I can't remember it myself."

"Do you know how your girlfriend knew this person?"

"Yes, Sophie had seen her last Christmas time and remembered her face."

"How and where did she see her last Christmas?"

"Sophie and I went to Telford to see Danny and his new flat. While we were there, we had a drink with him in the pub. Being the week before

Christmas there were, that night, a lot of the people from his works. It was their Christmas do. There were a lot of women and as I remember, a couple of them that Danny said he fancied the pants off. That was Danny. He always fancied the girls. We didn't speak to them, although they did wave to him when they noticed him. I remember that there was a big fellow there and seemed to be with them, but he spent most of the time at the bar talking with some other fellows. He didn't pay very much attention to the women."

"What you have told us, is indeed, interesting. Do you think your girlfriend would still be able to recall the name of the woman she recognised?"

"Maybe she would. She has a better memory for that sort of thing than I have."

"Could you arrange with her to meet us. We should be grateful to hear what she remembers of this woman and if she remembers her name."

"Sophie's away at the moment. She's in York visiting her sister who's just had a nipper."

"Have you any idea how long she will be away."

"A couple of weeks I think, but I'm not sure."

Knowing that they had all the information that could be gleaned from Paddy McGuire, the DI thanked him for his help, asking him to contact them when his girlfriend returned so that arrangements could be made for them to speak with her. Paddy assured them that he would do so, and with that they headed back to police headquarters.

After leaving police headquarters, they headed to St. John's Market and had a light lunch, before making their way to Lime Street Station. The next train to Crewe, was at three-twenty so they had plenty of time with no need to rush. This would give plenty of time to make the connection to Shrewsbury and then to Wellington. All in all, this had been a successful day, the only disappointment being that of not speaking with Paddy's girlfriend.

The journey gave them the opportunity to go over all the facts that they now had. They now knew that someone who worked for Salopian Industries had been to Eco-Tech, a competitor who had originally been a contender to take over Williams Bros. Ltd. and have the new type of insulation board. What was the reason for their visit to Eco-Tech? Was that person there, with the prospect of going to work there or was there a more sinister reason, such as delivering technical details. One fact that they were now certain of was that the unknown person was a woman. That narrowed down the field of enquiry, but there was a goodly number of women at Salopian Industries who could be that unknown person. To learn the name of the woman was crucial to the investigation and the sooner that they could speak with Paddy's girlfriend the better.

Paddy had mentioned two women they had seen last Christmas in the pub, who Danny had said he fancied. It was highly likely that one of them was Julie Phillips because he had mentioned the presence of a "big fellow" apparently being with them and Don Phillips was a big man. It was an established fact that Danny Drew and Julie Phillips were having an affair by her own admission. It was not plausible that the unknown woman at Eco-Tech was Julie because Julie had, herself, mentioned the comment made by Danny about the 'bombshell'. He had quite obviously known who it was and that most certainly was not Julie.

If this was, as suspected, a case of industrial espionage, then whoever the mole was, must be in a position to be able to extract the information and deliver it, by some method to Eco-Tech and in a manner undetected by her colleagues.

All these facts were discussed by the DI and Jane Todd during their journey. Another aspect was put forward by Jane Todd.

"Sir, suppose that there is more than one person involved. The unknown woman could be just the messenger. There could be, perhaps, a man involved. It was suggested that it was probably a man that killed Danny because of the manner, in which he was pulled, then pushed over the edge of the platform. That needed some strength to accomplish. We also know that Don Phillips was in the building when Danny's body was found."

"A good point, Toddy, although we must not forget that Don Phillips was himself murdered shortly after Danny. Was that because of his involvement and if so, by whom, or was death due to some other reason, which, at this moment, is unknown?"

9

Monday morning, the start of a new week in the Development Department and the start of new protocol as Arthur Brown explained to the assembled staff.

"You will all be aware that the computer, which to date has been for the use of all personnel, has been moved onto John Preston's desk. He, and he alone, will use it from now on. The new computer, which you will notice is now where the other one was placed, is for general use by all of you. It is for storage of information relevant to your work, for test results and for calculations in the manner that you have been used to with the other one. However, there is no internet connection. Such material to be sent to other recipients will be done by John himself."

"Are we not to be trusted to do that?" asked Lucy Thompson, one of the engineers, with a hint of umbrage in her voice. Lucy was the sister-in-law of Sue Thompson from the Sales Department. Lucy had married Gavin Thompson, the brother of Sue's husband Adam. Gavin, was a PC in the local force.

"That is not the issue," was the reply by Arthur Brown.

"Well, there must be some reason for the change. If it is not one of trust, I would very much like to know what it is," Lucy said, this time with distinct umbrage.

"If you must know, there is a strong suspicion that information has been leaked from this department to an unknown source, either accidentally or by intent. You are all aware of the critical importance of secrecy as we approach the time of applying for product patent, since we believe that there are other bodies who would like to get there before us. We are not completely sure who they are, but we do know that there were two other companies in the takeover bids for Williams Brothers and so it would not be surprising to learn that one, or both of them, were fishing for information. Our bid was the successful one, and so we have the new insulation board project. Bringing this product into commercial viability is vitally important, the financial rewards being enormous. Don't take these moves as a personal slur. That is not the intention. As I have already said, it is a matter of security."

With that, Arthur Brown left them to consider what he had just revealed to them. For a moment in time, there was a deathly silence, then an explosion of voices gabbling to each other. The news just given them had stunned them. They all realised that although Arthur Brown had not made any accusations or even hinted that anyone in the Department was under suspicion, there could be no doubt that they were all suspects in the eyes of management. A day that began as most days usually did, had suddenly changed. The news just revealed to them by Arthur Brown, coupled with the recent murder of a colleague on these very premises gave them all a surreal feeling. Whatever next could be coming down the track, time alone would tell.

Construction work on the plant had resumed after forensics had given clearance. Although there was the appearance of normality, that was, far from the truth. For those working on or around the tank platform there was an eerie atmosphere which no one could explain. There were many rumours circulating, none of which had any factual basis, but as is usual in such cases, stories and speculations tend to grow out of all proportion when compared to known facts.

The investigation team were assembled at Headquarters waiting for the morning briefing. The DCI entered the room, said 'Good Morning' and went straight to the incident board, looking at it for several minutes, before turning and addressing the assembly.

"Let us consider, once again, all the facts known to us. The first murder, that of Danny Drew, was in a place that he had no reason to be in according to his superiors. Death was due to a fall from the platform but since he would have been unconscious beforehand due to the head injury sustained by his head striking an angle curb by either falling backwards or being pushed, he must have been pulled up and pushed over the curb. Such an action would, in my opinion, require a good deal of strength because the body would have been dead weight. That suggests the work of a man. The only man in the vicinity around the time of the incident, so far as we can establish, was Don Phillips, the senior production foreman. However, he was found dead, recovered from the river a short time afterwards, reason being unknown, but away, from the factory. He had been fishing. His death was suspicious and may or may not have been connected to that of Danny Drew. We have now learned that Danny had been told something, by his pal in Liverpool, that Danny thought would be a bombshell if it became public knowledge. We now know that that "something" was the name of a woman, who had been seen at Eco-Tech by the girlfriend of Danny's pal. She recognised the woman from the time last Christmas when she saw her in a pub here in Telford, when a lot of the employees of Salopian Industries were having their Christmas do. Unfortunately, we don't know the name of the woman, but hopefully, we should be able to speak with Sophie Langford next week who I am sure will be able to give us that name. We can then determine the reason for her presence at Eco-Tech and be able to confirm if there has been, as is suspected, industrial espionage which is a crime apart from the homicide now being investigated. The DCI summarised what they already knew. Are there any questions or comments?"

"How did the girlfriend of Danny's pal know the name of this woman?" Was the first question put by DS Larry Robb.

"She saw her in reception, recognised her as I have already explained, and out of curiosity, asked the receptionist who she was. The receptionist had no idea but said she had come to see Mr Eardley, one of the company's partners. However, Sophie looked in the Visitor's Book and saw the name. This was the information that Danny had said would be a bombshell if known. The name of this woman I am sure is highly significant and will have a major bearing on the solving of this case. This information must, for the time being, be kept within this investigation team. I don't want anyone at the factory to be aware of this knowledge, and that includes Patrick Evans."

"Why can we only see Sophie, whatever her name is, next week," continued Robb.

"Her name is Sophie Langford. At the present time, she is visiting her sister in York, who I understand has recently had a baby. She is expected to return next week according to Paddy McGuire, Danny's pal. We shall interview her at the very earliest time possible."

"I presume that she lives in Liverpool. Will that be any problem?

"No problem whatsoever. As you know, DI Grant and DC Todd have already been up there and received full cooperation from our counterparts up there. Until that interview with Sophie Langford, we need to examine the circumstances of the death of Don Phillips in more detail. According to Mrs Addison, the lady who runs the B&B, frequently used by him when on his fishing trips, she had not seen him recently before his death. I wonder if she is being completely truthful in that statement. Robb, check that out more thoroughly. Also, speak with her husband. He works at the fire station and does shift work. Check his whereabouts at the time Phillips was killed. Now, I think that I have said all that is necessary, you all know what needs to be done, so get out there and do it."

As they were all leaving to go about their own individual tasks, DS Robb said to Harry Davies, "Sir, is there no indication, as to who this mystery woman might be?"

"None whatsoever, Robb. She could be any one of several women. There are three working in the Development Department for instance, any one of them being in possession of information useful to a competitor. The Supplies department, as you know is staffed entirely by women. However, let us not get too far ahead in our speculations. The presence of this person at the premises of a competitor of Salopian Industries, does not necessarily mean that they were there for underhand purposes. They could well have been seeking a new job. When it is possible to interview Sophie Langford and get to know the name of the woman concerned, we will then interview her and get to the truth and determine if there is any connection to the homicides."

10

Patrick Evans, having parked his Mercedes GLS in a side road, walked the hundred or so metres to the terraced cottage of Sharon Sumner. He didn't want his car to be seen in front of the property at six o'clock in the evening. It would be difficult to give a suitable or believable reason should it be seen by anyone who might recognise it. His wife, Amanda, believed him to be dining with a business associate. This was not unusual these days, particularly since becoming CEO. Often, he would be late home in the evening because, he explained, there was so much demand on his time during normal hours, he found he could get so much done when everyone in the office had gone home. These occasions of course were spent with Sharon, doing things other than business activities. They were times that he looked forward to, hardly able to contain his urges until the office block had been vacated and Sharon came into his office in that alluring manner she had. She would walk to him, pushing up close to him and putting her arms around him. Lifting her head to him, an invitation for him to kiss her, which he always did with gradually increasing passion.

Walking down the short pathway to her front door, he knew that she would be watching him as he approached, opening the door before he rang the doorbell. This was exactly what happened, and as the door opened, he slipped inside as she closed the door behind him neither of them saying a word. Then she was in his arms while he kissed her, both moving slowly into the room. Breaking for breath, Sharon whispered, "I'm so glad you are here, darling." Patrick's reply was by means of kissing her again.

"Dinner won't be for at least half an hour. I hope that's all right for you," she said when he paused from his amorous embrace.

"That's perfect. It will give us time to go upstairs won't it."

"You mean that you want desert before the main course," she replied with a little laugh and in the tone of voice that one could only describe as sexually charged.

"You know me so well. But don't tell me that you don't want it too."

"I think you know me just as well," she replied, as she took his hand leading to the stairs, still holding his hand as they climbed upwards. Inside her bedroom, which was decorated in a delicate shade of pink and with the soft furnishings perfectly arranged in a feminine manner, Patrick, once again drew her to himself. His hands began to explore her body with a freedom that excited Sharon to a feeling of utter desire. Slowly, Patrick began to unfasten the buttons of her blouse until finally, with all undone, he slipped his hands inside and removed it, letting it fall to the floor. With that, Sharon took off her bra. throwing it onto the bed as Patrick caressed her. Sharon, breaking away, quickly undressed and throwing back the duvet slid into bed watching Patrick as he also quickly undressed. He moved to the bed and slid in beside her. The next few minutes were engulfed in a passion that left them both totally drained of energy. Afterwards, they lay for a short while, silently relaxing, before getting dressed and going downstairs.

Sharon finished preparing dinner, which was lamb cutlets, new potatoes and mixed vegetables with of course, as Sharon expressed it, the essential mint sauce. She had also made a cod- mornay starter. The meal was enjoyed with a bottle of Burgundy in relaxed atmosphere and as Sharon said, the perfect finish to a wonderful evening.

"Patrick, I hope that we can do this more often."

"My darling, as often as will be possible I promise, but I have to be careful because I don't want Amanda to become suspicious."

Sharon felt the surge of a sharp pang of jealousy. The way he spoke of his wife made her feel belittled and nothing more than 'the other woman', a bit on the side. She covered her feelings by quietly saying, "I understand, darling, but if we are going to move forward together, your wife will need to be told sometime, or other." She reached across the table putting her hand on his, looking into his eyes with that almost indescribable expression that she alone could conjure up, an expression that was hypnotic.

"Yes, you are quite right, and I do understand how you feel, but this is not the right time to come out into the open. We must put our professional life first. We must get the patent granted and I must have the chairman's appreciation to the extent that if I get a divorce, it will not put me into his disfavour. After that there would need to be a suitable time delay before we dare openly be together. Do you understand what I am saying?"

"Yes, I do understand what you are saying, but you must also realise how frustrating it is for me. I love you so much and want to be with you properly. This evening has been a small taster of how things could be if we were married."

That word, married, startled Patrick to an extent that could be described as a shock. He had never had the intention of divorcing Amanda and marrying Sharon. Although Sharon was so sophisticated, attractive, intelligent and wonderful in bed, he didn't think of her in the position as his wife. The shock of the intensity of her feelings however, he covered well, and said with that smooth, silky voice he had, "My darling, I love you too, and it would be wonderful to have every evening as wonderful as this evening has been, but we must have patience."

"How long do you think it will be before we get the product patent?"

"I can't give a definite time, but we are very, close now. I am concerned though by the opinion of the police, that there may have been information including technical details given to one of our competitors. If they are correct in their suspicions, depending on just how much information has been given away, that competitor whoever it may be, could be granted the patent ahead of us. That for Salopian Industries would be a disaster. As for myself, my ambition of being the future company chairman whenever Sir Ian retires, would I think be forlorn hope. In other words, my future, prospects would be over."

"Patrick, my love, you would always have me, whatever happens. Anyway, I don't think for one minute, that Sir Ian or the shareholders would blame you for industrial espionage. It is, after all, a type of theft, the work of a burglar or burglars. It is a crime when all is said and done. I am sure that the police will sort it out."

"I hope that you are right," was his reply.

They moved from the table and sat on the sofa, Patrick's arm around Sharon as she rested her head on his chest. There, for a little while they sat in silence, enjoying their closeness.

Patrick's wife, Amanda, had finished her evening meal and now sat alone in the lounge, scrolling down the television guide, in the hope that she could find a programme that would be suitable to watch. Evenings, such as this, when Patrick was entertaining business associates, could be lonely and of course boring unless there was something of interest on TV or she had a good book to read. Unfortunately, she had not been to the library to change the book she had now finished, so the TV was the only option on this occasion. Having made the decision of which programme to watch, poured a glass of wine and sat down to relax. Taking a first sip of the wine, she was startled by a ring of the doorbell. Carefully putting down the glass, she went to open the door.

"I hope I'm not disturbing you Amanda, but I was only twiddling my thumbs and not seeing Patrick's car outside, I thought you may be on your own and would like a bit of company."

"Come in Karen, good to see you. Yes, you are quite right, I am alone and would love some company." It was Amanda's neighbour, who she liked very much, and they had much in common. Her company was always welcome.

"Come through, take a seat." Amanda switched off the TV and said, "You will join me with a glass of wine," and immediately began to pour a glass.

"You know me, I will never say no to a glass of wine." Taking the glass from Amanda, she said, "I presume that Patrick is on business this evening."

"Yes, entertaining a business associate and dining out."

"He seems to have a lot of these evening appointments lately. He must get fed-up with them taking up time when he could be relaxing at home with you."

"Yes," Amanda replied, but without conviction. She knew that Patrick always put work before her. His desire to 'be in charge, of matters' and to impress others, particularly his superiors, such as Sir Ian Leighton-Boyce, took precedence over anything and everybody. In all matters he wanted to be at the top of the 'pile'. She didn't like this side of his character, but there was another side of him that could be kind and considerate. She thought him to be an enigmatic person and had thought so when she had married him. He would never change his ways because his ambitions would not allow it, and so she was prepared to accept him for what he was.

Amanda, sat down and raising her glass, said, "Karen, here's to us."

Karen responded with enthusiasm, and so the evening for them began on a happy note. Their conversation ranged over many subjects but eventually came to the recent events at Salopian Industries. The homicide of Danny Drew had been the major content in the local newspaper resulting in the incident being the hub of conversation with most people.

"The newspaper accounts I am sure don't give all the details. Poor young lad, to come to such a horrible end is too much to comprehend," said Karen, shaking her head slowly from side to side.

"Absolutely. I feel so sorry for his mother, who I believe is a widow. She must be heartbroken, especially that he was her only son," replied Amanda.

"Do you know if the police are anywhere near to catching whoever did it. Has Patrick given you any idea of where they are up to?"

Amanda was aware that Karen was fishing for information. She was always curious and liked to get to know all the details of whatever was the topic of the day. The more lurid the details, the more she revelled in them. She enjoyed sensation.

"Patrick hasn't told me anything more than what has been reported in the newspapers. I don't think that the police would divulge all the information they have to Patrick. I expect that everyone in the company could well be considered as a suspect."

"What, even Patrick?" Karen said in astonishment.

"I suppose so. They must consider everyone as a suspect until they can eliminate them from their enquiries."

"I would imagine that Patrick has been eliminated by now. After all, he is the CEO of the company. Whatever reason would a CEO have to murder a young engineer in the company?"

"What reason indeed. That is exactly the question I imagine the police would ask themselves and only when they can satisfactorily answer it will they eliminate him from their enquiries."

"That other man that was found in the river also worked at Salopian, I understand."

“Yes, he was a senior production foreman. It is all very strange, almost surreal. I don’t think that they are sure that the two incidents are linked but I am certain that they will be making enquiries on that line.”

“This is the most exciting news we’ve had for a long time. I wonder what the next revelation will be,” mused Karen, who was thoroughly enjoying the sensational speculations.

The two women chatted on, analysing every aspect that they could think of that related to what Karen had described as the most exciting news for a long time, but without reaching any conclusions. Having exhausted the subject, Karen turned the conversation to the possibility that they could treat themselves to a little retail therapy.

“We could go to Shrewsbury or maybe Chester. What do you think?” Karen asked her.

“What a lovely idea,” Amanda replied. “I would like to go to Chester because it’s quite a long time since I was there. We could have a most enjoyable day, so, let’s make it soon.”

At this moment, they heard the front door opening and then closing. Amanda glanced at the clock. It was almost ten o’clock.

Patrick came into the room and seeing Karen, greeted her in his most charming of ways. It was his manner, especially with the ladies, to greet them with that smooth, silky voice that so enthralled women. Then to his wife, “Hello darling, have you had a pleasant evening?” Then seeing the two glasses and the almost empty wine bottle, “I’m sure you must have.”

“Yes, we’ve had a very pleasant evening, trying to analyse the events which are now the hot topic of conversation with most people, and with a bottle of wine,” Amanda replied, glancing at the depleted bottle on the coffee table.

“Splendid, and did you reach any conclusions?”

“No, we didn’t which is not surprising. However, we did conclude that we both deserve a day out with some retail therapy.”

“A good idea,” Patrick said. “Go for it. As a matter of fact, I need to go to Cardiff next week for a couple of days, so perhaps you could have your expedition then. Where are you planning to do your shopping?”

“We thought Chester would suit our needs very well. We intend to spend a full day, but if you are going to be away for a couple of days, then perhaps we could stay overnight. What do you think Karen, would your better half be ok with that?"

"I'm sure he would have no objection," was her reply. "There is a probability that he would be glad to get rid of me for a couple of days," she said with a laugh.

"I am sure that's not the case," said Patrick. "He thinks the world of you"

"How well was your meeting. Did you manage to get what you wanted from it?"

The question, as put by Amanda, was to say the least, ironic. She was totally unaware of the apparent implications embodied in the question. Patrick was, however, immediately on his guard, unsure if there was a hidden meaning in the question.

"Everything was fine, I'm quite sure we can make good progress," was his reply, watching her carefully as he was speaking, but could not detect anything in her expression to give him any concern. Perhaps I am becoming over sensitive, he thought.

"When will you be going to Cardiff?"

"I think that I will drive down there on Sunday afternoon, stay overnight, so that I can have a full day on Monday. During the morning, I will pay my periodic visit to Williams Brothers and lunch with the Sales manager and later, in the afternoon, I will pay a courtesy visit to John Williams. We may be able to get a round of golf at his club. I will then stay overnight and drive back on Tuesday morning. I should be back in the office around lunch time."

"In that case, Karen, we could go to Chester on Monday, stay overnight, giving us most of Tuesday, to complete our retail therapy. What do you think of that for a plan?"

"Absolutely perfect. I will tell Geoff what we are planning. I'm sure he won't object."

With that, Karen prepared to leave. Giving Amanda a hug, then Patrick, she said 'Good Night' and made her way home. Happy, having spent a pleasant evening with Amanda and having a good gossip, finally making the arrangements for a couple of days away, which she was already looking forward to, like an overgrown teenager.

11

Victor Eardley, or Vic, as he was generally known, was engaged in a lengthy 'phone conversation and expressing considerable concern about actions that must be taken quickly. His agitation manifested itself in the tone of his voice and in the volume, that was now steadily rising. As a director of Eco-Tech Limited and as the senior partner, such information that was being discussed must under no consideration, become public knowledge. That was the general gist of the conversation.

"Do something about it, and for goodness sake, do it quickly," was his last retort, then he switched off his mobile. He sat, motionless, in his chair for a couple of minutes or so, feeling almost out of breath. Then, his hands trembling, he reached for the top right-hand drawer of his desk, opening it and taking out a glass and a bottle of single malt, he poured out a good measure. His mind was in a whirl, and he felt powerless in circumstances for which he had not bargained and over which he had no control. This, for Vic Eardley was a new experience. His sharp thinking and quick wit were usually enough to get him through any problem, but this was very different to anything he had ever experienced in the past. The realisation that he could be drawn into a murder investigation terrified him. Obtaining information about a competitive company could, perhaps, be explained away as getting market intelligence, providing that the manner, in which the information was obtained, was not disclosed but, when murder was brought into the equation, the matter was entirely different.

Vic Eardley decided to walk into the factory to check on progress being made in the special area which was reserved for experimental work associated with the improvement of products or new and improved methods of production. The work, now being carried out, was the development of a manufacturing process for the insulation board that Salopian Industries were developing from the preliminary work carried out by Williams Brothers of Cardiff. His disappointment at the acceptance of Salopian's bid, for the takeover of Williams Brothers, was beyond measure. He wanted that company, for the prospect of launching the new type of insulation board onto the market was overwhelming. The possible financial rewards were immense. Being the type of man that he was, the decision to obtain technical information by underhand means was the best way to proceed. All that was needed was someone within Salopian's premises who, without raising any alarm, could obtain the information required and to keep him up to date with whatever progress Salopian were making. In practical terms, he needed a mole. He very quickly put his plan into action, and it was not very, long before technical information was being passed to him, in sufficient quantity and quality, to enable development work to begin.

This subterfuge was of course known only to his mole and himself. Had his partners been aware of what was going on, they would have stopped it immediately. The work being done however, was inevitably, always behind Salopian because he was reliant on receiving, from the mole, information 'after the event'. Because of this, he had pushed the mole a little too hard, with the result that her identity was jeopardized. His instructions to her were to 'fix it' without making too much fuss or letting the matter become public knowledge. The phrase, 'fix it', didn't in any way imply murder, either intentionally or accidentally. But murder had been the result and now he was terrified. His last words to her on the 'phone, to do something about it, was an instruction given in desperation, without any idea of what that 'something' could be.

***

DS Larry Robb had driven to Ironbridge to speak with Mrs Addison, who ran the B&B often used by Don Phillips when on his fishing trips. Robb could not understand why Phillips would stay overnight in Ironbridge, when his home was only a few miles away in Wellington. The fact that his marriage to Julie was going through what might be regarded as a rough patch, in his view, didn't present a good enough reason to stay at a B&B just a few miles away. There must be another reason and the one that he could not get out of his mind was that Don Phillips and the landlady were having an affair. Angie Addison was an attractive, forty-year--old woman, married to a man who worked on shifts at the local fire station. Shift work could well provide opportunities for her to engage herself in 'amorous, activities'.

Before going to the B&B, DS Robb read though the crime reports to familiarise himself with all the facts known to date. Don Phillips' body had been found in the river, caught up in the riverbank, downstream from where his fishing gear was situated, on the south bank at Buildwas. He had a head injury which originally was thought to be the cause of death but later refuted by forensics, who declared that death was due to drowning. The head injury had occurred post-mortem. There was a dog bite on the left thigh, sustained shortly before death. There was evidence of a struggle where the victim's fishing gear was situated and two distinct but different footprints had been found among the blurred impressions, caused by what was believed to be a struggle, neither of which matched the footwear of the victim.

It was Mrs Addison who answered the door to DS Robb.

"Good morning, DS Larry Robb," he introduced himself, showing her his warrant card. "May I come in. There are a few questions I would like to ask regarding Mr Don Phillips, who I believe was a guest here on frequent occasions."

"Yes, Mr Phillips stayed on many occasions when he was fishing," she replied as she ushered him into the lounge area. "The news of his death was a terrible shock."

"Did you ever think it strange, that he should stay overnight here when his home was only a few miles away in Wellington?"

"It never crossed my mind."

"At the time of his death, you claimed not to have seen him for a couple of weeks. Did you think it unusual for him to be fishing without staying here, since that had been his usual custom?"

"No, he was his own person and could do whatever he wished," she replied but with a tone in her voice that caught Robb's attention.

"Having stayed here on so many occasions, you must have become friendly."

"I am friendly with all my guests. It is a must in this business."

"Yes, of course, but with a gentleman who was a frequent guest, I should have thought that your relationship would have been more friendly than with a comparative stranger."

Robb detected a slight colouring of her cheeks, so he pushed on. "Did he perhaps, have dinner with you in the evening or did he go to a local pub, since this is a B&B?"

"All right, yes we did usually have dinner together. So what?"

"Mrs Addison, I want you to think very carefully before answering my next question and I would remind you that to lie or give misleading information to a police officer, is an offence for which you could be prosecuted. Do you understand?"

"Yes," she replied with a tone of resignation in her voice.

"Where you, having an affair with Don Phillips?"

"We did have a fling for a while, but I ended it. That is the reason that I had not seen Don for a couple of weeks before he was killed." The reply was given with reluctance.

DS Robb felt a surge of satisfaction. Her admission to have had a fling, as she put it, with Don Phillips opened up various possibilities for lines of enquiry. It most certainly, in his opinion, explained the reason for Phillips staying at a B&B within a few miles from his home, and maybe, the coldness that had developed between himself and his wife. Perhaps, he was in full knowledge of his wife's affair with Danny Drew, and being a jealous man, had been galvanised into carrying out that threat, which, according to his wife's statement, he had once made, "to break his bloody neck."

"Was your husband aware of your fling?"

"Heavens no, and he must never know. I love him and it would break his heart as well as ruining our marriage. Please, promise me that you will not tell him."

"Mrs Addison, I cannot make promises. It will all depend upon how the investigation develops, but I can say that he will not know unless it becomes necessary."

"Thank you. It was an aberration in my life that I deeply regret."

"Life is full of mistakes, but we all make them. I imagine your husband is at work?" Robb said as a question.

"Yes, this week he is on the day shift. He finishes at two o'clock this afternoon. He will get home at around half past two."

"I need to speak with him, so I will come back this afternoon."

With that, he made his departure. Driving back to Divisional Headquarters, he went over all the information he had gleaned from Angie Addison. The sum total was not very much, but the fact of an affair between Angie and Don Phillips was confirmed. If her husband had found out about it, that would, perhaps, be a motive for murder, if indeed it was murder. What had been substantiated was that the cause of death had been drowning. The cause of him being in the river was unclear. Whether he had fallen accidentally or been pushed was debatable. There was evidence of a struggle having taken place and that, being on the riverbank, either way was possible. Two separate footprints had been found and casts made, but the owners of them, so far, were unidentified. One print appeared to be that of a trainer but the other had the distinctive tread of a work boot. The ground around the area where the victim's fishing gear was found was badly churned up, as the result of a struggle, but who and why had anyone, or even two people started a blazing row. It most certainly was not for robbery, because his wallet had not been taken and the fishing gear was undisturbed. In Robb's opinion, the husband of Angie Addison, had a lot of questions to answer, and his work boots needed to be checked against the casts of the footprints found at the scene.

***

It was a bright and sunny Monday morning in Liverpool and pleasantly warm, ideal for getting on with those outside jobs that had been on hold throughout the winter months. So it was, that when the car pulled up and stopped outside the house of Sophie Langford, her next-door neighbour had already made a start on the task of painting the house front window frames. A young lady alighted from the car and walked along the short pathway to Sophie's door, saying good morning to her next-door neighbour as she rang the doorbell.

"Good morning, I'm DC Smart," quickly showing her warrant card. "May I come in?"

Sophie stood aside to let her in, closing the door behind her, then leading her through to the living room.

Some ten minutes later, Sophie's door opened, the police officer said thank you, the door closing behind her and nodding to Sophie's neighbour, she walked back along the pathway to her car. She paused for a couple of minutes, checking her papers, then drove away.

DI Grant and DC Todd, once again, were travelling to Liverpool by train. Waiting at Crewe for the connection to Liverpool, Lime Street, they sat in the buffet enjoying tea and toast. They discussed the procedure they were to take. First to police Headquarters, then by car to the home of Sophie Langford, who lived at Sephton Park. They had been told that she would be returning home yesterday evening, so she would be available for interview today. They didn't want to go to Eco-Tech to see her at work, that would have alerted the management to the interest the police had in their 'goings-on'. It was prudent to wait for Sophie to be at home when they interviewed her. They needed to know the name of the woman she had seen and recognised visiting Eco-Tech having seen her in Telford and knowing that she was an employee of Salopian Industries. DI Grant was certain that whoever it was, she was the suspected mole and probably responsible for the murder of Danny Drew. Whilst they continued with their tea, DI Grant's 'phone rang.

"Grant here," then he was silent, obviously listening intently, his face taking on a grave expression. "When exactly was this?" He continued to listen intently. "Yes, Sir, I will." Grant switched off the 'phone and sat, for a moment, without saying a word and still with that grave expression on his face.

"Is there something wrong, Sir," Jane Todd asked.

"It's bloody well unbelievable," was his reply without further explanation.

"What's unbelievable, Sir?"

"Sophie Langford is dead. She's been murdered."

"Murdered, when?"

"Must have been this morning. It has only been discovered a short time ago. The DCI wants us to continue to Liverpool and see DCS Stuart, who will fill us in with the details. This incident is of course on their patch and so they will be investigating the case, but as the DCI says, there is obviously a connection with our investigation, so there will necessarily be some cooperation between us."

"Where does this leave us, not having obtained the name of the unknown woman?"

"Back at square, bloody, one, but I am sure that we are on the right track. There is a mole in Salopian's place and somehow, matters have gone pear-shaped which has led to the death of Danny Drew and maybe Don Phillips. There is now an effort to cover up, and, conceal the identity of the mole at all costs, even to committing murder yet again."

Immediately on arrival at police headquarters, DI Grant and DC Todd were directly shown into DCS Stuart's office. Greeting them cordially, Stuart went on to describe and explain the events of about three hours previously. At around midday, Paddy McGuire had gone around to see Sophie. Ringing the doorbell, but receiving no reply, he went to the front window to peer through but saw nothing. The next-door neighbour, who was still painting, told Paddy that Sophie was in because he saw her, earlier in the morning, when she had opened the door to a police officer. He knew it to be a police officer because he had heard her announce herself as such. The officer had gone inside and was there for about ten minutes, or so, then left. He heard her thank Sophie for her help, as she was going, and she had nodded to him as she walked down the path, then got into her car and drove away. McGuire then went to the back of the house to look through the living room window. What he saw was Sophie lying very still on the floor. He called 999, asked for police and ambulance.

"So, who was the officer who called earlier in the morning?" DI Grant asked.

"Grant, no such visit by an officer from this department was made this morning, or at any other time. Whoever went there this morning was a phoney, and since the neighbour was painting at the front of the house all morning and saw no other caller, she must have committed the offence. Sophie Langford was stabbed in the stomach, and then had her throat slashed, severing the carotid artery. The poor girl collapsed and bled out. Whoever the perpetrator was, she was a cool customer, and had obviously gone there to do exactly what was done. There was no weapon found at the scene. There is a possibility that it was a burglary, 'gone wrong', because Paddy McGuire drew attention to the fact that her laptop was not where she normally kept it. The whole property has been searched but her laptop has not been found, suggesting that it was taken by the perpetrator. My own opinion is that this tragic crime was not a burglary but an act of deliberate and premeditated homicide. That, however, begs the question, for what reason was the laptop taken?"

"Did the girl live alone, Sir?"

"She lived with her widowed mother. However, her boyfriend, Paddy McGuire told us that her mother is in Australia, visiting her sister, who has been living there for the last ten years."

"I would like to speak with Paddy McGuire, Sir. As you know, it was he who told us about Sophie Langford."

"Yes, Grant, I, am aware, of the circumstances, and yes you should speak with McGuire. I will arrange for a car to take you to him. The investigation into the girl's death, will however, be conducted by DI Ken Abbott."

"I quite understand, Sir, but would it be possible for DC Todd to be present if or when you visit the premises of Eco-Tech during your investigation?" was Grant's request. "We at Telford believe there to be a connection, with the unknown visitor to the Eco-Tech company and the homicide of Danny Drew and maybe Don Phillips."

"I see no problem with that. I will speak with DI Abbott and explain the circumstances. This will be a complex investigation which I think will require the combined input of both forces.

Paddy McGuire was distraught when DI Grant and DC Todd went to see him. He explained that Sophie had phoned him last night, after arriving home, and said that she would see him today. If he could get time off from work, they could go out for lunch and have the rest of the day together and as your visit was expected, they could wait, together, for your arrival. She wasn't going back to work until tomorrow. Having arranged with his boss to have the day off, he had been home, washed, changed and gone to Sophie's around twelve o'clock. As he explained seeing her lying on the floor, tears were streaming down his face, his voice faltering and he just flopped into a chair, burying his head in his hands.

"Who would do this to her?" Paddy asked, looking up to DI Grant in desperate appeal.

"That is what we intend to find out," he replied.

***

DS Robb returned to the B&B in Ironbridge at three o'clock, to speak with Mr Addison. To begin, his attitude tended to be a little truculent, but Robb reassured him by saying that he was trying to build up a picture of the type of person Don Phillips was and he could only do that by getting the opinions of people who knew him. He explained that he had spoken with Mrs Addison earlier that day.

"I didn't know him very well because being on shift-work, I was often working when he stayed here. I couldn't understand why he stayed here, living only a few miles away in Wellington. I could only assume that his home life wasn't good."

"Do you think that there could have been any other reason?" Robb asked, carefully watching the expression on Mr Addison's face.

There was a marked hesitation in his voice and a slight pause before saying "I don't know. I didn't care for him very much, but his way of life was his business."

"There were a couple of different footprints found at the place where his fishing gear was located. We are trying to identify them, so we are asking anyone who, regularly, walks along the river to show us their footwear, to enable us to rule them out of our enquiries."

Mr Addison looked at DS Robb, then said, "or rule them in, isn't that what you really mean?"

"Do you walk regularly along the river, Mr Addison?"

"Yes, I do, and I have a confession to make."

DS Robb looked at him in a questioning manner, certain in his mind that he was going to admit seeing Don Phillips on the fateful morning.

"I walked along the river that morning, up towards Buildwas and saw the fishing gear in place. I knew it must have belonged to Don Phillips because the initials D P were stencilled on the basket, and it was in a place that he frequently used, but there was no sign of him anywhere in the vicinity."

"Why did you not come forward with this information when we were making our initial enquiries?"

"I didn't want to become involved and I couldn't add more than what I have just told you"

"But you are involved Mr Addison. You have admitted to being at the scene of a suspicious incident and I have only your word, that Don Phillips was not there at the time. Had you not admitted it, I believe it would have been proved that you were there by comparing your boots with the footprint cast taken at the scene. I need to take your boots to do just that."

"Very well, I will get them for you"

When Mr Addison returned with the boots, DS Robb remarked, "A little earlier you said that you didn't much care for Don Phillips, why was that?"

Addison was silent for a little while but looking at the DS with an expression which could only be described as one of uncertainty. DS Robb waited patiently for his reply, returning his stare with a steady gaze that implied that he was prepared to wait but demanded a reply.

"I had the feeling that Phillips was becoming too familiar with Angie. Not that I ever saw anything untoward, you understand, but as I have already said, staying here when his home was only a few miles away, well it didn't make a lot of sense to me."

"Did you ever express your concern to your wife?"

"No, I didn't. I trust her and didn't want her to think that I was jealous or paranoid."

Robb nodded his head in an expression of understanding and then said, "Mr Addison, I will return your boots when they have been checked and I shall probably need to speak with you again." With that Robb took his leave and returned to Headquarters.

12

Once again, DC Jane Todd stayed overnight in Liverpool. The plan for today was to accompany DI Ken Abbott on his visit to the premises of Eco-Tech. The reason being that of obtaining information relating to Sophie Langford. DI Abbott was of course the investigating officer, since the incident of Sophie's death was in the jurisdiction of the Liverpool police, whilst DC Todd was there to observe and take notes. There was the added purpose of speaking with Victor Eardley and seeing whatever was possible of the premises, without raising suspicions that they were concerned about anything other than the death of Sophie Langford. Arriving at the premises, their driver parked in the visitors' section and remained with the car.

Entering the building, they went directly to the reception desk. DI Abbott introduced himself and DC Jane Todd, showing his warrant card and said, "I should like to speak with the senior partner, Mr Victor Eardley"

The receptionist acknowledged them and speaking on the 'phone to Eardley's secretary, told her that there were two police officers wishing to speak with Mr Eardley. She listened for a few moments and then putting down the phone said, "Mr Eardley's secretary is trying to locate him. Please take a seat, I am sure he won't be long."

Vic Eardley was sitting at his desk going through some papers when his secretary came in from the adjoining office and told him that there were two police officers at reception who wished to speak with him. He felt a chill run through his entire body and suddenly, his tongue felt hot. A feeling of panic was beginning to take hold. Looking up to her, "Did they say what they want?" he asked.

"No, they just said that they needed to speak with you. I told reception that I would try to locate you."

"Good thinking. Give me five minutes, then go to reception and bring them up here."

Eardley's mind was racing. Had they come to confront him about his activities of espionage, had they discovered the identity of his mole at Salopian's place. If they had, would they link it with the deaths of those two men. Oh, God, how can I talk my way out of all this, he asked himself.

His secretary popped her head round the door, "I will go down and bring them up now, if you are ready."

"Yes, do that." He sat waiting for them, forcing himself to stay calm or at least to give the impression of being calm. He hoped that his usual quick thinking would save him, from a situation that he was beginning to feel, was a disaster that was about to happen.

With a tap on the door, Vic's secretary opened it and ushered in the two officers, introducing them as she did so.

DI Abbott showed Vic his warrant card, and they shook hands.

"Please, take a seat. How can I be of help?" he asked, surprising himself by the steadiness of his voice and the calmness of his attitude.

"I understand that you have in your employ, a lady by the name of Sophie Langford?" Were Abbott's opening words.

Oh God, here it comes, thought Eardley. Sophie Langford was the girl who had recognised his mole and discovered her name from reception. The one who's boyfriend had a close friend, by the name of Danny Drew, who worked at Salopian Industries and undoubtedly had become acquainted with the details. He had, regrettably, pushed his mole to prevent Danny disclosing her presence at Eco-Tech by saying "do something about it." That something ended in the murder of Danny Drew and now was the day of reckoning.

"Yes, that is so. She works in our sales department," Eardley replied.

"I am given to understand that she has been on vacation for a couple of weeks?"

"I'm not sure about that but, I can ask my secretary to check if you wish."

"That won't be necessary. I am afraid that I have some bad news. Miss Sophie Langford was found dead yesterday." DI Abbott watched Vic Eardley's face intently as he spoke, watching for any sign of unease or discomfort. The response was that of total shock.

"Dead, but how?" was his verbal response.

"She was murdered, Mr Eardley."

"Murdered, where was this?" he asked with a tone of incredulity in his voice.

DI Abbott observed him with a very, serious, and determined expression on his face and making a short pause before replying, a pause that to Vic Eardley seemed like an eternity. "The young lady was stabbed to death, in her own home, Mr Eardley." There was a stunned silence. Vic Eardley just sat there in bewilderment, then DI Abbott went on, "have you any idea who may have wished to do her harm?"

"No, I haven't," was his immediate reply. "She was a very popular girl and got on very well with everybody."

"Well, it is obvious that someone had intent to harm her, because evidence suggests that this was a deliberate and premeditated crime."

"What evidence to that, is there?" Eardley asked.

Both DI Abbott and DC Todd, picked up immediately, the note of cautious curiosity in his voice and they cast a brief glance to each other before Abbott said, "we cannot discuss the matter at this time, however, I should like to see her place of work, will you take us there, please."

"Yes, of course," and with that he led the way, downstairs and along to the sales office.

On their entry, the girls looked up, and seeing Vic Eardley with the two plain clothes police officers, but not knowing that was who they were, expected their boss to be showing around potential customers, which he usually did in an attempt to impress. Then with serious gravity, he said, "ladies, please pay attention for a moment. This lady and gentleman are police officers, and they have some grave and disturbing news," nodding to DI Abbott as a gesture of handing over to him.

"Good morning, ladies. Yes, sadly, I must inform you, of the death of your colleague, Sophie Langford." As Abbott paused, there was a general sound of the sharp intake of breath in combination with exclamations of "Oh, no" and "Ah," the typical sounds of mass surprise and shock.

One of the girls asked, "when was this, Sir?" then continued, "Sophie's been away in York visiting her sister. Was it an accident?"

"It was no accident, she was murdered, in her own home," replied Abbott. Then to Vic, "Will you show me her desk, please? I would like to look through the contents and of course we will take possession of any of her personal effects."

The two officers, spent the next half hour, examining all the contents of the desk drawers, separating personal effects from those appertaining to her work and when they had finished, DI Abbott thanked Vic Eardley for his cooperation, telling him that in all probability, they would wish to speak with him again and of course would keep him informed of any developments that had any connection with her place of work. With that, they made their departure.

They had barely left the premises when Vic Eardley, using his mobile, made a call. The call, to his utter frustration, went to voice mail. "What the hell have you done, you bloody fool? When you get this, call me immediately. I've just had the police here telling me that the girl is dead, murdered." With that, he switched off the 'phone, gave a deep sigh and sat back in his chair, feeling totally exhausted. He realised that his world was about to implode.

13

The journey to Cardiff had been easy and, in relatively light traffic, quite speedy. Patrick Evans made his way into the hotel and directly to the reception desk. Being a frequent visitor to the hotel, the receptionist recognised him immediately and with a delightfully warm smile greeted him and welcomed him, once again, to the "Three Feathers Hotel," giving him the customary registration form to complete. Having complied with her request, he passed it back to her as she gave him his room key card.

"Your usual room, Mr Evans. We wish you a pleasant stay with us once again."

"Thank you, so much, Janice. I'm sure everything will be perfect."

Janice's thoughts roamed wildly. Everything, she suspected, would be perfect because of his familiarity with the deputy hotel manager, Bronwen Jenkins. This was well known among the staff. She was the daughter of John Williams, the now retired businessman, who was also a regular guest at the hotel. Bronwen Jenkins was now divorced and there had been speculation among the staff, that she and Mr Evans would get together.

Patrick walked over to the lift, entered and selected the first floor. His first-floor room had a pleasant outlook across the city and having had this room on so many occasions it felt like home. Putting his suitcase on the stand in the corner of the room, he then took off his jacket and hung it in the wardrobe. It was a lovely sunny day and the light streaming into the room, through the large picture window, reflected on the tastefully decorated walls, giving the room a feeling of homely warmth. Patrick walked over to the window and gazed across the city and whilst doing so, his mind went back to the events that took place during the lengthy negotiations prior to the takeover of Williams Brothers Limited. This was when he was sales manager at Salopian Industries and accompanying the old managing director before he retired. He thought of the time he first met John Williams' daughter, Bronwen. She was, he thought, quite stunning but unfortunately, married. However, they got along perfectly, and he was aware that his smooth and silky voice and his gentle attitude towards her impressed her enormously. On the evening that the takeover had been signed and sealed, she had invited him back to her home for "celebratory" drinks. Her husband was away on business, so they had the place to themselves. It was the first occasion that they had been alone together but there were no inhibitions on either part. They were perfectly relaxed and comfortable with each other. Bronwen opened a bottle of Champagne. This she had remarked was the drink for celebration. They sat together, on the sofa, and with glasses charged they drank a toast to the future. For some time, in a relaxed and intimate manner, they talked about the possibilities of the future. Finding that their glasses to be empty, Bronwen, filled them up again and sat down again next to Patrick. She clinked her glass against his, and with the feeling of a degree of liberation, courtesy of the first glass of Champagne, said that they should drink to their own personal futures to which Patrick agreed readily. Gazing steadily into her eyes, he said that he hoped that her future would be wonderful and that she would have everything she desired. Bronwen responded by leaning forward and kissing him on the cheek, saying that she wished the same for him too. She then drew back abruptly. "Sorry," she had said. "I should not have done that." Patrick, in his usual suave manner, put his glass on the coffee table in front of him and deliberately drew her towards himself, telling her not to be silly, it was a lovely gesture and with that kissed her very gently, pulling her even closer. She didn't pull away but responded eagerly. Patrick for a moment broke the embrace, took the glass she was still holding and put it on the coffee table next to his own. He then put his arms around her, pulling her towards him, and kissed her again. Bronwen responded by putting her arms around his neck and gently caressing his head and face. Patrick gradually turned her so that she was lying back on the sofa and turning himself so that they were lying alongside each other. He then began to explore her body gently with his right hand whilst his left hand pulled her closely to him. Bronwen didn't object but kissed him with an energy fuelled by passion and Champagne. Patrick took advantage of the situation and with his increased passion she succumbed to the moment and they both experienced an ecstasy neither would forget.

Patrick's memory of that night was as fresh now as it was the morning after. As he looked out, through the window, he thought of all that had happened since then. He was now the CEO of Salopian Industries, he had shifted Leslie Anderson sideways, putting him under the control of Frank Ebbs, the new company chief engineer. Now, he had power of control of the company and he was the person to whom everyone looked up to because of it. He had a gorgeous PA in the person of Sharon Sumner, who was now his mistress. He was aware that Sharon wanted to become Mrs Evans, she had told him so, but that would never be. He would keep promising her, and his ego assured him that she would continue to believe his promises. Whenever he was here in Cardiff, he was sure that his pleasures would always be satisfied by the company of Bronwen Jenkins. Now divorced from her husband, a man that nobody liked, she was now a young lady free of ties. Having hinted to her that his own marriage was a sham and about to collapse he was certain in his own mind that Bronwen thought that one day they would be together.

The thoughts of Patrick were interrupted by a knock on the room door. He went over and opened it. Bronwen, with a broad smile moved quickly into the room, took the 'Do Not Disturb' notice off the inside handle of the door, placed it on the outside handle and closed the door without saying a word. Then she moved quickly to him and in each other's arms, she looked up to him and in her delightful Welsh accent said, "Oh, my love, it is good to see you again."

"To see you too, my love," he replied, then kissed her with his usual passion.

Bronwen took off her jacket throwing it onto the chair and again put her arms round him. Patrick began to undo the buttons of her blouse, beginning at the top, moving down to the bottom. Then, with the front of her blouse open, he deftly slipped his hands into the shoulders, slipping it off and letting it fall to the floor. They gazed at each other for a moment, then they quickly undressed and slipped into bed.

Their passion had in no way diminished and, as on that very first time that they had made love, the climax came as a simultaneous explosion.

They lay for quite a long time in total contentment not speaking but with Bronwen's head resting on Patrick's shoulder and his arm over her. Eventually, Bronwen broke the silence.

"I was shocked to read about the terrible happenings at your factory. To have a murder committed on your premises is almost unbelievable. Are the police sure that it was murder and not an accident?"

"Oh, yes. They are quite certain of that. Forensic evidence proves it to be so. They think that the motive was associated with industrial espionage which sounds fantastic to me but, they are of the opinion that the new type of insulation board, we obtained from your father's company and that we are developing into a commercial product is the focus of the crime. The police suspect the company, competing against us when we were bidding to purchase your father's company is at the heart of the matter. We are nearly ready to apply for a product patent but if there has been information stolen from us, how near they are, to applying for a patent, we don't know. They could possibly beat us to it, which would be an absolute disaster. Hopefully, the police will apprehend the murderer very soon and all will be brought to light."

That evening, they had dinner in the hotel. Bronwen had arranged for a table in a quiet corner of the large dining room where each could indulge themselves of the other's company in comparative privacy. For Bronwen, these moments were precious interludes in a life that hinged around the hotel and the unsocial hours that were demanded of her. She still had hope, that one day, Patrick would leave the wife that he described as unreasonably demanding, selfish and boring in every respect and whom he didn't love. He could then ask her to marry him, to which she would say yes, without hesitation. And, so the evening passed as they talked pleasantries. He told her of his plans for the following morning, to visit Williams Brothers as he regularly did and then, in the afternoon, he was hoping to have a round of golf with her father. Bronwen knew that her father had a high regard for Patrick and that, if ever she and he got together, she would have her father's blessing. There was no doubt that Patrick had a captivating personality. He was the type of man that Leslie Anderson had described to his wife, Jenny, as being able to 'charm the birds out of the trees'.

The following day, Patrick picked up John Williams from his home and drove to the Golf Club. On the way John asked about the reported murder at the factory in Telford, expressing his shock, when reading the details in the national press. Patrick gave him chapter and verse of events, telling him of the suspicions the police had of industrial espionage being the catalyst to the tragic event.

After signing Patrick in as his guest, they went to the dining room to have lunch before going out onto the course. The club was highly rated for its cuisine and the range of single malts, well-displayed on the shelves behind the bar. The ambience of the establishment was first class. John selected a table by the large panoramic window, which looked out over the course that they would soon be enjoying. In the foreground, the paved area, in front of the clubhouse, was bordered on either side by herbaceous borders behind which were flowering shrubs and trees. At this time of year, the appearance was at its finest, showing the early display of spring in all its glory. The magnolias, although just beginning to fade, had laid a carpet of the delicate petals that was beautiful to behold. There were several huge berberis bushes now displaying their magnificence with a mass of yellow blossom and some cherry trees almost ready to burst forth to augment their counterparts of nature. Observing Patrick's attention to the scene, John said, "It's quite lovely at this time of year."

"Quite magnificent, John. What a beautiful scene to enjoy whilst having lunch."

Out on the course, teeing off at number three, Patrick told John that he saw his daughter on the previous evening.

"I had dinner with your daughter last evening. It was most enjoyable to see her again."

"How splendid. I'm sure she thoroughly enjoyed your company too," he said with that lovely Welsh accent he had. "Bronwen likes you very much, you know."

"I like her also, John. I enjoy her company so much. Our conversation is always so easy and spontaneous."

"I worry about her sometimes. Since her divorce, she seems to have nothing in her life other than her work at the hotel. Being deputy manager, is of course, a good position to have, but the downside is the unsocial hours that come with it."

"She doesn't seem to mind and obviously enjoys dealing with people."

Having driven off from the third tee, they walked down the fairway, talking as they went.

"She should never have married Hugh Jenkins. He was not right for her and without interfering, I tried to let her know, in a roundabout manner that I didn't care for him, but to no avail. Bronwen should have married someone like you Patrick."

"Oh, John, life is full of 'should-have-been' and 'if only'. For myself, things have worked out very well."

"For me also," John replied. "But I was fortunate to have a younger brother, who was more academically inclined than me, and had ambition beyond my comprehension. Had it not been for David, I suppose I would still be in the Rhonda, and out of work since the closure of the coal mines. I left school at sixteen and went down the mine. Not as a miner but as an apprentice fitter. I can remember well the smell of 'oily dust' as we descended, at quite high speed, in the cage to the bottom landing. There, the warm air felt unnatural in an area that was quite large but cave-like. Then in the tunnels, dank and smelly, poorly lit in many places so that you needed the lamp that was fixed to the front of your helmet, you crawled through towards the coal face. There perhaps, would be a broken-down coal cutter that you were expected to fix as fast as possible, in often difficult positions. David stayed on at school and gained a scholarship to Bangor University. Chemistry had always been his great interest since a young boy with his chemistry set given to him one Christmas. At school he earned the nickname of 'Stinker Williams'. He gained a first-class honours degree and came here to Cardiff to work. His ambition was always to have his own business, and so he started in the insulation installation of domestic households. That is when he persuaded me to join him. My da, thought me to be very foolish leaving a steady trade in the mines. He thought that I would regret leaving his beloved Rhonda. We eventually moved into the fabrication side of the industry, which is when we became customers of Salopian Industries. The rest is history."

"At the time that we were bidding to purchase your company, there was that other company from Liverpool, Eco-Tech who, like yourselves, was in the fabrication side of the insulation industry."

"Yes, I remember the company quite well."

"What was your opinion of the people that you dealt with?"

Taking his time in preparation to play his ball, John Williams swung his club and executed a lovely stroke, putting him nicely on the fourth green. Turning to Evans, he said, "Vic Eardley was the man that I dealt with mostly and I didn't care for him. In my opinion he is a 'Barrow Boy', masquerading as a high-flying businessman. Certainly, a person that I would never trust. His partners seemed all right and were of better character than Eardley.

The round finished, John Williams being the winner, they made their way to the place of that hackneyed phrase, the nineteenth hole. Indulging themselves in a single malt, they sat in relaxation, chatting, until finally, Patrick said that it was time for him to leave. He had arranged to have dinner again with Bronwen and didn't want to be late. He took John home and returned to the hotel, arriving about five o'clock. This he knew would give him time to shower and change before six o'clock, when Bronwen would go off duty. He knew that she would come to see him before they had dinner. Hopefully to have 'dessert before the main course'.

They enjoyed the meal and bottle of Burgundy at the same table as the previous night. Conversation as always being easy and pleasant and importantly, in relative privacy.

"Patrick, I have so enjoyed your company this last couple of days. I'm going to miss you. Have you any idea when you may be able to come down here again?"

"I must be honest, at this present time, with all that's going on, it is impossible for me to say, but as soon as I am able, I will come, I promise."

It was almost ten o'clock, when Bronwen said that they should move and allow the staff to clear the table. Patrick walked with her to her car, and they kissed passionately before she got into the car and drove away into the night, back to her home that she knew would seem empty and that she would feel very lonely once again.

14

The police divisional headquarters building was by design utilitarian, referred to by many of the locals as a blot on the landscape. Relatively modern, being constructed at the turn of the millennium, it housed the constabulary responsible for Telford and surrounding districts. Entering through the large glass doors, there, immediately in front of the doors was the front desk, the domain of the duty sergeant. To the left-hand side, was a waiting area with relatively comfortable chairs, for those who came either to report an incident, give testimony, or request assistance from 'The Boys in Blue'. Also, to the left-hand side was a door through which those who came under arrest, were taken to the custody suite. On the right hand-side of the building was the doorway, which led to the offices, interview rooms and locker rooms of the uniformed branch of the service, all on the ground floor, whilst a broad stairway led up to the first floor which housed the CID Department. There was of course a lift connecting the two floors. The CID area was basically a large open-plan communal office, with several individual offices along one wall, specifically for the officers of high rank. DCI Harry Davies had one of these. The offices all had large windows, giving not only good light but also a pleasant western aspect of the countryside and of course the benefit of afternoon sunlight.

DCI Harry Davies was sitting at his desk looking out of the window, from which he could see the famous landmark of the Wrekin, a hill about five miles to the west of Telford, standing 1335 feet high and popular with locals and tourists alike. He thought, as he gazed out, of the local legend that he always found amusing. The legend that a giant had dumped a spadeful of earth there, after changing his mind from dumping it in the River Severn, to flood Shrewsbury, because of his grudge against the townspeople. He then scraped the mud off his boots, which became the Ercall Hill nearby. Ercall being pronounced as 'arcle'. Smiling, he thought how Shrewsbury often flooded without the assistance of the giant's spadeful of earth, as did various locations along the path of the Severn, including the Dale End at Ironbridge. The day was bright and sunny and so he could see the landmark quite clearly, which prompted his thoughts to a local joke, that if you could see the Wrekin, it was going to rain but if you couldn't it was already raining.

Bringing his mind back to the reports in front of him, he pondered on how next to proceed. He had received from DCS Stuart in Liverpool, the report of all the information they had to date that applied to the murder of Sophie Langford. The cause of death was due to haemorrhage following the severance of the carotid artery. The secondary, and associated cause, was that of stabbing in the stomach. The weapon was thought to be a kitchen type knife with a blade about fifteen centimetres in length, although no such weapon had been found at the crime scene. The time of death was specified as being mid-morning. There was no evidence of forced entry into the property, implying that the victim had let the perpetrator in, either because she had known the visitor or had been persuaded to do so. This gave credence to the statement made by the next-door neighbour that a woman, claiming to be a police officer had called mid-morning and gone into the house. His description was that she was of medium height, fair-haired and was wearing black trousers and black jacket. She also had a shoulder bag and her car was dark blue of indeterminate make. He estimated that she was there for about ten minutes. It had also been established that the victim's laptop was missing, presumed taken by the perpetrator. There were no unidentified fingerprints found, which suggested that the woman had been wearing gloves, but when questioned, the next-door neighbour could not remember if the woman he saw was wearing gloves.

DS Robb's enquiries concerning the death of Don Phillips were not entirely conclusive. Although Robb's opinion was that Mr Addison was not involved, but had been at the place where the deceased had his fishing gear, after whatever had happened there had taken place, as Mr Addison had explained. However, this was not confirmed. There was also the unidentified footprint of what appeared to be a trainer. That certainly needed further investigation.

The identity of the woman, who had been recognised by the now deceased Sophie Langford, visiting Eco-Tech was perhaps, the most frustrating thing in this saga. All that was needed was a name, the name which Sophie had known, crucial information that was now denied to them. That, most certainly, was the motive for Sophie's murder. The DCI remembered that although Sophie had recognised the woman, she didn't know her name but had found it in the visitor's book. She had remembered the woman, having seen her with a lot of the staff members from Salopian Industries last Christmas. Perhaps, he thought, there were photographs taken at the time by someone on their mobile. A line of enquiry worth pursuing. Often on such occasions, little groups would form according to their liking of each other. Danny Drew had at one time, when seeing some of the girls, made the remark that he 'fancied the pants off them'. If only those girls could be identified, it may lead to identifying the unknown one, since for Sophie to have remembered someone from such an occasion, her attention to that someone, must have been drawn for some reason, which could easily be Danny's comment about his 'fancies'. Scrolling through the reports, he paused to read again the one appertaining to the incident reported about Julie Phillips being very nearly hit by a car in a narrow lane, which led to Julie's mother's house. Julie had been staying there since her husband's death and on that occasion was cycling there. At the time, the DCI had thought that Julie had, perhaps, over-reacted to what was an example of bad driving along a narrow country lane. She didn't get to see the registration number of the vehicle but had said that it was dark blue and of medium size. The car used by the unknown caller to Sophie Langford's home was described as dark blue. Perhaps there was a connection.

In the main office, DCI Davies called for attention. "There are several lines of enquiry that we must re-examine. Firstly, the suspicious death of Don Phillips. One of the footprints found at the scene has been identified, and whether or not the owner of the boot that made that impression is in some way responsible for the death, it is vitally important that the person responsible for the second footprint be identified. Evidence at the scene indicates that an altercation, of some kind, had taken place, which no doubt resulted in the victim being in the river.

"Secondly, Danny Drew had commented on one or more of the women, saying that he fancied the pants off them. That would have drawn Sophie's attention, I am sure. Maybe the woman we are seeking was one that Danny fancied the pants off. On such occasions it is usual for somebody to be taking photos with their mobiles. We must make enquiries to find out if anyone has photos." Pausing to allow what he had said to sink in, and give time for anyone to comment, or ask questions, and receiving none, he continued.

"Grant, speak again with Julie Phillips about the incident in the lane and take Todd with you. Try and get a bit more information from her if you can. Then speak with anyone that was at the Christmas do. Ask if there are any photos available and if so, let us have look at them. DS Robb, you and I will go to see Don Phillip's ex brother-in-law's. I seem to remember that he lives in or near Buildwas. Check through Julie Phillips' statements. She gave his address. We were made aware that Phillip's first wife died in tragic circumstances. The coroner's verdict was accidental death, a verdict that Phillip's wife's brother didn't agree. It is known that the two men argued whenever they met. It seems that Phillips was suspected by his brother-in-law, of physically abusing his wife and that had led to her death. Let's see what he has to say."

15

DI Grant turned off the main road into the lane that led to Julie Phillips' grandmother's house. He said that he was taking this lane, the way that Julie had taken, when the incident occurred, to get an actual feel for the situation as Julie had described it. The lane was, as Julie had said, very narrow with high banking on either side. The banking on both sides of the lane were well overgrown with grass, weeds and all kinds of wild plants. The perfect habitat for all kinds of wildlife and insects. There were passing places at intervals, but it was quite obvious that anyone driving along this lane needed to do so with caution, as not only was it a single-track road, but one that was twisting with many blind bends to contend with. DI Bob Grant was beginning to believe that Julie's account of her experience was not imagined.

They eventually came to the main road and turning right, drove for a further two hundred yards to where, on the right, was Julie Phillips' grandmother's house. It was a very, attractive building from the early nineteen twenties, set well back from the road, with high hawthorn hedges giving privacy but blending in perfectly with the countryside.

Julie's grandmother opened the door in response to the doorbell and recognising both Bob Grant and Jane, from their visit following Julie's harrowing experience, invited them in, leading them through to the lounge.

"Please, do take a seat," she said. "I imagine that it is Julie you wish to see."

"That is so, Mrs Hampton. We just want to check up on a few details in connection with the frightening experience she had recently," the DI said. "It won't take up much time."

"Julie is not in at the moment. She's gone to the shops to get a few things for me, but I am sure that she won't be very long. Would you like tea or coffee, whilst you are waiting?"

"Thank you, that would be very kind," the DI replied. "Tea would be lovely."

After about five minutes, Mrs Hampton came back into the room carrying a tray with a teapot, milk jug, sugar basin and tea strainer. "I only use leaf tea," she said. "I am rather traditional in my habits, as you may well have noticed," indicating the tea strainer as she was speaking. Then regarding the mugs on the tray, "I thought that you would prefer mugs, rather than cups." They were not ordinary mugs, but of bone china, with an attractive floral decoration. Mrs Hampton was a lady of taste.

Having poured the tea and offering a plate of assorted biscuits, she sat down opposite to them with an elegance that surprised Bob Grant. She was eighty-four years of age, but, to Grant, she looked to be twenty years younger. Tastefully dressed, with a figure that was very trim, her appearance was enhanced by her hair that was of a distinctive iron-grey and which was beautifully arranged.

"This is a lovely room, Mrs Hampton," the DI remarked, taking in the ambience of his surroundings. "In fact, a lovely house."

"Please, Inspector, call me Eleri, it's less formal."

"Forgive me, but that is quite an unusual name."

"Not so in Wales."

That she was Welsh, was of course no surprise, for her accent gave confirmation to that.

"How long have you lived in Telford?" Jane asked, speaking for the first time.

"Long before Telford existed," she replied. "I came to work as a nurse at what was then the cottage hospital in nineteen fifty-six, when I was twenty-one, and just qualified as a state registered nurse. I met my late husband, a couple of years older than me, and teaching here at the village school. The school was only a small affair with just four classes taking the children from this village and surrounding areas. Two years later, in nineteen fifty-eight, we married and went to live in a small house in Wellington. We were happy there. It was convenient for both of us, because in those days we cycled to work. We didn't have a car. Being recently married, we couldn't afford to have one." She was silent for a few moments, as she gazed wistfully out of the window.

"It must have been very different in those days," Jane said, breaking the silence.

"Oh yes, it was indeed." Looking at them, with the faintest of smiles, "The village that you now see, has essentially replaced the old one. Well, what was more a hamlet with no more than a couple of dozen cottages, one of them being what could very loosely be called a shop. They were quite primitive, with no power, gas or electricity, no running water and no mains sewerage. At one time the water supply was from a village well. In reality, it was a piped facility from a natural spring. I suppose that is why the houses were built there in the first place, way back, in the middle of the eighteenth century. They were built to accommodate miners and furnace workers of the day. It was the beginning of the industrial revolution. Some time, after the First World War, mains water was brought to the village in the form of a village hydrant, but it was not piped into the houses. The inhabitants had still to collect their water in a bucket to take back to their houses, and this had to be done at least a couple of times each day, whatever the weather. Those houses were only demolished in the early sixties. There is a typical example of such a cottage in the Ironbridge Gorge Museum."

"How incredible it all sounds, especially when this is within living memory," Jane said.

"It's amazing that the authorities didn't take action years before,"

"I suppose the Second World War had something to do with that," Grant said.

"I'm quite sure that was the case. One must remember that the early sixties was less than twenty years after the war ended and we were only just beginning to see modernisation.

As I have already said, the village was built in the middle of the eighteenth century, to provide homes for the miners, who worked in the numerous pits in the area. Most of those pits were drift mines, those that one walked into, down an inclined tunnel because the coal seams around here were close to the surface. However, the coal was of the quality that suited the process of 'coking', which was required at that time for the iron furnaces."

"Why would people choose to live in such deprivation in the twentieth century?" Jane said in astonishment.

"Most of the inhabitants had been born and bred there, but I think that mostly, they had no other choice at that time. However, in the early sixties, all the properties were condemned by the council and demolished. Two hundred years of history gone for ever and that of course included the school. This house, in which I have lived since the early sixties, had always been called the Schoolmaster's House because it was always the residence of the headmaster, a perk of the job. Two years after our marriage, the headmaster retired and my husband was offered that position, which he accepted without hesitation, so we came to live here. A couple of years later, the decision to close the school was taken and we were offered the opportunity to purchase the house at sitting tenant rate, which of course we did, and so I have lived here ever since. The 'new town of Telford', only came into being some years later. So, you see, I was here long before Telford existed." With a broad smile, she offered them more tea.

"Do you think that there is any connection between Julie's experience in the lane and the suspicious death of her husband and of that young man Danny?" Eleri asked the DI.

"There are several lines of enquiry that we are pursuing. I don't rule anything out."

"I was rather shocked, to learn of Julie's affair with that young man. I never liked Don Phillips, and in my opinion, she should never have married him. I was aware that he didn't treat her very well, and I think he was a bully, but that is no excuse for what she did, and I told her so. Although I love my granddaughter very much, I could not condone her conduct. Happiness is rarely the outcome of extra marital relationships, only hurt to many." The following silence was broken by the sound of a door closing and then the voice of Julie.

"Hi, Gran, I'm back. Where are you?" Julieentered by the kitchen door.

"In the lounge, dear. We have visitors"

Julie came into the lounge and greeted the visitors warmly. Since her long talks with Jane, in an atmosphere that was friendly and relaxed, she now felt comfortable in the presence of the police.

"Julie, we should like to confirm one or two facts about your frightening experience. At the time that we spoke to you after the incident, you thought that the colour of the vehicle was dark blue. Do you still believe that to be so?" were the DI's opening words.

"I think it was. It all happened so quickly, and I was in total shock," she replied.

"Do you always use the lane when coming to your grandmother's?"

"Yes, until the incident, but I've kept to the main road since then."

"Am I right in assuming that all your colleagues at work know that you are staying with your grandmother, and have been since the death of your husband?"

"Yes, I think they do. I told Sharon Sumner to let them all know, so that if anyone wanted to contact me, they would know where to find me."

"I would now, like you to cast your mind back to last Christmas time, to the Christmas celebrations at the pub," the DI said. "Were most of your work colleagues there?"

"Oh, yes, they were all there, I'm sure. You see it's an annual event when all the staff get together. Yvonne Baxter, Sir Ian's secretary arranges it. There is a buffet, and we all contribute. She gets a price per head, and we pay her accordingly. It's something for all the office staff. The managers don't come, because they have their own dinner at the hotel."

"Was there general mixing of people, or did you stay in particular pairs or groups?"

"There was general mixing throughout the evening, but most people did for most of the time stay with their particular friends and colleagues of their own particular department."

"I imagine that somebody would have taken photographs. Have you any idea who may have done so?" the DI asked in the hope that her answer would be in the affirmative.

He was not disappointed, for without hesitation she told him that Adrian Hopkins, one of the assistant engineers was taking photos all through the evening.

"Adrian Hopkins, I presume works in Mr Anderson's department?"

"Yes, he does. He's been here for quite a long time."

"I would like to look at some of those photos. Do you think he will still have them?"

"Adrian is a keen photographer. It's his hobby, so I think that he would have taken only pictures that he thought were worth keeping."

The DI thanked Julie for her help and, also her grandmother for her kind hospitality, saying that they must now take their leave, there was still a lot of work for them to do.

Driving back, the DI remarked on the elegance and sophistication of Julie's grandmother.

"A very remarkable and knowledgeable lady," was his comment.

"Yes, there's no doubt about that," Jane agreed. "I think she gave one of the most interesting history lessons I have ever had," laughing as she spoke.

"I think we should now call in at the factory and ask Adrian Hopkins if we can look at those photos that he took but, as a courtesy, we should first speak with Leslie Anderson. Who knows what gems of knowledge, we may learn?"

Leslie Anderson welcomed them into his office, asking how he may be of help.

DI Grant explained that to assist in their enquiries, it would be very, helpful if they could see any of the photos that were taken at the last annual Christmas event.

"I am given to understand that one of your engineers, Adrian Hopkins, did take quite a lot of photos throughout the evening."

"That may well be so. I was not there so I don't know if photos were taken, but we can ask him. We managers don't attend because it is an event that the staff have arranged for themselves for many years. Yvonne Baxter, I believe is the main organizer."

"Yvonne Baxter, she is Sir Ian Leighton-Boyce's secretary, if I remember correctly."

"Yes, that is so," Anderson replied.

Buzzing through on his phone, to his secretary, he asked if she would locate Adrian and ask him to come to his office.

When Adrian arrived, he looked taken aback to see the two police officers sitting there.

"Nothing to be alarmed about, Adrian," Anderson said, seeing the discomfort on his face. "The police officers would be pleased to have your assistance."

"We are given to understand that at your last company Christmas event, you took quite a few photographs during the evening, is that correct?" asked DI Grant.

"Yes, I did. They were just shots of everybody having fun. Nothing very fancy."

"Do you still have them on your memory card. I presume the photos are digital?"

"Yes, I still have them. Would you like to see them?"

"I most certainly would. Are you able to send them to me digitally?"

"Yes, I will do that when I get home."

"Thank you very much for your help. I look forward to receiving them."

When Adrian had left the office, Leslie Anderson asked the DI if there had been any progress in the investigation.

"Progress is being made along several lines of enquiry. I'm sure you realise that I cannot say too much at this time or discuss the case with you."

"Yes of course. It was silly of me to ask."

"However, we would appreciate any information that you can give that will help us in our enquiries. Please feel free to contact us at any time."

"The horror of murder, especially here in the factory notwithstanding, I am totally perplexed by the fact that Danny was where he was at the time of the incident. I can think of no logical reason for him being there," Leslie said, with the sound of exasperation in his voice.

"I quite understand your feelings, because that is a fact that we have not yet been able to find an explanation. That he was in contact with someone, if only the perpetrator of the crime, is obvious, but whether it was just one person, or more than one person is still unclear. I have no doubt that such a traumatic incident must have given you many practical problems."

"Absolutely. It's almost two months now, since that terrible day, and of course during that time, with Danny no longer with us, I have had to do so many extra things myself, which has not been easy because the rebuilt production plant has come on stream. The first couple of weeks, at such times are the worst. That is the time when all the 'bugs' are sorted out. However, there is some light at the end of the tunnel. There is a possibility that I shall soon have a replacement for Danny, and believe me, it can't come soon enough."

The DI thanked Leslie Anderson for his help, and he and DC Todd took their leave.

True to his word, Adrian Hopkins sent the photos to DI Bob Grant and so the next morning he spent a considerable time looking at them along with Jane Todd. The names of most of those in the pictures, they knew from the questioning sessions that they had held.

"We don't need to pay too much attention to the men, it is on the women we should focus our attention. Take notice who are in groups, or in pairs and of course any shots of anyone alone. Danny made his comment about fancying the pants off them'. A phrase in the plural. That may be significant. Firstly, let us look for pairs."

There were shots of Lucy Thompson with another girl from the Development Department, Julie Phillips and Sue from the Supplies department, also Yvonne Baxter with Sharon Sumner. Scrolling through there was Sharon Sumner with Julie Phillips and Lucy and Sue together also, there was Frank Ebb's secretary, Tamzin with Racheal, the secretary of Leslie Anderson. Then there were photos of various groups from Sales, Supplies and Transport.

"Toddy," exclaimed Bob Grant, "who, would you think out of that lot, would Danny be referring when he said he fancied them?"

"I'm not at all sure, Sir. There are some very, attractive women among them, that would most probably have appealed to someone like Danny Drew. Although there are distinct groups together, mainly departmental groups, there was obviously a lot of mingling throughout the evening. He could have been referring to any of them."

DI Bob Grant had a distinct feeling of deflation. He had hoped that by viewing the photos there may well have been some indication as to whom Danny had been referring, that someone being the person remembered by Sophie Langford.

***

DCI Harry Davies and DS Robb drove to Buildwas, to pay a visit to Don Phillips' ex-brother-in-law, Steve Smith. The knowledge that he was known to have disliked Don Phillips, could not be dismissed. They knew that Smith blamed Phillips for the tragic death of his sister, Don's first wife, in contention to the coroner's verdict, so could be regarded as a suspect associated with the suspicious death of Phillips. Living where he did, Smith could quite easily have walked alongside the river, seen Phillips and accosted him.

Stopping outside Smith's house, they saw him on the drive, washing his car. The DCI approached him and showing his warrant card asked if they could go inside for privacy purposes.

"What do you want to speak with me about?" he asked in a belligerent tone.

"If we could perhaps, go inside, it would be preferable."

With reluctance, he led them into the house and into the living room. The DCI very quickly took in the general appearance of the room. It was tastefully decorated with comfortable furniture, tidy and obviously well cared for, probably with a woman's touch. Looking through the window, he observed a large, and well cared for garden. On the lawn was a dog, a German Shepherd, lying contentedly, chewing at a bone.

"Well, what is it?"

"When did you last see Don Phillips?"

"Can't remember. Obviously before he died," was his sarcastic reply.

The DCI had noticed the trainers that Smith was wearing and wondered whether they could be a match for the unidentified print found at the position of Don Phillips' fishing gear.

"Mr Smith, I should like you to think very carefully, because your answer could be of considerable importance. I will repeat the question. When did you last see Don Phillips?"

Smith still said that he couldn't remember. The DCI then asked where he was on the morning of that fateful day.

"At home, as I have been since I was made redundant about four months ago."

"Did you by any chance take a walk along the river?"

"Might have done, I can't remember," was his reply.

"There seems to be a lot of things that you don't remember. Tell me, how long have you had the trainers that you are wearing, can you remember that?"

"About six months and I wear them regularly."

"At the place where Don Phillips fishing gear was found, there was evidence of a scuffle. There were two different footprints found there, one of which has been identified but the other one not. Perhaps, Mr Smith, your trainers might supply the answer."

"Are you accusing me of killing him?"

"I'm not accusing you of anything Mr Smith, I am just speculating. However, I would like to take those trainers for forensic examination if you wouldn't mind."

Smith complied with the request and handed his trainers to DS Robb, saying, "You won't find anything."

"Thank you, Mr Smith. They will be returned as soon as forensics have finished with them. I apologise for the inconvenience."

With that the two officers left and returned to Divisional Headquarters. On the journey back, the DCI remarked on Smith's belligerent attitude and his comment that "we won't find anything."

"I think that perhaps these particular trainers will prove 'clean', but that doesn't mean that he wasn't at the scene. He could have been there but wearing different footwear. I didn't like his unhelpful attitude, for whatever reason that was, so I think we'll make him sweat a little. It may persuade him to be a little more cooperative."

16

Frank Ebbs, the Company chief engineer, rang Leslie Anderson asking him to go to his office saying that he had some news regarding a replacement for Danny Drew.

Leslie breathed a sigh of relief. Perhaps, very soon things would become a little easier.

"Do take a seat, Les," Frank Ebbs said cheerfully, pointing to a chair in front of his desk. Then he buzzed for his secretary, who came in through the connecting door from her office. "Tamzin, will you please bring two coffees, and if you have any biscuits left in the tin, some of those too."

"Yes, of course. And you haven't eaten all the biscuits yet, so I'll bring those too," she replied with a laugh, to which Frank responded likewise.

There was obviously a good rapport between them, which was reassuring to know. Tamzin was, in Leslie's opinion, a very, nice young woman, highly intelligent and with a kindly disposition. His own secretary Racheal was, he knew, very friendly with Tamzin. They made a good pair.

"The other day, I mentioned to you that there was a possibility that there was someone who may be suitable as a replacement for Danny Drew. He is someone that I have known for a considerable time and so I know him to be of good character and, also, to be a good engineer."

Tamzin brought in the coffee and a nice selection of biscuits. She never made instant coffee, but always a nice Continental blend, this being freshly percolated.

Frank Ebbs explained to Les, that several days previously, he had received a text message on his mobile. It was from a former colleague, who he had not seen for a considerable time. His name was Rowan Chapman. Rowan, he said was the son of a farmer from somewhere near Worcester, but had no intention of following in his father's footsteps He wanted to be an engineer, so having studied at Liverpool University, he graduated and took up a position at Aerospace where they met and became good friends. Eventually, he met a girl who came from up north, in fact Southport, and they married. She had a widowed mother, who was in poor health, and so to be near her, she and Rowan moved to Southport. He got a job at a firm in Liverpool. That firm was Eco-Tech Limited. He had worked there until twelve months ago, when he had a disagreement with one of the partners, Vic Eardley, and decided to leave. His new appointment was at a company in Manchester that manufactured special purpose machinery. They were also, precision engineers. This appointment suited Rowan perfectly.

"What was the disagreement he had at Eco-Tech?" asked Leslie.

"It was all to do with professional ethics."

Ebbs went on to explain that Rowan was employed there at the time that Salopian Industries acquired Williams Brothers. Rowan had said that Vic Eardley was hopping mad because he desperately wanted the opportunity to develop the new type of insulation board. He had said that they would pursue the product on their own account, although he didn't indicate how they would do that, in view that the formulation for the product was secret and would be subject ultimately to patent application. However, work was started, and over the next twelve months considerable progress was made, a rate of progress that surprised Rowan. How the formulation had been achieved he had no idea. They had employed a chemist, but to Rowan's knowledge, he had no idea of the formulation when he took up the post. About twelve months ago, Rowan was in Vic Eardley's office and he saw a drawing on Vic's desk. The drawing was folded up and so he was unable to see what it was but, what he did see was the title box which of course displayed the company name. The name was Salopian Industries Limited. He asked Vic Eardley what the drawing was, being surprised that they would have anything from their rivals. Vic Eardley was not pleased by the question and said that it was for he, Vic Eardley, to know and for him, Rowan, to wonder about. The incident worried him, because the only way in which something of that nature could be in the possession of Vic Eardley was by direct theft or by someone obtaining it for him. That was, in Rowan's opinion, corporate espionage. It was the only term that could be used, and which he believed could carry severe penalties. He made the decision to find other employment. He applied for a post at a Manchester-based company in response to an advertisement in the newspaper and was successful. By this time, tragedy had struck. His life had been changed forever. Six months previously, his wife had been fatally injured in a motorway pile-up and since then, his wife's mother had died. There was nothing to keep him in Southport, and so he moved to Manchester. That was about twelve months ago, but last week he was informed that the company was going into administration. Two of their biggest customers had been declared bankrupt, which left them in the present position, due to insufficient cash-flow. He suspected that whatever the outcome, he would be made redundant.

"That was the reason he contacted me. He hoped that I could offer him something or that I may know someone who can. I immediately thought of you Les. You need someone to replace Danny Drew, because I am fully aware that you are being stretched and with the prospect of the new insulation boards on the horizon you need someone capable of getting to grips with everything quickly. I am sure Rowan could meet the challenge, but I told him that I would leave the final decision to you. If you feel that he may be a solution for your needs, I will call him and arrange for him to come for interview."

"Frank, he sounds to be the ideal solution. Please invite him to see us as soon as possible."

"I'll do it right now, whilst you are here."

With that he rang Rowan Chapman and arranged for him to come to Telford in two days' time, telling him that he would book overnight accommodation for him. It would give time for them to catch up with each other.

That evening, Leslie told Jenny, about the new prospect of someone to take some of the daily strain, which felt to be getting worse with every day that passed. He felt assured that this man, being known to Frank Ebbs, whom he had come to regard with respect, would fit in very well. The one thing that surprised him was that at no time had Frank mentioned having spoken to Patrick Evans about the matter. It was obvious that Evans didn't try to manipulate Frank or try to dictate to him in any way, in the manner he used to do in the old days. Of course, now, he supposed, there was no need to do that, because he had wormed his way into the top job, pushing him, Leslie Anderson, into subservience at the same time. That was the sort of person Patrick Evans was. He absolutely detested the man.

A call from the gatehouse to Tamzin, announced the arrival of Mr Rowan Chapman, to see Mr Ebbs. "We'll bring him over Tamzin, so you stay where you are." There were always two security officers on duty, night and day. One would always remain in the gatehouse whilst the other one would, at regular periods, patrol throughout the factory. This time, they were both there and so one of them was able to escort Rowan Chapman to Tamzin's office. This was quite the opposite to the situation on the day and at the time of Danny Drew's demise. The duty security officer at that time was at the opposite side of the factory in the Development Department, so was unable to report having seen anything unusual or indeed anyone being in the vicinity of plant repair site.

Tamzin greeted Rowan and gave him an application form for him to complete. In this instance it was purely a matter of form rather than a necessity, but it did put on record Rowan's personal details. Returning it to her, duly completed, Tamzin showed him into Frank Ebb's office.

"Good morning, Rowan, it's good to see you again," said Frank, shaking hands and then introducing him to Leslie Anderson. "Please have a seat."

Tamzin came into the office, through the connecting door, bearing a tray with coffee and biscuits, placing the tray on the corner of Frank's desk, then carefully passing a beaker to each of them. "Gentlemen, please call me if you would like more," and with that warm smile that she always seemed capable of displaying, she returned to her own domain, closing the connecting door as she did so.

"Rowan, welcome to Salopian Industries. If you join us, Leslie, here, will be your superior. The position we can offer is that of deputy works engineer. I will say no more for the present. I will hand over to Leslie."

Leslie Anderson outlined the duties entailed in such an appointment. He went on to explain the added responsibilities that would soon need to be addressed, as and when, the new type of insulation board went into production. “I’m given to understand, that you are to some degree familiar with this product?”

“Yes, I am. I suppose that is, in a very roundabout way. That product is the reason that I am here this morning. It is of course, twelve months since I left Eco-Tech so I am sure that the development will have advanced considerably. At that time, Eco-Tech were just able to make a board but with quite a long forming period, a long way from the speed that would be necessary to make the product financially viable.”

“We here at Salopian, can now produce at a viable rate. The design people are now finalising the whole plant design, and so we shall soon begin the construction of the new plant.

We shall begin with one line, iron out any inherent ‘bugs’, and as product demand increases, we can easily duplicate lines.”

They discussed all the usual matters of interest, conditions of working, salary, vacation allowances, all of which were acceptable to Rowan, and so Leslie Anderson offered him the job. Rowan accepted the offer with thanks and agreed to a starting date ten days later.

The three of them finally adjourned for lunch. On this occasion they sampled the cuisine as presented by the works canteen, but in a side room so that they could continue talking in privacy. Rowan made it quite clear that he was grateful for the job offer. Not only grateful but relieved and looking forward to beginning his new role.

The matter of housing was discussed, and Frank Ebbs suggested that he arrange for temporary B&B accommodation at the Queen’s Arms Hotel, whilst he looked for permanent housing. Frank explained that the wife of the landlord, looked after the catering side of the business and that she was good. “Evening meals you can have there of course if and, when you wish,” he explained. Rowan thought such an arrangement would be ideal, giving him the time to search for a suitable property to either rent or purchase. Frank said that he would, himself, speak with the landlord and make the necessary arrangements if Rowan so wished. Rowan accepted the offer with gratitude. His next task, as he put it, was to arrange for his furniture to be put into store until he had somewhere to relocate. They arranged to meet at the Queen’s Arms at seven o’clock to have dinner. With that they left the canteen, Frank Ebbs and Leslie Anderson, returning to carry on with their work, Rowan Chapman to explore Telford, and possibly to speak with an estate agent, to see what housing was available. For Rowan this was an exciting time, and a wonderful opportunity for a new beginning.

17

Following a telephone conversation between DCI Harry Davies and DI Ken Abbott in Liverpool, DI Abbott made the decision to visit once again, the company of Eco-Tech. Davies had explained the situation of Rowan Chapman, now being employed by Salopian Industries Limited, and what he had revealed regarding his time at Eco-Tech. The DCI had made it quite clear that, in his opinion, there had been underhand activities undertaken, in the acquisition of the chemical formulation for the new product, also information as to the sort of equipment used for its production. He also reminded Abbott about Sophie Langford's discovery of someone, known to be employed by Salopian Industries, being a visitor to Eco-Tech, suggesting that Sophie's murder was the result of her making that discovery. "What is desperately required," the DCI had said, "is the name of that unknown person, who we know was a woman."

DI Abbott with his sergeant paid the visit to Eco-Tech going directly to reception, but to the surprise of the receptionist he didn't ask to see any person, but rather to see the visitors' book. Flicking through the pages until he came to the period known to be the time that Sophie had made her discovery, he was astonished to find a couple of pages had been removed.

"What's happened here?" DI Abbott asked the receptionist. "There are some pages missing."

"Oh, that. Mr Eardley was looking through the entries and accidentally knocked my coffee cup over the whole contents going over those pages. I tried to dry them off with a tissue, but Mr Eardley told me not to bother. Cut them out he told me. They are past now and of no importance. So, I did just that."

DI Abbott was nonplussed, and addressing his DS, said "there is nothing more we can do at the moment." Thanking the receptionist, they left the premises, to return to Headquarters.

On their return journey, the DS was driving, and DI Abbott sat in the passenger seat, quite obviously fuming with frustration. "That was no accidental knocking over of a coffee cup. If coffee was spilled, that bastard Eardley did it deliberately, or more likely, the receptionist had been told to give that excuse. No, Eardley removed those pages deliberately to get rid of the name we need to know, the name for which Sophie was killed."

"Then, what do we do next, Sir?"

"I'm going to speak with the super and ask to have a search warrant. We are going to turn that place upside down. Homicide is the prime reason for our investigation, but my opinion, is the same as that of DCI Davies from Telford. The murder, of Sophie Langford, is connected, with the suspected corporate espionage at Salopian Industries, and so, anything we may turn up during a search of the premises could possibly give us a lead in our murder enquiry.

DI Abbott and his DS arrived at the premises of Eco-Tech followed by two squad cars. At reception, DI Abbott asked to see Mr Victor Eardley. The receptionist rang through and a few minutes later, Vic Eardley came to meet them. On seeing the police team, standing in the vestibule, a surge of panic came over him once again. In an effort, to appear calm, he greeted the DI cordially.

"Good morning, Inspector, you appear to have come in force. hHw can I be of help?"

"Good morning, Mr Eardley. Yes, we are in force, because we have a warrant to search these premises and so we have much to do," DI Abbott replied, at the same time handing him the search warrant.

"What on earth you are hoping to find, I cannot imagine, but please, be my guest. You will of course be wasting your time."

"I will be the judge of that, Mr Eardley. We will be careful and will let you know when we are finished. We will start in your office and although we shall be very thorough, we shall try to be as quick as possible."

The team began, with Eardley's desk drawers, then by going through the filing cabinets, drawer by drawer. Vic Eardley stood watching them, helpless to prevent them looking at anything that was of interest to them. This was a situation that was, absolutely, new to him, being told what was to happen rather than he, dictating what was to happen. The feeling of total helplessness, and not to be in control was an experience very strange to him. His quick thinking and, often ready wit, that so many times had got him out of trouble was no help on this occasion. These men, going through his domain, were officers of the law and there was no way that he could prevent them doing a search into what he regarded as his personal records and information.

"Sir, take a look at this," called one of the search officers.

The DI went over to the cabinet to look at something the PC was holding. It was a folded drawing, the title box displaying the name, Salopian Industries Limited. Seeing this, Vic Eardley was stunned. This document he had concealed at the back of the drawer in between other papers totally unconnected. The DI took it and opened it out on Eardley's desk. It was obviously an engineering drawing showing an arrangement of machinery, to which the title shown on the drawing designated as Super Board Plant.

"What is this Mr Eardley?"

"Oh, that. It is something that I have had for a while. It's of no great importance. That is the reason that it was at the back of the cabinet," Vic replied, thinking rapidly for a reason.

"Why does it bear the name of Salopian Industries, and how did it come into your possession?"

"Somebody who used to work here brought it in some while ago, thinking that it might be of use."

"How did he come to have it?"

"I don't know because I didn't ask him," replied Eardley.

"Are you saying that the 'somebody' doesn't work here any longer?"

"Yes, he left some while ago. I don't know where he went to. I would have to look at past records."

"I may ask you to do just that. I'll let you know before we leave, if I need you to do that."

"I find it difficult to believe that you didn't ask how this drawing came to be in his possession." The DI was playing with Eardley. He could see the consternation in his eyes, and he could tell that he was beginning to squirm. Then to the PC, he said, "bag it. It may be evidence."

"I am telling you the truth. I have no idea how it came into his possession," was Eardley's response.

The police officers went on with the search, the DI being certain that what Eardley had just told them were lies to cover up the truth of how the drawing had been obtained.

The two other partners of the company came into the office, having been told by the receptionist that there were police officers with Mr Eardley and they had a search warrant. They introduced themselves and asked the DI, the purpose of the search.

"It is in connection with the murder of one of your employees, Sophie Langford. We believe that the crime is connected to something involving this company, and so we are searching for anything that might substantiate that belief." DI Abbott then took the evidence bag and taking out the drawing, said, "Gentlemen, have you ever seen this before?"

They both looked at it, and with a shaking of heads, said "no, never, this is from Salopian Industries. Where did you get it from?"

"This was found in Mr Eardley's filing cabinet. He says that one of your previous employees gave it to him, isn't that so, Mr Eardley?"

DI Abbott was now enjoying himself, watching very carefully, Eardley's reactions.

"Who was that Vic?" the question being asked, almost in unison, by Eardley's two partners.

"I can't remember his name. It was some time ago," he blustered.

The DI and Eardley's partners knew that he was lying. DI Abbott folded up the drawing and, handing it back to the PC, said, "we shall of course keep this for the time being, it may be used as evidence."

Leaving Eardley's office, they went into the factory and began looking at the various work areas until they came to an area set aside from the main production section.

"What do you do here" DI Abbott asked.

"It's our product development area. This is where we develop new products and sometimes better methods of production," was Eardley's reply.

There was, to the DI's untrained eye to machinery, a machine that was used to make a board that looked different to other materials around. It was black in colour and of some sort of foam.

"Is this something new?" indicating the black coloured boards.

"Yes, it is. This is of course in the early stages of development," Eardley replied.

DI Abbott knew, instinctively, that this was a similar product, to that which had been described to him, being developed at Salopian Industries. It was beginning to appear that the suspicions of DCI Harry Davies were correct and that here was the evidence, along with the drawing from Salopian Industries found in the possession of Vic Eardley, that corporate espionage had taken place. Here was the link with the murder of Sophie Langford and inevitably with the homicides at Telford. What was now most importantly needed, was the name of the unknown woman from Telford, who had visited this company to see Vic Eardley, she, probably being the bogus police officer who had visited Sophie and had killed her.

The police search team having now departed, the three partners of Eco-Tech were in Vic Eardley's office. Gerry Ewing and Bill Astley, sitting in front of Eardley's desk, glum faced and angry at what Gerry Ewing described as "one of the most humiliating moments in my life," and Bill Astley's outburst of, "You've lied to us and deceived us."

"Gerry, mate, and you Bill, don't let the accusations and innuendos of those buggers upset you. All I have done is for the future of this company. I acquired information about a competitor's production plans and strategy. I didn't break into their premises or hack into their computer system, so the police can't accuse me of anything illegal."

"How did that drawing, belonging to Salopian, come into your possession?" asked Gerry Ewing, "and, why not tell us about it, instead of hiding it away. You have led us to believe that the progress we have been making has been due to our own expertise, but now, I realise that you have been stealing information from the originators of the product."

"That's where you are wrong. I didn't steal it, I acquired it," countered Vic.

"Is there someone at Salopian, with a grudge against them strong enough for them to come to you with their product secrets?" chipped in Bill Astley, sarcastically.

"Of course not. As I have told you, I found a way of acquiring the important information needed without which we would never have got off the ground."

"As far as I am concerned, it all stops now. The reputation of this company will be in tatters if this becomes widely known," said Gerry Ewing, angrily. "You have continued to do exactly what you decide to do, even when Bill and I have expressed different opinions. Get this straight, Vic, you will no longer ignore us and what we have to say. I am going to call the accountants, and get them here, whilst we go through the accounts. We had an agreement on the amount we were going to spend on the development of the new product in this financial year. I no longer trust you to keep to any agreement. You think that you are God's gift to industry, well let me tell you, you are not. I am sure Bill agrees with me."

"Look, both of you, there's no need to go off the deep end. What I have done, has been for the good of the company," Vic burst in, before Bill could add his agreement.

"For the good of the company," Gerry repeated, in contempt. "For the gratification of your own ego, more like."

"Can't we sit down and talk about this, like responsible adults," appealed Vic, with a hint of concern in his voice.

"Like responsible adults," mocked Gerry, "you don't know the meaning of the word, responsible. Did you, for one moment, think of the possible consequences of your actions, in what can only be described as corporate espionage. I am not entirely sure of the law, in this case, but I would not be surprised for it to carry a custodial sentence. That is why I am calling the accountants in, to examine in detail the expenditure, and the details will be recorded in the minutes. Those minutes will be taken by your secretary and examined for accuracy. Make no mistake, Vic, the days of you doing just what you want to do, are well and truly over." With that, both he and Bill left, Vic being silenced by Gerry's verbal assault.

In the conference room, the three partners sat at the table with the accountant and Vic's secretary. The company's accounts were dissected and everything appertaining to the development programme receiving special scrutiny. Apart from the usual, and expected expenditure, there were regular payments going out but with no specific application recorded. Gerry having his suspicions, asked Vic to clarify the purpose of this expenditure. His glib reply was that this money was a bulked figure to cover all miscellaneous costs. Bill pointed out that the figure depicted every three months was a regular amount. which was strange if it was covering all miscellaneous costs. Vic's quick thinking gave the answer. It is the same in every three-monthly period, because that was the way he kept control of expenditure. The figure for each separate month would of course vary, according to activities undertaken during that period. In other words, if expenditure were high in one month, the expenditure would be limited in the next month so that the quarterly figure would correspond to budget.

It was, obvious, to both Gerry Ewing and Bill Astley that Vic was covering his tracks. They were sure that the so-called, 'miscellaneous expenditure', was in fact, the cost incurred in 'obtaining' the information from Salopian Industries. Payment made to a spy. That payment was high, equating to what would be a good salary if it were paid to one person. The other disturbing fact that had emerged from the meeting with the accountant, was that the project to date, was over budget to an extent that could cause a problem with cash flow. They may be forced to seek a loan from the bank, or to be more precise, an extension to the loan they already had.

A further worry was the impending action of the police, with regard to the discovery of the drawings belonging to Salopian. If charges were brought, they would be charges against the company, not just against Vic and that meant they both would be involved. They were both horrified by the thought and felt helpless in being unable to resolve the situation. There was also, the death of one of their employees to consider. Not just death, but murder. It had been said that it was a deliberate and premeditated crime. That being so, were the actions of Vic, in any way, associated with the murder of the girl. The police seemed to think so. It was time to confront Vic, and to demand to know who the spy was.

Vic refused to enlighten Gerry and Bill with details, saying that what they didn't know, they could not tell.

"You are a cheeky bastard," Gerry exploded in anger. "You have deliberately brought this company, of which we are a part, into disrespect and with the possibility of police action against us. The company finances have been depleted to such an extent that if any of our creditors are late paying or, heaven forbid, become incapable of paying, our cash flow could become negative. The only recourse then would be to ask the bank for an extension to our existing loan facility. If there were a police action pending, the bank would not even consider it. There is the possibility the bank could foreclose and then that would be the end. Bill and I demand that you tell us how you obtained the information from Salopian."

"All I will say, is that there is a woman involved. She is someone I met a while ago at Haydock Park races. We began talking about odds and favourites at the time of placing our bets and enjoyed a very pleasant afternoon that extended into the evening. She was at the races on her own as I was, so the company was welcome."

"A woman at the races alone, sounds like a pack of lies to me. I would hazard a guess that she was up to no good," Bill said with disbelief in his voice.

"We arranged to meet again for the next race meeting and had another enjoyable day which on that occasion extended into the following day. The rest is history," he said with a smirk on his face.

"How did she become involved in your devious activities?" asked Gerry.

"We agreed a price, and with that, I am going to say nothing more. The less you know the better it will be for all concerned."

"In other words, she became a paid informant."

"Vic smiled and shrugged his shoulders," turned and walked out of the office, heading for the factory.

DI Ken Abbott sat at his desk, turning his ball point pen first one way and then the other. He was in deep thought. The search at the premises of Eco-Tech Limited had revealed the fact that underhand practises had been carried out, and in his opinion, by Victor Eardley. From his observations of the other two partners, Gerry Ewing, and Bill Astley, they appeared to be, not only surprised, but shocked by the discovery of the drawing. The atmosphere in that company was, to say the least, fractious. He was sure that Vic Eardley was lying when he said that the drawing had been given to him by an ex-employee and by the look on the faces of the other two, that was also their opinion. It was certain that a woman was involved, and that woman worked for Salopian Industries. Whoever she was, she had to be in a position, to obtain information considered highly confidential, possibly her workplace being the Development Department. An alternative, being that she was not operating alone, someone else was passing the information to her, and she, delivering it to Vic Eardley by some means or other. The drawing must have been passed, either by hand or delivered by post, because it had been computer generated and there was no digital printer for large size drawings on the premises of Eco-Tech. The perpetrator of Sophie Langford's murder was probably a woman and likely to be the unknown woman seen at the premises of Eco-Tech. His musings were interrupted by one of the young officers putting a fresh mug of tea on his desk.

Having spoken to D Supt. Stuart, giving all the relevant details of the search, he phoned DCI Harry Davies in Telford. It was the Superintendent's opinion that the whole investigation should be carried out as a combined effort. The murder of Sophie Langford in Liverpool was, without doubt, connected to the murders of Danny Drew and possibly Don Phillips in Telford and since there was evidence of corporate espionage, that was perhaps the motive for all three deaths. It was the superintendent's opinion that he passed to DCI Davies.

DCI Davies, having listened intently to everything that Abbott had to say, said that he would immediately set in motion, an in-depth enquiry into all personnel that worked in the Development Department. There was a high probability that someone in that department was the mole, since being directly involved with the project, would know exactly the information that would be necessary for a competitor to have to make their own progress with the product development.

The DCI called for everyone's attention. He then briefed them on the development of the investigation in Liverpool and how that linked up with all that was known in Telford. Then after a brief pause, he went on to remind them that there was one matter, the death of Don Phillips, the cause of which was drowning, that carried a lot of uncertainty. That death may, or may not be, connected to the rest of the case and so he told them that he himself would look further into that along with DS Robb.

"As for the rest of you, I want an in-depth investigation of all Development staff. Where did they come from, how long have they worked for the company, to what depth are they involved in the project, and who are their friends, you all know the drill. Pay especial attention to the females in the department because we know that a woman is involved, either working alone or with an accomplice who could be a man or a woman."

The DCI called DS Robb over. "Take a seat Robb, and read the forensic report, on Don Phillips' death," handing over the paper.

Having read through it, Robb summarised. "Death was due to drowning. There was a head injury but sustained post-mortem, also a bite on the left thigh, attributed to a medium to large size dog, sustained shortly before death."

"When we visited the victim's brother-in-law, Steve Smith, there was a dog, a German Shepherd, outside in the back garden," remarked the DCI. "When Smith takes a walk along the riverbank, I would guess that he takes the dog with him. What if he was walking along the riverbank with his dog, came across Don Phillips fishing, then got into a argument with him, which resulted in a physical struggle, at which point the dog attacked, what it considered to be a threat to its master, biting Don Phillips, on the thigh and possibly jumping up at him. That could have caused Phillips to lose his balance and fall backwards into the river. He would no doubt have struggled in the water. Remember that he was wearing a heavy jacket and, also wellington boots which, even if he could swim, would have made that very, difficult. The river current would soon have taken him down stream and probably beyond any reach where Steve Smith could have helped. As we know, the body was seen and ultimately recovered from the side of the riverbank, a distance downstream from the place where he had been fishing. If that were the case, he should have raised the alarm but didn't. I wonder why that was."

"That all sounds very feasible, Sir. It would make sense of a number of things and, if that were to be the case, it would appear that the death of Don Phillips was not connected to that of Danny Drew and may not necessarily be construed as murder."

"Quite right, Robb. I think we should pay Mr Steve Smith another visit."

Steve Smith was just as belligerent when he opened the door to the DCI and DS Robb as he had been on their first visit.

"Now what?" was his immediate greeting.

"May we come in Mr Smith?" asked the DCI.

Smith made no verbal reply, but stood aside, nodding his head as an indication of invitation to enter. They once again went into the living room, where Smith gestured for them to sit down.

"Mr Smith, when you walked along the riverbank on the morning of Don Phillips' death, did you take your dog with you?"

"Of course, I did. I always take the dog with me," he replied.

"You saw Phillips fishing ---"

"I told you I never saw Don Phillips, just his fishing gear," Smith interrupted, before the DCI could finish what he was about to say.

Looking steadily at Steve Smith, he said with determination, "I don't believe you. However, I will tell you what I believe happened."

Smith was taken aback by the DCI's directness and felt uncomfortable under his steady gaze. DCI Harry Davies put to him his theory as he had put it to DS. Robb watching Smith's reaction as he was speaking. When he described what he believed the dog had done, he knew that he had hit on the truth. "Mr Smith are you going to deny what I have outlined, or are you going to be sensible, and admit that what I am saying is what happened?"

Steve Smith looking at DCI Davies with utter dejection, "yes, that is basically what happened. I didn't push him into the river or hit him. We started to argue and had a blazing row, as we always did whenever we met, because I hated the man and that I will not deny. I will never accept the verdict of the coroner about my sister's death. I am certain that he killed her, even if that was not his intention, and made it look as though she had tripped over the vacuum cleaner's power cord. I believe that he pushed her, and she fell striking her head on the hearth. He had hit her on several occasions during arguments. He was a bully. That morning, at the river, he stood up to me in a bullying manner and gave me a heavy push in my chest with his fist. That is when the dog leapt at him with a ferocious growl and bit his leg, but the weight of the dog put him off balance and he just fell backwards into the river. It all happened so quickly that there was nothing I could do to help. The current took him downstream and I can't swim so I was unable to do anything to save him."

"Why did you not raise the alarm and call for help, instead of walking away?"

"I didn't have a phone with me, so I couldn't raise the alarm. At that time, there was nobody else in the vicinity. I knew instinctively that he would not survive because he was wearing a heavy jacket, he had on wellies and I don't think he was a good swimmer. He had no chance. My thought was to get away from the scene so as not to be implicated."

"A cowardly attitude, I would suggest, Mr Smith.

He just shrugged his shoulders but made no reply.

"Stephen Smith, I am arresting you on the suspicion of the manslaughter of Don Phillips." The DCI then cautioned him and escorted him to the car,

18

The morning of Rowan Chapman's first day at Salopian Industries was taken mainly in his introduction to the personnel, not only with whom he would be in contact from the outset, but also on a frequent basis. This included the staff in the Supplies Department, in the general, as well as the engineering Stores, and now that the new product was nearing the time when construction of the production plant would begin, the personnel employed in the Development Department.

Everyone greeted Rowan warmly, welcoming him 'onboard' and assuring him that should he require assistance, help would be there at any time. He need only to 'ask'. Finally, Leslie took him to see Patrick Evans, purely as a gesture of courtesy, because he avoided seeing Evans as much as was practically possible. However, this was one of those occasions that could not be avoided.

Leslie knocked on Sharon Sumner's door and entered, introducing Rowan. "Good morning Sharon, may I introduce Rowan Chapman, my newly appointed deputy," and to Rowan, "Sharon Sumner, Mr Evans' PA." Leslie always referred to Sharon as, PA, knowing that Evans insisted in referring to her with that title.

"I am so pleased to meet you, Rowan," she said with a warmth, so welcoming. Shaking hands, she said, "Mr Evans told me that you were starting with us today. I do hope that you will be happy here. We are a friendly set of people, and should you need help of any kind my door is always open." Then with that captivating smile that she had, said "I'll show you in to see, Mr Evans." Opening the communicating door, she announced Rowan.

"Pleased to meet you Rowan," Patrick said, standing and walking around to the front of his desk, offering his hand. They shook hands, Patrick then inviting them both to sit. All this before Leslie had any chance to speak and make the presentation.

Leslie Anderson was not surprised by this manner displayed by Evans. It was, once again, his way of side-lining him, but to others, the intent would not be obvious.

"Frank Ebbs has told me all about you, and I am sure that Leslie here, is delighted to have you in his department. I know that he has been under significant pressure of late."

They conversed for a short while, then Patrick, standing, said, "I imagine you have a great deal to do this morning, Leslie, so I will let you get on with it," then finally to Rowan, "welcome to our world, and I do hope that you will be happy here."

"I am sure that I will be, and thank you Mr Evans," he replied.

Then with that smooth voice that he had, said, "please, in informal situations like this, call me Patrick. Formal occasions are, of course, a different matter."

Back in Leslie Anderson's office, they had coffee whilst Leslie outlined the various problems that had plagued him for some considerable time, and how, now that he had Rowan's input available, those problems would be resolved. One problem that had not yet manifested itself was of course the taking into the production scene of the new production plant now designated as the Supa-Board Plant. The word, "Supa" meaning, Special Utility Panel. The actual product having the title, Supa-Board 300 the number 300 being a reference to the ultimate temperature of 300 degrees Celsius that the product could withstand before combusting.

Having gone through most of the necessary matters, Leslie asked Rowan about his plans to find permanent accommodation.

"The day I came for interview, I spent some time looking for an estate agent. I found the office of Broughton's and had a good browse at the properties advertised in the window. There were a couple of the properties that interested me and so I have arranged to see the one that appealed to me the most, tomorrow afternoon. I hope that is all right with you."

"Of course, it is. I told you to take whatever time is necessary, to get things sorted."

Rowan took from his pocket, the leaflet giving the descriptive details of the property along with a photograph and showed it to Leslie.

"That is most attractive and in a nice part of the world. Buildwas, pleasantly rural. I hope you are successful."

The morning had passed with great rapidity and so Rowan realised that it was lunch time. He went to the canteen and selecting his meal at the service counter made his way to find a table. Looking around he saw two of the women he had been introduced to in the Supplies Department, earlier that morning and so he made his way to their table and asked if he could join them. Julie Phillips and her colleague Sue Thompson welcomed him warmly. Their conversation ranged over many topics, mostly connected to their place of work.

"I understand that you have come from up north. Manchester, was it?" asked Julie.

"Yes, quite right, although I am not from the north originally. I was born in Worcester and lived there until I went to Uni. in Liverpool. After I graduated, I went to work in Bristol for a while. It was while I was there that I met my wife to be, but after we were married, we moved up to Southport, and I had a job in Liverpool for a while, then I moved to Manchester."

"Has your wife come down with you or is she going to wait until you find somewhere down here?" asked Julie.

There was a slight hesitation before Rowan replied, which Julie noticed and wondered if she had asked the wrong question.

"I'm sorry Rowan, please forgive me. I should not ask personal questions."

"Not at all," Rowan replied without hesitation. "My delay in answering you, was not intentional. You see, I am a widower."

Both Julie and Sue, for a moment, looked at him in stunned silence.

"Oh, I am so sorry," said Julie, then referring to Sue, "We had no idea."

"It's not a problem. You couldn't possibly have known. The fact is that when we were up north, my wife was involved in a fatal motorway pile-up. I later moved to Manchester. Now that I am here in Telford, I intend to purchase a property because I have no plans to return to the north. As a matter of fact, I have seen a couple of properties advertised by Broughton's Estate Agents, that I rather like. The one that would be my first choice, I have arranged to view tomorrow afternoon." Rowan took out of his pocket, the leaflet he had shown to Leslie Anderson, offering it to the women to see.

"I know this cottage very well indeed," Julie exclaimed. "I once had an uncle and aunt who lived there. Oakwood, oh it's lovely. "They both passed away, long ago, but I remember having some wonderful times there, with my cousin, their only son. After they both died, the cottage was sold, and I believe that it had an extension to the rear added and the whole place was modernised."

"The description says that it's just off Buildwas Road."

"Yes, it's on a short farm track that leads to Johnny Price's farm. It is surrounded by trees and there is woodland to one side, with mainly oaks in it. That is probably why the cottage has the name "Oakwood."

"I don't want to sound too forward, but would you like to come with me?" Rowan said, addressing Julie. "You know exactly where it is, and it would be a chance for you to have a look at the place again and recall happy memories."

Julie paused before replying. "It would be lovely, but I will of course be working so I have to say no, but thank you for the offer."

"I could ask Leslie Anderson if you wish. Supplies comes under his jurisdiction. I think he may say yes."

"I am tempted to say yes, but he may not approve. I have had a lot of time off recently."

"Leave it with me. I will ask him. If he doesn't approve, he can only say no."

Leslie Anderson had no hesitation in agreeing that Julie could have the afternoon away from the office. As he expressed it, she would be assisting the new deputy works engineer, to find suitable accommodation. In other words, a form of work by the Supplies Department.

Later that day, Rowan told Julie that all was arranged and told her the words Leslie had used, and not to think of it as taking time off but rather to think of it as an extended duty of the Supplies Department. She could not help laughing at this statement.

"Mr Anderson is a lovely man, with a most generous nature. Rowan you have one of the best bosses that you could possibly have," she said. "I am really looking forward to seeing the place again. It's lovely country there and so much of interest. There is the Abbey on the far side of the river and its only about a couple of miles from Ironbridge."

"Perhaps we could have a look at the Abbey after viewing the cottage," suggested Rowan.

"I don't think there will be time for that," she replied, "I will need to get back for my bike to go home." She was really making an excuse because she didn't want him to think that she was in any way being too friendly. Although she liked this man, and he was without doubt courteous, gentlemanly in his attitude and mature, but she didn't know enough about him to fully trust him or indeed her own judgement. Julie was too aware of her unhappy marriage to Don, a person that she had misjudged, or she would not have married him. Then there was that fling she had with Danny Drew, a situation that could have only led to yet another disaster. The often, repeated words of her grandmother were now indelibly imprinted on her mind. 'Extra marital relationships rarely lead to happiness, only hurt for so many'.

"You could pick up your bike later, just ask at the gatehouse, but there is no need to do that. I will take you home and pick you up in the morning to go into work. How does that sound?"

"Yes, that's fine, if you don't mind doing that," she found herself saying and regretting it the moment she had said it.

"Wonderful," he replied. We can have lunch in the canteen and then leave in time for the appointment at two o'clock. After the viewing we can pay a visit to the Abbey and before going home, how about afternoon tea?"

"Yes, that sounds fine," she said, although she didn't feel comfortable with the arrangement. Why, oh why did I agree to all this she thought. Too late to have a change of mind. You are a fool, Julie, she told herself, but you will now have to make the best of it.

The following morning passed quickly and soon it was time to have lunch. He met Julie in the canteen and having selected their meal, found a table by one of the windows. Once again, the weather was fine and sunny, and perfect for a trip to the Abbey, Rowan thought. Since yesterday, he had thought of little other than the viewing of Oakwood and the visit to the Abbey. He hoped that Julie hadn't thought him to be too forward or pushy but he really felt relieved that someone else would be there to see the cottage and whom he could ask for an opinion, especially as she was familiar with the property on a personal basis.

For her part, Julie also had thought of little else since yesterday, and agreeing to accompany him for the viewing. That part was fine, but she kept telling herself that she should never have agreed to his suggestion of a visit to the Abbey. How weak she had been, unable to say, no. Laying, awake for some time during the night, she had hoped that it would be raining today. That would have prohibited the visit to the Abbey, because it was a ruin, open to the elements and although quite delightful on a beautiful sunny day, to visit in the rain was a 'no-go'. But, today had dawned sunny and warm. She really had no other option, than to go through with Rowan's plans.

Rowan drove from the factory in Ketley, along the A5, and then taking the road to Coalbrookdale and onto the Buildwas Road, arriving at Oakwood five minutes early. "That was nicely timed," Julie said, looking at her watch.

"Yes, it was indeed, but not too early," pointing to the car parked outside the property.

The lady from Broughton's was already inside, opening the door for them as they arrived.

The property was for sale as vacant possession, the owners having moved from the district. This was much better in Rowan's opinion, as he felt able to look more intimately into everything, including fitted cupboards. Also, with the rooms being empty, he could best imagine his own furniture in place. The extension to the rear of the cottage that Julie had mentioned was as he had hoped, giving a spacious lounge area and provided a ground floor shower room and toilet. The first floor provided an extra bedroom and an enlarged bathroom and toilet. The lady from the estate agent's left them alone to inspect the property but told Rowan to call her if there was anything that he wished to ask or discuss.

Julie was in her element as she went from room to room with Rowan, recalling events from the past that now gave her happy memories. The tour took about three quarters of an hour, and at the end of it, Rowan had made up his mind that this was the property that would suit his requirements and set in an area that appealed to him.

“Well, what do you think of it?” he asked Julie, being certain what her opinion would be, having so many happy memories of the place.

“Oh, Rowan, I love it. I always have, but I admit that it is even nicer now with the extension and having been modernised inside. More importantly, what is your opinion?”

“I like it very much and I have already made up my mind to make my offer for it.”

Saying goodbye and shaking hands with the lady from Broughton’s, he assured her that he intended to go into the office and make a formal offer.

Leaving Oakwood, Julie directed him to the Abbey, turning off the Buildwas Road, across the bridge over the river following the road to Much Wenlock and in a short distance, reached their destination. Entering the site, now under the hospices of English Heritage, they crossed the beautifully tended grass into the heart of the ruins.

“This was a Cistercian monastery founded in 1135, by Roger de Clinton, who was the Bishop of Coventry and Lichfield. It was dedicated to St. Mary and St. Chad, as is Lichfield Cathedral. It flourished well and was enlarged until it became a very, beautiful building,” Julie explained, enjoying the opportunity of airing her knowledge of a subject that had fascinated her for many years.

Rowan stood in what had once been the nave of the Abbey, looking towards the east end where the altar had been. All that now remained where the pillared walls, which even now, after eight hundred years, and around four hundred years of ruination following the dissolution of the monasteries, still exhibited the beauty and skill of the masons who were the craftsmen responsible for the building of the nation’s castles and cathedrals. As he stood in silence, his imagination took him back over the centuries, to the time when this was a beautiful building, and the stalls that would have been in the chancel, occupied by the monks.

“Julie, I can imagine, in the day, the monks saying the Service of Compline in this place that would have then been majestic.”

“What’s Compline?” Julie asked.

“Compline is one of the most ancient rituals, rarely, if ever, now celebrated. It was the last service of the day, before retiring to sleep. It had some very colourful and often figurative prose.”

"What do you mean, colourful and figurative?" Julie asked, now intrigued by his knowledge of a subject that she would never have thought him to be interested.

"At the opening, the cantor would say, 'Brethren be sober, be vigilant, remember that your adversary the Devil goeth about like a roaring lion, seeking who he may devour, whom, resist steadfast in the Faith.' Colourful, don't you think? Then, later, in supplication for protection, the figurative phrase, 'keep me, as an apple of thine eye, hide me under the shadow of thy wings.'."

"You are right, beautiful and certainly of an age so different to our own."

They wandered around the site enjoying the peace and tranquillity of the place on a lovely sunny day, Rowan happy that everything had been cordial and successful. He could hardly wait to go into Broughton's and make his offer for Oakwood.

Returning, Julie suggested going to Ironbridge and to the Dale End. There they would be able to have a pot of tea and perhaps a toasted tea cake.

"That sounds perfect," said Rowan and so that is exactly what they did.

Sitting in a very pleasant café, a pot of tea, large enough to provide two cups each and to Rowan, the nicest toasted tea cakes that he had ever had, he thought that the day had not only been successful, it had been very pleasant indeed.

"Thank you so much for coming with me and giving me your opinion," he said to Julie.

"Glad to be of assistance," she said with a laugh. "The Supplies Department is always ready to oblige."

"Thank you also, for taking me to the Abbey. I thoroughly enjoyed the visit and it was the icing on the cake."

As Rowan had suggested, he took her to her grandmother's house and told her that he would pick her up in the morning in time for work, promising her that he would not be late.

True to his word, Rowan arrived the following morning at eight o'clock, which was a little earlier than Julie had expected. Her Grandmother invited Rowan in, saying that Julie would not be long. "I take it that you are Rowan," shaking his hand. "Please come through and take a seat," Julie's grandmother said, showing him into the living room.

"Julie tells me that you are proposing to buy Oakwood."

"Yes, that is so. I was impressed when I saw it yesterday, and in a lovely area."

"It is indeed. We have many happy memories of the place. I hope that your offer is accepted. I am sure that you would be happy there."

"Thank you, Mrs Hampton, I shall keep my fingers crossed."

Julie appeared, somewhat flustered, and hastily finishing a piece of toast, declaring that she was now ready to leave.

***

In the interview room, Steve Smith sat glum faced as DCI Davies went through the questions once again, that he had previously put to him and again received the same answers.

"Mr. Smith, I put it to you that following the blazing row that you have admitted to having with Don Phillips and if, as you say, he fell backwards into the river when your dog attacked him, you deliberately left the scene without making any effort to raise the alarm. This you did knowing that he would drown".

Smith replied, "No, that's not true".

"You have already said that you left the scene so that you wouldn't be implicated".

Steve Smith remained silent, unable to refute this statement. Then, after a short pause, the DCI charged him with the manslaughter of Don Phillips.

***

At Liverpool, DI Ken Abbott, was reviewing the search carried out at the premises of Eco-Tech. His task was essentially to bring to justice, the person or persons unknown, of the murder of Sophie Langford but there was evidence of corporate espionage, that being the belief of his colleagues in Telford and his own opinion was now in agreement. The drawing found at the back of one of Vic Eardley's filing cabinets, supported the theory but was not absolute proof. However, there was a notebook with the drawing, some of the notes being of significant interest. There were references to stages of progress of the project, one such reference that was most interesting, read, "Twelve boards successfully made, according to info. received but the cure time was far too long to be practical. More up to date info needed. There were other jottings and one significant comment that periodically appeared, "the usual to VSS." The questions that DI Abbott was asking, as he addressed the team were, "who or what is VSS, and what is, the usual?"

"I would think that Eardley was referring to his mole at Salopian," ventured his DS.

"Yes, I am sure that you are right, Bagley. But are those initials, those of someone's name, or do they refer to a code name?"

"Could stand for Victor's Super Spy," came a flippant comment from the back of the room.

"That is not so daft as you might think, Roberts," was the DI's reply. "Whatever you may think of Vic Eardley, he is no fool. Foolish maybe, but make no mistake, he is, in my opinion, devious and someone who quite regularly, sails close to the wind, regarding the law. Observing the reactions of his two partners, when that drawing was discovered, I am sure that they were totally unaware of its existence. He is a character ready to do a deal with anyone if he thinks that he will profit by it, whether it is legitimate or otherwise. Bagley, check him out, see if he has got form. Then there are those periodic notes, 'the usual to VSS'. Do they refer to requests, or do they refer to, payments made regularly to VSS? You and I, Bagley, are going to visit that company again. This time we shall interview each partner separately, taking Vic Eardley first."

"Inspector, Mr Eardley will see you now. You know where his office is, so please go through," the receptionist said, giving them a welcoming smile. "Mr Ewing will see you when you have finished with Mr Eardley."

Vic Eardley stood as they entered the office. "Good morning Inspector," and nodding to DS Bagley, "sergeant. Please take a seat. How can I be of help to you?"

"Good morning Mr Eardley," the DI replied, shaking hands with him. "You will remember that when we searched your office and found the drawing that had originated from Salopian Industries, you claimed that a former employee had given it to you. Unfortunately, you were unable to remember who that employee was, or where he had gone to, but you could look through past records."

"Yes, I did say that, but I am sorry, I still cannot remember his name, so looking through records is not of much use, if I don't know who I am looking for" Eardley said, shrugging his shoulders. "It is so embarrassing, for me to admit that I can't remember, but names are a problem to me."

"The date on that drawing, I can tell you is within the last four months, so whoever the employee was, cannot have left your employment more than four months ago. So, Mr Eardley, I ask you, how many employees are there that have left your company within the last four months?"

"I don't honestly know."

"Then I suggest that you look at your wages file and check. I presume that it will be computerised. Will you please bring it up now, whilst we are here?" DI Abbott's tone had changed to that of a person of authority demanding compliance to his request. "There is one more thing that I would like an answer to, before you begin your search of the wages file."

Vic Eardley was by now feeling the pressure. He felt cornered, without an immediate way of escape. The agony was now about to be compounded by whatever the DI's question was going to be. He was now perspiring, not because the office was over warm, but from the effect of pure anxiety. With a super effort to display calm and give an impression of confidence, he asked, "what matter is that Inspector?"

"In your cabinet in which we found the drawing, there was also a notebook, obviously used to record instances in the progress of the project."

"Yes, indeed there was. Is there a problem with that?"

"No problem with the book Mr Eardley. In fact, it is very revealing in many ways."

Oh, God, thought Eardley, his mind racing over the many details he had written in that book.

"There are some references that I would like you to clarify. Periodically, you make a statement, 'the usual to VSS'. Firstly, who or what is VSS, and what do you mean by 'the usual'. Is that something given physically or is it an instruction?"

"Oh, that. Well, it's a bit of my shorthand. Nothing mysterious."

"Would you care to elaborate?"

"Elaborate, in what way?" Eardley asked, fighting for time, as he tried to think of an explanation that would give credence to the periodic appearance of the note.

"Firstly, what is VSS?" the DI asked, impatience now showing not only in his voice but in his facial expression.

"Variable Specific Support," he blurted out, wondering how that would be received.

"What exactly do you mean by Variable Specific?"

"There are, throughout any project, times when certain aspects need extra finance. In order to keep within budget, since these certain aspects vary month to month, I collated them on a three-monthly basis. In other words, if this month I had an overspend, next month I would reduce expenditure. A sort of robbing Peter to pay Paul. As I have said, I found it better to have this expenditure collated over a three-monthly period. The expression, 'the usual', just refers to the principle, robbing Peter to pay Paul had been utilised" Eardley, looked at the two police officers, and then added, "Have I explained that clearly enough?"

"For the moment. However, please look through your wages file for the name of your ex-employee who gave you that drawing. He may well have come by it from an illegal source, in which case you would be in receipt of illegally obtained material. Do you understand what I am saying to you?" I will give you a little time to do your search, whilst we now go to speak with your partners.

Gerry Ewing was waiting for them in his office. His mind was full of dread and he was unsure how far he should go to enlighten the Inspector without compromising himself and Bill Astley. He knew that to say that he was unaware of what had been going on with this new board project, was not a legitimate excuse that would be acceptable in law. He knew that as a director of a company, it was his bounden duty to know exactly what was going on in every aspect of the business. Whatever wrongdoing there had been, both himself and Bill Astley were equally responsible. The terrifying thought that he had, was that if Vic had committed a criminal act in the name of the company, then he himself and Bill were equally guilty.

Both DI Abbott and DS Bagley, shook hands with Gerry Ewing and wished him good morning on entering his office.

"I assume your visit is in connection with your investigation into the murder of that poor girl, Sophie Langford," began Gerry, in overture that he hoped would direct the ensuing conversation away from the subject of corporate espionage, a hope that was, as he undoubtedly knew, forlorn.

"Yes, it is, in part. But you must realise that during our search of these premises, the indications that vital information about a project of a competitor has been obtained, as your partner, Mr Eardley put it, without the knowledge or agreement of that competitor. That in my view, constitutes corporate espionage, a very, serious matter. However, we have reason to believe, that the murder of Sophie Langford was also directly connected to those activities, and so our enquiries are covering both aspects."

The statement of the DI was to Gerry, the herald of total disaster. The death of the girl was now linked to improper company conduct, which inevitably involved both himself and Bill Astley. He realised that they had been, not only foolish, but negligent in assuming that what Vic had been doing was legitimate.

"Mr Ewing, we believe that regular payments were being made to a person or persons unknown, for the purpose of obtaining sensitive technical information from Salopian Industries. Such technical information was to enable your company to progress a project to develop a special type of insulation board ahead of Salopian Industries, and obtain patent rights."

"I honestly, have no idea about any such dealings. I am shocked at the thought of it."

The DI sat in silence for a few moments, allowing his words to sink-in, then, "I am inclined to believe you Mr Ewing. I would, however, ask you to look carefully through your accounts, covering the last two years, to see if there is anything not readily explainable. If necessary, get your accountants to do the same. Should you find anything that you think to be suspicious, please contact me right away. Thank you for your cooperation, Mr Ewing. I will now speak with Mr Astley."

DI Ken Abbott, spoke in similar fashion with Bill Astley and got the impression that he also was telling the truth when he declared that he had no idea that there was anything going on of an illegal nature. Bill was asked in similar fashion, to check the company accounts and get in contact should he discover anything suspicious.

Retuning to Vic Eardley's office, he was sure that Eardley, would have looked at the wages file, but equally sure that he would say that he couldn't find what he was looking for, or have some other excuse not to be able to give a name for the supposed ex-employee.

"I don't know why this is, but I can't find the name of the person who gave me that drawing. I promise, I will keep looking and hopefully within the next day or two, I will have success, then I will call you immediately."

"Thank you, Mr Eardley, I look forward to receiving your call."

Returning to Headquarters, the DI expressed to DS Bagley, his satisfaction at putting the wind up them. "We need to keep them under pressure, especially our friend Eardley. He is no doubt one slippery customer."

Within five minutes of the departure of the police, Vic Eardley made a phone call to a mobile number that he knew by memory. His call was answered almost immediately. The person who answered was a woman. "Activity must stop as of now," he said without preamble, "The police have been here, in connection with the murder of Sophie Langford. They are convinced that her death is connected with our activities. They found that bloody drawing you sent, along with my private notebook. They are putting me under immense pressure to tell them how it came into my possession. I made up a story which they don't believe, although they haven't said as much. I will have to think of some other way to get them off my back. Maybe you should consider getting out of there."

"No way," was the reply. "That could raise suspicions. Just keep cool and be very, careful what you say. Least said, soonest mended."

Switching off his phone, Vic Eardley sat at his desk in quiet contemplation. He needed to speak with DI Abbott again and modify his story as best as possible, then just hope that they would believe him.

DI Abbott made a phone call to DI Bob Grant in Telford, to update him with the progress of the investigation into the murder.

"Ken Abbott here, Bob. I thought it was time to bring you up to date with things this end. There is no doubt that Vic Eardley is one devious bugger. Quite definitely there is a woman at your end giving him technical information, but I wouldn't rule out the possibility of there being someone else working with her. Highly likely a man. Eardley is fully aware that we know that a woman is involved, but he has referred several times to a man, he says was once one of their employees, although he cannot remember the name. He claims that it was this man who provided him with the drawing, taken illegally from Salopian's files. I suspect him of lying but there may be some element of truth in his story. I would suggest it may be worthwhile to check up on male employees, starting to work there, within the last twelve months."

"If there is a man involved, it would support our original suspicions, that a man was most probably involved with the death of Danny Drew. Many thanks, Ken for your update. I will set in motion an investigation as you suggest and let you know whatever we may discover."

Carefully scrutinising the entries made in Vic Eardley's private notebook, DI Abbott could see a pattern of steady progress during the early stages of the project but of late, there was obviously a problem with rate of production, to such an extent, that a note stated, "that the rate achieved could never be financially viable. There must be a better way, VSS must cover the problem, whatever the cost." The drawing found in Eardley's possession, gave details of the production plant, designed at Salopian Industries. This must be the information he wanted. The method being used by Salopian, to give a rate of production necessary for financial viability. As he pondered all this, the desk phone rang. DS Bagley answered, and after a brief conversation, he handed the phone to DI Abbott, saying that it was Vic Eardley for him.

"Good morning, DI Abbott speaking."

"Good morning, Inspector. I have a confession to make."

"What might that be, Mr Eardley?" the DI said, looking up at DS Bagley and winking.

"I have not been telling the exact truth about the way I came to have that drawing. You see it was not given to me as I said. I received a phone call from someone, telling me that he had a drawing showing the final production plant for the new insulation board that Salopian had designed.

If I wanted it, I had to send five hundred pounds, in twenty-pound notes, to an address that he would give. When he received the money, he would send the drawing by post. He said that he was an ex-employee."

"That was a risky thing to do. Sending cash to an unknown person with no guarantee that he would send the drawing to you. What address did he give?"

"It was a PO Box number."

"Can you remember what the number was. Did you make a note of it?"

"Unfortunately, I didn't. I didn't think at the time."

"That is most unfortunate, Mr Eardley. It doesn't give us much to go on, but what we do know, is that you received the drawing. Thank you for letting me know." He put down the receiver, then with a little laugh said, "That man is the biggest liar I have ever had the misfortune to meet. He is really rattled and scared and he feels cornered. I have no doubt that the drawing was sent by post, but not in the manner he describes. We will let him sweat for a little longer."

The investigation team at police divisional headquarters in Telford listened to DI Grant as he related to them the essential details from his conversation with DI Ken Abbott in Liverpool. Taking into consideration, DI Abbott's recommendation that an enquiry into the background of any male employee who had joined the company within the last twelve months, Grant thought that it would be a useful move.

"Toddy, make a start on that," he said addressing DC Jane Todd. "It shouldn't take too long because I don't think that there will be many names to investigate."

19

The weekend had for Vic Eardley, been one of worry and anxiety. His inner self told him that his latest conversation with DI Abbott had done nothing to help convince him, of the manner, in which he came to be in possession of the drawing from the Salopian company. Perhaps, it had only succeeded in heightening his suspicions. This was a dilemma that he could not have foreseen by any stretch of the imagination. His intention, this Sunday evening, was to go to his local, have a couple of pints with his friends, in an effort, to relax his mind from this nagging worry.

The pub was about half a mile from his home and so he always walked there, which was good in the sense that he wasn't going to drink and drive. Leaving the house, he turned right and then crossed the road, unaware of the car that was parked some fifty metres behind him. Walking along steadily, he turned into an alleyway which was a short cut to a large playing field, with a pathway along one side that led directly to his destination. At the time of his turning into the alleyway, the previously parked car passed, taking the next turning to the left. Emerging from the alleyway, Eardley made his way to the footpath and after a short distance, he recognised a figure walking towards him. With a degree of shock, he stopped and waited for the person to come up to him.

"What on earth brings you here on a Sunday evening."

There was no reply, but a swift movement of the right hand plunged a knife into Vic's stomach. There was only a quiet gurgling sound from him as the hand holding the knife, quickly slashed his throat. Eardley dropped to his knees and then fell forwards onto his face. Blood flowed copiously from the throat wound, a wound that had severed the carotid artery. Death came quickly to Vic Eardley, and without a single witness to give testimony, his shady dealings, and the life of one of the world's wheeler dealers came to an abrupt end.

The body was found, early the next morning, by a man walking his dog, or to be more precise it was found by the dog. The dog was sniffing and investigating all the smells of interest, in the way that dogs do, when it stopped at what first appeared to be a bundle of clothes at the base of the hedge. The dog's owner called it to come on but with no response from the dog, its interest in the bundle was far too compelling to carry on walking. The man then went to investigate, and to his horror saw that the bundle was in fact the body of a man. A very dead man.

Having raised the alarm, it was less than five minutes before not one, but three police patrol cars arrived plus two police officers on motorbikes. All were in the vicinity of the incident when they received the call to go to the scene of a possible suspicious death. The area was immediately secured, and the dog walker questioned.

The next to arrive was DI Ken Abbott accompanied by DS Bagley. The body of the deceased had been turned onto his back, and so immediately that the DI saw him, he recognised the corpse as that of Vic Eardley, which was quite a shock.

"The contents of his wallet, identify him as Victor William Eardley, Sir, and he lives locally," said the patrol constable who had been the first on the scene.

"Yes, thank you Constable. I know this man. I interviewed him quite recently."

The scientific support vehicle had arrived, and the forensic team, clad in their white overalls were already busy examining the scene. Vic Eardley was pronounced to have been dead for between ten and twelve hours.

"The alarm was raised at about seven o'clock this morning, so that puts the time of death between seven and nine o'clock last evening when it would have been daylight tending towards dusk," said DS Bagley. "How could that be, and not for him to be discovered?"

"I think, anybody walking past at that time of the evening would not necessarily take much notice of what appeared to be a bulk of clothes at the base of the hedge. He was not killed where he lay. He was killed on the footpath and then dragged over to where he was found. The forensic people have found the spot on the path, from the amount of blood present and there is an obvious track across the grass to the base of the hedge where the body was dragged."

"It was a vicious attack, Sir."

"It, most certainly was, Bagley. I would say that it was an action performed quickly and skilfully. Two swift actions with a very sharp knife. The first, being a stabbing into the abdomen, then a quick slash across the throat, that being absolutely, fatal. This killing is identical to the killing of Sophie Langford. She was stabbed in the stomach, and then her throat was slashed in exactly the same way"

"So, the assailant was a woman, Sir."

DI Abbott was silent for a few moments before replying. His mind racing over all the facts that had emerged in their enquiries.

"I am not sure that that hypothesis is one that we should accept. The woman that we suspected, was the woman seen by Sophie Langford at the premises of Eco-Tech. The one that she had recognised at the pub in Telford and knowing that she was an employee at Salopian Industries," was his reply.

"Sophie Langford's neighbour saw a woman enter Sophie's house, a woman he heard identify herself as a police officer. We know that she was not, and according to the neighbour, he saw nobody else go to the house. She must have been the one who killed the girl," was Bagley's opinion.

"The more I think about it the more uncertain I become. If the woman that went to Sophie Langford's was the same as the one she had seen at the premises of Eco-Tech, why did she not recognise her when she opened the door to her. She may have been disguised to a degree, but it would have needed to be a very, good disguise when seen at such close quarters."

"If she didn't kill Sophie, Sir, what purpose had she to go to the house."

"The one item that we know was missing, when we examined the premises, was Sophie's laptop and it has not been recovered. For what purpose was it taken, and where is it now?" mused the DI.

"Are you suggesting, Sir, that it was just a robbery committed by someone posing as a police officer, and that it has no connection with the person Sophie had seen at Eco-Tech?"

"Not at all, Bagley. What I am suggesting is that the woman, posing as a police officer, went to the house for the purpose of getting the laptop because she suspected that there may be something on it that could identify her by name. Emails, for instance, sent to her boyfriend who you will remember was Danny Drew's pal. To do that she would have gone to great effort with her disguise. I would suspect the use of a wig, which can change the appearance of someone dramatically and the possible use of glasses, with plain lenses."

"If she was not the killer, then who do you think it might have been, Sir?"

"The people in Telford, originally thought that there had been a man involved in the murder of Danny Drew, in fact Don Phillips was their prime suspect, but he was also killed, which spoiled the theory, so the unknown woman was the only one being sought. She has still to be identified. The reason that the involvement of a man was suspected, was the way that the body of Danny Drew had been rolled over and pulled over the edge of the platform, which had needed a degree of strength. Now, we have here, the body of Vic Eardley, who has been dragged from the footpath for about fifteen metres, across grass and pushed into the base of the hedge. That would take quite a deal of strength, especially when I would suspect it would have been done as fast as possible, in case someone came along the path and saw what was going on."

"Are you suggesting, Sir, that whoever did this killing, was involved in the murder in Telford?" DS Bagley asked with some incredulity.

"No, I am not suggesting that for a moment. What I am saying, is that in my opinion, the theory of a man being involved in the Telford crime was probably correct whether, or not it was Don Phillips, is another matter altogether. In this case I believe that the assailant was a man. The method of attack is identical to the attack on Sophie Phillips, which makes me think that in her case she was killed by a man, and the thought of it being a woman is a red herring. If that is the case, it is my belief, the same man. We need to interview the neighbour of Sophie Langford again. We need to push him into deeper thought of his movements that morning. Was he continually at the front of the house all morning or, as I suspect, he may have left it if only for a short time, whereby a man could have gone into the house, after the woman had left, killed Sophie, then left the scene, unobserved."

A little later, the body of Vic Eardley was removed and taken to the mortuary. There, a post-mortem examination would be performed, and a full forensic report sent to the DI, probably by late afternoon. Once back at Headquarters, DI Abbott went to see the Super, to give him not only details of the morning's events, but to put to him the thoughts and reasonings he had discussed with DS Bagley.

DCS Stuart listened to DI Abbott, without interrupting him, and only when he had finished, did he speak. "What you are saying, Abbott, does have the essence of probability. I agree with your opinion, that both victims were killed by the same person. I think that the modus operandi, in both cases being identical, it would be stretching the possibility of coincidence too far to think of there being two separate assailants. However, there is no evidence that a man entered the home of Sophie Langford. On the contrary, the neighbour made the statement to that effect, saying he had seen only a woman there on that morning. Speak with that neighbour again. See if there is any way that he could have missed seeing a man, that morning."

As they arrived at the house of Sophie Langford's neighbour, DI Abbott and DS Bagley saw the neighbour weeding the border to the path. Hearing the closing of the car doors, he looked up, and recognising the two police officers, he put down his trowel and greeted them in friendly fashion. "Good morning, Sir," replied Abbott. "Getting some gardening done before it rains, I see. Are you taking some holiday?"

"Yes, I am, and no I'm not," replied the neighbour, commenting on the statement and answering the question in one sentence. "I have a milk round, so I begin work very, early, which means that I am usually finished by nine o'clock. It gives me the opportunity to do all the household tasks early in the day. After lunch, I am able to do whatever I wish."

"A splendid arrangement," the DI said, and DS Bagley nodding in ascent.

"How can I help. I suppose you've come to ask more questions?"

"Mr McKay, I have remembered your name correctly, I hope?"

"Yes, you have," he replied. "Your memory for names is much better than mine, because I have forgotten yours," he added with a laugh.

"I'm sorry, Mr McKay, I should have announced myself properly and shown you my warrant card," doing so as he gave his name and that of DS Bagley. "We have come to see you to ask you to think back to that tragic morning when poor Sophie was killed. You said at the time, that only a woman, purporting to be a police officer had entered the house that morning, and that you were here all morning but saw no one else."

"Yes, that is correct," McKay said, without hesitation.

"Mr McKay, I want you to think very carefully, because I cannot emphasise too much, the importance of your reply. Are you absolutely sure, without any possible doubt, that you didn't leave the front of your property at any time during that morning?"

"I have already told you that I was here all morning. I wanted to finish painting the door before lunch time."

"I understand what you are saying Mr McKay, and I am not trying to get you to say otherwise, but I want to be sure that you didn't move away from the front of your house at any time, even for the briefest of periods. Please take you time but, think carefully."

After a few moments, shaking his head, he began to repeat his previous statement, and then he paused, and said, "I've, just remembered that I heard the phone in the hall, ringing, so I went in to answer it, but the front door was still open because I was painting it."

"How long were you speaking on the phone?" asked the DI, with a degree of excited expectancy.

"It was my mother-in-law, and despite the usual quips, about mother's-in-law, we get along very well. We spoke for less than five minutes. But I remember that when we finished speaking, I decided to make a cup of tea."

"Mr McKay, thank you for that information. It is of immense value to us. I would now, like you to do something else. Will you please go in, and make a cup of tea, as you did that morning?"

"With pleasure Inspector, we can all have a cup. Please come in," he said, as he opened the front door. "Come through."

The purpose for the DI asking McKay to make tea was not because he wanted tea himself, but to time the tea making procedure. "That morning, did you drink your tea here in the kitchen or did you take it outside?"

"I drank it here, in the kitchen because I couldn't paint and drink at the same time. I would probably have got paint on the cup, in which case, I would have been in trouble with the wife."

"Where is your wife, Mr McKay. We haven't yet met her?"

"She has a part-time job at the local garage. She works mornings."

They continued chatting as McKay made the tea and afterwards as they drank it. The DI's impression of this man improved as they talked. He was obviously intelligent and quite observant. His only failure, when making his original statement, was that of not remembering to tell them about the phone call and most importantly, the making of the tea and the time taken in drinking it. DI Abbott had timed the tea making, from reaching for cups in the kitchen cupboard to the pouring of the tea. It had taken eight minutes. They then took a further ten minutes to drink it, a total of eighteen minutes. Adding the time of about four minutes for the phone call, McKay had said less than five minutes, it was obvious that he had been away from the front of the house for around twenty-two minutes. That was more than enough time for a man to have entered Sophie's house, killed her and left the scene before Mr McKay had returned to continue painting.

"Thank you for the tea, Mr McKay. Just one more question before we leave. Was the phone call from your mother-in-law before or after you saw the woman enter Sophie's house.

"Oh, definitely after. It would be about eleven o'clock, that is why I thought to make the tea after the call."

"Thank you, once again, Mr McKay, you have been very helpful."

Making their way back to Headquarters, DI Abbott reviewed all the facts that had come to light, during their visit to Mr McKay. "Do you know Bagley, the more questions we find the answers to, the more questions arise. We now know that there was a period of at least twenty minutes during which someone could have entered Sophie's house, killed her, and left without being seen. If that was a man, working along with the unknown woman, why did he go there after the visit of the woman. Was her purpose, to take the laptop, in which case why bother doing that, if he was intending to go there to kill her. He could have taken the laptop himself. It would seem to me, that the two visits were uncoordinated. That being so, why was there such a lack of coordination between them. If a man is involved, is he from this region, or is he from Telford.

There was a long telephone conversation between DI Ken Abbott and DI Bob Grant. Abbott explained the details of the murder of Vic Eardley in minute detail, emphasising the similarity to the murder of Sophie Langford. Also, his feeling that the way in which Eardley's body had been dragged a considerable distance, after the knife attack, demanded a good deal of strength in a similar way that the body of Danny Drew was manoeuvred over the edge of the platform also required strength. That a man was involved with the unknown woman was a possibility, that could not be ruled out.

DI Abbott suggested that to question the male employees both in Liverpool and Telford, as to their whereabouts on Sunday evening between six o'clock and ten o'clock might be a useful first move. DI Grant agreed with the suggestion, and when all information was obtained, he said that they should hold another phone conference and then make a decision about what their next move should be. With all of this agreed, the necessary procedures were put into motion.

***

Rowan was already seated in the canteen and had started his lunch, when Julie, having selected her meal and looking around for a table, saw him sitting and eating alone. She went over to him and smiling said, "May I join you?"

"Of course, please do," a true welcome showing in his facial expression. He enjoyed her company, a feeling he had realised when they had gone to view Oakwood and their visit to the Abbey afterwards. His mind had gone through many re-runs of that day, and privately he wished that they could have more days like that one.

"Have you had any word from the estate agents, about your offer?"

"Yes, I have. There was a letter waiting for me at the hotel reception this morning. The vendors have accepted my offer and the contract is now at the solicitors, awaiting my signature."

"How wonderful, I am so pleased for you," Julie exclaimed, "You must be very excited."

"Yes, I am, but of course now the work starts. The whole place will need to be cleaned, and then I will need to arrange for the removal people to get my furniture out of storage. Then it is a matter of arranging the date and time for them to do the actual delivery. A lot to sort out."

"Well, if you need a scrubber, I am willing to help," she said with a laugh.

"Julie, you are no scrubber, believe me, but I would welcome your help with open arms," he said this with genuine gratitude, but also with a warm sense of pleasure, with the thought of having her company during a time of what may be considered a personal occasion in life. The time of setting up a new home.

"When will you sign the contract?"

"Tomorrow, all being well."

When Rowan returned to his office, after lunch, Leslie Anderson phoned, asking to see him.

"Frank Ebbs has a problem, and he has asked me if I can possibly help. At the company in Cardiff, that we took over, Williams Brothers, they are having some mechanical problems with one of the laminating machines. Their maintenance man has been unable to find the problem, which is intermittent, and so they have asked Frank Ebbs for help. Unfortunately, Frank is short of someone suitable to send, because of the push to get construction started on the Supa-Board Plant, as soon as possible. He has asked if I could possibly manage without you for a couple of days and to send you down there and try to sort it all out. How would you feel about that?"

"If you are happy for me to go, then it is all right with me," Rowan replied. "However, I thought that it was now company policy, that we were only to do engineering in this works, company engineering doing everything else."

"That is the ruling, but Frank Ebbs, being the company chief engineer, has the authority to request whatever assistance he needs."

"Would the day after tomorrow be all right, because I am due to sign the contract for the house tomorrow, and I don't want to delay in case the vendors might think that I am wavering."

"I will tell Frank that you are unable to go tomorrow. The day after is the earliest possible time. When are you hoping to move into your new home?"

"When I have cleaned through and had my furniture brought here. Julie Phillips has kindly offered to help me clean the place, an offer I couldn't refuse. As you know, she came with me to view the place, because she knew it, having had an aunt and uncle once live there. I think that it was a chance to indulge in a little nostalgia."

"That's a very, kind offer. I feel sorry for Julie, because I believe that her marriage to Don was not a happy one, and then perhaps, unwisely, she became involved with Danny Drew both of whom have been killed in tragically suspicious circumstances. Both of her parents are dead and now she has only her grandmother, an educated, and intelligent lady. I have met her on a couple of occasions, and I have been impressed as has my wife. When you get back from Cardiff, should you feel that is necessary to have a little time away from work to get things sorted out at your new house, cleaning and of course getting your furniture installed, let me know. We could arrange that for Julie too, if you wish," he said with a knowing smile.

Visiting Cardiff was a new experience for Rowan. It was a part of the world that was totally unfamiliar to him. However, with the aid of his Sat-Nav, he found the Three Feathers Hotel with relative ease. He had driven down during the afternoon, so now at six o'clock, he was able to have a little time to relax, then a quick shower, before going to the restaurant for dinner, at seven thirty, which he had booked at reception when he arrived. Staying in hotels alone, had never held much appeal to Rowan. Hotels were usually busy places, people going here and there, activity all around but, alone, one always felt isolated, an observer watching life and the world go by but without any involvement.

Entering the restaurant, he booked in and was then shown to his table, a small one, suitable for two people, set in a corner of the room. This table was suitable for someone like himself, dining alone, but it would have been ideal, he thought, for two people hoping to dine with a degree of privacy. The waitress took his order for a glass of Shiraz, which was listed as a house wine, whilst he studied the menu. The waitress returned with a large glass of his choice, and took his order for cream of asparagus soup, to be followed by the main course of rib eye steak, chips and assorted vegetables. Rowan didn't go for exotic dishes, he much preferred, what he usually described as ordinary food.

Whilst, waiting for the first course and tasting the wine, he saw, to his surprise, none other than Patrick Evans being shown to a table, similar, to that of his own, but in the far corner of the room. A couple of minutes later he was joined by a lady, who was dressed with eloquence and appeared to be well-known by the staff by the manner that he could see they reacted with her, although from the distance he was from them, he could hear nothing that was said. He had not thought of it before now, but he realised that being CEO, Patrick Evans probably came to the factory here in Cardiff quite frequently. He wondered who the woman could be. Perhaps someone from the factory, who was giving up her evening to accompany the CEO for a meal.

If only, he himself, had some company, he would enjoy the meal more. Such were the thoughts and musings of a lonely man. However, he enjoyed his meal and having finished his glass of wine, retired to the bar for a night cap or two.

At the factory, the following morning, he soon became friendly and at ease with the production leader, Glyn Watkinson. Glyn outlined the problem that was causing large scrappage of product. Rowan was, of the opinion, that the basic trouble was one of inconsistent tracking of the laminate film being applied to the product. Tracking of laminate was controlled automatically by sensors and he believed that one of the sensors had an intermittent fault. He suggested to the maintenance fitter, that a change of Sensors be the first thing required, and left him to get on with the job. With the fitter now embarked on changing the sensors, Glyn showed Rowan around their production area.

"I was surprised to see Patrick Evans in the hotel last night," Rowan remarked as they were walking around.

"He visits quite regularly to keep hands-on, as he puts it. Having dinner with a lady, was he?"

"Yes, he was. From what I could see, she seemed to be well-known by the staff."

"Oh, yes, she is. You see she is the deputy manager at the Three Feathers," Glyn replied. "Whenever he is down here, they have dinner together. Her name is Bronwen Jenkins and she is the daughter of John Williams one of the old partners of this place before you took us over. She is now divorced from her husband, who I understand wasn't a very, nice person.

I have heard it said that her father didn't like him and didn't want her to marry him in the first place, but of course that is all hearsay. However, Bronwen is a very, likeable person, kind and down to earth in her attitude."

"That is a position that carries a lot of responsibility, being deputy manager," Rowan remarked.

"Oh, yes, it is indeed. It also involves working, what I call, unsocial hours, but she doesn't seem to mind that. Of course, living alone, I don't suppose it matters much."

"How long has she been divorced?"

"Several years now," then suddenly he said, "Patrick Evans is knocking her off, you know. It's common knowledge at the hotel. My sister works there, and whenever he comes to stay, Bronwen makes sure that she is off duty at six o'clock, so that they can have the evening together, usually having dinner in the restaurant. But when he arrives, which is usually about four o'clock, Bronwen disappears and you will see the 'Do Not Disturb' notice on the door of his room. It is invariably the same room on the first floor."

Rowan made no reply to that, but could not help remembering a comment he had heard back in Telford, concerning Patrick Evans and Sharon Sumner, intimating that they were having a fling and the opinion, that should the chairman of the company become aware of the matter, Patrick Evans would not remain in the position of CEO.

"Before Bronwen was married, she and Gwyn Thomas, the chemist who went up to Telford, were an item for about two years. Then suddenly, they broke up. We were all surprised at the time. It was not long after that, that she met that Jenkins fellow. It was a whirlwind affair, and then they married. I think she was on the rebound from Gwyn Thomas. How is Gwyn, by the way?"

"He seems to be quite well, although I don't see him very much," Rowan replied, but his mind now digesting all this information that Glyn Watkinson had so readily given.

"I think that John, Bronwen's father, has a high opinion of Patrick Evans. Whether or not, he suspects just how intimate they are, I have no idea, but I think that he regrets that Evans is a married man, and so there is no possibility that he and his daughter can get together."

The rest of the morning passed affably, the new sensors had been fitted and adjusted as Rowan had suggested and the laminating machine started. Everything worked well, and with a feeling of satisfaction, he thanked Glyn Watkinson for his assistance and said that he would leave and start his return journey. "Perhaps I will have the opportunity to come again in the not too distant, future."

"I hope so," was Glyn's reply. "I have enjoyed your company, not to mention your technical expertise."

***

DI Bob Grant had brought DCI Davies up to date with his discussion with DI Abbott from Liverpool and their agreement to question male employees with regard to their whereabouts on the night of Vic Eardley's murder, between seven o'clock and nine.

"Have you any particular suspects?" asked the DCI.

"There are, in my opinion, three possible suspects. First there is Arthur Brown. He was rather disgruntled when the new company engineering department was formed. He dislikes Patrick Evans because in his own opinion, both he himself, and Leslie Anderson were not moved sideways into different work positions but were, demoted, although neither of them lost out in salary. However, he considers that they lost status. Perhaps, in Leslie Anderson's case that is true, but as far as Arthur Brown is concerned, his position seems to entail some different responsibilities that don't constitute demotion. His antagonism could perhaps be a catalyst to lead him to join up with someone, whose purpose was to give away sensitive technical information to a competitor. However, the male counterpart of such a duo, assuming that there is a male counterpart, would be someone who would be vicious and without remorse. I don't think that Arthur Brown has either of those tendencies in his character. I will, however, check his whereabouts last Sunday evening."

"The second possibility is John Preston. A man who came to the company from Liverpool, as did Danny Drew. Preston is a family man, with a wife and two children. He claims to be happy here in Telford, and that his wife and children like himself, love the countryside. He appears to be genuine in his expression of satisfaction with his situation. The progress of the new type of insulation board project, is essentially in his hands, albeit that he is responsible to Arthur Brown. He has worked well on behalf of the company, does not seem to have any grumbles, is a family man and appears to be happy with his position. We don't know for certain, if he knew Danny Drew before coming to Telford, although he claims not to have done. As with Arthur Brown, I don't think that John Preston could be as vicious as the perpetrator of both the murders of Sophie Langford and Vic Eardley. Both those crimes were committed with purpose, speed and deadly results. Although, as with Arthur Brown, I will check his whereabouts last Sunday evening."

"The third possibility is that of Gwyn Thomas, the chemist in the Development Department. The man who has been the key figure in the formulation of the product, without whom the project would never have got off the ground. He did say that he was not enthusiastic to come to Telford, at the time of Williams Brothers being taken over by Salopian. He had hoped that one of the two companies from up north would have been successful in the take-over because he would have preferred to have moved to either Liverpool or Manchester, both being progressive cities. His absolute preference was that of remaining in Cardiff, but he would have needed to find a new job, since once the new board project was moved up to Telford, his presence was no longer required at Williams Brothers. He did suggest that finding a new job in Cardiff, equivalent to the job he had would be difficult. I think that there might have been other reasons, but be that as it may, he finally decided to move to Telford. He lives alone in an apartment, close to the factory, gets along well with his work colleagues and in all respects seems to be happy. I am given to understand that his mother, a widow, has now moved into a home. She has dementia, which is steadily becoming worse, and so the family home has been sold. Gwyn is an only child, so the proceeds of the house sale have been transferred to him. However, the cost of her stay in the home will be paid for from those proceeds. Once again, I don't think that the actions of the assassin could be carried out by Gwyn Thomas."

"Who else is there, that might have a grudge against Salopian Industries, or who may be tempted to betray the company's trust for monetary gain?" asked DCI Davies.

"The only person, in my opinion, who could have a serious grudge is Leslie Anderson. However, he is Organist at St. Chads Church, as you know, and on Sunday evening he was playing the organ, for the evening service from six o'clock until about seven forty-five. The first half hour being the organ voluntary period, so there is no possibility he could have left the Church and arrived in Liverpool before ten o'clock. Forensics put death having occurred sometime between seven o'clock and nine o'clock, so that rules him out."

"Perhaps this possible male accomplice is in Liverpool, which is more likely to be the case since the homicides of both Sophie Langford and Vic Eardley were in Liverpool," said DCI Davies.

"But what about the death of Danny Drew. We have established the fact that on the morning of his death, there were no visitors in the factory, so if there is a male accomplice, he must have been an employee of Salopian at that time."

"Perhaps, there are two accomplices, one in Telford and one in Liverpool," mused the DCI. "We had initially, Don Phillips as prime suspect and were astounded when he was killed. What if, he was the male presence that was suspected, the muscle power that pulled, then pushed the victim off the edge of the platform. His demise was not connected to the incident in the factory, as we now know, but it doesn't eliminate him from the perpetration of that crime."

"Yes, Sir, that is quite right," Grant agreed. "I will speak with DI Abbott and discuss this with him. Who knows, he may have highlighted someone up there, as a suspect."

The identification, of a suspect, was proving as difficult to DI Abbott, in Liverpool, as it was to DI Grant in Telford. He could find no one that didn't have an alibi. Both partners, at Eco-Tech were as helpful as they could possibly be, but could think of no one, other than the employees that the police had interviewed, that could possibly be implicated. As for the partners themselves, Gerry Ewing had been at home all that day, which was corroborated by his family, and although Bill Astley lived alone since his divorce, he had spent time on that Sunday evening at his local, as was his usual practise at the weekend. This was confirmed by the landlord. However, he did say that Bill Astley was there from about seven o'clock until eleven o'clock but could not "swear under oath," and had laughed when he had said it, that Bill Astley didn't leave the pub at some time during that period. It had been a busy evening with lots of people coming and going and he and his wife had been rushed off their feet behind the bar.

With some exasperation, DI Grant said, "Oh, Ken, it would appear, that you have had as much luck in identifying a possible suspect as I have myself. Maybe we need to look a little deeper into the backgrounds of these people. Who knows what may turn up?"

"Whatever the background these people may have, they all have an alibi for the time in question. Perhaps there are other male employees with a much lower profile than those we have so far considered," then DI Abbott said, "to use a phrase like the one by Fagin in *Oliver*, I think we had better think it out again." They both laughed.

Once again, in the canteen at lunchtime, Rowan was sitting at a table with Julie and her colleague, Sue Thompson, from the Supplies Department. Meeting up, and sitting together, had become the usual thing at lunchtime.

"Have you fixed a date to have your furniture delivered," Julie asked Rowan.

"Yes, the week after next, on the Friday. That will give me the weekend to get everything sorted out."

"Rowan, please don't think that I am poking my nose in, but have you given any thought to curtains. I strongly suspect that those from your old home are not going to be suitable for the windows in Oakwood, even if you have saved them."

"No, I haven't," he replied, rather taken back by the question. This was something that had not entered his mind. Trust a woman to think of something like curtains, he thought. "I suppose that I had better measure all the windows, to see what may be required."

"I think that you should, and quickly," she said with a laugh. "I know of a shop that have a good range of 'ready-mades' of excellent quality, and at reasonable prices, if you are interested."

"Oh, yes, I am interested. Would you come with me," he asked, hopeful that she would say yes.

"Of course, I will if you want me to," she replied with pleasure that he had asked.

"Would you be available on Saturday morning?"

"Yes, absolutely no problem. I have nothing special to do, so we could go whatever time is suitable for you."

"Splendid, then I shall pick you up at ten o'clock. Meanwhile I shall measure the windows and if you are available, you could hold one end of the tape measure for me," he said with a broad grin.

They went the following evening, the contract having been signed, he now had the keys. The lovely cottage called Oakwood, was now his. Julie had said that they could first give the place a clean as she had originally promised, and then measure the windows. While doing the cleaning, Julie asked how his trip to Cardiff had been.

"Oh, very well. In fact, much better than I was expecting" he replied. Then he went on to tell her of seeing Patrick Evans having dinner with a lady who he learned from Glyn Watkinson was Bronwen Jenkins. When he repeated Glyn's words that he was 'knocking her off', Julie just starred at Rowan for what seemed to be an age without speaking.

The revelation that Rowan had just made took Julie by surprise. She was not only surprised, she was stunned. She thought back to the time when Sharon Sumner, had confessed to her that she was having an affair with Patrick Evans. What would Sharon do, she wondered, if she became aware of Patrick Evans dalliance with Bronwen Jenkins. Perhaps, she might cause him considerable embarrassment by leaking the information about Bronwen, so that it became known to the chairman, and to Patrick's wife. Maybe, she would just leave the company, and say nothing to anybody, she mused.

"You have suddenly gone very quiet. Has what I have just told you been a shock?"

"Yes, it certainly has," Julie replied, deciding to say nothing to Rowan, about Sharon's affair with Patrick Evans. Least said, soonest mended, she thought.

"It was a shock to me too. Although, the hotel people could be putting two and two together and making five. After a drive to Cardiff from Telford, he perhaps wants a short while without being disturbed, so puts the notice on the door for that reason."

"Perhaps, that's so, but I am more inclined to think that the staff have seen many more indications, other than a notice on a door, to have the opinions that they hold."

***

The day finally came to receive his furniture. Rowan, once again, with Julie for company, had a pot of tea whilst waiting for the delivery van. Leslie Anderson had once again, kindly given his permission for Julie to help Rowan in getting everything sorted at the cottage. Just a little before midday, the vehicle arrived, and so as the removal men brought into the cottage, piece after piece of furniture, Rowan and Julie arranged them in the rightful places. It was a little after three o'clock before they could sit and rest, with everything in place.

"A good job well done," Rowan said with a sigh of relief. "Thank you so much, Julie. You are a star. My special star, because, there is no doubt that I would have struggled without your help."

"Rowan, I am only too pleased to have been able to help, and I have indulged in a little nostalgia being here at Oakwood," was her reply, with a slight colouring of her cheeks, which didn't go unnoticed by him.

Rowan was setting out the drinks and glasses on a worktop in the kitchen, whilst Julie and her grandmother were putting the final touches to the buffet that they had spent the past hour in preparation. Julie had proffered help, once again, this time to prepare the buffet for his, house-warming, which he had gratefully accepted. Rowan had picked up Julie and her grandmother, earlier. Since she had been invited, Julie's grandmother had insisted in lending a hand with the buffet, along with her Granddaughter.

The event was not intended to be a grand affair, but just an evening to enjoy a buffet and a few drinks, with a few of the people who had offered him such kindly friendship and help, since coming to Telford. Those people included Leslie Anderson and his wife Jenny, the girls out of the Supplies Department, Sharon Sumner, and from the Development Department, Gwyn Thomas, Lucy Thompson, Pam Briscoe, John Preston and his wife.

The evening was a relaxed time, when everyone present, mingled freely and all in the party mood, the evening was a huge success. It was a wonderful relief from the concerns and tensions that had pervaded every department of the factory since the tragedies of the deaths of both Danny Drew and Don Phillips. No one mentioned or referred in any way to either incident, not only because they intended to stay in a party mood, but because of the presence of Julie, who, everyone knew, would have been very sensitive to any reference to either incident.

Talking with Julie's grandmother, Eleri Hampton, Leslie Anderson and his wife, Jenny congratulated her and Julie on preparing such a lovely buffet.

"Julie wanted to do it, so I helped her, since I was here as a guest."

"Julie has helped Rowan considerably, in getting him settled in his new home," remarked Leslie. "She says that she has enjoyed the nostalgia of being in this cottage, remembering the happy days when her aunt and uncle lived here, although I think she has enjoyed Rowan's company also."

"I think that you are correct, Leslie, in both cases. Rowan is a very, nice young man, highly intelligent, and appears to have a sincere and honest character. I would be very, happy indeed to see them become closer. But of course, I would never make any inference as such. Their futures are in their own hands and should not be influenced in any way by me."

"You are absolutely right, Eleri," Leslie said.

"But being a romantic, I do hope that they get together," added Jenny, smiling at the thought. "Although you are quite right not to interfere in any way."

Rowan moved over to them, followed by Julie, at which the conversation was switched immediately to the pleasantries of the evening. “I hope that you are helping yourself to all this food. If there is much remaining at the end of the evening, I shall be upset because it means that I will be eating it for who knows how long.”

The evening passed all too quickly, and at eleven o’clock, Leslie and Jenny gave Rowan their thanks for a lovely evening and made their departure. After which, one by one, after giving their sincere thanks to Rowan for the kind invitation, and wishing him well in his new home, said good night and left. Sharon Sumner was one of the last to indicate her departure.

“I have just thought that I could take Julie and her grandmother home, since I will be going in that direction, that is if you wish.”

“That would be most kind,” replied Julie, then to Rowan. “That is if you don’t mind.”

“That’s fine with me. Thank you, Sharon, you are very, kind.”

When all had departed, he helped himself to another single malt as a night cap. The tidying up he would leave until morning. Settling down in his favourite armchair, he reflected on the evening, the absolute success that it had been, which had been largely due to the help of Julie, and of course her grandmother with her help with the buffet. But it had all started with the arrival of his furniture, the help given by Julie in getting things sorted and into place, not to mention the selecting of the new curtains and actually putting them up after getting the furniture in place. Rowan realised how much she had done for him over the last couple of weeks. As he sipped his whisky, his greatest wish was that she was here with him at this moment.

20

The aroma of freshly percolated coffee pervaded in the board room of Salopian Industries Limited. Yvonne, the secretary of Sir Ian Leighton-Boyce, had, as she always did, before a meeting of the board of directors made a fresh jug of coffee. The meeting was arranged to begin at ten o'clock. She had also put in place around the table the agenda, and a notepad together with a ballpoint pen. So many times in the past, the number of directors who had forgotten to bring a pen or those who had a pen that had decided not to function, had prompted her to avoid the fussing about, by ensuring that everything was there, that was needed.

The meeting, arranged for this morning, was not that scheduled on a monthly basis, but had been called by Sir Ian, to discuss the recent disturbing events, and the possible consequences that may ensue. Sir Ian was, although only fifty-four years of age, a person who could be considered as 'old school'. Not only in his devotion to the company of today, but resolute in preserving, what he always referred to as the company's proud history.

That history went back in time to the middle of the nineteenth century, when a gentleman by the name of Enoch Ewart, at that time recently married, set up his own business in Shrewsbury. He had served an apprenticeship and now considered himself fully qualified to fix a sign on the front of the small premises he now rented, stating that he was a 'Blacksmith and Farrier.' He was good at his trade and soon had a thriving and growing business, matched only by his thriving and growing family. His wife bore him five children, all of whom were girls, and he adored them all. His only regret was that he didn't have a son to whom he could pass on his skills and one day, the business. However, his eldest daughter, eventually married a man, although not a farrier, was himself a blacksmith and the son of a farmer. That led to much work being carried out on farm equipment, which by the year 1900, was the majority of work being undertaken. On the death of Enoch Ewart, the business was left to his daughter, and son-in-law, Ralph Shepherdson. Ralph was not only a good blacksmith but had a ready understanding of mechanical things, and soon he was undertaking the repair of such farming equipment as threshing machines, balers and reaper and binder machines. Such machines were becoming more into use as the years went by. Threshers and balers could be seen at harvest time outside a barn, coupled by drive belts to a steam traction engine. It was even becoming popular to have hay baled, rather than have the traditional haystack in the field.

Ralph decided to try building a baling machine, which he did with great success and it was not long before he was asked by some of the threshing contractors, for whom he did repair work, to build a baler for them. His next venture was that of building a threshing machine, which he did, again with great success. He was now not just a blacksmith, he was an agricultural engineer, and so he needed and acquired larger premises. The name was then changed to Shepherdson engineering Limited.

Ralph Shepherdson had four children, one of which, a son, married the daughter of a local coachbuilder. That company had been founded around the time that Enoch Ewart had started in business and in those days started by building farm wagons. Now the company was known as Crown Coachwork Limited, and the work now was mainly that of the coachwork for buses, coaches and special purpose vehicles. A second son had married the daughter of Robert Davies who was an iron founder in Ketley, a business that had prospered well over the years. Ralph's son was to become the owner of that foundry. The name was changed to accommodate the union of the couple and became Davies and Shepherdson Limited.

At the end of World War Two, the urgent need for housing due to the loss and severe damage to property in the major towns and cities by enemy bombing, brought about the evolution of the Pre-Fab, the prefabricated house that could be erected quickly and in great numbers anywhere in the country. One thing that was of great importance to such a structure was that of insulation. The main large companies were soon producing insulation from glass fibres and so it was that Shepherdson's and Crown Coachwork, together with the Davies Foundry, all related by marriage, made the decision to try to make insulation, a product of growing demand. They eventually succeeded in producing a glass fibre, quite coarse in nature but suitable for the purpose of insulating pre-Fabs, since once inside the structure, it was never to be handled again. The decision was made to establish a new company which became, also, the holding company of the three originals. The name given was Salopian Industries Limited.

To those three, original companies, there was now added the company of Williams Brothers, all four Companies being subsidiaries of Salopian Industries Limited. This very room, the board room where the directors met, to organise and control an establishment with such a proud and glorious history, was without doubt a place for those who had the power and the glory.

The first to enter the room was Patrick Evans, who as CEO, had a seat on the board, and whenever he attended a meeting of the board, he could not help but privately wallow in the sense of, the power and the glory, which gave him a feeling of exhilaration. He had climbed the mountain of ambition, reached the peak, and now able to partake in the pleasure of mixing with those who had the power of control, and who were, in his own egotistical view, admired by everyone subservient to them.

The room quickly filled with the other board members. With the exception, of Patrick Evans, as CEO, and Bruce Barnard, the company secretary, all the other directors were family members. Helping themselves to coffee and biscuits, they chatted among themselves, wondering why this special meeting had been called. Sir Ian Leighton-Boyce was the last to arrive and having availed himself of coffee and biscuits, took his seat at the head of the table.

Taking his cue, they all one by one took their seats.

"Good morning to you all," Sir Ian began. "I have no doubt that you are all wondering why I have called this meeting. Let me begin by reminding you of the tragic incident that occurred here with the death of one of our young engineers, Danny Drew. As you are all well, aware, the police are treating it as a case of murder. What most of you don't know, is that in pursuing their enquiries, the police have established, without doubt, that this company has been the target of corporate espionage."

A general murmuring immediately began, generally expressing in many, different ways, a feeling of shock and surprise.

"For what purpose?" asked Bruce Barnard, the company secretary. This was, as a solicitor, an obvious question to ask.

"To obtain technical details and information about the Supa Board development project we have continued since our acquisition of Williams Brothers. The police have established that the Eco-Tech in Liverpool is responsible. It is not my intention to say more on this subject because at eleven o'clock, the police will come and address us all on the situation as it stands, and I imagine on their recommendations as to how we proceed in the immediate future.

In the meantime, perhaps, Bill Hammond can give us an update, firstly on the progress of the Supa Board project and secondly, on the possibility of a new project to be undertaken at our Shepherdson factory. Thank you. Bill. Please carry on."

"The Supa Board project, as far as immediate development is concerned, is finished.

"We are now able to produce a good quality product, consistently, and at a production speed well in advance of the minimum required to make the product commercially viable. Patent application we believe should now be made. This to be on the formulation and method of producing boards of any thickness. Notably, I should say that in production terms, changing to a different thickness can be achieved within five minutes. Final design work for the production plant is now complete and construction may begin just as soon we, as a board, sign the Capital Expenditure Requisition." After a short pause he continued. "As you are all well aware, since we first listened to Keith Pritchard a couple of years ago, talking about the automation of the seed sowing machines, manufactured at Shepherdson's, a great deal of work has been undertaken by him. He is a qualified controls engineer, absolutely, up to date with the latest in digital technology and has also an innovative mind. He has now produced a document, outlining the possibility of using Sat-Nav control of seed sowing, which is already being used by some of the large and well-known manufacturers, but by similar technology, analysing the soil of any field and that analysis being used automatically to apply the correct amount of organic nutriment, no matter how much such requirements may change throughout any area. Also, he has an outline design of a driverless tractor capable of connecting to such equipment. However, before he embarks on any such trials, the cost of which I will leave with you, so that you can deliberate in your own good time, an approval of such expenditure will be required from us. I would suggest that this be considered and voted on at our next regular meeting."

"Thank you, Bill. I now have the Capital Expenditure Requisition, for the Supa Board plant which was passed to me by Patrick. Yvonne has made copies for each of you. I would suggest that as we are now running short of time, you peruse them when the police have left us, after which we can confirm our assent to proceed, that is assuming that we are all in agreeance.

At eleven o'clock, Sharon Sumner announced that DCI Davies had arrived and showed him into the board room.

Sir Ian welcomed him and introduced him to the rest of those present, which included Yvonne, who, had been taking the minutes of the meeting, a task that she did at each meeting and then issued those minutes to all concerned. One could say that she was acting as the secretary to the company secretary.

"Good morning ladies and gentlemen. Thank you for receiving me here, which hopefully, when you have heard what I have to say, will help you to understand the difficulties and complexities that my investigation team have experienced from the beginning. The death of the first victim, Danny Drew, was obviously one of homicide. What is more, the circumstances were such, that we believed the perpetrator to be male. We had a possible suspect, but he was also killed very shortly afterwards, leaving nothing substantial to work on. However, enquiries revealed that the girlfriend of Danny Drew's best friend in Liverpool, had seen and identified a woman visiting the Eco-Tech company, where she worked, as someone who was employed here in Telford. This she revealed to Danny, but he didn't pass the information on to you here. Subsequently, that girlfriend was murdered in her own home, shortly after we became aware of the unknown woman visiting Eco-Tech. A witness, told the Liverpool officers that a young woman had visited the home of the girlfriend, purporting to be a police officer. He had heard her say so. The Liverpool police had not sent any officer to that address, she was bogus and brazen. The Liverpool police visited the premises of Eco-Tech and in the course, of their investigations, became aware of documentation belonging to your company, being in the possession of one of the partners, a Victor Eardley. He was unable to give a satisfactory explanation for the manner, by which he had come by the documentation, and so it was concluded to be a case of corporate espionage. Before any further action could be taken, Victor Eardley was murdered, outside, in a manner identical to way that Sophie Langfordhad been killed. We here in Telford are working in cooperation with the Liverpool police and it is our collective opinion, that both were killed by the same assailant, and we think that the assailant is male. However, what we don't know is whether he is from here in Telford, or from Liverpool. This opinion gives credence to our original suspicion that the killing of Danny Drew was by a man. We are sure that the murders, here and in Liverpool are directly linked to the matter of corporate espionage I have mentioned, that of obtaining information regarding your development of your new type of insulation board. From the beginning of our investigations, we have looked at the death of Danny Drew as the principal point to work from, and I admit, so far, we have drawn a blank when trying to identify the name of the unknown woman. The Liverpool force have had no success in naming a prime suspect for the two killings there. We have decided to turn our attentions to the personal life of the deceased, Victor Eardley, and to widen our field of enquiry here, by looking for any connections with anyone employed at any of your other companies. Please, I ask you all, to say nothing outside this room, of what I have told you and the manner, in which we intend to proceed. It will be better for our officers to arrive unexpectedly, when questioning the employees."

When DCI Davies had finished speaking, there was a short period of silence from the assembly. Then, Sir Ian thanked the Inspector for his most enlightening appraisal and expressed his desire, on behalf of all present, that the work of the police be rewarded by success in the very near future and that the judiciary would dispense the justice that these heinous crimes so rightly deserved.

***

Sharon had prepared all that was possible before grilling the rainbow trout. The meal was for two, because this evening she would share a few hours with Patrick. She never cooked a meal for six o'clock, when he usually arrived, because he preferred an overture of a sexual nature before eating. This evening, she had prepared not only for the meal, but also herself, wearing a house coat over very, little else.

He parked his car, as he usually did, in a side road a little way from Sharon's house. Walking the short distance to the house, his mind still turned over the events of the morning. Whoever the spy was, there was no doubt about the audacious manner of operation. To obtain information, that until quite recently, had been strictly guarded from all but those in the Development Department working on the project, was almost unbelievable. If it were someone working on the development, why could the police be unable to make an identification. There had been an undercover officer in the department for a little while, but without result. The most, horrific thought, was that not only was the murder in the Telford factory linked with this spy, but also two killings in Liverpool. The killer was thought to be a man, but the police were quite certain that a woman was involved. Was this pair another 'Bonny and Clyde'?

Reaching the door, it opened before he could ring the doorbell as was usual. Sharon looked for him approaching the house and opened the door quickly to allow him in without delay. A small precaution to avoid the possibility of someone seeing him at her door. Patrick sometimes thought that she was becoming paranoid

Once inside, they were immediately in the arms of each other, then kissing her gently, he pulled open her housecoat, knowing that there would be little else underneath. He was not disappointed and as he ran his hands gently over her naked flesh, he felt a slight tremble. After a short time, Sharon broke away, and without speaking pulled him towards the stairs which they ascended quickly. Once inside her bedroom she flung off the housecoat, removed her smalls and slipped into bed, pulling back the duvet for him to join her.

For a few minutes, they experienced that bliss that is totally indescribable until with an explosive finale, they lay together completely exhausted. Sharon knew exactly how to satisfy this man that had become so much part of her life. When she took the position of his PA, she never imagined that she would become his mistress. That he would become so close to her, had certainly not been her plan. Her future was something she must now think about. Here was a man that was quite wealthy, had a position in life that was powerful and was respected by many people. The big drawback was him being a married man. Perhaps, if she kept up her urging, he would leave his wife. He didn't hesitate to tell her that his marriage was a farce, that there was nothing now between him and his wife. As her thoughts rolled on, she realised that he had said nothing as they lay there. He just lay there, gazing up at the ceiling.

"My darling, you are very quiet, is anything wrong?" Sharon, asked him, feeling a little concerned.

"Nothing wrong with you, my love. Sorry, my mind cannot forget all that was revealed at the board meeting this morning. As you are aware, that DCI fellow, Davies was there. You brought him to the board room."

"Why was he there?" she asked, then turning to him, running her hand over his chest, "I thought he had come to arrest you," and laughing, "I wondered how I was going to amuse myself this evening."

"He revealed much more about this espionage business and how they propose to proceed with the investigation." He began to run his hand over her body again. "They suspect that a man and a woman are responsible for the murder of not only Danny Drew, but two murders up in Liverpool, and that it is all connected to technical information being obtained about our development work here and being passed on to Eco-Tech."

Sharon drew herself closer to him saying, "Darling, you are beginning to frighten me. Whoever they are, to commit three murders, and steal information as you say, they are not only viscous but cold-blooded in their actions. Do you think that we are safe?"

"My darling, I don't think we have anything to worry about. We have no idea who these people are, but anyone that gets too close to them will be in mortal danger," was his reply, as he moved on top of her again.

She opened up to him, running her hands over his back. He kissed her gently at first, then more passionately as they once again experienced fulfilment in unison. Afterwards, they lay in the arms of each other, completely relaxed.

"Did the police say what they were going to do next."

"They are widening their investigation here in Telford. They are going to look at the whole of the Salopian Industries Group. There could possibly be someone with a grudge against the company, or someone who is prepared to get involved for money. The Liverpool police are widening their field of investigation also, by looking deeper into the background, not only of Vic Eardley, but of the other partners and employees."

"Oh, it makes me shudder, thinking of it all," Sharon said, and without further ado, said, "I think it's time to move. Don't forget, Patrick Evans, that I still have trout to grill."

"You are quite right, my darling, I am beginning to feel a little peckish."

"And, so you should be, after expending more energy than ever before," she replied with a tantalising laugh, that she knew, always turned him on.

They dressed and went downstairs. Sharon immediately started on the cooking, and Patrick opened a bottle of wine, pouring them both a glass.

"Patrick, take your wine and go sit and wait, while I grill these trout. It won't take long. Put a CD on. I'll let you choose which one."

They ate their meal, their conversation on other things, rather than the disturbing news that had dominated the time after they had made love. Dessert before the main course, as Patrick always called it, but this time the disturbing news seemed to have prompted him into having a second helping. She was not complaining.

After they had finished the meal, table tidied, all pots, pans and dishes in the washer, they sat together on the sofa, Patrick's arm around Sharon, her head resting on his shoulder.

"Patrick, darling, I wish that we could do this every night, don't you?"

He was immediately on guard, He knew where this was leading, because it had happened before. She was leading up to her usual question of when, he would leave his wife. His answer had always been when it was safe and expedient to do so. He had to be careful not to upset the chairman, Sir Ian, because it could damage his career. Sir Ian was very much a family man and would not take kindly to his CEO leaving his wife for his PA. The truth of course was that he had no intention of leaving his wife. How much longer he could put her off, he was becoming unsure. He didn't want their relationship to end. She was gorgeous and wonderful in bed. Who else could he come home to, and have dessert, before the 'main course', certainly not his wife. "My darling, it would be wonderful, and one day everything will be different, I am sure, but it cannot be now."

Sharon didn't say more, but she wondered how seriously Patrick wanted to be with her permanently and have her as his wife. She also wondered if it was only to have her in bed that appealed to him. She knew that her only choice was to be patient and wait.

It was ten thirty, when Patrick Evans arrived home. Entering the hallway, and closing the door behind him, his wife, Amanda, hearing the sound of him entering, shouted from the lounge "is that you, dear?"

"Yes, my love. Just hanging up my coat."

Patrick entered the lounge, gave his wife a kiss on the cheek and moved to the table on which stood a cut-glass decanter along with matching wine, whisky and brandy glasses. Patrick reached for a bottle of single malt and poured a generous measure. Turning to Amanda and holding up his glass, said, "would you like a drink dear?"

"I already have one," she replied, pointing to the small table at the side of the sofa.

Patrick moved around to the armchair by the side of the fireplace and sat down, sighing as he did so.

"It was another long evening for you. Did everything go well?"

"Yes, everything was quite successful. Things could not have gone better, really."

"Where did you meet this time?"

"Oh, that Inn on the A5, going towards Shrewsbury," he replied, "I can never remember the name. I have been there once or twice before."

This declaration came so smoothly and convincingly, that it would have fooled anyone into accepting it as the truth. Patrick Evans was, apart from anything else, a most accomplished liar.

"Is the food good?"

"Yes very, good. We had grilled trout."

"You must take me there, one evening, when you are not having to meet business associates. We haven't been out in the evening, for quite a while."

"You are quite right, my love. I suppose that I have been neglecting you recently. Never mind, I will make it up to you, when all these pressing things for work are over and done with. Although, sometimes I seem to be taking one step forward then two back," he said with a laugh.

"Have there been any further developments of this dreadful murder affair?"

"That Detective chief Inspector fellow, Harry Davies, came and addressed all the board members, this morning. He gave an update on the investigation, and the manner, in which they are planning to proceed. I thought it was odd, for him to do that. I always thought that the police do what they do, and don't reveal why or what they are doing, until they are ready to arrest and put the cuffs on someone. It all seemed to be staged, in a way that might upset one, if guilty. He did say that although they had suspicions that a man and woman were responsible for the murder here, and those two up in Liverpool, they had, so far, been unable to identify them. However, they are going to extend their enquiries into all our associate companies and working in cooperation with the police in Liverpool."

"Let us hope that they solve the case soon, my love, then perhaps you will be able to relax," Amanda said, raising her glass, not in a toast, but in a demonstration of sincerity.

Patrick didn't reply but sat there in serious contemplation.

21

The persistent ringing, of the mobile phone eventually penetrated the sleep-drugged brain, of a man, who always found it difficult to drag himself out of bed every morning and prepare for yet another day of work. His alarm clock was set for seven o'clock, but switching on the light, and observing this outrageous time of six thirty, he was about to switch off the phone, when recognising the number showing on the display, decided that it was important for him to reply. Picking up the phone and answering, he said, "what the bloody hell do you want at this God forsaken hour?"

"It is only God forsaken for lazy sods like you," was the woman's reply. "Listen to me and save your comments until I have finished."

"OK, get on with it."

"The police were here again yesterday. Well one of them. That DCI Davies. He came to speak to the directors and was here for about three quarters of an hour. From what I can gather, they are fairly, certain that they are looking for a man and a woman and are connecting what happened here with those things that happened in Liverpool. We need to meet urgently."

"Where and when?" was his curt reply.

"It has to be somewhere that is away from crowds, so not in a pub, and where it is unlikely that anyone from work might see us. You are originally from Wrockwardine Wood and so I presume that you know Holy Trinity Church."

"Yes, of course I do. My grandparents are buried there."

"Excellent. Do you know where the grave is?"

"Yes, but why do you want to know that?"

"Buy some flowers, and meet me there, this evening. Say half past six. I will be there a little before that and I shall be outside the east end of the church. Come and meet me there. We will then go to your grandparent's grave as a couple and put on the flowers. That way we will be inconspicuous, and we can talk freely," with that she switched off the phone.

He lay there, musing over what she had said, until it was time to get up at seven o'clock, heralded by the strident sound of his alarm clock, which he switched off as he hauled himself out of bed. What would she want this time? She had wanted something done about that girl up in Liverpool and when he had done it, she blew her top, saying she didn't mean murder. "Whatever possessed you to be such a bloody fool," she remonstrated. There were other ways that would have kept her quiet, ways that would never have alerted the law. Now, the police were investigating which was the worst possible outcome. Then when she became aware that, that fellow, Vic Eardley had been found to have the information in his possession belonging to Salopian, the information that had been the cause of that engineer's death in the first place, she was starting to panic. She couldn't trust Eardley to keep his mouth shut, so he had gone up to Liverpool, and shut it for him, permanently. This time she went ballistic. She had said that they would be very, lucky to get away with this, and to do nothing more, until he heard from her. He had now heard from her, at the ungodly time of six thirty this morning. Somehow, today, he had to go and buy bloody flowers to take with him this evening. He would have to go at lunchtime because he would have no other opportunity.

It was just as well, that he now lived alone, he thought. Nobody to be aware of what he was doing or ask where he had been. His partner of four years, had up sticks and left him six months earlier, because she suspected him of having an affair. Stupid bitch he thought. He couldn't tell her the truth about one of the women, that it wasn't an affair with her, but an alliance, for the purpose of feeding technical information, relating to the new insulation board development, to that firm in Liverpool. He couldn't tell her, how much he resented Patrick Evans, that egotistical bastard, and the pompous company chief engineer, Frank Ebbs, who had insulted him at his interview for the position of company controls engineer. Ebbs had said that his qualifications and overall knowledge of the subject, were not sufficiently advanced for that exacting position. However, there would be opportunities in the future provided, that he obtained a degree or gained membership of a professional institution.

They were satisfied with his work at Davies and Shepherdson, the Foundry where he was the works electrical engineer. Carry on there and have patience was the recommendation. What a load of shit he had thought. Then he had, by chance, met the woman that could change his life. A woman that had overheard him going on about the rejection and his perceived, degrading insult, when in the Queen's Arms Hotel and talking to one of his close colleagues. That woman had spoken to him later at the bar, and he offered her a drink, that she gratefully accepted. She told him that she had overheard his conversation earlier and sympathised with him. She fully understood his indignance and feeling of rejection. It had happened to herself in the past but not to give up. After all is said and done, we work for reward, she had told him. Reward can come from more than one direction. One has to keep on the lookout for the right opportunity, and for herself, she had at last found a way of earning extremely good money, although not without a little risk. But that risk gave some excitement in life. It sounded good he had said, but he couldn't see any such opportunity that could benefit himself. Then, putting her hand on his arm, and looking at him with a penetrating stare, she had told him to meet her again, the next night. She may be able to suggest something for him to think about.

He had met her the following night, again in the Queen's Arms Hotel, and having taken their drinks to a table in the lounge, she explained to him the way he could make substantial money, whilst at the same time extracting his revenge on those pompous idiots, who, thought themselves to be God's gift to British industry. All he had to do was give her advice on what technical information would be mostly needed by a competitive company. She would obtain it, pass it to him and he would send it to them, from his domain. Any further assistance she may need, they could discuss and agree terms as and when the situation arose.

The whole idea appealed to him instantly. Why not, he thought, what was there to lose?

Maybe, that competitive company might give him the sort of job he wanted. A job that would satisfy his interest in computer control, the work he had applied for with company engineering but for which he had been rejected. He knew that this would be industrial espionage, that it was illegal, and he didn't know what the penalty would be if discovered. But what the hell, he thought, it would be exciting.

That was just after the founding of the Company Engineering Division. He agreed with her there and then to do what she wanted and so the technical information for the new Supa Board development was passed to the competitive company, Eco-Tech in Liverpool. He had of course learned her identity and had great admiration for her. She was so cool and calm about everything, she was, in his opinion, the perfect spy.

Things began to unravel only when she had been seen and recognised when visiting Eco-Tech company. The death of that engineer had been the result. One of the extra bits of assistance she had asked him to do was to put the girl who had recognised her in a position that would keep her quiet. He had done just that. He had silenced her permanently. He could not ever forget the tongue lashing he received for taking the action that he had taken. Then when she was beginning to panic over Vic Eardley's possible arrest and what he would reveal, he had once again silenced the man, permanently. She went ballistic, but what was done was done.

As he had been instructed, having parked his car some distance from the church, he made his way there with the prescribed bunch of flowers, he had picked up at lunch time from the local garage. She was, as promised, standing at the east end of the church and awaiting his arrival. She was dressed in light blue jeans, black flat heeled shoes and wearing an expensive black leather jacket, a red scarf around her neck, and large framed sunglasses. She had selected this attire with the dark glasses to affect a disguise. She didn't want to be recognised by anyone that knew her, especially with Eddie Harper. It didn't matter that he was wearing jeans and bomber style jacket, clothing that he was often seen in, because he was just visiting a grave to place some flowers. As he reached her, she linked her arm through his, carrying a bottle of water with the other hand and said, "let's walk as though we are couple." They then made their way to the grave of his grandparents, arranging the flowers in the vase that needed to be washed out beforehand. It was obvious that it had not held flowers for some considerable time. This done and no one else anywhere around, she delivered the dos and don'ts to him now that she was sure that the police were stepping up their investigation, which would no doubt cover everyone employed by Salopian Industries, including the associate companies. Be absolutely, certain, she had told him, to have a plausible alibi for the significant times and dates that she knew would be the focus of any questioning.

It is often said that life is one big game of chance. That evening, chance played an unexpected card in events. DC Jane Todd, who lived in Wrockwardine Wood and was that evening off-duty, was walking past the church almost colliding with a man and woman who were coming out from the churchyard. The word, sorry, was exclaimed by all three in unison as they moved in the same sideways direction, although endeavouring to move in the opposite direction to avoid each other. Jane Todd laughed, as she managed to move around them, then turning her head towards them said, "a lovely evening," to which the couple turned, momentarily, replying in the affirmative, then carried on walking in the opposite direction to Jane.

Jane Todd was a very observant woman, maybe due to her police training. She had already registered in her mind, that the woman was of medium build, wearing jeans but had on an expensive leather jacket, probably Italian, a red scarf and had on a pair of rather large framed sunglasses. The leather jacket impressed her, because she had seen something similar in a shop in Shrewsbury the last time that she was there. It was very, expensive. Although casual dress, everything harmonised well with her dark shoulder length hair and the red, silk-like scarf, around her neck looked just right. The man was again wearing jeans and a light casual jacket. He was a big man, about six feet in height, solidly built, weighing perhaps fifteen stones and with a shaved head. Jane could not get out of the habit of estimating height and weight in 'old money' terms. The pair were in their early thirties was her estimate.

As the couple walked back to where they had parked their cars, the woman said with a degree of concern in her voice, "that woman we almost collided with I have seen before. She is police and was at the factory with the investigating team when Danny Drew was killed. I can't remember her name, but I never forget a face."

***

At police Divisional Headquarters, DCI Harry Davies had briefed the investigation team with the latest information that he had, and the outcome of conversations he had held with both DS Stuart, and DI Ken Abbott. The plan was now to expand the enquiry to cover the whole of the Salopian organisation. It was now the opinion that the unknown woman had a male accomplice and that they were both employed by the Salopian organisation but not necessarily at the same factory. Each factory would be visited, and the personnel questioned, covering the individuals' background and with, attention being paid to their whereabouts at the times of the murders of both Sophie Langford and Vic Eardley. The Liverpool team would be following the same pattern in their region. The DCI said that he would go to Cardiff, to speak with all at Williams Brothers, DC Jane Todd would go to Davies and Shepherdson, the foundry in Ketley, DI Bob Grant would go to Shepherdson Engineering and DS Larry Robb would go to Crown Coachwork both of which were in Shrewsbury.

The morning that DC Jane Todd went to her assigned company, she decided to interview all staff first and then deal with all the shop floor workers afterwards. Her reasoning was that it was more likely, that should anyone be involved in obtaining technical information from the parent company, a person at staff level was more likely to have such opportunity than someone off the shop floor.

Jane had interviewed the works manager and his secretary both of whom were most helpful with their answers to her questions. She had no doubt in her mind whatsoever, that they had not been involved in any way with the illegal activities or in any way connected to the homicide. Her next interview was with the works electrical engineer. The works manager's secretary had put out a call for him to come to the conference room, where all the interviews were being held.

"Good morning, my name is DC Jane Todd. You are, Mr Eddie Harper?" she said, looking up from the notepad on the desk, and immediately recognised the man standing before her. He was tall, well-built, and had a shaved head.

He was undoubtedly the man she had almost bumped into as he was coming out of the churchyard in Wrockwardine Wood, with the woman in the expensive leather jacket.

"Good morning, Miss," he replied. "Yes, my name is Eddie Harper."

"Please, take a seat. Mr Harper, I think we have already met."

Looking confused, and, realising that this was probably the woman that his accomplice had recognised outside the church, and said that she was police, although, he could not himself be sure of that, so he was immediately on guard. "I don't think so Miss," he said with a confidence that he didn't feel.

"Did we not, very nearly collide outside the church in Wrockwardine Wood, when you were leaving the churchyard with a lady?"

"I think you must be mistaken, Miss, I've not been to Wrockwardine Wood."

"They do say that we all have a double somewhere, I must have met yours. Have you got a brother perhaps?" Jane pressed, because she was sure in her own mind that he was indeed the man and that he was lying for some reason. Maybe the woman that he was with was someone that he should not have been with, she thought.

"I don't have a brother," he replied, truculence beginning to show in his demeanour.

"What is your full name, and address?"

He gave his full name as Edward Robert Harper and his full address in Oakengates

"How old are you, Mr Harper?"

"I am thirty-two"

"How long have you been working here?"

"Six years," he replied

"Have you ever lived in Wrockwardine Wood?"

"No, but my Grandparents lived there but passed away many years ago."

"What were their names?"

"Jack and Pat Davies. They were my mother's, parents."

DC Todd then asked him to give his whereabouts at the crucial times and days of the murders of both Sophie Langford and Vic Eardley, watching, carefully his reaction to the questions. She detected a degree of tension in him, beginning to take hold.

"I can't rightly remember. Is it important?" he said, uncertain of what he should or should not say.

"Yes, it is important. You are fully aware that we are investigating three murders, which we believe to be connected, with Salopian Industries, of which this company is part. Since you work here, we need to have such information, in order to eliminate you from our enquiries.

Jane noticed a slight relaxing in his demeanour when she inferred elimination from the enquiries. She could not be sure about his attitude, or why he was so adamant that he was not in Wrockwardine Wood, when she felt certain that this was the man, she had almost collided with outside the church. She was sure that he was lying, but why should he lie about visiting a churchyard.

"I think that I was fishing at those times that you asked about," he said, bursting in on her thoughts.

"Where would that have been?" she quickly asked.

"I was river fishing, up at Buildwas. It's nice and peaceful up there."

"Can anyone verify that. Did anyone see you there?"

"There were one or two people there at the time. They were fishing too, but I didn't know them. I didn't even speak to them. We were all at reasonable distance from each other. That's the way it is."

"Are you married, Mr Harper?" she asked changing the subject.

"No. I did have a partner, but we split up about six months ago. I live alone now."

"What was your partner's name?" Jane asked.

"Sian Gilmore," he replied. "Why do you want to know that?"

"General background information, Mr Harper. Do you know where she is now?"

"Back with her parents in Ironbridge. Her father has a bistro and she works there."

"Where did you live when you were together?"

"In Wellington. We were buying a house, but when we split up, it was sold. That's why I am now living in a rented flat in Oakengates."

"Thank you, Mr Harper, for your cooperation. You have been very, helpful." With that, Jane stood up, signalling that the interview was over and shook hands with him.

After Eddie Harper had left, Jane sat for a while going through the notes that she had made. Of all the people she had so far interviewed, this man was of the greatest interest. Despite his denial that he been in

Wrockwardine Wood and that he had been in the churchyard there, she was convinced that he had been. Jane was sure that he was the man with a woman that had nearly collided with her, as they came out of the churchyard. Why should he lie. Did he lie because he was with a married woman? Thinking about her and her appearance, there was someone she had seen in the Development Department, when they were questioning the staff following the death of Danny Drew, that bore a similarity. A woman of medium build, with dark shoulder length hair and about the same age. What if she was the unknown woman and Eddie Harper was her accomplice, the man that they had thought to have been present when Danny Drew was killed. Jane began looking through her notebook for the name. Turning page after page, she came finally to the description she remembered so well, the name was Lucy Thompson, and there was a note alongside that said, sister-in-law of Sue Thompson of the Supplies Department.

If Lucy Thompson was the woman with Eddie Harper leaving the churchyard, for what reason had they been there? The most common reason to go to a churchyard or cemetery was to put flowers on a grave. Perhaps, they had put flowers on his grandparents grave but why should he deny being there. Jane made a mental note to enquire at the church to find the location of that grave and then check to see if fresh flowers had been placed there. She also decided to speak with DI Grant regarding her suspicions concerning Lucy Thompson and ask him if she should re-interview her. Lucy worked in the department that the development of Supa Board was being carried out and her notes revealed that Lucy Thompson was an industrial chemist and was assistant to Gwyn Thomas, the man who had pioneered the chemical formulation for the product. She was in a perfect position to pass on technical information.

The following afternoon at Headquarters, briefing was underway, DCI Davies was going over the results of interviews carried out, so far, throughout the Salopian organisation. He was particularly interested in the information that DC Jane Todd had given. "Interview Lucy Thompson again, but speak with the company chief engineer, Frank Ebbs, before you do, as a matter of courtesy," he said addressing Jane. "There is a possibility that the two people you nearly collided with, could be the ones that we are seeking." The rest of the briefing didn't reveal anything worthy of following up. It was rather disappointing to the DCI, but such was police work. Slogging away, apparently getting nowhere, then suddenly, often from the most unexpected source, would come a breakthrough.

Frank Ebbs was very, helpful and respectfully suggested to Jane that she spoke to all in the Development Department, so as not to appear to be singling out Lucy. If she were in any way responsible for covert activities, it would be better not to alert her of their suspicions before they had all the facts.

Her first approach was to John Preston, telling him that it was necessary to confirm some of the information that had been gathered during the original interviews following the death of Danny Drew.

"If I may, I will begin with you Mr Preston." Then flicking through her notebook, she came to the page that had everything that he had said. Going through the various answers he had given, he confirmed that all was correct, as recorded. Thanking him for his cooperation she went to speak with Gwyn Thomas who confirmed all that she had recorded was correct, and she thanked him also for his assistance.

"Hello again, Lucy, I suppose that you remember me, DC Jane Todd," she said in the most, friendly manner that she could muster. "I am sorry to interrupt your work, but we are checking all original statements to ensure that we have everything right and to ask a few more questions to help us in building the overall picture of people's relationships, with one another."

"Well, for a start, as I think I said originally, I knew Danny Drew, but not in any personal way. He came in here from time to time, preparing himself for when he would have a day-to-day responsibility for the equipment on a production basis. He was a likeable person in general but rather forward with the women. I used to tell him to get lost, but he never took offence, only laughed it off. That of course was Danny."

"I don't think we established whether or not that you are married, although I can see that you are wearing a wedding ring, so I think that says all," DC Todd said, giving a friendly smile.

"Yes, I have been married for five years. My husband is one of your lot, PC Gavin Thompson. He is uniform branch."

"I know Gavin Thompson, but I had never connected him with you. What a small world. My notes tell me that Sue Thompson from the Supplies Department is your Sister-in-Law, so that means that you and Sue married two brothers."

"Yes, that is correct. As you say it is a small world that we live in."

"Tell me, do you by any chance know Eddie Harper, who works at the foundry?"

"Who doesn't?" was the reply. "He was a hot-shot rugby player until about a couple of years ago when he retired from the game. I don't know why he finished playing, unless he thought that he was getting too old at the ripe old age of thirty."

"He told me that his partner, had left him six months ago and that he now lives alone. Have you any idea or have you heard why she left?"

"It's no use asking me. I don't know him well enough. If you want to know the answer, ask him," Lucy replied with irritation in her voice.

"Yes, I might do just that. Thank you, Lucy, you have been most helpful."

DC Jane Todd continued to question the other members of the staff, but the information that she really wanted she now had. What she was unaware of was that the moment Lucy was away from Jane, she made a call on her mobile. That call was to Eddie Harper. The reason for her call being to keep him informed that the police had just re-interviewed her. The officer was DC Jane Todd who had asked if she knew Eddie Harper. Eddie told her that DC Todd had already re-interviewed him and had said that she recognised him, but he had persuaded her that she was mistaken. Lucy then said that they must be very, careful, because DC Todd was now aware that PC Gavin Thompson was her husband.

DC Todd made the decision to visit Mr Gilmore's bistro in Ironbridge. A talk with Sian Gilmore would, she thought, be interesting. Hopefully, a further insight into the character and life of Eddie Harper might be obtained. He appeared to be an intelligent man and had good manners, but there was something in his demeanour that Jane could not really understand. When she had questioned him, he was helpful and polite but there was an underlying tension there that displayed some truculence in his manner. Also, he had been, in her opinion, lying to her about his presence in Wrockwardine Wood. Jane wondered about the alibi he had given for the times of the two murders in Liverpool. Fishing, she thought was dubious, for in the first instance he had said that he couldn't remember, then had said he had been fishing almost as though he had suddenly thought of it, and that it was as good as any other validation. The location was of course a well-known place for anglers and there was a possibility that nobody that was there would remember anyone, unless known personally.

On entering the bistro, DC Todd went straight to the cash desk. The gentleman she spoke to was middle-aged, of medium build with iron grey hair and a distinguished appearance.

Jane introduced herself, showing her warrant card, and asked to speak with Sian Gilmore.

"Yes, I will call her," he said. "Sian is my daughter." With that he disappeared into a back room. After a few moments, he reappeared and said that his daughter would be along presently and invited her to take a seat.

"I am Sian Gilmore, how can I be of help?" Sian said as she entered and addressed Jane. Sian was in the working dress of a chef and had obviously come from the kitchen.

"I understand that you are the ex-partner of Eddie Harper," Jane began.

"Yes, that is so," then with a little anxiety in her voice, "Is there a problem?"

"No, please don't upset yourself. I just need some background information to help with our enquiries."

"Enquiries into what?" she asked with some suspicion.

"It is a murder investigation which I cannot discuss with you, but we need background information on all personnel employed by Salopian Industries. I think that your input might be useful to us in building an overall picture."

Sian called one of the waitresses over and ordered a pot of tea and toasted tea cakes for two, suggesting that they could make the interview a pleasant interlude in her daily chores.

Sian explained that Eddie had joined the army when he was eighteen and had served a total of seven years. It was in the Army that he learned his trade as an electrical engineer also where he gained his skill as a controls engineer. When he left the Army, he started work at the foundry. About twelve months later, the works electrical engineer retired, and Eddie was appointed in his place. Shortly afterwards, Patrick Evans became CEO and founded the new company engineering Division. Eddie applied for the position of company controls engineer but was rejected. He seemed to change after that. He became moody and easily lost his temper. Up until that time he had been a keen and renowned rugby player, but then decided to quit the game much to the regret of all his rugby associates. He took up fishing and joined a club, although he never seemed to be as keen as he had been with the game of rugby.

Sian explained that she had always worked in the bistro and had been to catering college to become a qualified chef. The one drawback to such a profession was the unsocial hours that were usually demanded. She explained that she shared the evening shifts with her mother. Since her mother was of course middle aged, Sian covered three evenings, her mother two of the five evenings that they opened, Tuesday to Saturday inclusive. However, her mother had always covered Friday and Saturday so that Sian could have all weekends free. Sian explained that her suspicions, that Eddie was seeing another woman, were aroused by the smell of perfume on Eddie's jacket. It certainly was not a perfume that she herself used. Not wanting to accuse him of being somewhere with another woman, she said nothing. Then when putting one of his shirts into the washer, she had noticed what appeared to be lipstick on the collar. Then Sian had tackled him about it, also about the smell of perfume on his jacket. He flew up into a rage, at the suggestion that he was seeing someone else, denying everything.

One week she had asked her mother if she would cover the Thursday evening, because there was something she needed to do, and so went home at teatime. Eddie didn't come home until ten thirty. He was flabbergasted that Sian was at home when he arrived because when she was working it was about eleven thirty when she returned. Sian demanded to know where he had been until that time, without coming home. He blustered but could give no reasonable explanation. She then accused him of having an affair and wanted to know who it was that he was with. There then erupted a horrendous row that resulted in him hitting her, something that had never happened before. Sian vowed that it would never happen again and walked out on him, there and then. She had driven back to her parents and only went back to the house to collect her things when he was at work. That was six months ago. The house that they were buying was sold, fortunately within the first two months of their separation. Eddie, she believed now had a flat in Oakengates.

He had displayed a violence in his temper that had scared Sian. It was her opinion that had she remained he would have beaten her with possibly terrifying results. Never, before in their relationship, had she had any indication that he had such a violent temper. It was frightening and something that she would never forget.

Everything that Sian Gilmore had revealed about her relationship with Eddie Harper had to an extent shocked DC Todd but not entirely surprised her. There was something about that man that she could not understand. He was without doubt, enigmatic. His was a character that could well fit the profile of the perpetrator of all three murders that they were now investigating. However, it was one thing to have suspicions but something quite different to obtain proof. His alibies for the Liverpool murders were tenuous but difficult to dismiss. As for the murder of Danny Drew, it was highly unlikely that he was anywhere other than at the foundry, which would eliminate him from that incident. Could there be two male accomplices working with the unknown woman, a possibility that had been considered before. If that were the case, who could possibly be the second man. Someone working in the Development Department was perhaps the highest probability.

The woman who was with Eddie Harper in Wrockwardine Wood, could be Lucy Thompson. With someone else from the same department along with Eddie Harper, Lucy would have all the support needed to obtain the technical information and pass it on to the firm in Liverpool. In DC Jane Todd's opinion, formed by all that Sian Gilmore had revealed, Eddie Harper had the character to have committed both murders in Liverpool.

Speculation is all well and good, often leading to a successful conclusion of a problem but in this case, there were a limited number of male members of staff in the Development Department to speculate about. Firstly, there was John Preston but the more she thought about him being the second man, the more she rejected the idea. He was a happily married man, with a family, who, according to his statement, liked being in Telford. Although all were from Liverpool and were used to city life, they loved the countryside, which, living in Telford afforded them some of the nicest countryside in England.

The second possible suspect could be Gwyn Thomas, the chemist from Cardiff. He was a single man and so, as far as she knew, didn't have a girlfriend. He lived alone in an apartment quite near to the factory, so there was nobody to confirm when he was at home. But there was no obvious reason for him to be mixed up in the covert work of selling company secrets, other than pure pecuniary gain. He certainly didn't exhibit a lifestyle that could in any way be considered as opulent. He appeared modest not only in his lifestyle but in his basic personality, and he appeared to have taken great pride in his work during the development of the new product. DC Jane Todd was running out of ideas.

Similar investigative work had been carried out by DI Ken Abbott in Liverpool. His focus had been on the background and past life of Vic Eardley. This was a man who had lived on the borders of honest work and illegal transactions and he wondered how his business partners, Gerry Ewing and Bill Astley had come to be tied up with him. They appeared to be honest men and were genuinely shocked at the discovery of information, obviously procured from the Salopian organisation covertly. Pressing them on the matter of payment being made for such information from their company funds, they admitted that they had not kept a close enough eye on the accounts, not from neglect but because Vic had a persuasive tongue and didn't keep them fully informed of his actions, always assuring them that all was well. Both Ewing and Astley bitterly regretted that they had not asserted more authority over the years but had put Vic under pressure to tell them how he had managed to obtain the information. This he didn't reveal but as Gerry Ewing put it, gave them a cock and bull story of meeting a young woman at Haydock Racecourse, who was on her own and, at the tote, began a discussion with him on possible winners. He claimed that everything had developed from that. For a woman to be at a race meeting on her own was, in the opinions of them both, highly improbable and verging on a story that could be attributed to someone like Hans Christian Anderson.

DI Abbott had not however, discarded the story entirely, but had followed up the story by going to Haydock, not as a police officer but as someone trying to contact an old friend by asking the bookmakers if they recognised the photograph he had of Vic Eardley. A couple of them had confirmed that they knew him but had not seen him for some time. One of them had seen him on several occasions with a woman, much younger than himself, but that was two- or three-years past. He thought that she was the daughter of a one-time, regular punter at Haydock but couldn't remember his name. It had been twelve to eighteen months since he had seen him and thought that he had perhaps died or moved from the district. DI Abbott was beginning to run out if ideas, in a similar way to that of DC Jane Todd back in Telford.

22

Patrick Evans asked Sharon to call Gwyn Thomas and have him come and see him. John Preston took the call and immediately told Gwyn that the Big Boss wanted to see him right away.

"What, I wonder, does he want?" Gwyn said in exasperation. "Usually it is, how soon can we have this or when will that be ready. He is a bloody nuisance."

"I dare you to tell him so," John replied with a hearty laugh.

"I might just do that one day," was the reply, the Welsh accent, markedly noticeable.

Gwyn went, as instructed, to see Patrick Evans. Tapping on Sharon's door, he went in and said, "Hi Sharon, I believe Mr Evans is after my blood."

"Oh, Gwyn, I don't think it's quite like that," and with that throaty laugh that was so alluring said, "I think that he wants to give blood rather than take it." Tapping on the communicating door and opening it she announced Gwyn's arrival.

Gesturing for Gwyn to take a seat, he said, "How is everything going on the Supa Board project? In your view, are we on schedule and almost ready to begin construction work on the production plant?"

To ask his opinion, Gwyn thought, was a first. Patrick Evans' conversations usually consisted of demands rather than requests. Guardedly, Gwyn gave his opinion. "Everything is going well and yes we are on schedule. Once we get the green light from the board, the construction work can begin."

"Good, that is what I was hoping to hear. Sanction to begin should be given within the next few days and that brings me to the reason that I asked you to see me. I want you to take the position of manager of the Supa Board plant when it come on stream. It needs a manager with a chemistry background, and you are the best person to take on the role. However, there is still the development of the product for pipe fittings and other specialities to be pursued and I want you to head that development but giving more input and authority to Lucy Thompson to free you up sufficiently to allow you to carry out your managerial responsibilities. Does that all sound reasonable to you?"

Here we go again, asking my opinion Gwyn thought, was most unusual. The real word should be unbelievable. Still wondering what might be coming next, Gwyn replied in the affirmative.

"I'm glad that you are happy with such an arrangement. I realise that it's a lot to ask, that is why I am saying that Lucy Thompson must step up more to the front. When the new plant comes on stream, I have instructed Leslie Anderson to delegate Rowan Chapman to take direct responsibility for the engineering side of things, so I would suggest that you and he get acquainted and plan your management strategy well in advance. Unless you have any further questions, I won't detain you any longer. Come and see me any time, should you be concerned about anything."

Gwyn left by the same route as the one he had entered, via Sharon's office. As he closed the communicating door, Sharon said, "what did I tell you? He was giving blood rather than taking it," again with that alluring throaty laugh.

"I am overwhelmed, I had been thinking about what to do when Supa Board is in the hands of the production people. Perhaps going back to Cardiff, but now I know that I shall be staying in Telford."

Gwyn had arranged to take a couple of holiday days and return to Cardiff to see his mother, now resident in a care home. Her house had been sold and so Gwyn had booked a room at the Three Feathers Hotel which was quite close to the factory of Williams Brothers. He planned to call in at the factory and see his old colleagues again and perhaps, go to see John Williams who along with his brother had been his joint mentors in those early days. It now seemed such a long time ago. They were exciting times, with the great expectations of where this new product could possibly lead them to as a company. As with all development projects, costs began to rise until serious thought had been given by the Williams brothers about their financial ability to continue the work. Of course, this was unknown to Gwyn. He was still in his 'blue heaven' especially because he had started dating Bronwen, John Williams' daughter. She was, in Gwyn's eyes, the loveliest girl in Wales. He still believed that today. Many occasions since leaving Cardiff, he had thought longingly about Bronwen and had inwardly cursed himself for being such an idiotic fool, walking away from her in the way that he had done. It had started as nothing more than a little disagreement but escalated into a row that was perhaps more his fault than hers. He was too proud and stupid to say sorry and patch things up and so they parted permanently. He afterwards, realised his mistake but could still not bring himself to go back to her and try again. He now knew that he had broken Bronwen's heart and she had on the rebound become involved with Hugh Jenkins, and in a very, short time had married him. It was a disaster waiting to happen. If only, Gwyn thought, he could have the time to go over again, all would be so different. Of course, if only, was a phrase often used to express something that could never be.

Gwyn began his journey early on Thursday morning and was in Cardiff by lunchtime. He went directly to the care home to see his mother. She was more confused than when he had last seen her. She didn't seem to recognise him when first he saw her.

"It's me, Mam, Gwyn. I know that I have put on weight but I had hoped that it wouldn't be too much to make me unrecognisable," he said to her, taking her hands that now seemed so fragile that they could easily break if not handled carefully.

Recognition then came to her. "Oh, it's you Gwyn, how lovely to see you. I haven't seen you for such a long time. How are you and how is Bronwen?"

She had forgotten that it was only a couple of weeks since he had been there and that he had not been with Bronwen for a long time. How tragic life can become, Gwyn thought, as he held her hands. His thoughts moved on. Perhaps it's worse for those who are left to care, than for the afflicted because they are unaware of their ability to grasp the present but regress into a past, which to them is the present. Gwyn was content that his mother was now being cared for and he could have the peace of mind knowing that although he could not be with her every day, she was safe and protected. He knew however, that her condition would deteriorate, and a day would come, when she would no longer recognise him, or the world around her.

That evening, he signed in at the Three Feathers Hotel, something now strange to him. In the old days he would of course have stayed at his mother's house, and in his old room. But that was a luxury of the past, a time that would be no more. Having obtained his room key, he went directly to his room put his small suitcase on the stand provided and proceeded to make a cup of coffee at the service table. The time was five thirty. He had booked a table for dinner at seven thirty, which gave him a couple of hours in which to relax.

Sitting in the armchair, sipping the coffee, which he thought was quite good, considering that it was of the instant variety typical of that to be found in hotels anywhere in the world. His mind wandered over not only his experience, earlier that day, at the care home, but of the future, which for him was to be in Telford. This was something that had never entered his mind when first he had moved there, to pursue the development of a project that at one time had meant so much to the Williams brothers. He would have scorned the idea back then. But now everything was changed, and life had moved on. He had been caught up in the flow and moved with it. His reverie was interrupted by a knock on the room door. Putting his cup on the small side table, he went to the door and opening it received a shock, for standing there was Bronwen.

"Please come in," he said, completely taken aback by her presence. "How lovely to see you after such a long time."

"I don't wish to intrude, but I heard that your mother is now in a care home and I just had to ask how she is getting along. I saw your booking entry earlier and so here I am," she hurriedly explained, almost breathlessly.

"Oh, Bronwen, it's wonderful to see you again, and you are not intruding in any way at all. I noticed that your name on the board downstairs listed you as deputy manager. Congratulations on your preferment." Then giving a slight pause as he adjusted his grasp on the fact of her presence, he continued. "My mother is physically well but she has dementia that is slowly getting worse. She didn't recognise me immediately when I saw her this afternoon. It was a while before she realised who I was, but such is the sickness. Please do sit down," indicating the chair.

"Thank you, this is fine," she replied, sitting on the edge of the bed.

Gwyn could hardly believe that she had come to see him. He knew that she had divorced Hugh Jenkins, but he really thought that he was at the bottom of her visiting list. What Gwyn didn't know was that she was now aware of Patrick Evans' affair with his PA, which was something that Gwyn didn't have any knowledge.

When Rowan Chapman learned about Patrick Evans dalliance with Bronwen and had told Julie what was, apparently, common knowledge among the hotel staff, Julie was astounded. Astounded because she knew about the affair he was having with Sharon, an admission made to her by Sharon herself. Although at the time that Rowan had told her, Julie had said nothing to him about Sharon, she had, however, eventually given him the facts after careful thought. Rowan's opinion was that Bronwen deserved better. If only she could be made aware of the fact that Patrick Evans was just using her. Another of those, if only, situations. It was Julie who had suggested that he, Rowan, could talk with the production man at Williams Brothers and 'let slip' the knowledge about Evans and Sharon's affair. Julie was sure that the information would get to her. What she did about it was of course her decision to make but she would know what kind of man Patrick Evans really was.

When Rowan had 'let slip' the facts about Evans, the first person to be told was John Williams, who was thunderstruck by the revelation. He admitted that he had always held Patrick Evans in high regard and had secretly wished that it had been possible for he and his daughter to get together. He knew that Bronwen and Patrick had become close and that whenever Patrick was in Cardiff, he and Bronwen dined together. Just how close they had become he was unsure, but one thing was certain, he would tell her what he had learned and hoped that this time she would take more notice of what he said, than when he had tried to advise her against Hugh Jenkins.

Bronwen had been shocked by what her father had told her. This time however, she decided to take notice of what he said and have nothing more to do with Patrick, other than on business terms. She had decided to say nothing to him about what she had learned. She was not going to behave like the 'wronged woman'. However, she was sure that Patrick would question her attitude and when he did, she would tell him, in no uncertain terms, exactly what she thought about his devious and philandering ways.

Bronwen started to speak at the same time as Gwyn, then both stopping and laughing Gwyn said, "ladies first."

"How are you Gwyn, is all well up in Telford?"

"Thank you, yes all is well. I didn't want to go there in the first instance but now I am quite settled. It took a little while, and there were times when I thought of returning, but all had changed here in Cardiff and there was nothing to come back for, so I immersed myself in work and began a new life."

"I am so sorry for the way things ended between us. It should never have happened." Bronwen fell silent but looked steadily at him, observing his reactions and wondering what he was thinking. This was the first time they had spoken since their break-up, so long ago.

Gwyn, returning her gaze said, "It is for me to be sorry. It was my intransigent attitude that was the real problem. I have regretted it ever since. When I learned that you had married Hugh, I assumed that you were happy again and forgotten all about me and my stupidity."

"Marrying Hugh was one of the biggest mistakes of my life, and believe me, I have made a few that I bitterly regret, but all that was my stupidity, so you see we are not that different in our lives."

"Perhaps, one day, we shall learn to live in a happier way," Gwyn said smiling as he spoke.

"I saw that you have booked to stay for two nights, tonight and tomorrow night."

"Yes, I have. Tomorrow morning, I shall visit the old factory and hopefully go to see your father. He was so good to me in the early days, and it would be nice to catch up with him. Tomorrow afternoon I shall go to see my mother again. Saturday morning, I shall drive back to Telford."

"Gwyn, tomorrow, I shall be off duty at one o'clock for the rest of the day. Would you allow me to come with you, when you go to visit your mother, I would love to see her again?"

"Of course, no problem. I could pick you up here at one o'clock."

“I don’t know what you have planned for tomorrow evening, but if you wish we could have dinner here in the hotel restaurant” Bronwen said tentatively.

“That would be very, nice. I shall look forward to it,” he replied. “It will be lovely to have the opportunity to catch up.”

“I must go now. I shall book a table for seven thirty tomorrow evening if that is all right with you.”

“That will be fine, and I will pick you up here at one o’clock to go to the care home.”

When Bronwen left, Gwyn made another cup of coffee, and sat in the armchair, his mind a mixture of shock, and exhilaration that made him feel light, headed. The sort of feeling he remembered as a teenager when contemplating a date with the girl he had been fancying for weeks. Bronwen had been the love of his life, a love that he had thrown away through his own stupidity, and now she had chosen to come to see and talk with him. Not only that, she had asked to accompany him to see his mother and to have dinner with him.

Reality eventually took over as he sat in the chair, his cup now drained of coffee. She had been friendly and had expressed regret at the way they had parted, but that didn’t mean that she still had the feelings for him that once she had. She had married that fellow Jenkins, and although that marriage had ended in divorce, it was an event in her life, after himself. Gwyn was now beginning to experience a feeling of deflation.

As Bronwen closed the door to his room behind her and began walking along the corridor towards the lifts, she was also suffering from mixed feelings. She had almost turned back, before knocking on his door, such were her feelings of trepidation, the uncertainty of his reaction towards her. As far as she knew, Gwyn had not had another woman in his life since their break-up, but she had herself a feeling of guilt because of her interludes with Patrick Evans since her divorce. The relief she had felt by the way he had received her was almost overwhelming. She was so pleased that he had agreed to her accompanying him to see his mother and she also had that feeling of exhilaration at the thought of having dinner with him. Descending in the lift to the ground floor had the effect of bringing her mind down to earth. She told herself, not to get carried away on flights of fancy. Gwyn had made a new life for himself and had said as much. When he returned to Telford, he would probably forget all about her and that was that. She told herself to be realistic, to enjoy tomorrow and be prepared to say goodbye at the end of the day.

The morning once again dawned bright and clear, which Gwyn hoped was the herald of a wonderful day to come. He went down to breakfast at eight thirty and having enjoyed fruit juice and his favourite cereal, was indulging in a Full English, when to his surprise and delight Bronwen came to his table, a small one in one corner of the restaurant. "I have to come to say good morning," giving him the most alluring and friendly smile that she could muster. She still felt tense, waiting for his reaction. She need not have worried, because his face lit up as soon as she spoke.

"Good morning. It's wonderful to see you," he replied. "It is a lovely morning out there, the herald I think of a lovely day to come."

They mutually relaxed, tensions and trepidation on both of their parts, now dispelled. There was something there between them, that still remained, from those halcyon days of long ago, when, in their minds, all the world was young.

The visit to the factory was a happy reunion with old friends. Gwyn and the senior production foreman had always been good friends. Glyn, or Taff as he was often referred to, had been upset, when Gwyn and Bronwen had split up. He was surprised beyond belief when Bronwen had married Hugh Jenkins and when they had divorced, he had said that it was inevitable in his opinion. He was amazed and disappointed when his sister had told him about the affair with Patrick Evans and didn't hesitate to let Mr John know about Evans and his PA. However, he would never tell Gwyn, something to forget, in the hope that one day the right outcome would prevail.

Late morning, Gwyn had gone to visit John Williams who was absolutely delighted to see him. They talked of old times and John wanted to know all about the progress of the new Supa Board development, which had meant so much to him in the old days. He tentatively asked if Gwyn had seen Bronwen in the hotel and was visibly pleased by what Gwyn had told him, especially that she was going to see Gwyn's mother and then have dinner with him later.

Bronwen was waiting at the hotel main entrance when Gwyn arrived. Dressed in a grey suit with a dark blue silk scarf and black moderate heeled shoes, to Gwyn, she looked like a million dollars turn out. Of course, he had always thought that about her, so this was no exception. Getting into the car, with a grace that was perpetually hers, reminded Gwyn of past times, times now long gone, but, he thought, no one can take away memories, other than the destructive sickness that had now afflicted his mother.

Entering the care home, they went to the lounge area, where most of the residents were sitting, having finished their lunch. As they approached his mother, Gwyn could tell that she had not recognised him.

"Hello, Mam. It's me Gwyn. I am here again."

Suddenly recognition dawned and she said, "Gwyn, how good to see you. It has been such a long time."

"I was here yesterday, don't you remember?" he asked, knowing that she didn't remember anything of yesterday.

"I must have forgotten. I sleep so much these days."

"Bronwen has come to see you. You remember Bronwen surely," he said but not having much hope that she would remember.

Bronwen had been standing next to Gwyn during the opening dialogue trying to come to terms with the situation and to put the person, now sitting before them, in place of the lady she had known so well, a few years past.

His mother looked at Bronwen for what seemed to be ages, then quite suddenly she said, "Oh, Bronwen, how lovely to see you and thank you so much for coming to see me. You are getting married soon, or are you already married, I am getting so forgetful these days."

"There is no date fixed, Mam," Gwyn said, taking her fragile hand in his and looking quickly at Bronwen as he did so.

Bronwen just looked at him, without speaking, tears streaming down her face. Gwyn put his hand gently on her arm with just the slightest suggestion of a squeeze. Bronwen immediately put her hand on his in recognition of his suggested movement of comfort. Then, with the greatest of effort to avoid breaking down completely, she asked if they would excuse her for a few moments, as she walked away to the doorway into the large entrance hall.

“Is Bronwen all right?” then, “I think that you should go to her.”

Gwyn left his mother and followed Bronwen into the hall. She was sitting on a chair and looked up as he approached. There were tears, still on her face of which she seemed unaware. Taking out of his jacket pocket, a clean handkerchief, he began to wipe her face and realising what he was doing, she took the handkerchief from him and completed the job herself.

“I am so sorry, Gwyn, I have let you down and I shouldn’t have come today.”

“Nonsense,” he replied, “You have not let me down in any way. I am so happy that you are here with me.”

“Do you really mean that?” she asked, hardly able to believe what he was saying.

“Of course, I do. I would not say it if I didn’t mean it. Then, taking her hand he said, “Let us go back to, Mam.”

“I am glad you have come back. Before you went out, I remember asking when you are getting married. I must know in good time because I need to buy a new wedding outfit.”

“I told you, Mam, that there is no date,” and catching Bronwen’s eye, Gwyn could see tears welling up again.

Gwyn managed to change the subject by talking about his mum and how well she was getting along in her new surroundings, being waited on hand and foot. The memory of him and Bronwen about to be married, gone from her mind completely. Not so with Bronwen. It was that question, when were they getting married, that had finally brought her into tears. Gwyn was aware of that and wondered just what those tears really signalled.

That evening, taking their seats at the table reserved for them, a waitress came over to them with the wine list. “Good evening, Ma’am, Sir,” she said, addressing them both with a warm smile. She liked Bronwen, as did all the staff. Everyone’s opinion was that she was a good boss, kind, considerate and fair in her dealings with them all. There were, however, those who could not understand her apparent attraction to Patrick Evans. Staff members’ opinions of him was divided. His suave manner certainly appealed to some, but there were others who regarded it to be false and that as a person, he was not as trustworthy as he portended to be.

For Bronwen to be having dinner with someone else, other than Patrick Evans, gave the staff something to talk about and to speculate on. Generally, the opinion they had of Gwyn Thomas was that he was a gentleman of taste, kind and without being a show-off in any way. A much nicer dinner companion for Bronwen than Mr Evans, was the thought of some.

It was obvious that Bronwen and Gwyn Thomas were well acquainted with each other and most of the staff who saw them together, wondered why they had never seen them together before now. His accent was proof that he was local, so where had he been hiding? Such was the chit-chat, that one might describe as domestic gossip.

Bronwen and Gwyn, were of course quite oblivious to it all. She wondered what Gwyn had really thought of her demeanour at the care home, and still felt embarrassed.

"Gwyn, I am so sorry for blubbing the way that I did this afternoon. I just couldn't help myself."

"There is nothing to be sorry about. Please don't think about it any more," Gwyn replied, giving her a comforting smile and at the same time, reaching across the table and putting his hand on hers in reassurance. At that very moment, the waitress brought the wine that Gwyn had ordered and poured a taster for his approval, simultaneously noticing, what she would describe as, the affectionate gesture of his hand on hers. Something to tell the others.

"It was seeing your mother like that, so frail now, unbelievably different to how I remember her. When she asked when we were getting married, I was choked. She had no memory whatsoever of us splitting up."

"Perhaps it is just as well that she has no memory of that. All I could think of saying was that there was no date for the wedding. If she remembers any of that again, hopefully it will be a memory of expectation."

"Yes," Bronwen replied, "hopefully."

They chatted on during the rest of the meal and having finished dessert, Gwyn topped up their glasses, then sitting back he said, "thank you not only for a lovely evening, but for a lovely day."

Bronwen didn't reply immediately but fell into silence. Gwyn felt his heart sink. He had no doubt said the wrong thing, implying that it was her presence that had been the catalyst for his 'lovely day'. Lifting her gaze from the glass in front of her, gently turning it by the stem with delicate and well, manicured fingers, she looked at him directly, with a serious expression on her face.

"I have a confession to make," she said without preamble.

Gwyn's heart sank even further. She was going to tell him that it had not been so enjoyable for her, especially when his mother had talked about wedding dates. The turmoil in his mind was suddenly stayed as she spoke again.

"I have had an affair with your boss, Patrick Evans. He comes down here about once a month and when he does, I have been with him. We always had dinner, like we have just had. But it is now all over and done with. I now know that he is having an affair with his PA and it has been going on for a long while. He told me that his marriage was over and that a divorce was imminent. I foolishly believed him. I had to tell you before either of us says any more of today. If you get up from the table, say good night and walk away, I shall fully understand and will not blame you for one moment. There, I have said it all," still looking at him directly, tears once again beginning to well up in her eyes.

"Bronwen, my love, you have nothing to be sorry about. You went with your heart, and there is no problem with that. That he is a philanderer and not worthy of you, is his fault not yours. But you now know what kind of man he is and have done something about it. Good for you. As for me walking away from you, all I can say is that I have done that once before but never again."

"Thank you," was all that she could manage to say, the tears were now running down her face. Taking a small handkerchief from her bag she wiped her eyes and face, then, "sorry."

Once again, Gwyn put his hand on hers, assuring her that all was well, his heart had now lifted figuratively to the heights beyond his imagination.

"Do you think that there is a chance to…" Bronwen said, tentatively.

"To begin again, yes of that I am quite certain, if you are too," he said, before she could finish her question. Fortunately, he was correct in assuming what she was about to ask.

23

DI Bob Grant had been perusing the notes taken during the recent interviews and reviewing the facts that they had so far established. The salient fact was, that 'bloody woman', so far unidentified by any of the investigating team, was without doubt the spy, or mole whichever term to be used, was installed at Salopian Industries. It was now certain that she had a male accomplice and a possibility that there were two male accomplices. The staff questioned, regarding their whereabouts at the times of the killings of Sophie Langford and Vic Eardley, all had suitable alibies with only one being tenuous. That being the alibi of Eddie Harper, who claimed to have been fishing at the time of both of those murders in Liverpool. Tenuous because there was no one to verify his claim.

The DI thought more deeply about the claim of DC Jane Todd, that of almost colliding with a man and woman as they came out of the churchyard in Wrockwardine Wood and later recognising him as Eddie Harper, although he denied being there at the time. Todd had established the whereabouts of Harper's grandparent's grave, and on examination had found that fresh flowers had, very recently, been put into the flower pot, something that by the appearance of the pot and memorial stone, didn't happen on a regular basis. Regarding the woman who was with him, the description given by DC Todd bore a strong similarity to one of the women working in the Development Department, namely, Lucy Thompson. The woman in question, having dark shoulder length hair, was wearing an expensive leather jacket with a distinctive red silk or chiffon scarf around her neck and had on a pair of large framed sunglasses.

"DC Todd, a moment please," he called, hailing her from across the room.

Jane Todd, arriving at his desk, "Sir, you wanted me?"

Still thumbing through the various reports and statements, "Toddy, I want you to ask that fellow at Salopian, the photographer chap, to borrow the memory card that has the photos taken at that Christmas do.

I have had an idea. I will get our photographic people to take one that has Lucy Thompson on it, and superimpose a black jacket, red scarf and add some sunglasses. You can then see just how closely that resembles the woman that you saw with the man you say was Eddie Harper.

Adrian Hopkins was only too willing to assist the police by lending the memory card to them. DI Grant selected the photo best suited for his purpose from the prints that he already had in the file and explained to the photographic people what it was that he required.

"I don't know how you will do it, but I am sure that you will find a way," he said, looking at the expert with hopeful enthusiasm, giving him the memory card.

"Our pictures taken at Scene of Crime, are as accurate as they can possibly be, but these days digital photos can be doctored as required. The old adage, that photographs never lie, is the biggest lie ever uttered," and with a grin, "leave it with us and we will do our best."

The result achieved was better than the DI had expected. The image of Lucy Thompson with dark shoulder length hair, now showed her dressed in a black jacket, a red scarf around her neck and she was sporting a pair of large framed sunglasses, as DC Todd had described.

"Perfect," said Jane Todd, "that is the person that I remember."

"I will ask just one question," DI Grant said, "can you, from that image, positively identify that person as being Lucy Thompson?"

The person in the photograph certainly bore a general resemblance to Lucy, but DC Todd had to say that a positive identification could not be made.

"Why is that, do you think?" asked the DI.

Jane looked at him with a thoughtful expression before saying, "it almost looks like someone in disguise."

"Exactly. Whoever it was that you saw coming out of that churchyard was dressed like that, to avoid the possibility of being recognised should she be seen by anyone that knew her. The question one has to ask again, is, "whoever the woman is, why should she be in a churchyard in Wrockwardine Wood, and be with a man, who was, almost certainly, Eddie Harper?"

"Perhaps they were there not to put flowers on a grave but to meet in a place that would have few people about, if any at all. A meeting to make plans or decisions of future actions. Maybe they are beginning to become scared that the net is closing in on their covert activities."

"Toddy, you may well be right. Although Eddie Harper denies ever being there, I feel sure that your recognition of him is right and he is lying because he doesn't want to be linked to a woman whose identity he would have to disclose if questioned. To refuse to identify her would be tantamount to admitting guilt. I think that we should leave him alone for a while but concentrate on Lucy Thompson. Let us squeeze her until the pips pop. She could well be the unknown woman."

DC Jane Todd couldn't help laughing at Grant's expression of popping pips. "If she is the one, then it is almost certain that Eddie Harper is the male accomplice. If we can break her down, then I think that it would be relatively easy to break him."

"The one concern that I have, is that Lucy Thompson is the wife of PC Gavin Thompson. He is a very, good officer, honest, pleasant and sociable. In whatever way that we may decide to tackle Lucy, there could be repercussions, and so before we go any further, I shall speak with the Super. And ask for his direction.

The detective chief superintendent listened carefully to DI Bob Grant, as he explained the situation as it was at the present time. He understood, perfectly, the dilemma that faced DI Grant and agreed that the outcome of putting Lucy Thompson under further questioning could well reveal marital infidelity and covert activity that would impact directly on PC Gavin Thompson. Of course, that should not, or indeed must not prevent the necessary investigative questioning.

"Continue with questioning Lucy Thompson," was the DCS's recommendation. "If she has nothing to hide, she will probably tell her husband, PC Thompson all about it. We can always ask Thompson if his wife has mentioned the goings-on at the factory in a casual conversational way. If she has, then in all probability she is not involved in any way. Otherwise, she should be regarded as a suspect. In which case she could be brought in for questioning under caution."

Lucy Thompson was surprised by yet another visit by the police to her department. She was beginning to feel nervous when she was singled out for further questioning, this time by DI Bob Grant with DC Jane Todd in attendance to take notes.

Without preamble, DI Grant said, "I want to confirm that your name is Mrs Lucy Thompson," his manner as formal as he could possibly make it. This was the beginning of making her pips pop as he had previously expressed his intention.

"Yes, that is correct," Lucy confirmed.

"I understand that your husband is a police officer stationed at our Divisional Headquarters. Would you please confirm that is correct?"

"Yes, his name is Gavin Thompson," she said, a slight tremor now noticeable in her voice.

Keeping up the formality in his attitude he said, "we have a witness that believes that you were in Wrockwardine Wood in the company of Eddie Harper and had attended the grave of his grandparents. I would like you to tell me why you were with Eddie Harper on that occasion."

"That is not true. I haven't visited Wrockwardine Wood with Eddie Harper, let alone his grandparents grave. Whoever your witness is, they are lying."

"Mrs Thompson, I believe that you are having an affair with Eddie Harper. Sian Gilmore, Eddie's partner found out and that is why they split up. Isn't that the truth? If you deny that, how do you explain not only your perfume being on his jacket but traces of your lipstick being on his collar. DNA these days is a wonderful science as I am sure you are aware."

Lucy was totally crestfallen. Her confident attitude had gone and that original defiant expression she had exhibited was replaced by a look of desperation and fear. There were tears in her eyes and were the representation of her figurative pips being popped.

"I admit that I did have a little fling with Eddie, but that is all over now. It was nothing serious on either of our parts. It was for me a bit of excitement. I think that it was the same for him. But things became complicated and when his partner accused him of having an affair, there was a big row, which turned to violence. Eddie hit Sian, and that was that. She left him, went back to her parents and would have nothing more to do with him. Our fling ended at the same time. I knew it was wrong and learning of him hitting Sian, brought me to my senses. I swear that I was not in Wrockwardine Wood with him at any time. Whoever your witness saw, it was not me. Inspector, can I please ask you not to tell my husband. I love him and it would break his heart."

"Mrs Thompson, I cannot make promises, but I will try to do as you ask. Thank you for your admission and for your assistance in our enquiries. As you are well, aware, we are investigating triple murders, that we believe are all connected to a well-organised plan of corporate espionage within this company. Perhaps, you should tell your husband, that you have been questioned and that you have been assisting us in our enquiries. Just a suggestion."

On their way back to Headquarters, Jane said, "that certainly made her pips pop Sir," unable to prevent herself from laughing. That expression had tickled her sense of humour. "I didn't know that we had DNA evidence linking her to Eddie Harper."

"We don't but she didn't know that. In fact, I reminded her that DNA was a wonderful science. I didn't say that we had any DNA evidence. She fell into the trap because of her guilt. Had she been innocent, such a statement would have been nothing more than a chance remark."

Breaking down Lucy Thompson was one hurdle out of the way, but it had not helped in identifying the woman behind this sorry affair. It seemed to the investigating team that for every step that they made forward they made two back. Every answer that they gained prompted yet more questions to be answered. The suspicion that Eddie Harper was the male accomplice must be either confirmed or proved to be false. But this was extremely difficult to do, because this man was like a slippery eel, wriggling out of one's grasp.

It was assumed that Sophie Langford's laptop had been taken by the woman portending to be a police officer and that she was killed by a man later in the morning. Again, that was also an assumption, because there was no evidence that a man had been there. It was an assumption based on the similarity of the killing to that of Vic Eardley which was almost certainly the work of a man because of the physical strength needed to drag the body a considerable distance in very quick time. If the killing of Sophie was the work of a man, could he have been the one that had taken the laptop? But should that be the case, what was the purpose of the visit of the bogus police officer. If Eddie Harper was the guilty one, and he had taken the laptop, it was possible that he had it at his place of residence.

With all these possibilities considered, DCI Davies made the decision to make application for a search warrant of Eddie Harper's residence. If the laptop, was found there, they would be in a position, to charge Harper with the murder of both those victims and almost certainly he would then reveal the identity of the unknown woman. It was also possible that there would be evidence to link him and whoever the woman was to the corporate espionage, the very root of the case.

At seven thirty in the morning, Eddie Harper was making toast in the kitchen which was to be a quick breakfast before leaving for work. He was not in the best of humour because of a phone call he had received the previous evening. The woman's voice that he recognised instantly, told him that all activity must cease immediately and not to contact her under any circumstances. When the time was right, she would contact him. She made it quite clear to him, with language that was unbecoming of any woman, that the potential trouble that now faced them both, was entirely due to him and his bloody stupidity.

He had just taken a bite of the toast he was holding in one hand as he poured boiling water from the kettle, onto the tea bag in his beaker when there was a ring of the doorbell. He was very, surprised, because he rarely had callers at this early hour. Putting down both the kettle and toast he opened the door and was immediately shocked. Standing there was DCI Davies accompanied by DS Robb and two uniformed officers.

"Good morning Mr Harper, I have a warrant to search these premises. Please remain in the property because, in due course, I shall need to speak with you," the DCI said, offering the warrant to Harper.

"But I am due in work at half past eight," Eddie said, as the DCI and the other officers made their entrance.

"Call your work and tell them that you are engaged at the moment, helping the police with their enquiries," the DCI told him.

The officers began the painstaking search, leaving nothing uninspected. In a cupboard among various papers DS Robb found a drawing with the title block bearing the name of Salopian Industries Limited.

"Sir, look what we have here," said Robb hailing the DCI.

The DCI seeing the title 'Control circuit arrangement — Supa Board Plant', said to Harper, "Mr Harper can you explain the reason for this drawing to be in your possession."

"I have it because I am instituting something similar at the foundry and wanted to compare my principles with those of company engineering," was Eddie's glib reply.

"Do the people in company engineering know that you have this drawing?" Davies asked, suspecting that they didn't.

"No, I asked Lucy Thompson to get it for me without anybody knowing about it."

"When was this?" the DCI pressed.

"About a couple of weeks ago."

DCI Davies remembered that Lucy had told them that she had ended their relationship when Sian Gilmore had left him. It was in Davies's opinion, highly unlikely that Lucy Thompson would have obliged him, knowing the risk she would be taking in doing so. Taking DS Robb aside, he asked him to make a call to Lucy and ask when she had last supplied Harper with drawings and other information in connection with the Supa Board plant.

Robb, having made the call as requested told DCI Davies that Lucy had denied ever supplying him any information and certainly not drawings. For her, that would not have been possible because she would have needed to go into the Drawing Office, obtain the relevant disc and then operated the digital printer, a task she had no idea how to perform. That could only have been done when no one else was around. DCI Davies was quite satisfied with that testimony. It was as he had thought. Eddie Harper was lying again, to shield that unknown woman, for it was in all probability, she who had obtained the drawing and passed it to Eddie to send or take to Eco-Tech. in Liverpool. That of course was no longer possible because of the police investigation.

A call from one of the uniformed officers drew the attention of DCI Davies to the bedroom, where he had found in the bottom of an underwear drawer, a knife with a pointed end and one extremely sharp edge.

"Mr Harper, can you explain what this knife is doing under a pile of underclothes?" DCI Davies asked.

"It must have been there for a long time. I was unaware that it was there."

"Are you telling me that the lower layers of underclothes have been in that drawer, unused, for so long that you had forgotten putting a knife there?" Before Eddie Harper could make any reply, he said to DS Robb, "bag it," then to Harper, "it is a bloody strange place to keep a knife."

Not only was the flat being searched but also Eddie's car. The constable performing the task found in the glove compartment, a pair of driving gloves that were stained and showed some attempt of being cleaned in some manner. It was the opinion of the DCI, that the staining could well be blood and that although an attempt had been made to clean them, in all probability there would be sufficient forensic evidence to link them, and consequently Eddie Harper to the Liverpool murders. Speaking with DS Robb, he believed that they had enough evidence to charge him.

"Edward Robert Harper," the DCI began, "I am arresting you on suspicion of the murders of Sophie Langford and Victor Eardley. You don't have to say anything, but it may harm your defence if you don't mention, when questioned something which you later may rely on in court." Then to the two uniformed officers, "take him away."

On returning to Divisional Headquarters, DCI Davies put through a call to speak with DCS Stuart in Liverpool. He explained how with a search warrant for the residence of Eddie Harper, they had found evidence of the espionage that they had suspected, but also a knife and driving gloves suspiciously stained both of which were being examined by forensics. Harper's car was also being examined by forensics. The DCI said that Harper had been arrested on the suspicion of the murders of Sophie Langford and Victor Eardley and thought that the presence of DI Ken Abbott may be desirable. DCS Stuart agreed and said that DI Abbott would attend.

Edward Robert Harper, along with an appointed solicitor, sat in the interview room awaiting the arrival of DCI Harry Davies. Harper's solicitor had listened to what Eddie had to say and questioned him about the knife, found in such an unusual place as underneath a pile of underwear. Eddie claimed that he had forgotten about the knife and couldn't remember ever putting it there. He was asked by his solicitor, who else could have put it where it was found, without his knowledge. Without hesitation, he said that it must have been his ex-partner, Sian Gilmore.

He then told his solicitor that he had become afraid of Sian before the break-up. In his opinion she had become paranoid, accusing him of having an affair with another woman. He was, at that time, beginning to wonder if she was mentally unstable. The solicitor's next question concerned the driving gloves. Had he recently attempted to clean or wash them in any way and if so, for what reason. His answer was as glib as that regarding the knife. He had indeed tried to clean them by washing because he had accidentally cut his finger when doing a wheel change due to getting a puncture. The gloves also had some grease staining. He had thought that he should throw them away, but they were so comfortable, that he had decided to try to clean them up by putting them in the washing machine. The result was not perfect, but he thought it was passable. When asked about the drawing found in his possession, he reiterated what he had told DCI Davies.

"Mr Harper, you must be absolutely honest with me and you must tell me everything if I am to defend you in court. DCI Davies has told me that Lucy Thompson has denied giving you the drawing or any other information concerning her work at Salopian Industries."

"Then she is lying. She is probably afraid to admit it, especially with all this talk of espionage or something. It all sounds too cloak and dagger to me."

The solicitor looked at Eddie with a long penetrating gaze and said nothing for a couple of minutes, weighing up, in his mind, how much of what Eddie had told him was the actual truth and how much may be assigned to the realms of fiction. The solicitor knew from experience that DCI Harry Davies was a man that rarely made an arrest without good evidence to back up his case. This time, however, was different in that he had made the arrest without waiting for the forensic report on the knife and, also the driving gloves. There must be a degree of assumption and perhaps speculation by the DCI. Should the forensic report be negative on the knife and gloves, there would be no justification to detain the accused and he would be released.

Entering the interview room with DCI Davies was DC Jane Todd and DI Ken Abbott of the Liverpool force, who had driven down immediately that he had been told by DCS Stuart. He had arrived only twenty minutes earlier at four o'clock. The reason Davies had chosen DC Todd to sit in on the interrogation was because of her previous experience of questioning him, also her statement about seeing him in Wrockwardine Wood although he had denied that he had been there. The DCI had told them that he would lead but at any time they wished to ask a question to do so.

Putting his case file on the table, he took his seat as did DI Abbott and DC Todd. She then switched on the recorder.

"For the benefit of the tape, I am DCI Harry Davies and accompanying me is DI Abbott of Liverpool and DC Jane Todd. Mr Harper, the accused, is also present with his solicitor Mr Simon Ward. Mr Harper are you fully aware of the charges against you?"

"Yes Sir, I am," Eddie Harper replied with a confidence that he didn't feel but nevertheless, it made the DCI feel that this interrogation was not going to be easy.

"Have you anything that you wish to say?"

"Yes Sir, I deny the charges."

"Then explain the reason for a knife being found under underclothes in a drawer in your flat. A lethal weapon that you had concealed, obviously for it not to be easily found."

In confident manner, Eddie Harper reiterated what he had previously told his solicitor.

"Mr Harper, I saw you in Wrockwardine Wood, leaving the churchyard with a woman, in fact, I not only saw you, but we nearly collided. When I asked you about this at a later interview, you denied being there. Why did you make that denial?" asked DC Todd.

"Simply because I was not there. I told you that you were mistaken. I remember you saying that I must have a double," Eddie answered with a slight smirk on his face.

"What do you know about the corporate espionage at the premises of Salopian Industries?" DCI Davies asked.

"Nothing more than what I have learned through interviews and company gossip."

"Explain the reason you had in your possession a drawing of the new plant, which we know has been the target of espionage, initiated by a director of a competitor in Liverpool.

"I have already explained that it was to help me in my work at the foundry, which, may I remind you, is an associated company of Salopian."

"That drawing was from the offices of company engineering Division. Had you have asked for a copy would they have given you one?"

"No, that's why I asked Lucy Thompson to get it for me."

"Lucy Thompson denies having done so. She has stated that not only was she unable to get the information, she had no idea how to operate the digital printer. In any case you had that drawing illegally. That drawing was in your possession in order, for you to pass it on to the competitors. It had been given to you by a woman who we believe to be the spy. I also put it to you, that because the identity of the spy had been discovered by Sophie Langford, you murdered her to prevent her revealing what she knew. The Liverpool police, during their investigation into the woman's death, discovered the covert activity between a director of the competitive company, namely Victor Eardley and the spy at Salopian Industries. To prevent him making any revelations you murdered him in a similar manner to the killing of Sophie Langford."

"I deny everything that you have just said. I have murdered nobody, and I know nothing about any espionage," Eddie Harper protested. "You have no proof of any of this, you are using circumstantial evidence in an attempt to convict me."

"Mr Harper, we don't convict, we accuse. A jury in a court of law convicts by finding an accused person to be guilty. I shall now terminate this interview at eighteen fifty," the DCI said, noting the time on the wall clock. He and the other officers left the interview room.

After the interview with DI Grant and DC Todd, Lucy had thought very deeply about the DI suggesting she tell her husband. She realised that the possibility of the truth about her fling with Eddie Harper becoming known by him was very real. That was undoubtedly the reason that the DI had made that suggestion. Her mind was made up, she would tell Gavin everything. If he decided to divorce her on the grounds of her infidelity, she would accept it as the punishment for her own stupidity.

Lucy was very quiet throughout their evening meal. So much so, that Gavin asked what was troubling her.

"I have a confession to make. I have done something that I bitterly regret, and if you are unable to forgive me, I will understand. I will do whatever you wish but I want you to know that I love you and always have done. Whatever the outcome I will never stop loving you," Lucy, having gabbled this, sat, breathless due to stress. "I had a brief fling with Eddie Harper, the ex-rugby player. It didn't mean anything. It was pure stupidity." Lucy sat looking at Gavin with tears in her eyes, not daring to say more.

Gavin rose from the table, not speaking, and walked around to where Lucy was sitting. Standing behind her, he placed his hands on her shoulders. He felt her tense, then with just a slight squeeze with his fingers, he said, "I know," and after a pause that to Lucy seemed like an eternity, he continued. "I have known all along, and I know when it stopped. I didn't say anything because I hoped that you would one day decide to tell me. I still love you and we should now forget about it. Water under the bridge."

Lucy sprang up from her chair, almost knocking it over doing so, and turning to him, she flung her arms around him quietly saying, "thank you my darling, thank you. I am so sorry." Then she kissed him, a feeling of utter relief surging through her and an elation in her soul that surpassed anything that she had ever experienced before.

Back in the interview room, DCI Davies and DC Todd sat at the table facing Eddie Harper and his solicitor Simon Ward. Davies had in front of him the forensic report on the knife and on the driving gloves. Harper was beginning to feel more confident as he studied the DCI's expression whilst reading the report. DCI Davies was just looking through the papers noting certain aspects he felt were particularly important. He had read the report before coming into the interview room and was aware that it contained, for his purposes, good news and bad news.

"Mr Harper, this Forensic report states that there is nothing to link the knife and the driving gloves to the murders of either Sophie Langford or to Victor Eardley," the DCI said, looking sternly at Harper.

"I could have told you that without a forensic examination," was the terse reply.

"However, examination of your car, particularly, the glove compartment, has revealed traces of human blood. Those traces have been identified as belonging to Sophie Langford and Victor Eardley. The only possible way that those traces could have been in the glove compartment is from the knife or gloves, or both, having been put there immediately after the crimes were committed. Have you any comment to make on that conclusion?"

"I don't doubt the conclusion of the forensic report. However, that doesn't make me guilty. I have told you that I have killed nobody. Lucy and I were having an affair and she used my car on many occasions. She must be the one to have put the knife and gloves in the glove compartment. That being so, she must have been the one who committed the murders."

Simon Ward, the solicitor asked for an adjournment while he conferred with his client. This was granted by DCI Davies, who, along with DC Todd retired from the room.

The solicitor wanted to know the reason that Harper had not told him about his affair with Lucy Thompson earlier. "You should have told me about the affair. That fact may prove to be significant in your defence. I must know everything if I am to help you. You must realise that you are facing a charge of double murder and that if you were to be convicted of those crimes, the chance of you being an old man before ever leaving prison is a stark reality."

"I didn't think it relevant at the time. I didn't want to get Lucy involved but I now realise that she is the only person who could have committed those crimes and had the opportunity to clean the knife and put it where it was found," Harper said, in an effort to convince Simon Ward how innocent he was.

When they all reconvened, Simon Ward explained to the DCI, why his client had not previously revealed his relationship with Lucy, and that there was compelling evidence that Lucy Thompson had the opportunity to have committed both murders.

"Mr Harper, what motive would Lucy Thompson have had to have murdered those two victims?"

"The only reason that I can think of is that she is the spy at Salopian Industries, and she killed both to prevent them identifying her," was his reply.

"Such revelations need to be investigated as I am sure that you are aware. You will therefore be detained in custody while the necessary investigations are made." The interrogation terminated, the DCI and DC Todd left the room.

24

Friday morning, the last day of the working week, always held that pleasant feeling of expectation for Sharon Sumner. The anticipation of a little longer in bed, and a leisurely beginning of Saturday, a day when one can usually do the things that one chooses to do rather than having to do those daily tasks demanded of one's working life. She had arrived in the office at eight fifteen and was busying herself percolating coffee that Patrick liked at the start of his day.

Sharon glanced at the headlines of the local newspaper she had collected on her way into work and now lying half folded on her desk. The bold headlines read LOCAL MAN HELD ON SUSPICION OF DOUBLE MURDER. There followed an account of the arrest of local Telford resident, Mr Edward Robert Harper, an engineer at a local foundry, and who had been arrested on the suspicion of the murders of a woman and a man both of whom resided in Liverpool. He had been detained on the previous day, pending further investigation.

Sharon was still reading the account when Patrick Evans arrived in his office. Before pouring coffee, she went straightway into his office carrying the paper, which she placed on his desk, and in utter astonishment said, "Have you seen this?" an irrelevant comment to make as he had only just entered the office.

"Seen what, and a good morning to you."

"This report," she said indicating the bold headlines.

"Good God," he exclaimed in shock. "It would appear, that he is the male accomplice of the unknown spy in our midst. I have no doubt that we shall be having a visit from the police this morning. It may be necessary to rearrange my diary accordingly. If you have made coffee, I would love a cup right now." With that, he sat down and began reading the paper.

Saturday morning in Ironbridge was relatively quiet, with just a few people walking around. At eleven o'clock, the only people in Gilmore's bistro were the Gilmores. Sian was standing by the pay desk talking to her father when, with a ring of the bell actuated by the opening of the door, she turned to see who was entering. A woman of medium height, with dark shoulder length hair, wearing a black leather jacket, a red silk scarf around her neck and a pair of large framed sunglasses walked to a table by the window and took a seat. Although now indoors, she didn't remove the sunglasses.

The duty roster had remained unchanged since Sian had split up from Eddie Harper, and so at weekends, it was Sian's duty to act as waitress, while her mother was in the kitchen. But from six o'clock on Saturday evenings, Sian was free and a young woman from Buildwas took the role of waitress.

Sian walked over to where the woman who had just entered was sitting. "Good morning, what can I get for you?" Sian said, order book in hand and pen poised to take down the woman's requirements.

The woman, looking up from the menu she had been perusing, gave Sian a charming smile and asked for coffee latte and toast. Sian having gone to the kitchen to process the order, the woman gazed around the dining area, taking note and being impressed by the standard of decoration. The atmosphere was also notable for its freshness, without a trace of cooking smells, so often encountered in such establishments.

Sian served the coffee and toast and said 'enjoy', as she turned to return to the pay desk. She had only advanced a couple of steps when the woman addressed her.

"Am I correct in assuming that you are Sian Gilmore?"

Sian stopped abruptly, turned to face the woman who had asked the question. "Yes, I am Sian Gilmore. Do I know you?" she said, surprise and curiosity evident in her reply.

With a little laugh, the woman said, "Oh, no. I am sure you don't. Please if you are not too busy may I speak with you for a moment?" giving a charming smile.

Sian returned to the woman's table, curious to know how this person could possibly know her and why she wished to speak with her.

"Let me introduce myself, I am Annie Morten and I am a journalist working for the periodical, 'The Salopian Oracle'. The case reported in the newspaper yesterday, concerning a local man being charged with murdering two people in Liverpool is interesting. It aroused my curiosity and so I have been making enquiries into what I am sure is an interesting story. Certainly, a story that will interest our readers. Tell me Miss Gilmore, I am given to understand that you were at one time very, close with the accused, is that correct?"

"Who told you that?" Sian asked with suspicion evident in the tone of her reply.

"I am afraid that I cannot tell you that. We journalists never reveal the source of our information."

"Eddie Harper and I parted company six months ago and we have not been in touch since that time."

"Why did you split up, Sian. Ho, I am sorry, may I call you Sian?" she asked appealingly.

"That is a question that I am not going to answer. In fact, I am not going to answer any further questions that you may have." With that she turned away from the woman and returned to the pay desk at which moment four new customers entered and took a table at the other side of the room from where the so-called journalist was sitting. Sian went to them, once again, with order pad in one hand and pen poised for action in the other. Having taken their order, she crossed to the kitchen but noticed that the journalist woman had gone. Sian was immediately furious. The woman had left without paying. Sian gave the order of the new customers to her mother in the kitchen and told her everything about the questions the journalist woman had asked of her and that she had refused to answer.

"I don't understand how that woman could have known about my past association with Eddie Harper. Who she could have spoken with, so soon after the newspaper report, that would have known my history, and where I live and work, is mystifying and scaring, not only that, but she left without paying her bill."

"Ring the police station. Tell them what happened and that she left without paying."

Sian went to the pay desk to make the phone call. There on the counter was a ten-pound note and a written note that just said, 'Sian, thank you'.

The call was taken by the duty sergeant, who after listening to Sian's story asked her to hold and he would transfer the call to someone who would be able to deal with her.

It was DS Larry Robb who responded and having noted all the details that Sian had given him, told her that someone would be in touch later. Going to DI Grant, "Sir, I have just taken a very, interesting and curious call from a Sian Gilmore in Ironbridge. She is the daughter of the Gilmores who own the Bistro. He then described the visit of the journalist. Then while Sian was dealing with another customer, the woman left unseen by Sian, who at first, thought that she had gone without paying. But at the pay desk there was a ten-pound note with a written note saying, thank you. The most interesting thing is that Sian described the woman as being of medium height, about five foot six, with dark shoulder length hair and wearing a black leather jacket, a red scarf around her neck and a pair of large framed sunglasses, which she never removed."

"Bloody hell, that is the exact description that Toddy gave of the woman she said was with Eddie Harper as they left the churchyard in Wrockwardine Wood. The photo we had of Lucy Thompson, that we had doctored in accordance with that description is here." DI Grant picked up the said photo from his pending tray and they both stared at it. "One thing that I am certain of is that, Annie Morten doesn't exist and neither does the Salopian Oracle. Check that out Robb. That woman I am sure is the unknown woman we have been chasing our tails to identify. The woman responsible for the espionage and highly likely the murders. Eddie Harper might be the one who perpetrated the crimes, but that woman is behind it all. There is one other fact to bear in mind, Eddie Harper didn't kill Danny Drew, neither was he involved. He was not on the premises of Salopian the day that Danny was killed. That killing I am sure was down to the unknown woman, and perhaps, a male accomplice." He sat and pondered for a few minutes. The big question uppermost in his mind being the purpose of her visit to Sian Gilmore. What, did she hope to confirm or to discover from her conversation with Sian. Obviously, it was directly connected with Eddie Harper. Maybe, she wanted to know what, if anything he had said to Sian that could potentially be a risk to her anonymity. If there was something that threatened her, she would no doubt take action to eliminate that threat as soon as possible. This woman was dangerous, cold and calculating. Sian had refused to answer her questions and so it was possible that to be on the safe side, the woman would attempt to silence her in whatever way she felt appropriate. Sian's life could be in danger.

Staring long and hard at the doctored photo of Lucy Thompson, DI Grant wondered if they had made the right decision to eliminate her as a suspect of being the unknown woman. Whoever she was, she was devious, calculating, and he believed, vicious. He made the decision to visit Sian in Ironbridge, taking DC Jane Todd with him. This time they would make a display of their visit. They would go in a squad car, highly visible and perhaps they might use the blues and twos just before arrival to advertise the fact. If anyone was keeping the bistro under surveillance, police presence might just dissuade them from taking any specific action against Sian.

There were a dozen or more startled pedestrians in the vicinity of the bistro when, with the noise of the blues and twos, echoing around the area, DI Bob Grant arrived outside the bistro accompanied by DC Jane Todd. Not only were the pedestrians outside startled, so were the customers inside. Being lunchtime, almost all the tables were occupied and as the two plain clothes officers entered, all eyes were directed towards them, the diners in various stages of mastication, just staring and wondering who had committed what offence.

Sian recognised DC Todd immediately, from the recent interview. With a friendly smile, the officers shook hands with her, and Sian invited them into a small office at the back of the building. The diners, realising that there would be no further drama, reverted their attention back to the meal before them.

Sian explained the sequence of events earlier in the morning and again gave a full description of the so-called journalist, which tallied with the description of the woman seen by DC Todd. It was while Sian was expanding on the general attitude of the woman and how she had left the bistro unseen by her, and then finding on the pay desk a ten-pound note and a handwritten note just saying, 'thank you' that DI Grant's mobile rang. He listened for a few minutes then thanking the caller, switched off.

"That was DS Robb. He has checked and found that there is no such periodical as the Salopian Oracle and so there is no such journalist as Annie, whatever name she gave. A total fabrication which I believe was an attempt to discover what, if anything, you Sian, know about the covert activities of Eddie Harper and his relationship with her. In other words, had there been too much pillow talk. She is, without doubt, the unknown woman that we are trying to identify. She is the mastermind behind the corporate espionage and undoubtedly has pulled the strings of Eddie." After a few moments of thought, the DI asked, "What did she order, to drink and eat?"

"Coffee latte and toast. Typical elevenses."

"For which, she left a ten-pound note and a thank you message. That was quite an expensive cup of coffee and toast. She left quickly and without speaking but ensuring that she paid, forfeiting the change due to her, rather than speak to you again. I think that there is a streak of honesty, somewhere in her character but she is up to her neck in possible trouble and is fully aware of that. She knows that Eddie Harper can and probably will, disclose her name. But how much that will be of use to us will depend on what name he knows her by."

Briefing was underway at Divisional police Headquarters and again DCI Harry Davies was emphasising the salient points that were known to them.

"Whoever the spy is, must have had connection with Vic Eardley in Liverpool. He was the man who instigated the espionage. So, let us take that fact one stage further. Did he recruit someone from his own region, or did he know someone from this area well enough to be persuaded to do the work. In either case, does that person work at the Salopian Industries factory, or did Eddie Harper have someone on the inside to obtain the information as required, then pass it on to the unidentified spy. Eddie Harper, an employee of the Salopian Group, is well-known, both in the company and of course generally because of his rugby career, so if he had an insider, it could be anybody."

"We do know that he was close to Lucy Thompson, they did have a fling, Sir," Larry Robb said. "I know that she was thought to be clear of suspicion but we are talking of covert activity and surely anyone involved in any way is going to give the most convincing performance that they possibly can to throw suspicion away from themselves. Eddie Harper said that it was she who had obtained the drawing that was found at his flat. He also suggested that she had done the killings. We believed that he was lying but let us not lose sight of the fact that he could be telling the truth, or at least, some of it."

"A good point, Robb. Let us look a little deeper into that possibility," said DCI Davies.

"I interviewed Lucy Thompson, and it was me that decided on her innocence," put in DI Bob Grant. "I'm still of that same opinion, but I accept that to look a little deeper would do no harm. My considered opinion is that we should look deeper into the backgrounds of people who to date have not been in the forefront of our investigation. Questions such as, how long a person has been employed and worked here? Where did they originally come from? We do know that there are a few members of staff that are not local people. There are some that we know are from Liverpool and though that doesn't make them guilty, it cannot be denied that anyone from Liverpool could have known Vic Eardley."

"You are quite right in what you say Grant. We have been chasing our tails far too long. Our opinion that the spy that we are looking for is a woman I am sure is correct. The evidence that we have indicates that fact. We have considered several women as possible suspects and have ruled them out for one reason or another. Perhaps we should rule them all in again and delve more thoroughly into their backgrounds. At this moment in time, we have Eddie Harper in custody, charged with the murders of Sophie Langford and Vic Eardley and I am sure that we have the right man, also that he is the male accomplice, but he didn't kill Danny Drew, the crime that started this investigation.

"It was our opinion, at that time, that a man had been involved in the incident and so when delving into the backgrounds of the women, let us look into the backgrounds of the men who could have been in on that killing and as being a second male accomplice."

"Another business meeting this evening, my love," had been the words Patrick Evans had said to his wife, on leaving for work on what was going to be, for her, yet another monotonous day and lonely evening. Amanda understood the reasons for these late homecomings, Patrick had explained to her that so much more could be achieved after normal working hours and away from the office, a fact that in, reality for him, was the absolute truth. He was under a great deal of strain these days, especially since all this terrible trouble had flared up. Goodness only knows what may be next. First, the talk of espionage then murders to contend with was almost more than anyone could stand. But she knew her Patrick, resolute, and determined to shine through all adversity.

Sharon tapped on the communicating door to Patrick Evans office, opened it and announced Detective chief Inspector Davies.

"Thank you, Sharon," then to the DCI, "would you like coffee or tea?"

"Tea would be most pleasant Mr Evans, thank you," the DCI replied.

Sharon having heard this, Evans just nodded to her and she withdrew to make tea. Busying herself, setting the tray, she was always most fastidious when doing this, she couldn't help but wonder what the chief Inspector was here to talk with Patrick about. Whatever, she thought, either time or Patrick would reveal all. Maybe this evening. She now looked forward to these evenings with almost the excitement of a teenager.

The tray now finally set with milk jug, sugar basin and cups and saucers, always cups and saucers and not mugs when taking in a tray with a teapot. A plate with an assortment of biscuits completed the arrangement. Sharon tapped on the door, entered and placed the tray on Patrick's desk. "Would you like me to pour or would you prefer to do it yourself, Mr Evans," she said, displaying her professionalism for the benefit of the chief inspector.

"Thank you, Sharon, I will pour myself," Patrick said by way of dismissal.

Patrick poured the tea, offered the plate of biscuits and sat back. "I presume you have come to bring me up to date with all that is happening. I was stunned to learn of the arrest of Eddie Harper. He is a well-known employee of the Group, and to think that he is capable of murder is almost beyond comprehension."

"Mr Evans, it is said that we are all capable of murder. It is just that some commit to it on the spur of the moment, due to pressure that overwhelms them. Often in the attempt of self- preservation. There are those, however, that commit murder by premeditation. They are the people that may be regarded as evil. Eddie Harper committed those crimes that he has now been charged with by premeditation. It will be the case of the prosecution that he travelled to Liverpool with the intention of killing both those victims. Premeditated murder, which will carry the maximum sentence. He has so far pleaded not guilty, but there is now forensic evidence linking him directly to both crimes."

"Is he responsible for the corporate espionage that we have been subjected to," Patrick asked, hoping that would be the case and that he would be able to report to Sir Ian that all was now under control.

"I wish that I could say yes to that question, but we still believe that there is a woman involved because of what the young lady who was murdered had revealed before her death. We don't know whether she is employed here or in one of your other associate companies, as was Eddie Harper, or if she is an outsider but with the ability to do the string-pulling of Harper and maybe another within this particular factory. We still believe that a man was involved in the murder of Danny Drew. If that theory is correct, that man must be employed in this factory."

"Have you any suspects, chief Inspector?" Evans asked.

"Not at this time. We have interviewed personnel in the various departments and have so far ruled them out of our enquiries, for one reason or another, but we shall look more deeply into the backgrounds of those that would be in a position to obtain sensitive technical information, in whatever department they are employed. Your help would be appreciated by giving us a list of staff who have been employed within the Group since Salopian Industries acquired Williams Brothers and the new product development that is the purpose of the covert activity."

"I will get the Personnel Department to get onto it right away."

"Might I suggest that you ask your human resources manager to do this, and to keep this approach confidential. To alert the culprit before we have the opportunity to follow this line of enquiry could be counterproductive."

"I understand exactly what you mean. I will do what you ask whilst you are here and can hear exactly what I say," said Patrick and he then rang the manager concerned.

Patrick Evans was once again at the home of Sharon, and having taken off his coat on entering, he took her into his arms and kissed her gently, then as he began to run his hands over her body and he could feel her eager response, his kisses became more passionate. Sharon broke away and taking his hand, pulled him to the stairs. They ascended quickly and once in her bedroom, they stripped and were quickly into the bed, where they were both transported to a realm of sensual pleasure.

Totally spent, they lay for a while quietly relaxing, the only sound being the ticking of Sharon's bedside clock which, to Patrick, seemed to be getting louder as the minutes passed by. It was beginning to irritate him but before he could voice his irritation, Sharon turned towards him, saying, "I thought we would have seen the last of that Detective Inspector, having arrested Eddie Harper. I was surprised to see him this morning."

"I must admit that I was a little surprised myself. They still believe that there is someone else involved, but they don't seem to be getting much information out of Harper. He is still denying the charges and was blaming Lucy Thompson which I think is highly unlikely, as do the police. They have found forensic evidence in his car that they believe will connect him to both murders in Liverpool. They also have evidence of his connection with the espionage business."

"What about poor Danny Drew. Have they any suspects for his death because that cannot be put down to Eddie Harper. He could not possibly have been in the factory."

"I think that they are still struggling with that problem,"

They lay there for a little longer until Sharon said that it was time to move, otherwise it would be time for him to leave before they had eaten. She quickly dressed and went downstairs to complete the final preparations before serving the casserole. Patrick quickly followed and sat down to enjoy the meal and wine with his gorgeous PA. How lucky he thought, to have chosen Sharon from all the other applicants for the position of PA. His only problem with her was her hints for them to be together permanently. He now, often wondered how much longer he would be able to put her off.

Detective Chief Inspector Davies, was browsing through the list of employees who had been engaged by Salopian Industries since acquiring the company of Williams Brothers. There were a couple in Shepherdson Engineering, one in Crown Coachwork, none of which appeared to have any connection whatsoever with anyone in the Telford factory. There were however, seven names on the list for the Telford site. Four men and three women.

Frank Ebbs the company chief engineer, John Preston the design engineer, Gwyn Thomas the chemist in the Development Department and Rowan Chapman the deputy works engineer were the men listed. The women were Tamzin Littler, secretary for Frank Ebbs, Racheal Stubbs, secretary for Leslie Anderson and Sharon Sumner, PA for Patrick Evans. Looking at the names before him didn't inspire much hope in formulating a possible suspect.

His mind wandered back to the murders in Liverpool, both of which had identical characteristics and totally different to the killing of Danny Drew here in Telford. Two different perpetrators but connected by the espionage carried out at the instigation of Vic Eardley, himself being one of the murder victims. Eardley had given a cock and bull story of meeting a young woman who was at Haydock Park Racecourse on her own but DI Abbott, had discovered, when showing a photo of Vic Eardley to the Bookmakers at Haydock Park, that he had been seen with a woman much younger than him. Someone had said that she was the daughter of a former regular racegoer that had not been seen for a considerable time. It was thought that he had perhaps died. The DCI began to wonder whether that young woman was the person he had persuaded to obtain the technical information from Salopian Industries. Somehow, he needed to trace her, but where to start was a major problem. If she were the daughter of a regular racegoer, she would probably be known at racecourses other than Haydock Park. Doncaster or Chester could be possible venues where they may be remembered.

A talk with DCS Stuart in Liverpool was the DCI's next move. Maybe he would be able to arrange for the photograph of Vic Eardley to be shown to bookmakers and regular racegoers at Doncaster, whilst he himself could arrange for something similar at Chester. His idea was thought to be good in principle and so DCS Stuart agreed to set the wheels in motion at his end, leaving DCI Davies to do the same in Chester.

To deal with the Cheshire force was a new experience for Harry Davies. He was unsure how his request would be received, as there was nobody there of any rank, that he knew or had previously dealt with. He need not have worried. Having listened to DCI Davies' story, and how the people in Liverpool were cooperating, DCS Frodsham agreed that one of his officers would accompany an officer from Telford to question people at Chester Racecourse. He was of a similar opinion to that of Davies, that to identify the young lady with whom Vic Eardley had become friendly, may well identify the woman believed to be the perpetrator of the covert activity at Salopian Industries.

25

Confirmation of race meetings at Chester showed that there was activity Wednesday to Friday, inclusive and so DI Bob Grant went to Chester on Wednesday and with DS Zoe Ford, of the Cheshire force, set about the task of asking all the bookmakers if they recognised Vic Eardley from the photograph that they had. To trudge around at a race meeting, looking for what is tantamount to looking for a needle in a haystack, can be a tiring task. The two officers were beginning to feel that they were wasting their time when quite unexpectedly, one of the men at the tote claimed to recognise the person in the photo.

"Yeh, I know that fella," the man exclaimed. "Not seen 'im round lately."

"Do you know his name?" DI grant asked.

"Yeh, Vic Eardley. At one time he was a regular at meetings 'ere, though as I said, I 'avn't seen 'im for a while."

"Did he come alone, or did he have company?"

"Last few times as I remember, he 'ad a woman with 'im. Younger than 'im, a bit of all right she was. Vicki, I think he called her, but I don't remember her second name. I think she was the daughter of another old regular that I 'avn't seen for ages. I remember 'is name was Jimmie"

"I don't suppose you remember his second name," said DS Zoe Ford.

"No, sorry. I know that he often stayed at the Royal Alfred when there were meetings over a few days instead of driving back and forwards to Liverpool. That's where he came from. Somebody at the Royal Alfred might remember his name."

DI Grant and DS Ford, feeling the effect of walking round and round for what seemed like an eternity, decided to have a break and have a pot of tea from one of the catering stands.

There they relaxed with the cup that cheers and discussed the little bit of luck they had just had.

"I know where the Royal Alfred is and it's only a short walk from here," Zoe said. "Perhaps we should go there next, we may be onto a lucky break."

Entering the Royal Alfred Hotel, they went straight to the reception desk and DI Grant having introduced himself and DS Ford, asked to speak with the manager, who appeared quickly following the call put out by the receptionist. DI Grant explained that they were trying to identify a man of middle age and a younger woman believed to be his daughter who used to stay in the hotel when visiting the races.

"We get a lot of people staying here during race weeks. Have you no idea of their names?"

"We only have their first names, but not their surnames. We believe that the man's name was Jimmie and the woman's name was Vicki."

"Come into my office and I will check with some of the staff that may remember them. Have they, to your knowledge, stayed here recently?"

"I don't know, but I would hazard a guess that they have not been here for about a couple of years," was Grant's reply, as they were ushered into the manager's office.

"I will leave you and speak with some of the staff, meanwhile would you care for coffee?"

Thanking him for his kind offer, they sat, thankful to take the weight off their feet. A short time afterwards, a waitress came into the office with coffee and biscuits which they enjoyed at leisure and patiently waited for the manager to return, hopefully with some positive information. DS Zoe Ford was interested to listen to DI Grant as he explained the complex case that this had turned into. The thought of an unidentified woman, operating in the midst, of the investigation, being able to avoid detection was to Zoe, absolutely, fascinating. That not only was she the perpetrator of the espionage, but also the instigator of three murders was almost unbelievable.

"I think that the murders, which were not committed by her, happened outside her control. As I am sure that you know, we have made an arrest and charged a man for two murders in Liverpool. He is denying the charges, but forensic evidence I am sure will convict him. However, he is trying to blame someone else and we must investigate accordingly.

It is possible that he may divulge the name of the woman in time, but to do so now would negate his claim of innocence, so I think that if he is found guilty, he may give the name of the woman as a platform to launch an appeal. But I am sure that she will by then, have woven a shield of defence that will be hard to break.

"Do you think that this woman called Vicki is the unknown woman you are seeking?"

"It is highly likely. Vic Eardley, before his death, did infer, to his business partners, that a woman was involved but gave no further information. They were furious with him for bringing their company into what they considered to be disrepute. He claimed that he had not stolen sensitive information but had acquired commercial knowledge of a competitor's business strategy. The woman he had referred to, being the supplier."

The hotel manager returned with a waitress who, he said, remembered a middle-aged man and his daughter staying on many occasions during race weeks. She says that he was always generous with his tips.

DI Grant asked, "do you remember the man's name?"

"I am not a hundred percent certain, but I think it was Holden or Holding. I do remember he called the young woman Vicki. She was his daughter."

"Thank you very much, you have been most helpful," the DI said as she was leaving. Then to the manager, "would it be possible to look through back records of guests?"

"Yes, but we only keep records for three years, so if their stay was further back than that, the records would no longer exist," the manager said.

He accessed the registration records on the computer and scrolled back. At two and a half years previously, he suddenly stopped. There was a Mr James Holden, the address was West Derby, Liverpool. The booking was for two single rooms and was for two nights.

"Wonderful," exclaimed DI Grant. "I feel sure that this is the man we are looking to speak to." He thanked the manager for his invaluable help and for the coffee, and he and DS Ford, left the hotel.

A lengthy explanation of the discovery made in Chester by DI Grant was received with great interest by DCI Harry Davies, who, when he had all the facts, put in a call to DCS Stuart in Liverpool. DCI Davies gave him all the relevant information and asked if a check could be made at the West Derby address to see if James Holden still lived there and if they could find the location of his daughter, Vicki. It was promised that this would be done immediately, and they would call him in Telford with the results as soon as possible.

About forty minutes later, DCI Davies' phone rang. "Davies here." He listened intently to the caller, then giving his thanks, he put down the receiver. Disappointment showed on his face as plainly as one of the well-known posters displayed on almost every hoarding in the town. "Holden passed away about two years ago. The whereabouts of Vicki are unknown, but all is not lost. Apparently, Holden had three children, two daughters and a son. Vicki was the eldest. Our colleagues in Liverpool are trying to locate either the son or the other daughter, both it is thought are still living somewhere in Liverpool." It was now a waiting game, with no idea whatsoever how long it would be before one or both, of these people were located.

Forensic evidence found in the car belonging to Eddie Harper was twofold. There were three predominant but different sets of fingerprints, one set belonging to Harper, the other two having nothing on the database that corresponded. Examination of the glove compartment had revealed blood stains that were human but belonging to two separate people. They had been identified as Sophie Langford and Vic Eardley. These stains were probably from the knife, used in the attacks, which had been hastily put into the glove compartment when fleeing from the scene in haste. Harper was now saying that he was innocent, and that Lucy Thompson must have committed the crimes at times when she had used his car.

Following DCI Davis' opinion that Lucy Thompson should be interviewed again having heard DS Robb's reasons not to rule her out of suspicion, DS Robb went to interrogate, rather than speak with Lucy. He told her that Eddie Harper was denying the charges against him and blaming her for the crimes in Liverpool.

"Have you at any time driven Harper's car?" he asked her.

"A couple of times, to pick up something from the shops, but I have never driven to Liverpool in my life," she pleaded desperately. "I have already confessed to having had a fling with Eddie Harper, something I deeply regret. But as I have already told you, it ended six months ago. DI Grant, very wisely, suggested that I tell my husband and that I had been questioned in connection with the espionage here, together with the link to the murders in Liverpool. My husband told me that he knew about my dalliance with Eddie and that I had ended it six months ago. I have not been with Eddie Harper since and so could not have committed those killings. My husband has forgiven me, and I really thought that the whole sorry affair was closed." Lucy by this time was very, close to tears.

DS Robb had listened carefully as Lucy explained her situation, watching her general demeanour. He could see that she was becoming distressed, but he thought not from guilt but from a feeling of helplessness and was beginning to feel sorry for her. This was a young woman, who like so many, had made a mistake in life but had realised her own wrongdoing and not only put her life back in order, but had confessed her infidelity to her husband. That, Robb thought, took a lot of courage. "I am sure now that you are telling the truth and I am sorry that I have had to question you again. However, with Harper denying the charges and naming you as the possible perpetrator of the crimes, we must investigate and present evidence of your innocence to prevent any possibility of a miscarriage of justice. I suggest that you check your whereabouts at the times of both murders in Liverpool with verification and that will then eliminate you from the enquiry."

"I remember quite well where I was at the time that woman in Liverpool was killed. I was in Ludlow with Gavin, my husband. We were visiting an elderly aunt of his. We stayed at a hotel and there you will have the necessary verification if you speak to them. I was at home when the second murder took place, with my husband. I trust that his word as a serving police officer will be accepted."

"I am sure all will be satisfactory, so please don't worry." The DI was of the opinion that she was telling the truth. He would, as a matter of course check with the hotel in Ludlow and PC Gavin Thompson, her husband but he had no doubt that Lucy Thompson was finally off the hook. Now they were back to square one, still looking for a spy who was at least an accomplice to murder and believed to be a woman. She had been seen by DC Jane Todd, of that he was certain, but nevertheless, unidentifiable. She was without doubt, very resilient, with a controlling personality and audacious. If she was working as an outsider to the company, her method of obtaining the technical information from within was very sophisticated. If, however she was someone working within the company, her audacity was almost unbelievable. DS Robb's opinion was that she would be well-suited to work for either MI5 or MI6.

26

Bill Hammond, the technical director went to Leslie Anderson's office to have a talk with Leslie not only to enquire how he was getting along, but to speak of matters that were now giving him some concern.

Bill Hammond had always had the highest regard for Leslie Anderson. He was not happy with the board's decision to appoint Patrick Evans to the position of CEO. His preference was Leslie Anderson. He felt that Evans was a showman, with a glib and smooth tongue that could easily persuade people to believe that he was correct in his opinions and that his executive ability was of the highest calibre.

"Have you a few moments to spare, Leslie" he asked.

"Yes, of course I have Bill, please take a seat. Would you like coffee?"

"Leslie, what I would like is a cup of tea. We have so much coffee these days, that I fear that we are beginning to forget that we are traditionally a nation of tea drinkers," he replied with a smile. "Whether it's another bit of European influence, or because so many people visit places abroad these days, I am not sure. I like coffee, but there is nothing quite like a cup of tea."

"I couldn't agree more," Leslie replied, and with that he asked his secretary to do the honours.

Bill Hammond had made the decision to talk with Leslie because the company was at a stage of bringing the culmination of the development work into the real world of production on a commercial scale. Such a move was always critical in the progress of any company, large or small. It was Bill Hammond's opinion that someone with the right technical ability and, also the right commercial attitude was essential to be in control from day one. That person was, in this case, Leslie Anderson, but he had wondered for some time, how much longer Leslie Anderson would be with Salopian Industries. Bill Hammond could only imagine the degradation that must have been felt by Leslie, when Patrick Evans had founded the new Company Engineering Division and on the issue that it was a new department, Leslie Anderson would have to apply for the position of company chief engineer along with all other outside applicants. He was, at the time, convinced that Anderson would resign and leave the company, and he for one, would not have blamed him. It was blatantly obvious that the move by Evans was to give him the power of control over all engineering and development work on a Group basis. He would choose the new company chief engineer, over whom he would be able to impose control, and he would effectively have pushed Leslie Anderson out of his way. Evans had secretly detested Anderson because in the past, he could not have all his own way. With Anderson in the subordinate position of works engineer, he could control him by proxy, through the new company chief engineer.

Whether or not Leslie Anderson remained with the company, although to him of great importance, Bill Hammond was seriously concerned by another problem that involved the integrity of the present CEO, Patrick Evans. The worrying information he had recently learned was from John Williams in Cardiff. Since Salopian Industries had acquired Williams Brothers Limited, he had kept in touch with John Williams on a regular basis. He regarded the man as one of the most pleasant people he had ever met. A man of honour and a man of integrity. He was quite a good golfer too, that being the icing on the cake, having spent a few wonderful days in Cardiff with John on the golf course.

Whenever they met, they would go into detail about progress that was being made with the development of the new product, John listening avidly to everything that Bill Hammond could tell him as they progressed around the course. This was always much more than could be spoken of during the time of a normal telephone conversation. Initially, he had expressed regret that Leslie Anderson would not be leading the development, because during the latter stages of negotiations with Salopian Industries, Leslie had visited Cardiff several times with the then managing director. In John's opinion, Anderson had exhibited a remarkable grasp of what was required to bring the idea into a full-scale production unit that was financially viable. Not only that, but had in mind, the direction that engineering design work should take in order to achieve that goal.

He was surprised when it was announced that Patrick Evans was to take over as CEO, the modern name for managing director, but on meeting him, he considered him to be an affable man, a smooth-talker perhaps, but very much a get-up-and-go person. Someone who would push the development with purpose. His plan of forming a department, within the Salopian Group, to devote itself to all aspects of engineering and development, was in John Williams' opinion, one that would be beneficial not only to the company but also to the progress of development of the new product. He was astounded however, when it was announced that a new company chief engineer had been appointed and that Leslie Anderson had been moved sideways, with no input whatsoever to the development programme. This, John Williams regretted most sincerely, but during the following months he came to regard Patrick Evans as a person one could rely on, apparently a man that was honest and plainspoken to everyone.

During those early months, Patrick Evans spent a considerable length of time in Cardiff and it was then that Bronwen, John's daughter, recently divorced from Hugh Jenkins, renewed her acquaintance with Evans. Bronwen, being deputy manager of the Three Feathers Hotel, met Evans quite frequently, since he always stayed at that hotel when in Cardiff. Their friendship had made such a difference to Bronwen's mental state since the divorce. She was obviously happier than she had been for several years and much more outgoing. In truth, a return to normality, was John's opinion. He secretly wished that Patrick Evans was not a married man, because he felt that he and Bronwen, despite him being twelve years older than her, would have made a good couple.

The problem now concerning him was the information that John Williams had given to him on the previous day. Bill Hamond had bounced it around in his mind ever since, even during the night it had disturbed his sleep.

Sipping his tea, Bill Hammond looked steadily at Leslie Anderson, then put down his cup. "Leslie, how are you getting along now. To have had your assistant murdered here in the factory must have been a traumatic experience for you."

"It still troubles me. The whole episode is bizarre. Danny Drew murdered for no apparent reason was bad enough, but then to learn that the company has been subjected to espionage, followed by two more murders perpetrated, possibly, by an employee of this Group is almost beyond my comprehension."

The troubles of corporate espionage, and murder, was not what Bill Hammond wished to discuss, but his opening question had prompted that direction of conversation. He changed tack. "Is it your intention to remain here in the company or are you thinking of moving on?"

The question came as a shock to Leslie. What reason Bill Hammond had for asking in such a blunt manner, left him temporarily mystified. "I have no immediate plans to move, but I don't understand your reason for asking."

"To be frank with you, I would not be surprised if you did move. Your put-down by Patrick Evans must have humiliated you. It was my opinion then, that you would leave the company. I was surprised and thankful that you remained."

"The only thing that kept me here was the schooling of my two children. As teenagers, the disruption to their education would have been too much, because for me to have found a comparative job, would have required me to have moved a significant distance from here. Changing schools at such a critical time in their education, was in my opinion the worst possible thing for them to cope with. My decision was to swallow my pride and stay at least until they have completed their A levels, after which I shall be free to do whatever, I think best."

"I am so pleased, and I admit, relieved to hear you say that. The new Supa Board plant will in the near, future, be coming on stream. It will need the right technical oversight as well as the right commercial control and I want you Leslie to supply both those requirements. I am aware that it will put extra workload onto you, but you now have Rowan Chapman as your deputy, so I feel that you will be able to cope."

Leslie Anderson was silent for a few moments before making any comment. Those few moments gave Bill Hammond the feeling that his proposal was going to be rejected. It was a feeling that inwardly, he had expected. For anyone to have felt the degradation that Anderson must have felt when dealt with in the way that Patrick Evans had deliberately done, the urge to do something against the company would have been quite natural.

"If that is your wish, my answer is yes, I will do that. Had it been the request of Patrick, my answer would have been a resounding no."

"Thank you, Leslie. Please be assured that it is my wish and that Patrick has no knowledge of my intentions." A worrying thought however had come into Bill Hammond's mind. Leslie Anderson's obvious antagonism towards Evans was strong and unrelenting. Maybe time had turned that hostility to hatred. Could that be a catalyst for corporate espionage and for murder. Surely a person like Leslie Anderson would never kill anyone. But it is said that we are all capable of murder if pushed far enough. The police strongly believe that a woman is involved, but if Leslie is involved, who could his female accomplice be. He was brought back to reality by Leslie speaking.

"You do realise that Patrick is CEO, and as such could overrule you personally. He could do whatever, and put in place whoever he wishes unless it is a board decision."

"Yes, you are quite right, Leslie." He paused in thought. "That brings me to my second reason for me speaking to you this morning. I was speaking on the phone yesterday with John Williams in Cardiff. He told me that he has been informed, on good authority, that Patrick Evans is having an affair with his PA, an affair that has been going on for a considerable time. He also told me that Evans had become very close to his daughter Bronwen. He had told her that his marriage was on the rocks and that a divorce was imminent which as far as I know is not true. He always goes out of his way to give the impression that he and his wife Amanda are a devoted couple. John told Bronwen, who was absolutely furious, indicating that their association was more than just friendly. She has however met up again with the first love of her life and it would appear, that they are getting together again which pleases her father, because it is Gwyn Thomas, our chemist here in Telford."

Leslie Anderson was shocked with the revelation. "Evans is having an affair with his PA, Sharon Sumner?" He could hardly believe what he was hearing.

"I would hazard a guess that he has told Sharon the same story. His marriage is on the rocks and a divorce is imminent. His ability to persuade anyone to believe whatever he says by his smooth-talking, is the method by which he gets whatever he wishes."

"Does anyone else on the board know about it."

"Not yet, but it's only a matter of time. When Sir Ian hears about it, Patrick Evans is likely to be dismissed. Meanwhile keep this to yourself. Let us see how matters evolve."

27

Patrick Evans arrived at the Three Feathers Hotel at his usual time of four thirty which he knew would give him time to relax for a short time before Bronwen would come to him. He always liked to have that short time to himself before she arrived. It gave him the time to contemplate on the sensuality they mutually indulged in whenever she came to his room. She always tapped on the door, entered and before closing the door, put the 'Do Not Disturb' notice on the outside handle. Then when she came to him, they would embrace, his hands exploring her body until with an urgency that was sudden and deliberate, they would undress with great rapidity.

As was his normal sequence of moves, he made a coffee at the side table provided for the purpose and then sat in the easy chair to await for that knock on the door that excited him beyond measure. The minutes passed by, his coffee cup now empty, but still no knock on the door. He looked at his watch, five fifteen. What, he wondered was keeping her? Usually, she came about a quarter of an hour after his arrival.

On arrival, he had registered as usual, collected his room key and come up to his room. He had not booked a table for dinner because Bronwen always did that, arranging for a table for two in a corner of the restaurant that gave them a degree of privacy. Looking again at his watch, it was now six o'clock and still Bronwen had not appeared. This was most unusual. He picked up the phone and rang reception. "Can you tell me if Mrs Jenkins is off duty yet."

The receptionist, giving a grin and nod to her colleague, paused. "I am sorry, Mrs Jenkins is not on duty today. She has however booked a table for you in the restaurant for seven thirty."

"Thank you," he said, putting down the phone. He felt shocked. She had not called him to explain why she wasn't on duty. There was nothing to indicate to him whether, or not she would join him for dinner. This was most unusual.

Patrick went down for dinner at seven thirty. A waitress showed him to the table reserved for him. It was not in the usual corner but a little further into the room. The table was set for one.

It was obvious that Bronwen was not going to be with him. He would be dining alone, something he had not done for a considerable time. This was so unlike Bronwen. Whatever could be the reason for not being here as usual. Patrick's mind raced around and around. Not to be on duty when he arrived was something new. He could think of no logical explanation. No doubt she would be on duty tomorrow morning and would explain everything.

The meal satisfied his gastronomical needs but gave no pleasure whatsoever. He could not come to terms with Bronwen not being with him. He felt alone. Not a state of mind that he was accustomed to having. The poignant issue was not receiving an explanation or apology. The meal over, he made his way to the bar, ordered a double Highland Park single malt and found a seat in the lounge area. There his mind gradually smouldered to a state somewhere between disappointment and anger. Bloody women, he thought, unpredictable and selfish. They deserve to be treated in the same manner. To be flicked aside and made to realise that they could not treat a man in whatever manner they chose. He was slowly becoming maudlin, he realised. Pull yourself together he told himself. Tomorrow she would probably have a good explanation.

Thinking of tomorrow, a round of golf would be good in the afternoon. A call to John Williams was called for. Using his mobile, he made the call. "Good evening John, Patrick here. How about a round of golf tomorrow afternoon?"

"Sorry Patrick, I cannot play tomorrow, but I would like to see you. Perhaps you will be able to call on me at home."

"Yes, I will do that. Say about two o'clock."

"That will be fine. Good night." John Williams ended the call without further conversation.

Evans was taken aback by the curtness of the conversation. It was so unlike John to end a call so abruptly. He usually had a few snippets of news or gossip to chat about. Tomorrow would be a new day. Maybe things would be better than they appeared to be right now.

Breakfast was again a lonely experience. There was no sign of Bronwen, which was again unusual, because she was normally on duty early and would come to say good morning. Not a thing he could do about it. He decided to go to the factory of Williams Brothers early. Get the business side of the day over, have some lunch and then go to the home of John Williams. A pity that he was unable to play golf but no doubt he had a good reason and would explain when he saw him.

The morning passed surprisingly quickly. Everything was good, with no problems to deal with. His report to the board would be short and simple but positive in every way. He made his departure at midday and called for lunch at a small pub on the way to John's. He often used it because they offered one of the best mixed grills that he ever had, anywhere. That with a pint of the local bitter was perfect and all that Patrick desired at lunchtime.

When he arrived at John's, the greeting was courteous but strangely cool. Patrick was aware of a difference in John's attitude. His handshake was normal, his smile was normal but lacking the warmth that was part of John's character. Leading Patrick through to the lounge, John poured two drinks, handed one to Patrick and at the same time gesturing for him to take a seat. John sat in the chair opposite.

"You may be wondering why I have asked you to come here, rather than have a round of golf."

"The thought had occurred," Patrick replied, beginning to feel uneasy. There was undoubtedly something in John's demeanour that was distinctly unusual. His attitude was formal rather than friendly. This, Patrick had never experienced with John. Not even in the early days when they were just beginning to get to know each other.

"I will not prevaricate. I will come straight to the point. I have learned from a reliable source that you are having an affair with your PA. I believe that her name is Sharon. This I would not have expected to hear about you. I am also aware that you have been intimate with Bronwen, giving her the impression that your marriage is over, and a divorce is now imminent.

"That, I am informed, is not true. You always give Sir Ian the impression, that you and your wife, are a devoted couple because you know that he has strong opinions on family values."

"This is all rubbish, John. I have had dinner with my PA on a number of occasions, but not an affair." Patrick was trying his smooth, confident way that he usually used when trying to convince people what a genuine and upright person that he was. "I have never given your daughter the impression that there could ever be anything serious between us. We share a lovely friendship and enjoy each other's company which, I may add, I missed last night."

"You may deny this as much as you wish, but I know that what I am saying is the truth.

"The reason that you didn't have my daughter's company last night was because she has driven up to Telford." John recognised the anxiety now showing on Patrick's face. Fear that Bronwen was in Telford for a confrontation. That would be a disaster for him. He would be exposed as the philanderer that he was, not only to Sharon his PA, but to Sir Ian Leighton-Boyce and of course to his wife, Amanda.

"Why has Bronwen gone to Telford?" A question that he feared to hear the answer.

"She has gone to see Gwyn Thomas, your resident chemist."

"But for what reason does she want to see Gwyn Thomas?" He was now showing puzzlement, being unable think of a plausible reason for such a visit, but with a degree of relief that she hadn't gone for a confrontation.

John was beginning to enjoy the task of putting Patrick into a vulnerable position. To watch the changing facial expressions, going from a suave confidence through anxiety to fear. This man for whom he had developed a genuine liking and who he had secretly hoped that one day could be with Bronwen, was now just a contemptable being. He deserved to be treated as such. "Bronwen has gone to spend a couple of days with Gwyn, who for your information was the first love of her life about ten years ago. That was before she married Hugh Jenkins, another waste of space. She married him on the rebound after she and Gwyn foolishly split up. Thankfully, she and Gwyn are back together, hopefully for good."

"Oh, I see. Good for them." Patrick's suave and genial manner was gone and replaced by one of acceptance by inevitability. Comparable to a popped balloon, John thought.

"One more thing Patrick. Don't think for one moment of causing difficulties for Gwyn in the workplace because of this, for if you do, your indiscretions will be made public. That is not a threat. It is a promise. I can also tell you that all is already known by Bill Hammond, who I can assure you, is not pleased, not pleased at all."

For the first time in his life, Patrick Evans was nonplussed and uncertain of what lay ahead in the future. He was guilty of leading Sharon to believe that one day, when the time was right, he and she would be together. It was a ploy to keep their affair going and he had wondered many times how long she would accept this state-of-affairs. He had no intention of leaving Amanda. She was the bedrock of his respectability that could maintain the status that he now had. He was the CEO of Salopian Industries Limited, a position that gave him the power, but it was also a position which people looked up to. In olden days, a position to which the surfs would have touched their forelocks. A position of glory.

In Telford, Bronwen was already resident in the Queen's Arms Hotel. She had driven up from Cardiff on the same day that Patrick had gone in the opposite direction. She wondered what he would be thinking and if her father had spoken to him, which he had told her he was going to do. What his reaction would be, she could not imagine. Probably an attitude of denial, she thought, but her father would not let him off the hook, of that she was certain. She had herself been furious and hurt when she had learned about the affair with his PA. But on reflection, Bronwen admitted to herself that she should have had more sense than take his word that his marriage was finished and waiting for a divorce. He was a married man and she had fallen into the age-old trap of a philanderer. Caught on the rebound from her disastrous marriage to Hugh and inevitable divorce, that being a rebound from her split-up from Gwyn, the first and only love of her life. Bronwen accepted that her life had been a total mess until now, but she was now determined to change her ways and make sure that her reunion with Gwyn was going to be successful. She knew that Gwyn loved her and that she loved him and the words of the poet, Robert Browning came into her mind 'And God's in His Heaven and all's right with the world'.

This morning, Gwyn was taking her to Much Wenlock and then to see the Abbey. They would have lunch and then drive to Wenlock Edge. The weather was perfect, being sunny and clear. The view from Wenlock Edge, Gwyn had told her, was quite stunning. The steep drop away of the land from the Edge running out to rolling countryside as far as the eye can see is wonderful. Bronwen was looking forward to all this, the thoughts and feelings connected to Patrick Evans now but a memory.

28

In Telford, Leslie Anderson was thinking about the news of Patrick Evans and his affair with Sharon Sumner. In Leslie's opinion, Sharon was a much nicer person than Patrick. Whatever had persuaded her to get involved in a sexual relationship with her boss he could not imagine. It was a course of inevitable disaster. Knowing Evans as well as he did, Leslie thought that somehow, Evans would wriggle out of it and blame Sharon for talking with some of her colleagues and perhaps boasting of the familiarity they shared in private, and those boastings being exaggerated into common gossip. He would then use it as a reason to dismiss her, so getting her out of the way and discrediting her at the same time.

The news that Gwyn Thomas and Bronwen Jenkins were back together after so many years, which for Bronwen had been years of turmoil, pleased Leslie. However, the question uppermost in his mind was where would Gwyn be in the next twelve months? Would he go back to Cardiff to be with Bronwen, or would Bronwen come to Telford to be with Gwyn?

Bill Hammond had asked Leslie to take overall control of the new Supa Board plant when it came on stream and Leslie had agreed to do that, but he would need Gwyn to be in charge of the plant because of the chemical requirement in the process, with Rowan Chapman taking control of the engineering maintenance of the machinery and equipment of the plant. If Gwyn returned to Cardiff, life could become difficult and he, Leslie Anderson, would be required to sort it all out. Leslie wondered what he had let himself in for.

Bill Hammond pondered the problem of what to do about Patrick Evans. If he said nothing about the affair, and Sir Ian became aware of it and then discovered that he, his technical director, knew about it but had said nothing, there would be terrible trouble. On the other hand, to inform Sir Ian of what he knew would probably mean the dismissal of both Patrick Evans and Sharon Sumner, not that he would be troubled by seeing the back of Evans, but he would feel sorry for Sharon. He had always liked her because she was polite, sophisticated and there was no doubt that she was efficient. There was of course one other significant factor to consider. Patrick was a married man, so what would such a revelation do to the marriage. It could lead to divorce and he would not be comfortable with the knowledge that he had been the catalyst for the break-up.

An alternative would be to talk to Patrick privately. Tell him that it was only a matter of time before the fact of his affair with his PA became public knowledge and advise him to finish it and do whatever possible to cover up the matter. The more he thought about it, the more he thought this to be the better way forward.

Driving back from Cardiff, Patrick was in a mood that was sullen and distraught. Who, he wondered had discovered the truth about his relationship with Sharon and put the word out at Williams Brothers with the obvious purpose of informing Bronwen of his duplicity? The thought of her being with Gwyn Thomas infuriated him and filled him with jealousy but he was powerless to do anything about it. John Williams had, in no uncertain terms told him that if he did anything against Gwyn in an act of retribution, action would be taken. John had said that it was not a threat, it was a promise.

The only way to deal with the problem would be to tell Sharon that someone had discovered their secret and fight fire with fire. Come out and make it known, publicly, that there was someone making wicked statements that they were having an affair which was totally untrue. Perhaps before doing so, he should speak with Sir Ian, and tell him how upset he was that such lies were being told and Sharon was both bitterly upset and angry. With luck, they might convince enough people of their innocence and get away with it.

The only problem he could envisage to this strategy was Sharon's reaction. It was possible that she would want to come out in the open and say that it was not an affair but a genuine romance, and that it was their intention to marry once his divorce was granted. A divorce he had spoken of but with no intention of ever getting one. Maybe he would be able to persuade her that this was not the time for that course of action. It would cause more trouble than it was worth. There was the possibility that they would both be dismissed and that would be an absolute disaster. Hopefully, she would listen to him and agree to deal with it in his way.

***

In Merseyside, the problem that DI Ken Abbott had was tracing Vicki Holden. Her father, Jimmie Holden's last address, so far as they knew was in West Derby. Here, the DI learned that Jimmie Holden had passed away about a couple of years previously. The present occupants of the property had bought it, vacant possession, through an estate agent in the city. The property was sold on behalf of the late Mr Holden's children.

The DI visited the estate agent, requesting the names of the children and their addresses. Both the son and second daughter lived in West Derby so contacting them was easy. The home of the son, whose name was Keith, was a semi-detached property in a pleasant area.

A young woman in her late twenties answered the door to DI Abbott. She was well-dressed, her hair, the DI noticed, was immaculate, as though she had perhaps just returned from the hairdressers. Her left hand bore a wedding ring and an engagement ring, exhibiting three large diamonds arranged in a beautiful setting. The occupants were not poor.

"Good afternoon, I am Detective Inspector Abbott, may I speak with Mr Keith Holden?" He showed her his warrant card. "You are Mrs Holden?"

"Yes, I am Mrs Holden, please come in and I will fetch my husband." Leaving Abbott standing in the hall, she went off to find her husband, who, after a couple of minutes appeared from the back of the house.

"Good afternoon, Inspector. How, may I be of help?"

"I understand that you are the son of the late Mr Jimmie Holden and that you have two sisters."

"Yes, that is so. I have an elder sister, by the name of Vicki, and a younger sister named Sue."

"How old is your sister Vicki?"

"She is thirty-two and my sister Sue is twenty-six. What interest have you in my sisters?"

"We wish to speak with Vicki in the hope that she can help us with an ongoing enquiry."

"Neither my sister Sue or I have seen or heard from Vicki since Dad's funeral and I am afraid that I don't have her address. The last address that I have for her was in Sephton Park, but she told us that she was moving down South and would give us her address in due course. Unfortunately, she hasn't been in touch since."

"Do you have a telephone number or mobile number for her?" DI Abbott was beginning to clutch at straws.

"No, I am sorry."

"Thank you, Mr Holden for your help. If Vicki does get in touch, please tell her that we would like to speak with her as soon as possible." The DI's hopes had just evaporated.

We are back to square one was the only thought in DI Abbott's mind. The Telford people had managed to track down the name of a person who could, possibly be the 'unknown woman', traced her original address and now she had disappeared as quickly as a morning mist. Not even her brother and sister knew where she was. No doubt, Vicki was keeping her whereabouts secret for good reason.

DI Abbott called DI Grant in Telford to give him the latest news relating to the search for the elusive Vicki Holden who had disappeared without trace.

"I'm sorry that I cannot give you better news. Maybe if you could look for someone with the name Vicki Holden who has some connection to Salopian Industries, and moved into your area within the last couple of years, which I imagine sounds like a load of tripe to you." He gave a short laugh, emphasising his frustration.

"Ken, I thank you most sincerely for your painstaking efforts. I know how frustrated you must feel, but the feeling is exactly, the same here in Telford. Whoever this woman is, she is bloody good at covering her tracks. Vic Eardley certainly knew what he was doing when he got her to be his spy. One frustrating fact is that we don't know whether she is working from within the company or from the outside. Now that the spying activity has been revealed, she will no longer be operative which makes it more difficult to get a trace on her. Another view that we should not neglect is that she may not be known here as Vicki. She could be 'Bertha' or 'Dolly' or whatever bloody name you could think of."

"You are quite right Bob and all we can do is keep going and hope that she makes a slip somewhere along the line. We will keep on it at our end and if we find anything of interest, I will give you a call. 'Bye for now."

Mulling over all that he and DI Ken Abbott had discussed, DI Bob Grant began thinking of all the possibilities. They had questioned, exhaustively, the personnel within the company and other than Eddie Harper, now under arrest, they had been unable to site anyone as a prime suspect of being the 'unknown woman' or an accomplice. What to do next was the 'million- dollar question'.
Look for someone by the name of Vicki Holden, with a connection to Salopian Industries, having moved into the area within the last two years. The jovial suggestion, of DI Abbott, may not be the tripe that he had suggested. A check on all those registered to vote might be a first step. Scrutiny of the Electoral Roll, although large for an area such as Telford, would not be too exhausting, because only the entries of females, need be considered. It was not necessary to look at the full detail of each entry, just look for the name. If the name, Vicki Holden appeared, or possibly Victoria, only then would full detail of the entry be required. However, if no entry of that name be found, it would be a strong indication that the real Vicki Holden, was operating under a different name, a fact that may well be the case. DI Grant made the decision to get DC Jane Todd to make a start immediately.

***

The problem that concerned Bill Hammond was how best to approach Patrick Evans. He had pondered about this for the last twenty-four hours. Having now made up his mind, he went to Patrick's office via Sharon's adjacent office. Sharon was busy percolating coffee, as usual, first thing in the morning when Bill entered.

"Good morning Mr Hammond." She greeted him with a lovely warm smile.

"Good morning Sharon. Is he in yet?"

"Yes, do go through."

Bill Hammond went into Patrick's office, approaching his desk directly.

"Good morning Bill. Do take a seat," indicating the chair by his desk. "What can I do for you on this fine morning."

Bill sat on the chair indicated, looked steadily at Patrick before speaking. "I have been informed by John Williams, in Cardiff, that you are having a sexual affair with your PA. He assures me that this information has come from a reliable source. I need not remind you that if Sir Ian is made aware, your time here will be finished, as will Sharon's. Not only that, but your marriage could also be in jeopardy. I advise you to finish it now before it's too late."

For a moment, Patrick just looked at him, then throwing back his head, began to roar with laughter. "Sharon come in here." Then he continued to laugh.

"Yes, Mr Evans, you called."

"Sharon, did you know that we are having an illicit affair?" He continued to laugh.

"No, Mr Evans, you haven't told me. Sorry, If I had known I would have dressed differently for you."

Now in a more serious mood he spoke with determination. "I have never heard such tosh in all my life. Unadulterated lies. I will find out who has dared to perpetrate what is nothing more than slander and they will be out of this company faster than they can draw breath."

Bill Hammond looked at him with that steady gaze, for which he was well known before speaking. "I will speak with Sir Ian and explain all to him. Put a lid on things before they get out of hand."

"No need. I will speak to him myself. Thank you for letting me know what is going on. Will you stay for coffee, Sharon has just made some?"

"Thank you, but no. I am quite busy this morning." With that Bill Hammond left Patrick's office.

Patrick Evans looked at Sharon, a look that she returned as he blew a long blast of breath through pursed lips. He didn't speak, just sat there in deep thought. Sharon returned to her domain, poured coffee for them both and took both beakers into Patrick's office. She sat in the chair just vacated by Bill Hammond. "Patrick, what do we do now?"

That was a performance that deserved an Oscar, thought Bill as he returned to his office. He had obviously briefed Sharon on how he would, 'play-things', if, and when he was confronted.

It was possible that he had not expected to be confronted in his own office but to call Sharon in and speak to her as he did, was good spontaneous thinking. Sharon's response was given with perfection. To anyone who didn't know Patrick Evans well, they would have been convinced of his innocence and that of Sharon. But Bill Hammond was not fooled.

To trawl through the Electoral roll was a task that DC Jane Todd had never been asked to do before. She wasn't very enthusiastic about it, but it was something that needed to be done and so with the hope that something positive could be learned she made a start. Name after name, name after name. Tedium was almost about to set in, then the name Victoria made her stop the trawl. Several times she had seen Veronica, Vera and Valerie, names beginning with V, and each time she had stopped before realising that they were not the name she was seeking. Here though was that all important name of Victoria. Jane read the full entry. Disappointment struck immediately. The entry was for VICTORIA SHARON SUMNER. Not Holden, the surname she was seeking. This was of course Sharon Sumner, Patrick Evans PA.

Jane was about to continue the trawl, when she remembered something that had been considered a puzzle when the investigation was made at Eco-Tech. When trying to find evidence of payment being made by Vic Eardley to someone for covert activities, the initials in his notebook, were VSS. Eardley had said that it was his shorthand for covering miscellaneous payments during the product development process. Jane couldn't remember the exact words that he said they were short for, but at the time everybody thought his explanation dubious. VSS, those letters were the initials of Victoria Sharon Sumner. Could she be the woman by the name of Vicki Holden? If she were the same person, why had she changed her name?

Still staring at the screen, she called. "Sir, I think you had better look at this."

DI Grant went over to see what it was he should look at. "What have you found?"

"Sir, those letters that were in Vic Eardley's notebook, VSS. They are the initials of none other than Victoria Sharon Sumner, Patrick Evans PA. Do you think that Sharon could be Vicki Holden?"

"Bloody hell, Toddy, you could be right. She may not have changed her name deliberately, because registering with official departments like Work and Pensions and HM Revenue and Customs could have complications. She may be or may have been married. I'll call Liverpool and speak with DI Abbott. He can check with Vicki Holden's brother."

The word that came back from DI Ken Abbott was positive. Vicki Holden had been married to a Richard Sumner. When Keith Holden was asked why he had not mentioned this earlier in their conversations, he had just said, 'you never asked'. He went on to tell them that Richard Sumner had been convicted of drugs trafficking and had received a lengthy custodial sentence.

Vicky had sued for divorce which had been granted three or four years ago, after which she went around with her father, attending many race meetings at the popular racecourses.

DI Grant informed the DCI, putting forward the theory that the unknown woman that they had been seeking for so long, the woman suspected of killing Danny Drew, and being the spy responsible for the corporate espionage as well as ordering the murders of Sophie Langford and Vic Eardley was Victoria Sharon Sumner.

The investigating team were assembled ready for the briefing to be given by DCI Davies. They were all aware of the recent developments. The next move would be explained to them by the DCI, and they were all feeling that excitement that was always there when a significant move was about to be ordered.

The DCI came into the room and stood before the incident board, looking over all the evidence notes, scene of crime photographs and numerous indicators before turning towards them and speaking. "I believe that we are on the verge of cracking this case. Sharon Sumner is perhaps the least likely person to be suspected of the crimes that we are investigating. We know that she didn't commit the crime of murder in the cases of Sophie Langford and Vic Eardley. We have already got the perpetrator for those crimes under arrest, but we may be able to prove that Eddie Harper carried out those crimes under her direction. As for the killing of Danny Drew, Sharon Sumner must be considered as the prime suspect, although it is still my opinion that she had a male accomplice and that cannot have been Eddie Harper, because he was working at the foundry at the time. Whatever we do, we must not give Sharon Sumner any hint of our suspicions before making the next move."

"What is our next move, Sir and when is that likely to be." The voice of DI Bob Grant interrupted the DCI's flow. Excitement and eagerness sounding in every word.

"I shall be making an application for a search warrant to search the residence of Sharon Sumner. If she is indeed the 'unknown woman', she is the person who posed as a police officer and entered the home of Sophie Langford. She must therefore be the person who took Sophie's laptop, in which case she probably still has it somewhere in the house. Also, if she were the woman seen with Eddie Harper, by DC Todd and the woman who posed as a journalist, asking questions of Sian Gilmore, she will have in her wardrobe a leather jacket and in a drawer maybe, one red silk or chiffon scarf and a pair of large framed sunglasses. All these items will be the evidence we need to charge her. We can link her directly to Vic Eardley and Eco-Tech, and hence to the corporate espionage. The moment I get the warrant, we go into action.

It was seven thirty in the morning. Sharon Sumner was getting herself ready to go to the office. With quietness and without flurry, two police squad cars and a police personnel carrier arrived outside the residence of Sharon Sumner's home. DCI Harry Davies alighted from the lead car and made his way along the short path to the front door followed by the other accompanying officers. He rang the doorbell and waited.

Sharon opened the door, expecting to see either the paperboy or the postman, although it was rather early for him, she thought. She was totally shocked to see DCI Davies standing there with what appeared to be an army of police officers behind him.

"Sharon Sumner, I have a Warrant to search these premises." He showed her the warrant. He then brushed past her followed by the rest of the team. He directed them to the various locations in the house and the search began.

"What on earth are you looking for. What do you expect to find?" Sharon was trying to remain calm but wondering what kind of information they had to prompt a house search. What, could she have done to make them suspect her of a criminal act because she knew that was the procedure taken when seeking evidence. She had first-hand experience of that, at the time her ex-husband had been arrested. This was a nightmare she had not anticipated.

There was a call from upstairs, a call from DS Larry Robb. "I have something, Sir."

There on the bed he had placed a laptop. "It was at the bottom of the wardrobe."

The DCI looked at the laptop and at the case lying at its side on which were the initials S.L. "I think that this is the evidence that we need. Let us see what is on the hard-drive that can prove that it belonged to Sophie Langford." He pointed to the initials on the case as he spoke. "Get it over to forensics."

Another call came from DC Jane Todd. "Look what I have found." In her hand was a black leather jacket, the sort she had described seeing the unidentified woman wearing.

"Have you managed to find the red scarf and sunglasses?" The DCI was beginning to feel jubilant.

"Not yet, Sir, but I think that there is every possibility that they will be in one of these drawers." She indicated a chest of drawers standing in the corner of the bedroom.

The bottom drawer revealed the items in question. "Bingo," Jane exclaimed, holding up the red scarf and sunglasses.

"Good for you, Toddy. Let's go downstairs and confront the unknown woman." The DCI lead the way down and into the living room where Sharon was sitting and looking very uncomfortable. Addressing Sharon, he said. "Can you explain why you have a laptop, the case of which has the initials S L. in gold-coloured letters."

"Oh, it was one I picked up cheaply at a car boot sale." Fast thinking was one of her many attributes.

"You also have a black leather jacket, a red scarf and a pair of large framed sunglasses. We found the scarf and sunglasses in the bottom drawer of the chest of drawers in your bedroom. A woman wearing similar attire was seen by DC Todd, with Eddie Harper in Wrockwardine Wood, although he denies the fact."

At that moment, DC Jane Todd entered the room carrying the items to which the DCI was referring and, also, a dark-haired wig. "I found this in the other room, Sir." Holding up the wig for the DCI to see.

Addressing Sharon, he said. "I must ask you to accompany me to the station for further questioning." With that the search was completed, Sharon locked the door and she was then led to a squad car and assisted into the back, DC Jane Todd sitting beside her.

The formal questioning began, headed by DCI Harry Davies. Sharon began by insisting she had bought the laptop at a car boot sale some time ago. She couldn't remember exactly when. Questioned about the leather jacket and red scarf, she shrugged and said that she often wore them. The jacket, which was rather expensive, she had bought in Shrewsbury because she liked it and of course the red scarf complimented it perfectly. As for the sunglasses, she often wore them when it was bright, who doesn't was her confident remark. Sharon categorically denied being with Eddie Harper in Wrockwardine Wood. Why on earth would I be with him of all people? Was her indignant response. The DCI accused her of wearing the apparel and the dark haired, shoulder length wig as a disguise. This she categorically denied.

The interrogation was interrupted by DS Robb. "Have you a minute Sir, there is something you should see."

DCI Davies left the interview room. DC Jane Todd remained and was joined by a uniformed PC who stood just inside the room. No one spoke. They just awaited the return of DCI Davies.

About fifteen minutes passed before the door opened and Davies re-entered the room. Taking his seat once more, he looked directly at Sharon, who sat pensively opposite to him.

"Forensic examination of the laptop found on your premises, confirms beyond all shadow of doubt, that it belonged to Sophie Langford. That same laptop was removed from the home of Sophie Langford by a woman, posing as a police officer. I believe that woman was you and that you told Sophie Langford that the laptop was needed for examination. You were afraid that there would be something in the memory that would identify you as the industrial spy, a fact that you could not allow to become known. Danny Drew had already been killed simply because Sophie Langford had recognised you at Eco-Tech, and told her boyfriend, who then told his best pal, Danny Drew. Danny Drew had to go."

"It's not true. I didn't kill Danny Drew." Her voice now had the sound of desperation.

"I believe that you did." Then with gravity he spoke the words that Sharon was dreading. "Victoria Sharon Sumner, I am arresting you on suspicion of the murder of Daniel Drew and complicity in the murders of Sophie Langford and Victor Eardley. You don't have to say anything, but it may harm your defence if you don't mention, when questioned something which you later may rely on in court." Then to the constable who was still standing in the room, "Take her away."

29

Sir Ian Leighton-Boyce was sitting at his desk and listening to DCI Harry Davies give the full account of the arrest of Eddie Harper on suspicion of the murders of both Sophie Langford and Vic Eardley and now the arrest of Sharon Sumner. The charge against her being the murder of Danny Drew and complicity in the murders of Sophie Langford and Vic Eardley. This was almost beyond the comprehension of Sir Ian. All this, stemming from the desire of one man, Vic Eardley, to obtain a patent on the new insulation board ahead of the application by Salopian Industries. This, he could do only by obtaining the technical details by covert means. His efforts Sir Ian knew had put Eco-Tech Limited into financial difficulties and had been the cause of three deaths, including Vic Eardley himself. The whole sorry mess was a human tragedy.

The affair between Patrick Evans and Sharon Sumner had been made known to Sir Ian, who was furious that the CEO of the company could behave in such a manner. It was something that he neither could or, would tolerate. In a conversation he had with John Williams, he had learned about Patrick's dalliance with his daughter Bronwen, which had sealed his decision to dismiss Patrick Evans from the company. In both cases, Evans had inferred that he was about to obtain a divorce from his wife, a ploy to make them more susceptible to his advances and ultimate seduction. In Sir Ian's opinion, the work of a despicable creature.

Patrick Evans had received the call from Sir Ian, summoning him to his office. Patrick's mind was still reeling from the news of Sharon's arrest. He could not believe that she could be guilty of either espionage or murder. Her behaviour with him, and indeed everyone else he could think of was not that of someone who could kill in cold blood and to engage in covert work under the noses of so many people.

Sir Ian's face had a grave expression. "Take a seat." His abruptness heralded something that sent a chill down Patrick's spine. "I think that perhaps you know why I have asked you to come to see me. It's not about the arrest of your PA, Sharon Sumner, but of your conduct with her."

"But Sir Ian." Evans didn't get any further. He was silenced immediately.

"Don't interrupt." Sir Ian's voice was harsh and with authority. "You may protest your innocence for as much as you wish, but we both know what the truth really is. You have engaged in a sexual affair with your PA, Sharon Sumner and intimated that you were about to get a divorce from your wife. That is shameful, and something that I will not tolerate. To add to your shame, you were conducting a similar association with the daughter of a good friend of mine, in the person of Bronwen Jenkins. You had no concern for the feelings of either of those women or for the potential humiliation of your wife, a lady worth far better, than you. You will collect your personal effects from your office and leave these premises within the hour. Anything that you cannot take today, will be deposited at the gatehouse for you to collect later. You will be escorted from here by a security officer who will remain with you until you are off the premises. Do I make myself absolutely clear?"

"Yes, Sir Ian, I am sorry for what I can only call a regretful aberration."

"I think that you are nothing more than a degenerate philanderer. Now get out."

The security officer was waiting in the corridor. Without a word being exchanged between them, Patrick Evans returned to his office for the last time. He collected his personal effects and then was escorted to his car and checked at the gatehouse as he left the premises.

Leslie Anderson was shown into the board room by Sir Ian's secretary, Yvonne. The sight that greeted him was rather daunting. At the head of the board room table, that hallowed piece of furniture made from the finest walnut, sat Sir Ian Leighton-Boyce, chairman of the board. Chairs either side of the table were occupied by the other directors, and company secretary.

"Good morning Leslie, please take a seat." He indicated the chair at the opposite end of the table to himself. At the same time Yvonne took the chair next to the company secretary, ready to take down the minutes of the meeting in shorthand. It was obvious to Leslie that there was going to be a meeting, but he was rather puzzled as to why he had been asked to attend. He was probably going to get a grilling on the progress he was making in preparation for taking the new Supa Board plant into commercial production, he thought. His thoughts were suddenly brought back to the here and now.

"I am sure that you are by now fully aware of the traumatic events that have taken place over the last few days. Events of a gravity, the kind of which I have never before experienced in my life. I hope that I shall never experience the like ever again. There is now a vacancy for the position of chief executive officer of the company." He paused to take a draught of water. "We, the members of the board, have discussed at length this matter and have unanimously decided to offer that position to you, that is if you wish to accept."

Leslie Anderson was stunned by what he had heard or thought that he had heard. This was to him, unreal. He realised that every eye in the room was looking at him and all the people were waiting for him to reply. "You want me to be CEO?" He stared at them in disbelief.

"That was the general purpose of the offer." A smile now beginning to show on Sir Ian's face.

"My answer is yes. I would be honoured to accept the position. I do apologise for my initial hesitation in answering but in truth I wasn't sure that I had understood correctly, what you had said. However, I can assure you that I will give of my very, best to the job."

"I am delighted, as we all are, that you have accepted. We have every confidence in you. Please consider that you are operative in that role with immediate effect."

"Thank you, Sir Ian and of course my thanks go also to you all for the confidence you have afforded me."

"Leslie, you will need a new PA. Yvonne will place an advertisement in the local press."

"Before she does so, may I have a day or two to pursue someone who I believe would be excellent in that position. She is a person who I have known since she was a teenager."

"May we know of whom you are thinking?" Curiosity showing on Sir Ian's face.

"Bronwen Jenkins, the daughter of John Williams. You may or may not know that she is now, shall I say, close to Gwyn Thomas our resident chemist. He was her first love before she married that fellow Jenkins.

Bronwen is at present, the deputy manager of a hotel in Cardiff. If she remains there, and she and Gwyn decide to marry, which is highly possible, Gwyn would, return to Cardiff leaving us needing another chemist to manage the new plant. If, however Bronwen came here as my PA, Gwyn would remain, and all would be well. I am quite sure that her experience as deputy manager of a busy hotel would be perfect as a PA."

"Leslie, you are thinking like a CEO already. I believe Bronwen would be highly suitable. Like you I know Bronwen because her father and I have been good friends for many years. Make your approach as soon as possible."

Leslie Anderson called Gwyn to his office to outline to him his plans for the management of the new Supa Board plant when it came on stream. "I want you to become the plant manager and when product demand becomes such that another production line is needed, you would be in overall control. Now that I am CEO, I shall appoint Rowan Chapman as works engineer and he will arrange for an engineer to look after all your needs."

"Thank you for the offer, Leslie, but can I have a couple of days to think it over?"

"Are you thinking of how your relationship with Bronwen Jenkins may be affected?"

"Yes, I am. I was contemplating returning to Cardiff, if I can find another job, so that we can be together."

"Do you think that Bronwen would come to Telford if she had a suitable position to come to?"

"I think that she would because she likes the area. I have taken her to quite a few places which she thinks are wonderful, but for her to get a suitable job here is very doubtful."

"How do you think she would react if I offered her the chance to be my PA?"

Gwyn was visibly shocked. "Are you serious?"

"Of course, I'm serious. I am sure that you are aware, that I have known Bronwen, since she was a teenager because of my association with Williams Brothers and her father. With her experience in the job she has, I am sure she would be perfect as my PA."

"Would you like me to put the proposition to her?"

"Yes. Why not call her now. If she is interested, arrange for her to come to Telford and we can sort out all the necessary details."

When Gwyn spoke to her, she was overjoyed by the offer and agreed to visit Telford within the next couple of days. This was, she felt, a heaven sent, opportunity. It was now, only a matter of time before her life would change from the mundane to one of joy and happiness.

The full board of directors, sat once more at the boardroom table. Now, as CEO, Leslie Anderson took his place along with them. They were meeting to discuss a proposition that had been put to the chairman by Gerry Ewing and Bill Astley, the remaining partners of Eco-Tech.

The company was now in serious financial difficulty, due to the irresponsible dealings of the late Vic Eardley. He had negotiated a Bank Loan to cover the development and purchase of the necessary machinery and equipment for the new type of insulation board, a large percentage of that loan being paid for the covert activity at Salopian Industries. The figurative thunder bolt had struck without warning. One of the company's biggest customers had gone into liquidation owing Eco-Tech, a considerable amount of money. The cash flow, as Gerry Ewing had put it, no longer existed. The bank was going to foreclose within seven days unless sufficient funds were introduced from elsewhere. The bitter truth was that there was nowhere else from where sufficient funds could be raised.

Had it not been for the bank loan, the company could have weathered the storm, but in the present circumstances there were only two options. The first was to declare insolvency, and that would be the end of Eco-Tech Limited, or for some other company to take them over, including the debt. Gerry Ewing had asked Sir Ian Leighton-Boyce if Salopian Industries would do just that. As he put it, the loan had paid for the development equipment, so taking over that debt would be an investment by Salopian Industries rather than taking over a complete loss. The board meeting now convened, was to discuss such a move and to decide whether, or not, to proceed with a take-over.

Sir Ian began by outlining the potential benefits of taking over Eco-Tech Limited. "To take over the debt would not be a problem to us." A bland statement by Sir Ian. "To then offer the same figure for complete purchase, would again be no problem. Looking through the company's accounts, and the potential order book, to lay out the total sum that I have mentioned, assuming, that the partners agree, would be for us an absolute bargain. We would gain a substantial piece of the market in that part of the world, whilst the products made would be made using our own base materials supplied from this factory. Regarding the equipment, already in place for producing the new Supa Board, we could install what is necessary to bring it into commercial production as and when it is suitable to do so. Eco-Tech Limited could be an extended arm in the north of England." Sir Ian paused to look at the others around the table, waiting for comments on his proposal.

"How would you suggest the company be managed and by whom?" A pertinent question from Bill Hammond.

"The two existing partners, could carry on as managers, doing effectively what they would still be doing had it not been for the stupidity of Vic Eardley. Obviously, they would come under the control of this board, strategically and financially."

It was a unanimous decision to go ahead with the acquisition of Eco-Tech Limited, on the terms outlined by the chairman, subject to the agreement of Gerry Ewing and Bill Astley. There was no doubt in any one's mind that the offer would not be accepted. Ewing and Astley had no choice other than going into liquidation and being declared bankrupt.

30

A meeting of the board had been called by the chairman, to confirm that the acquisition of Eco-Tech Limited had been confirmed. The company was once again doing normal business with Gerry Ewing and Bill Astley performing their usual managerial duties, although they were now, employees of Salopian Industries. For them, a bitter pill to swallow, but they were aware that if they had been firmer with Vic Eardley, even to have had a massive row with him, things would perhaps not have developed as they had done. Although he was such a determined character, that even a row may not have deterred him. It would have been better had they never had him as a partner in the first instance.

The chairman also confirmed that Leslie Anderson had now appointed Bronwen Jenkins as his PA gesturing in Leslie's direction. "An excellent choice Leslie, and I am sure that we will now have the continued service of Gwyn Thomas, who will be a great asset to us as the new plant comes on stream and eventually when we begin that operation in Liverpool."

The other purpose for the meeting was to listen to DCI Harry Davies, who had requested the meeting, to bring everyone up to date with the police investigation that had become so protracted. The board now awaited his arrival.

With all eyes on DCI Harry Davies, everyone, alert, eager to learn the outcome of the investigation that began with the death on the premises, of Danny Drew and the discovery of corporate espionage being perpetrated within the company. Then the murders of two people in Liverpool, closely, connected to the espionage. The DCI began a full disclosure.

The saga began when Salopian Industries acquired Williams Brothers Limited and included in the acquisition, the partially developed product to become known as Supa Board. Two other companies had made bids for the acquisition, one being Eco-Tech Limited of Liverpool. Salopian Industries and Williams Brothers had for many years enjoyed a close business relationship. That fact plus the generous bid by Salopian Industries ensured the success of that bid, Williams Brothers becoming an associate company of the Salopian Group of Companies.

Vic Eardley, a partner in Eco-Tech, was bitterly disappointed by the outcome. He wanted the partially developed new product. Being the character that he was, he was prepared to obtain the necessary technical information by covert means, pursue the development at Eco-Tech and hopefully obtain a patent on the process ahead of Salopian Industries.

At that time, he was seeing an old acquaintance on a fairly, regular basis at horse racing meetings. His name was Jimmie Holden. He had a daughter, Vicki, recently divorced and so accompanying her father for pleasant days at many of the well-known racecourses. She and Vic Eardley became friendly and when the advertisement for a PA for the new chief Executive officer of Salopian Industries was published, he suggested to Vicki that she apply for the position, since at that time she was unemployed. It was a vague hope of Eardley's that Vicki might get the job and then maybe he could persuade her to obtain technical information for him to develop the new type of insulation. Beyond Vic Eardley's wildest dreams, Vicki got the job. He then persuaded her to get the technical information he needed, offering monetary reward that Vicki couldn't resist. The die was cast. Vicki was engaged in corporate espionage.

When she applied for the job, she had presented herself as Sharon Sumner, Sharon being her second name, and Sumner being her married name. She had only been in the job for about six months, when Patrick Evans made his first amorous advance. She was not only flattered, but she rather fancied him and so she responded in like manner. Of that, the rest is history.

During the following eighteen months she obtained information on a regular basis for Vic Eardley but needed an accomplice to pass on the information from an outside source to avoid any possible discovery being, as she thought, traced to herself. She recruited Eddie Harper, an employee of the Group, but working at the foundry. Harper, who had a chip on his shoulder and a grudge against the company, was easily recruited by the promise of large monetary gain.

All went well for her and her romance with her boss, Patrick Evans. It was blossoming in a way that she had not thought possible when it had all started. Patrick had, in a roundabout way, mentioned divorce. She had visions of becoming Mrs Evans.

Things began to unravel when she was recognised as an employee of Salopian Industries, when paying one of her rare visits to see Vic Eardley at Eco-Tech. At the time, she was unaware of the problem. Sophie Langford, an employee of Eco-Tech and the girlfriend of Paddy McGuire, Danny Drew's friend, was the person who had recognised her having seen her at the works Christmas do in Telford when she and Paddy visited Danny. She told Paddy, who then told Danny.

Sharon was certain that Danny had seen her in an embrace with Patrick Evans and was very wary of him. One day, after normal office closing time, Sharon had gone into the drawing office to get some more technical information after everyone had left for the day, when Danny, who was also staying late, saw her through a window. Knowing of her visit to Eco-Tech, and seeing her in the drawing office where she had no right to be unaccompanied, he put two and two together, went into the office and said to her 'you are caught and rumbled. Now I know what you were doing at Eco-Tech. Sophie Langford saw you and recognised you'. He laughed and being 'the kind of lad he was with the ladies', he suggested that his silence was worth a few favours. Sharon laughed and teased him saying she would give it some thought. Not to be put off, Danny said ring me tomorrow. Tell me when and where. Sharon had said it would be in the control room on the tank platform. She would let him know when. With that, he left her and went on his way.

Sharon knew about Julie's fling with Danny, and knew that Julie's husband Don Phillips, was suspicious that Danny Drew was seeing Julie when he was at work. Julie had told her that Don had threatened to break his neck if he caught him. With this, in mind, Sharon devised a plan to lure Danny to the tank platform area, when all the workmen were in the canteen at lunchtime and shout for help when Danny arrived. Don Phillips, who she had confided in, saying that she was tired of Danny's advances, had agreed to run to her aid when she shouted, and both would accuse him of sexual assault on Sharon and have him dismissed from the company. That would get him out of the way.

When Danny arrived, Sharon had already climbed the steps onto the platform, and she called for him to come up to her. This he did. When he went to put his arms around her, she had pushed him away and shouted for help as previously arranged with Don Phillips. Unfortunately, as she pushed Danny, he was caught off balance and he fell backwards, his helmet falling off and he struck the back of his head on the angle curb around the edge of the platform. He was out cold. Don Phillips ran up the steps joining Sharon on the platform. Don took one look at the prostrate form and with no hesitation, hauled up the body turning him in the process and pushed him over the edge of the platform. The body of Danny lay on the concrete floor, twenty feet below them. Sharon and Don ran down the steps and made their escape from the area where the body lay.

Sharon was mortified by what had happened. Don Phillips had deliberately thrown Danny off the platform with the purpose of killing him. She toyed with the idea of going to the police to explain that it was an accident due to her pushing Danny but was afraid that they wouldn't believe her. Then, shortly afterwards, Don Phillips was found drowned in the River Severn. Sharon made the decision to keep quiet and say nothing.

The thought that she had been recognised by the woman called Sophie Langford, filled her with dread. When asked, Vic Eardley had given Sharon the address of Sophie and so Sharon devised the plan of going to Sophie's address, knowing that Sophie would recognise her immediately and spinning her the story that she was police working undercover. She was investigating the possible theft of valuable technical information from Salopian Industries. She would ask Sophie for her laptop for forensic examination and have her swear to keep the visit secret, promising to return the laptop as soon as possible. That, Sharon would have done after checking that there was nothing on it that would incriminate her. However, her accomplice, Eddie Harper, panicking that this woman, Sophie Langford, was ready to expose them, decided to quieten her permanently. So, knowing that Sharon was going to visit Sophie, Harper shadowed her and after Sharon had left, took the opportunity of going to the house, gaining entry and killing Sophie in cold blood.

Sharon was incandescent when she learned what he had done but could do nothing about it. Then, disregarding Sharon's anger and threats, he made the decision to silence the other potential threat to his and Sharon's anonymity, namely, Vic Eardley. It was the reason that Sharon had arranged to meet Eddie in Wrockwardine Wood, a place she thought would be quiet, especially in the churchyard, and where it would be unlikely for them to be seen and recognised. She would give him instructions of future procedure should any enquiry involve them. Fate dealt them a devastating blow when leaving the churchyard and almost colliding with none other than DC Jane Todd, who later recognise Eddie Harper during enquiries and questioning at the foundry, linking him to the unknown woman who they were seeking. It was DC Todd who had connected the initials VSS with the notes in Vic Eardley's notebook, leading to the true, identity of Sharon and her relationship with him.

Following the arrest of Sharon and having charged her, she had opened-up and told them the full story. DCI Davies looking at the assembly and having told them everything about the case, took a draught of water.

"We have charged Sharon Sumner with accessory to murder in the case of Danny Drew and complicity in the murders of Sophie Langford and Victor Eardley. She has also been charged with impersonation of a police officer, theft of a laptop and corporate espionage. A lengthy list to say the least and it's probable that she will be convicted on all counts and receive a lengthy custodial sentence."

"I'm amazed that a woman like Sharon, sophisticated and eloquent, could be responsible for crimes such as these," remarked Sir Ian, slowly shaking his head, illustrating his amazement.

"Sharon Sumner is a cold, calculating woman with a criminal mind. She is, capable of manipulating any situation and anyone for her own purposes, as is evident by the manner she used Eddie Harper."

After the departure of the DCI, the board members broke up and returned to their daily activities, but with the knowledge of all that had happened, and the words of the DCI indelibly imprinted on their minds.

At seven o'clock that same evening, Leslie Anderson, accompanied by his wife, went to St Chad's Church where he was the official organist. She sat at the back of the church alone at first but was quickly joined by four young people, who knew that Leslie would be here at this hour to play the organ. Gwyn Thomas, Bronwen Jenkins, Rowan Chapman and Julie Phillips, were those young people, who believed that the happiness in life that they now shared was in no small measure due to the kindness of the man that was now about to play that mighty instrument.

Leslie Anderson didn't disappoint. He began by playing Widor's *Toccata*, that piece of organ music that is the very epitome of power and glory.